To J

DANCING FOOLS AND ALL THAT JAZZ

love
Becky
Fleetwood
xx

4/9 Julie

love
Rach
Fleetwood
xx

DANCING FOOLS AND ALL THAT JAZZ

B Fleetwood

First published in Great Britain in 2025 by
The Book Guild Ltd
Unit E2 Airfield Business Park,
Harrison Road, Market Harborough,
Leicestershire. LE16 7UL
Tel: 0116 2792299
www.bookguild.co.uk
Email: info@bookguild.co.uk

Copyright © 2025 B Fleetwood

The right of B Fleetwood to be identified as the author of this
work has been asserted by them in accordance with the
Copyright, Design and Patents Act 1988.

All rights reserved. No part of this publication may be
reproduced, transmitted, or stored in a retrieval system, in any form or by any means,
without permission in writing from the publisher, nor be otherwise circulated in
any form of binding or cover other than that in which it is published and without
a similar condition being imposed on the subsequent purchaser.

The manufacturer's authorised representative in the EU
for product safety is Authorised Rep Compliance Ltd,
71 Lower Baggot Street, Dublin D02 P593 Ireland (www.arccompliance.com)

This work is entirely fictitious and bears no resemblance to any persons living or dead.

Typeset in 11pt Minion Pro

Printed and bound by CPI Group (UK) Ltd, Croydon, CR0 4YY

ISBN 978 1835742 440

British Library Cataloguing in Publication Data.
A catalogue record for this book is available from the British Library.

In memory of Sandra Murphy,
a wonderful friend and fellow dancer
with an amazing sense of humour.
Miss you, lovely lady.

Music Playlist
SPOTIFY – DANCING FOOLS AND ALL THAT JAZZ

Expression Paris
[Excerpt from the competition programme]
Dance Excellence – Clarissa Kirkland (North West, United Kingdom)

Three entries:
"Rolling in the Deep", Adele – contemporary jazz
"Dancin' Fool", Barry Manilow – upbeat jazz fusion
"The Humma Song", OK Jaanu – Bollywood spectacular

Principal Dancers:

Monica Thornton	Asha Gupta
Ruby Anderson	Bonnie Manford
Ingrida Valenko (Reserve)	Cath O'Reilly
Fay Langridge	Janine Young

1

MONICA THORNTON

'Balance step to the left. Then to the right. Midnight… la-la-la… sleeping…' Clarissa's shrill just-off-key voice is amplified by her radio mic. Her lyrics are fragmented and lag slightly behind those of Shakin' Stevens' "Green Door". She gives a flick of her hand towards me.

'Good evening, Monica.'

So much for creeping in unseen.

With a cursory wave back – head down – I make a beeline for the bench and hurriedly change into my jazz shoes.

I know the other ladies will have glanced quizzically over to me.

Monica is never late – I can almost see their thought bubbles.

Normally, Ruby and I arrive a good fifteen minutes early to help Clarissa set up, plug in the sound system, turn on the spotlights, the air con and all that. Normally Clarissa tells us how Hazel's treatment is going as we prepare the studio... Normally – ha. Things will never be normal again. I swallow hard.

Clarissa changes direction. The dancers behind her – clad in black leggings and the black floaty tops I designed – are reflected in the full-length wall mirrors. They follow her every move.

'Join us when you can, Monica... dum-dum-dum...' Her tone and smile are friendly, not critical. Ruby's covered for me, thank goodness.

A sharp pain flickers across my forehead. I can still barely believe it.

Ruby briefly turns my way. Her eyes urge, 'You can do this.'

I respond with a weak smile before joining the end of the row at the back to get into step with the others. We move in synchronisation with the heavy beat, and I force myself to concentrate on the steps.

'Now triple walks. Arms up in a Vee. Bonnie, get your arms higher. Da-de-da... green... no, even higher...'

I glance critically at my reflection in the mirrors as we leap in unison. OK, I look better than anticipated. The bright lights blot out some of the puffiness, so I just look a little tired. Waterproof mascara works.

'Box step left. Dum dum... flick kick and turn.'

Ruby winks at me in the mirror. She frequently impersonates Clarissa mumble-singing out-of-time and out-of-tune. In the fleeting glance we know we're thinking the same, Ruby taking Lady C – as she's dubbed her – off to a tee. A loud snort bursts from my nose. It takes me and Bonnie, who's dancing next to me, by surprise. I bite my lip and look apologetic. Bonnie merely shrugs it off.

My emotions are swinging wildly out of control, and I determine to fix my thoughts on the music, the beat.

Shaky sings out about the secrets behind the door as Clarissa calls, 'Reach out to each corner and kick…'

Secrets. All those ones you've been keeping… I kick sharp and high.

'Come on now, practise those winning smiles. Dum-de-dum da-da… Swing those arms.'

I imagine swinging for Vince.

He'd tried to phone me as I'd hurried from my car to the studio. I'd dismissed the call, stabbing a finger on his details and hitting edit. With a flourish, I changed his name to *Cheating Bastard*, shoving the phone back in my bag with a disproportionate degree of satisfaction.

Now righteous fury and utter dismay fight for the spotlight in my turbulent thoughts.

'Cross through… No. Janine! Wrong way – dear, oh dear. Pay attention. La-la-la door…'

I force my focus on the other women. We thread in and out of each other before returning to our original places.

Ruby gives my hand a glancing squeeze as she passes.

When she called earlier to find out where I'd got to, I barely managed to stammer out my words.

'Monica, what the hell's happened? Talk to me.'

'Vince… he… for years… he's been…'

'What?'

'…with other women…'

'What the…?'

'And I just can't… can't…'

'Frigging hell. What a toerag. Look, Monica, skip dance. It won't matter for once, will it? Although thinking about it, Lady C will effing flip if you're not there.' Ruby's voice switched to Clarissa's, '"Ladies, Expression Paris is only two weeks away and these last rehearsals are not, I repeat *not* optional"'

'No, I have to… I *need* to come.'

'You're right. Look, think of it as displacement activity. I'll go ahead and make up some excuse why you're late. We'll talk after – I can come back to yours.'

'No, not here. Not with the twins in earshot.'

'OK, we'll talk at the studio. Just get yourself there when you can. And when you do, give that dance floor hell.'

Dear Ruby. She's right. She wouldn't allow someone like Vince to make a fool of her. She's strong, independent, always in control. Oh, to be more like Ruby.

Reminding myself of her words, I throw myself into the dance, my whole effort channelled into executing the steps within the complex patterns of direction. The lyrics thump into my muscles and I begin to unwind.

'Ensure you stretch out each move to fully warm-up, ladies.'

The routine demands full concentration and by the end of the number we're all breathing quickly and have broken into a sweat. I feel distanced from the earlier revelations, which seem almost surreal.

We dive for our bags and rummage for our hats for the next dance.

Ruby leans into me. 'You OK?'

I smack her hand lightly. 'No being nice,' I hiss. 'I need to stay furious and focussed.'

Ruby grins. 'Furiously frigging focussed. Atta girl.'

I stare at the floor and through clenched teeth ask, 'How did I not know? Am I utterly stupid?'

'Whoa. Stupid you are not. Come on, Monica. This dance floor needs a kicking.'

Clarissa calls from the front. 'Ladies, "Dancing Fools" next. Positions… Janine, further forward… Fay, two steps back… and… Five – six – seven – eight…'

*

The class flashes past. An hour and a half of solid dance. By the end, the tension has ebbed from my body, and I'm in a much better frame of mind. We stretch out, Ruby next to me. My muscles are warm with exertion and my head's clearer.

'Endorphins work.' Ruby nudges me, dabbing the perspiration from her brow.

'Too right.'

'Excellent rehearsal, ladies.' Clarissa gently claps the fingers of one hand onto the palm of the other as she smiles her approbation. 'Remember, when you dance, everyday life evaporates. Our troubles float away…'

If only.

'…Nothing matters but your moves and your focus. This is what engages your audience. You are taking them on a journey, a flight of fantasy. Capturing their hearts and souls. You must put every ounce of your being into each single move from your toes to your fingertips. So, practise daily at home. The competition is very close now.'

As we change back into our shoes, other dancers edge towards me.

'Everything OK, Monica?' Cath asks. 'Your solo was bang on. Best I've seen you dance it.'

'Thanks, Cath.' A bubble of anguish starts in my chest.

'What on earth happened to you, Monica?' Bonnie leans over Ruby to pat my leg. 'I don't think I've ever seen you arrive late. Everything all right?'

'Yes, fine thanks, Bonnie.' I keep my head down.

Fine. Just peachy. Oh, apart from discovering your husband's a rotten dirty cheat. I feel myself starting to slip.

Clarissa calls for silence. 'Ladies, our new dance school badges have arrived, and I have to say Hazel's design is marvellous. They will need to be sewn onto our tops in time for the competition. Right-hand side, between the chest and the shoulder.' She indicates the required position.

I join the others as they pool around Clarissa to see the new insignia. We'd all agreed the old 'Dance by Clarissa' next to a top hat had desperately needed updating.

Eagerly, everyone takes a new patch.

Ruby hands me mine and gives me her 'What the F?' look.

I stare at the sewn patch, and have a terrible urge to laugh, which I quickly suppress.

An artistic representation of a dance figure denoted by bright blue fluid curves stands poised on one leg, the other outstretched in a high kick. This, I can see, has Hazel's brushstroke genius. What can't be Hazel's work is the rest of the design. Our new group name – only Clarissa could have come up with this – has been embroidered in a tiny blue font below and along the line of the extended 'leg'. Instead of capitals the first letter of each word is in lower case but enlarged and in a flowery silver font quite different to the blue lettering. The eye is immediately drawn to the four standout letters sparkling in silver thread. I stare, lost for words, at the bespoke badge and quickly exchange looks with Ruby.

'What do you think, ladies?' Lady C beams at us all.

There is a stunned silence before Bonnie gushes out her praise. She appears to be the only one, other than Clarissa, who hasn't clocked the unfortunate result.

'Oh, isn't it lovely?' Bonnie holds her patch high, squinting at the lettering. 'I'm not wearing my glasses but these lovely sparkly letters, I can see the "d" must be for dance and the "c" and "k" for Clarissa Kirkland. So I am guessing the "i" is for inspiration?'

'It is *not* an "i".' Clarissa's indignation is palpable as she gives Bonnie a piercing stare. 'It is an "*e*" and it stands for *excellence*.'

'Oh, silly me. An "*e*". Well, what a lovely name for us, "Dance Excellence – Clarissa Kirkland". How marvellous. Did Hazel design this? Clever lady. We'll be the buzz of the town.'

Fay instantly corrects Bonnie in her usual annoyed tone. 'Talk, Bonnie, for goodness' sake, it is *talk* of the town. Dear me.'

Ruby, still looking aghast, points to the kicking leg and opens her mouth. 'But…'

'Very nice,' I say and grab Ruby's arm as I steer her away.

She clamps her mouth shut and shakes her head as we cross the studio on Fay's heels to pay our lottery and Paris money to Janine.

'Really?' hisses Ruby. 'I mean DECK's a bad enough name but that definitely reads "DICK". Even that ruddy leg looks like a ginormous...'

'Shh, she'll hear you.'

'Unbelievable. Well, I'm not sewing that on my top!' She leans into me as she adds, 'Talking of almighty di—'

I shush her with my hands. There're too many flapping ears in here.

'Monica, how did you find out?'

I put a finger to my lips. 'We need to pay Janine first and then get out of here.'

We stand behind Fay waiting to hand over our money and my mind lurches back to Vince.

I knew – of course I knew – deep down. All the signs were there but I chose not to look closer. Why didn't I confront you? Daft question. I didn't have any proof until today.

Prickling with anger, the now-blatant clues slam into my head.

Your flat. All the nights you stay away in Birmingham. No wonder you didn't want me at your city centre pad, purchased with our joint savings (I bristle at the added injustice) just before I fell pregnant with the twins. Our conversation replays from the first and only time I saw the damn place when you got the keys. What an innocent I was.

'This is amazing. Views over the city too. We can

come and stay here when there's a dance show on at the Hippodrome…'

'Monica, please. I will not mix work and pleasure. This is purely an investment and somewhere for me to stay midweek. Besides, can you really see me going to a dance show? No, I think not.'

'Well, we can stay here if we go to the NEC or fly from the Midlands airport or…'

'Monica, no. Now drop it.'

Fay's loud irritated voice temporarily interrupts my thoughts.

'Janine, you should really have given us each a full record of our payments…'

Payments. Credit card bills. It's so obvious now. Vince's oily voice reverberates, 'Those are my work credit cards, Monica. For business expenses. Of course you don't see them, they go straight to head office.'

I shake my head and picture the nicely furnished city apartment. A fleeting glimpse of Vince, naked on top of me, flashes unbidden across my mind. I feel nauseous. You did this with all those other women? My chest compresses and I barely notice Asha has come up next to me and started talking.

'Monica, can you possibly show me the moves of the tricky section in the Adele number, the bit after the cross through? I missed the class when Clarissa slowed down the sequence and I just cannot get the hang of it. The way you move your arms full circle before the chassé turn looks so elegant, I want to be able to do the same. I hope you do not mind me asking?'

I stare vacantly at Asha's mouth and dazzlingly perfect teeth – the reason Ruby has given her the nickname Gnasher-Asha, well this and the fact she's a dentist – before rewinding her words in my head.

'Yes, sure. Can I show you next week, Asha? I'm in a bit of a rush tonight,' I mumble.

She studies my face and gives me a concerned smile. 'Sure. Thank you, Monica. I hope everything is OK with you?' Her eyes beg an explanation as she stands her ground.

I feel a flush of emotion and shake my head before looking anxiously past Asha to see why there's a hold-up with the payments.

An argument has broken out between Fay and Janine about how much money she owes. I can barely focus on what they're saying. I just want to get out into the fresh air.

'Come on,' I mutter under my breath, but now Ruby has gone and joined in.

'Why are they charging us extra?' Ruby asks.

'I definitely paid more than that.' Fay turns her back on Ruby to face Janine.

'Fay, you were up to date, but now they've put up the cost of the airfares. Some sort of airport tax increase. It's not my fault.' Janine's voice is quiet, and she doesn't lift her eyes from her notebook.

I step impatiently from one foot to the other and realise Ingrida is now making a beeline for me, her face smiling and eager. I bow my head and look studiously at my watch, biting my lip. She takes the hint and returns to the back of the queue.

A dull buzz sounds from inside my handbag. I ignore it.

'Is that your phone, Monica?' Asha points to my bag.

I shrug, ignoring her and the persistent buzzing.

Buzz… buzz… No bloody wonder you never answered your phone when you were away. Well, two can play at that game. Come on, Ruby. I need to get out of here.

I march past Fay to interrupt the argument. 'Look, it's not Janine's fault if the prices have increased, and it's only fifteen pounds more. Janine, here's mine. Ruby, are you coming?'

Fay firmly folds her arms, her glare turned on me.

Janine quietly reminds Ruby she still owes five pounds from the previous week.

Ruby rolls her eyes to heaven and pulls out the one and only note from her purse. She jokingly clutches it to her chest and strokes it lovingly before reluctantly peeling it away and handing it to Janine. 'It's all I have. But it's yours. And as our numbers haven't come up on the lottery – I'm assuming you've checked we don't have that unclaimed winning ticket – I may just have to go and beg on Cheadle High Street or turn a few tricks to pay the extra next week.' She turns and winks at Bonnie and Cath.

'Oh, you are terrible, Ruby.' Bonnie and Cath laugh.

Fay's face twists into a sneer. She looks at Ruby as if she's something unpleasant on the underside of her shoe.

'Got a problem, Fay?' Ruby flashes Fay one of her massive white toothy smiles.

'My problem is not helped by continuous interruptions, Ruby.' Fay lifts her chin and turns to Janine. 'Now look here, Janine. Your records are most definitely wrong.' Fay grabs the notebook from Janine's hands to examine the entries.

I feel sorry for Little Janine Young. Ruby added the 'little' because she's both petite and also the youngest of our group at only twenty-three. 'Sounds like a character in a nursery rhyme.' Ruby had laughed when she first came up with the nickname. 'Little Janine Young has lost her tongue.' Poor girl. In truth, anyone would be dumbstruck with Fay giving them the evil eye, let alone a quiet shy girl like Janine. Ruby's nickname, Frosty Fay, has never been so apt.

Janine has turned lobster red and is trying to stutter out an explanation. I would normally have stayed to smooth things over, but in truth I am relieved when Ruby leaves them to it and steers me toward the door.

'Ouch. Just got frost bitten. Now it's poor Little Janine Young's turn,' she murmurs.

'What's the matter with that woman?' I glance back at Fay berating Janine as we leave the studio and step into the dark car park. 'She prickles at the slightest thing, and she seems to really have it in for Janine.'

'Don't think she's too fond of me, either.' Ruby exaggerates Fay's clipped tones, '"My problem is not helped by continuous interruptions, Ruby!"'

I smile as Ruby replicates Fay's sneer perfectly.

'Hey, Frosty and I will never be on the same wavelength. Her loss.' Ruby shrugs.

Reaching my car, Ruby stops, grabs me and wraps her arms around me to give me a bear hug.

I swallow back a sob and with no warning, a wave of anger judders through my body, making me produce a guttural groan.

Ruby, sensing my teetering emotions, pulls back. 'Sorry. No being nice. Stay furiously frigging focussed.'

I smile. Ruby's language is as colourful as her bright clothing. When we first met, I'd found her swearing disconcerting, but I soon realised it's part of her 'say-it-as-it-is' psyche. From her wide smile to her closely cropped hair and her sparkling teak eyes, I love her loud, brash manner.

Bonnie and Cath head for the vehicle next to mine and Cath calls in her lilting Irish accent, 'You be sure to take care of yourselves ladies. We need you fighting fit to have any hope of winning this competition in Paris.' She bursts into song as she's prone to do with the slightest association. This time it's something about a night in Paris being like a year elsewhere.

I quickly get in my car.

Ruby jumps into the passenger seat, all ears. 'Now, tell me. Vince. What have you found out and how?'

'I have you to thank for that…' I begin.

Ruby raises her eyebrows.

'SE. I wouldn't have known about SE. Would have had no idea it was a dating app if you hadn't shown it me on your phone.'

'Spontaneous Encounters. God, is that still going? I haven't used it since Max and I hooked up again… sorry, go on.'

'Well, Vince left his tablet. It was down the side of the

settee – I found it when I was tidying. I mean, I thought it was James's, and I was worried he'd been playing games instead of doing his homework. So, I scanned through all those icons across the screen and there it was, the same dating site you used to use. I was horrified. I thought, what's James doing on dating sites when he's only fourteen? Especially knowing all the things you got up to with the blokes you met. I mean, no offence intended.'

'None taken.' Ruby's eyes twinkle.

'But then I realised the tablet was a newer model. It wasn't James's and then I saw Vince's work stuff and I knew it had to be his. He can't have realised he'd left it. Then it...' My words dry up.

Ruby waits patiently.

I swallow and try again. 'It hit me like a hammer. Vince was using Spontaneous Encounters.'

Ruby presses her lips together.

'He couldn't have known he'd left it at home. I mean, it was easy to open the app. The password was the same as our alarm code – the date we got married. What a joke. And then I saw them...'

'Go on.'

'All the encounters... A whole history. I was shaking as I hit the home button. He seemed to have several profiles. I clicked on one of them and there was a picture of him from years ago. It was taken on our honeymoon. I had been photoshopped out.' I clench my fist.

Ruby squeezes my hand.

'Honestly, I wanted to throw up. He was using another name. On this profile, he was Ben Johnson. I felt so repulsed I had a sort of tunnel vision; I could barely see the detail. But, Ruby, the dates, they went back years. And the lists of women he'd met. So many. And as I took it all in, I realised these encounters were all arranged for midweek when he was away from home.'

'How many?'

'At least ten. I started to count, but then one date struck me. The earliest entry. Ruby, it was…' I choke out the words, 'It was fourteen years ago. Just one week after the twins were born, when I was still in hospital.' I thump the steering wheel. 'One damn week.'

'Frigging hell. The shit.' Ruby shakes her head.

'There were no other dates for a good few years – from what I could see – but then the numbers started increasing. First one, then two a year, then more. One part of me wanted to smash the tablet against the wall, the other part to examine every detail. Then mother arrived to look after the twins so there was no time to delve any further.'

'Did you tell her?'

'My mother? Heavens, no. Speak a word against Vince? She thinks he's God's gift. Besides, she was too busy moaning about having to drive over to sit with Joanne and James on her Cheshire Ladies' night.'

'What did you do with the tablet?'

'I shoved it under my bedcovers and now I can't think… I mean, what do I do? Ruby, I must look a complete fool…'

'Foolish you are not.'

'But I should have known. Hell, what am I saying? I did know… I immersed myself in my dress design, in dance, yoga, Pilates, running… anything but face up to it.'

'Hey. You're not the one at fault here. He needs to go.'

I rub at my brow and realise my teeth are clenched. It is easy for Ruby to have such clarity. She has never known the complexities of being married. She's free and utterly liberated.

My phone starts to give a low buzz, vibrating inside my bag. Ruby grabs the bag, pulls out the device and switches the call to divert before throwing it back inside.

'You need time to plan your next move. When's the scumbag due back?'

'Tomorrow evening, I think.'

'OK, you've time to decide what you're going to do. Do you want me to come round in the morning? I'm working from home again and can slip over to yours after the school drop off.'

I nod. 'What would I do without you?' A small wail of anguish escapes my mouth, and I bite my hand.

Ruby places a firm hand on my shoulder. 'You're going to be OK. Come on, Monica. Go home. Don't look at that tablet again. Resist. Take a bath, have a stiff drink and go to bed. We'll look at it together in the morning and work out what to do.'

I give a shudder and suddenly feel exhausted.

Ruby takes my hand and gently strokes it as we sit quietly for several minutes. A calm descends on me and I breathe deeply.

'Please don't tell anyone about this.' I sniff and start to rummage for a tissue.

'My lips are sealed.' Ruby pulls a fresh pack of tissues from her coat pocket and puts them in my hand before opening the car door to get out. 'Sure, you'll be OK?'

'Yes, I'll be fine.' I remove a tissue and blow my nose loudly, causing Ruby to jump back.

'God, I've never known anyone blow their nose so loudly. That snort would give a demon a fright.'

We smile and I suddenly know I *will* be OK. Ruby has her life sorted – she'd never let someone walk all over her. Hell, I can be like Ruby.

'Ruby, I really appreciate your help. See you in the morning. By the way, who was calling?' I indicate my bag she's placed back on the passenger seat.

'Someone called *Cheating Bastard*.' She winks at me, and we both laugh.

2

RUBY ANDERSON

My fingers hover over the keyboard of my laptop as I sit at the worktop in my kitchen. I stare at the screen, shaking my head as I read this year's three-hundred-and-sixty-degree work appraisal task.

Present yourself as the latest new product. What are you? What do you do? How do you work? What is your unique selling point? How will you become an invaluable asset to the First Bite company?

The format is a variation on the same tedious theme repeated every year by the IT recruitment company I've worked for these last eight years.

Present myself as a product. Again? I groan. I'm not in the mood for this.

I'm scheduled to give my – as yet unwritten – presentation to my team via shared screens later today. I'll be expected to use all the management lingo I can muster. Blue-sky thinking, cross-pollination, ideation… My boss and my peers will then give their feedback on my performance.

I realise the point of the process is to emerge from the appraisal with a new sense of self, intended to trigger change and improvement.

It's the usual corporate exercise bollocks. Nothing but a stupid game.

I remember last year's fiasco.

'Ruby, you are giving the impression you are not taking your job seriously,' Giles, my Eton-educated boss had remonstrated. 'Comparing yourself to a new fertiliser spreading much-needed nutriment in the company served only to bring into question the calibre of your colleagues, let alone prompting a distasteful image in our minds.'

I could hardly say that was my whole point. Since Giles took over the company, it's all turned to chicken shit. He got rid of all the decent workers, replacing them with his cronies. How I'd love to shovel manure all over them. I should've been made team leader long before it finally happened. I mean, I brought in more frigging deals than the rest of them put together. The gobshite even had the cheek to expect my gratitude when he alluded to operating positive discrimination when I finally got my promotion. Little toerag.

I snap the laptop shut and head into my handkerchief-sized garden. The welcome April sun warms my face as I sip my coffee and look at the clouds skittering across the sky.

Who am I? What does make me tick?

My colleagues would be shocked to know the real Ruby. I keep her well-hidden from most people, but especially when I'm at work. I close my eyes and smile as

I imagine a true presentation of myself to my colleagues – one they will never see.

Hi. I'm Ruby Anderson. I'm forty-four, a single parent with a fourteen-year-old son, Will. Yes, I know. My name matches my status, Ruby-and-her-son. Glad you find that amusing. So, you want to know all about me? Well, politically, I'm left of centre. I believe women rock, Black Lives Matter and plastic should be outlawed. I hate dog poo, misogynists, and any kind of pastry. I love music, dance, festivals – Glastonbury, Leeds, Creamfields… basically anywhere where you can dance all night – and my tipples are gin or red wine.

Oh, and by the way, I'm a sex addict.

I imagine their mouths dropping open.

I refuse to apologise for my addiction. I love sex; it's true. I love getting naked, I love the buzz, the intimacy, the orgasms. Hell, I like sex more than music and dance, but the music and dance of a good festival with sex thrown in is the dream combination.

Pardon?

Yes, I know nothing at work would indicate this side of my character. When I'm at work, I'm at work.

I can see from your faces you want to know more…

So, I prefer men to women, although I've been with both and sometimes both at the same time.

I picture Giles's eyes so wide they're nearly popping out. I'm enjoying this.

If I can't have sex at least once a week, I have to turn to my appliances. Yes, I said appliances. Sex toys, dildos, vibrators. I have several. I picture the photos of each little beauty flying up on the PowerPoint screen in glorious technicolour.

My team's reaction would, I'm sure, match Monica's shock at my Ann Summers party a few years back. She'd never seen a vibrator, let alone used one. She'd had a glass too many when she confided in me. 'I have never had an orgasm.'

'You're frigging kidding me? Never?'

She clammed up when Asha interrupted, wanting to know what we were talking about. I never managed to get Monica to discuss it again. So, I got her a Rampant Rabbit for her birthday. She nearly died when she opened it. In fact, she was so embarrassed she told me she'd hidden it deep in her wardrobe so her husband and kids wouldn't find it. Mind, she didn't throw it away. I smile.

Back to my presentation.

But my crazy sex life is now past tense. I've changed.

I can see you all sighing with relief. Oh, I'll always be a sex addict.

Consternation.

However, I'm contemplating becoming a sex addict with one person. You may well ask, what's caused this change? One word. Max.

Max. It all feels a bit surreal. I said I'd never go monogamous... The imaginary office scene melts away as Max's face, Max's body fills my mind. His beautiful, thick curly hair, his brown eyes, his toned stomach. He may be ex-army, but he still keeps ultra-fit.

I met Max through the dating app. We only dated the once. We barely spoke over our single drink before going back to his. Hell, I barely made it into work the next day. The memory makes me quiver.

Then the following week I checked the app to approach him for another date, but he'd disappeared without a trace.

I think back and picture Max's genuine smile of surprise when we met by chance a few months later. Monica and I had been to see a dance show at the Royal Northern College of Music in Manchester. We walked to Piccadilly to catch the train home and there he was, all by himself. He sat next to us on the train, and we talked all the way back to his stop, a few before ours.

We swapped numbers – that was a first – and he suggested we meet up again. I had to confess my name was not Scarlet.

'I like Ruby better. Deeper shade of red,' he'd muttered with a lascivious smile.

We've been seeing each other for almost a year now. He said he'd acted completely out of character on that first date. He made me agree we wouldn't have sex for at least a month until we'd got to know each other better. Going home after only one chaste kiss each time we dated – excruciating. But the restraint thing, if I'm truthful, it made it even sexier.

He came to a weekend festival with me last autumn, us and a few mates. After dancing in the mud and the rain twenty-four-seven, I knew he was my kind of guy.

'Ruby Anderson, you're starting to turn my head.' Those words still ring in my ears.

Heck, even Will likes him; I can tell. And I know

Monica will like him when they meet properly. He's like her, completely genuine.

I think back to Monica's reaction that night on the train going home from Manchester. Monica insisted on knowing how we'd met. She could sense the chemistry sparking between us and was intrigued as to why Max thought I was called Scarlet. Well, I'd had a few drinks and felt on a high after Max took my number, so I ended up confessing the whole meeting-others-for-sex thing.

Wow. Was Monica shocked. She didn't believe me at first. I had to show her the app on my phone.

'God, Monica, have you really not seen a dating app?'

'Why on earth would I have seen one?'

'Jeez, you have to get yourself on social media, woman.' I told her. 'You haven't a clue what you've been missing.'

Her astonishment soon turned into an insatiable appetite to know everything. She wanted all the gory details.

I smile as I recall our conversation. Now that would have made some presentation.

We giggled all the way home as I told her about my spontaneous encounters. I deliberately kept it light. The good, the bad and the downright comical. And there was a fair variety of each. Snatches of our exchange replay in my head.

'How do you choose which ones to meet? I mean they could make up any of that stuff they write.'

'And believe me, they do. I send a tester email first. If I think they're too serious or dull or creepy, I say thanks, but no thanks. Then I always ask certain questions.'

'Like what?'

'What's your favourite food? No, seriously. You can tell a lot about a person by what they eat. And if they mention meat and two veg…'

'Stop.'

'Which brings Freddy to mind. Big on his roast dinners…'

'Ruby.'

'He was a sound engineer with a touring show performing in Manchester. Only here for a few months. Unusually, we met a second time. He'd rented out one of those Salford Quay apartments. Had no conversation whatsoever. God, was he dull. I was going to make excuses to leave early on our first date, but the minute he turned the lights down and put on tracks from Orchestral Manoeuvres in the Dark, he transformed into a gyrating, sexy beast. Wow, was he hot. You do realise you are showing a very unhealthy interest in this, Mrs Thornton. Should I be worried?'

'What? This is better than the erotic book I purchased on my kindle by mistake. Tell me more.'

'OK. Well, at first, I thought I'd find my match, settle down and do the whole commitment thing. But I soon got bored. I rarely went out with someone more than two or three times. The serious ones scared me. I mean, Will and I are perfectly happy by ourselves – no one else to interfere with my parenting or disrupt our lives. Besides, I love the thrill of being with someone for the first time. Sadly, it soon wears off. I confess it, I'm an addict and why stick to one man when you can have loads?'

'I only had a couple of boyfriends before Vince.'

'Honestly?'

'I was barely out of college when we married. But stop changing the subject Ruby Anderson, or should I call you Sassy Scarlet? Tell me more about all these dates.'

'Oh, many are instantly forgettable, but a few stick in my mind. One chap looked at me in horror when I turned up for our rendezvous. I quickly checked my boobs hadn't escaped my dress and asked him if he was OK. You know what he said? "I hadn't realised you were black". Yeah. Ridiculous. He mumbled something about not paying photographs much attention, but I didn't give him a chance to finish. I got up and walked out. He followed me to ask why I was going. So, I told him, "I hadn't realised you were an arsehole". That shut him up. Opened and closed his mouth like some beached fish. Come to think of it, his skin was really pasty – looked like a blanched piece of cod. It's true. Who wants to have sex with a fillet of fish? Mind, even the good-looking ones can be a pain. There was one who spent his entire time looking at his reflection in huge mirrors on his bedroom ceiling.'

'Whoa. Kinky.'

'He kept moving me to one side to admire his beautiful body. He called himself Apollo – I know, loads of bizarre names on the app. Clearly thought of himself as a right sex God. More like Narcissus. Totally in love with his fake-tanned six-pack. Then there was this guy who wanted to have sex in the bushes of the park…'

'What?'

'I said no at first, but it was a warm, dry night, and the park was empty.'

'You didn't?'

'I did. And I have to say, it was exhilarating. Hilariously, his name was Rowan.'

'Ha ha. You have definitely made that up.'

'Or maybe it was his berries I remember…'

Monica snorted into the back of her hand.

'Hey, if you really want something to laugh at, I can tell you about the ones who want to dress up. Close your mouth. I'm OK with it if it's not too weird. It's just a bit of innocent fun. I happen to have built up a small wardrobe of erotic gear.'

'Seriously? I need details.'

I smile as I picture Monica's face when I replied. Her bright blue eyes were alight with a combination of curiosity and scandalised delight.

'I knew you would. Oh, you know, stuff like nurse and doctor, pilot and air hostess, wench and master… that sort of thing. One chap got us both *Flintstones* outfits.'

'Yabba-dabba-doo.'

'Best if I don't mention his club.'

'Stop it.'

'Then there was a guy who was into cowboys. What did he call himself? Oh yes, Clint Westwood.'

By this time, Monica was laughing aloud.

'His bedroom was done out like a tacky wild west stage set. Saloon doors, beer barrels – I think plastic shotguns were part of the decorations. I was hammered, so it's all a bit of a blur, but it was a total turnoff when he started shouting "Yeeee-ha".'

'Time to get out of the saddle?'

'You betcha. The showdown morphed into a total letdown. Clint was all boots without spurs and pistols without shots.'

Our laughter petered out and Monica suddenly turned serious.

'Will you tell Max about all the other sex dates?'

'It's none of his business.'

'So, no?'

'OK, I guess I've already told a little white lie. I intimated that like him, I'd only had a couple of dates via the app. Hey, stop shaking your head. I barely know the guy.'

Monica smiled as she sent her lovely long auburn mane swinging around her head. 'What are you like?'

A year on, I still haven't told Max the full story, not that he needs to know. In fact, I hadn't confided this aspect of my life to anyone until I told Monica. I guess I did enjoy raising her eyebrows. She's normally so serene and collected. Everything about her, from her perfectly made-up symmetrical face to her beautifully manicured nails, speaks calm and poise. She could easily come across as a bit remote, but when she lets her hair down, the real Monica emerges, and she's full of fun.

We had a ball when we went to Glastonbury together, just us with our kids. I asked her after mistakenly assuming she was a single parent like me.

Her face had lit up when I described it as a welly-wallowing-wet-wonderland.

'So, let me get this straight. We'll be staying in tents among crowds of people, with barely any facilities, in the mud and the rain?'

'All that and worse. But there's music, dancing, atmosphere... Oh, and Kylie...'

'Kylie? Deal breaker. OK, yes.'

'Really?'

'We'd love to come. The twins'll be so excited, and Vince is away on a work trip.'

That was the first I'd heard of the bloke. I'd been chatting to Monica intermittently for maybe six months and she'd never mentioned him before. Anyway, our kids – pre-teen – adored the freedom of the festival and we all got on famously. The weather was phenomenal – dry and hot – and Monica and I laughed the entire weekend. It was the start of our close friendship. We would've gone every year since, but sadly the pandemic put paid to that and we couldn't get tickets to the ones since.

Kylie's "Spinning Around" plays in my head and I can picture Will, Joanne, James, Monica, and myself all copying the moves of Kylie's stage dancers with thousands of others. We still jump to our feet every time we hear it to relive the moment.

A cool breeze prompts goosebumps, and I come back to the present, opening my eyes to see a threatening cloud starting to blot out the sun. I head indoors, downing my remaining coffee.

I can't think of a better mate than Monica. I can tell her anything. If it hadn't been for our lads accidentally swapping mud-covered PE kits at school, I'm not sure we would've ever spoken. At first, I was a little wary of her. I mean, it's slightly intimidating to be with someone who looks so perfect, but once we got into conversation, she and I just gelled.

Monica introduced me to Clarissa's dance class. Lady C might be somewhat regal, but her careful tuition and attention to detail has transformed my dancing. It's going to be great to be performing on stage in Paris.

I wonder why Monica cancelled on me this morning. Her text was brief.

Do not come to my house.

She would only ward me off if Vince had arrived home early. He must know she's discovered what he's been up to. The bastard. She needs to kick him out.

Hopefully, she'll phone soon, but I know better than to try calling when she's having it out with him. Besides, if she doesn't manage to send a message, we'll be able to catch up before dance tomorrow when she picks me up.

Monica deserves someone way better than Vince. Would I like to give him a piece of my mind…? I furrow my brows. I can't picture him. He's never at the school – Monica does all the parents' evenings and events – and I never go over if he's at home. It struck me as odd at first, but we got in the habit of it just being us and I never thought any more about it. Well, I hope for Monica's sake, he goes quietly. In her shoes, I'd ditch the crappy husband and, come to think of it, the crappy job; she's paid an absolute pittance for her incredible wedding dress designs.

Talking of crappy jobs, I must go back to my laptop and work on this groan-worthy presentation. Time to put aside the true Ruby. My team will see the efficient business-like, down-to-earth Ms Anderson.

I glance at my phone to see if Monica's texted. I can't resist quickly scouring my chats. And then I see it…

No. I stare in disbelief. I've made a total balls-up.

It's right there above the *do not come to my house* text. The recorded message I thought I'd sent to Max last night, telling him all about Vince, I sent it to Monica by mistake.

Oh my God. How on earth did I do that? I quickly replay it, slowly covering my mouth with my hand.

Hi, Max. Missing you like crazy and guessing with you being several hours ahead, you're already tucked up in bed. I can picture you lying there, curly hair all ruffled. So, you'll get this message when you wake… sexy man.

Just back from dance. You should come over here after one of my classes. Dance always puts me right in the mood. A nice rub down in the shower would be the perfect way to end the evening… My voice makes loud panting noises.

This whole being-apart-for-an-entire-fortnight is beginning to drag. You'll have to tell your firm they can't send you away like this. Never mind you being their senior engineer, it is tantamount to torture.

OMG, Max, there's been a real crisis with my mate, Monica. Before you ask which mate, Saint Monica. You know, Practically-Perfect-In-Every-Way-But-Never-Had-An-Orgasm-Monica.

Anyway, she found out today her husband's been cheating on her for years. What a prick. While I've always wondered if she was happy with him, she doesn't deserve to have been treated like that.

Seems he's been with dozens of women. Even when their twins were born, he was playing away. And they're now the same age as Will. That's fourteen frigging years. Monica says she suspected but only got the proof today. I can't understand why she didn't confront him before, the horrible toerag. Why she ended up marrying such an arsehole, I'll never know.

I hope you manage to get back before we leave for Paris. I miss you. Well, your body, obviously. And I guess your mind isn't so bad either. So, hurry home. Your Racy Ruby is waiting.

No, no, no. I shake as I hurriedly delete the recording, but there's no way Monica hasn't heard it. It was sent at midnight, that's almost twelve hours ago. No wonder she hasn't called. She won't see those comments as a joke, or even remotely funny. The message I'd read as a warning to say Vince had returned early now looks like an angry and final dismissal.

Shit, what have I done?

I dial her number but all I get is *number unobtainable*. She's blocked me.

3

INGRIDA VALENKO

Barry Manilow's song, it play inside my head and my feet tap out the steps on the kitchen floor as I prepare the meal.

I place the empty colander on my head and check my fingers are in correct position in the reflection of the eye-level microwave. I can also see Neil, behind me at the table, bent over his computer. He is concentrating very hard and does not notice my jazz hands or my movements as I triple walk to pick up the salt. I twist and leap before adding a grind of salt to the saucepan, then lift the colander from my head to sweep it around my body, switching hands on the way.

The routine, it varies depending on whose position I take. As the reserve, I will need to step into someone's place at a moment's notice so I must know the moves of everyone else.

Neil does not look up as I repeat the dance first as Ruby then Fay, Janine, Bonnie, Cath, Asha, and Monica – though

God forbid Monica does not make it to Paris. I do not think we will do well in the competition if she is not there.

I taste the beef stew and, satisfied with both this and my dance practice, I check the clock and go down the hall to the lounge and turn off the television just as the *CBeebies* programme has finished.

'Children, dinner is almost ready. Wash up your hands.'

Returning to the kitchen, I smile at Neil who glances up at me, his brows furrowed.

'Is everything with your work OK, Neil?' I ask him this question almost every day, but he answers me the same each time.

'Nothing I can't sort.' The frown on his face melts away.

I would like him to share with me his problems. After all, we are now married – I smile every time I think of this. Perhaps English men do not tell their wives about work troubles?

I give the stew a quick stir and start to chop the salad.

'Come here.' Neil beckons me over. 'Love the dance steps, by the way. You must remember to pack the colander for Paris.'

I laugh, discard the salad and cross to him. He grabs me by my waist and squeezes me. I wish my waist was not quite so big. I know I have put on much weight over the last year, I think two sizes of dress. But Neil, he does not seem to care. He pulls me close for a kiss. I am still pinching myself to think, in actual truth, I am Neil's wife. It all happened so quickly. Our secret – for now – and it make my heart sing.

We hear the children thump down the hall, and I quickly pull away.

They have completely accepted me as their new mama, but I do not like them to see Neil and I embrace. It seems wrong, even though Maya – God rest her soul – passed away almost two years ago. Lizzy was just a tiny baby, Theo was toddler and Grace barely four-years-old when Maya become ill. When Lizzy began to talk, she start to call me Mama, but I tell her, no – her mama is in heaven – and I insist she call me Ingrida like her siblings. She could only pronounce my name as Guy-da and this name, it stick. Both the older children also now call me Guy-da. I warm inside when I hear it. Inside my head, where I am now thinking almost all the time in English, I give a new translation to this word Guy-da. It means the same as Mama to me. I have come to love these children as much as if I had birthed them myself, and I hope Maya approves of me from her place in heaven.

I will look after them for you, Maya. It is my promise.

Theo, he bounds into the kitchen followed by Grace who is straining to carry her little sister. They first hug their father, then me, before sitting down at the table. I thank God they accept me with – how do you say in English? – ah yes, without reserve. Perhaps it is because they were so young when their poor mama died. She had the diagnosis of advanced-stage cancer and was in hospital for many months.

I felt so sorry for her. I know what it is like to have cancer. I was very lucky to recover from mine. Poor Maya she was not so lucky. We get to know each other when I nursed her in St Ann's Hospice. It was where I met Neil.

He was forced to look on without any way to help as his wife grew weaker by the day. I took the children to the play area so Neil could be alone with Maya. Grace help me give Lizzy her bottle, and we both pushed Theo on the swing. We grew so close.

It seemed like most natural thing to say yes when Maya ask me to help with the children. Neil had to return to work part-time – he does an especially important job and supplies medical equipment to the poor countries of the world – and he could not do this and look after the children by himself. So, I change my shifts at the hospital and spent as many hours as I could with them.

When Maya, she pass away, Neil said it was crazy for me to pay rent for my flat. He said I could move into his spare room and become a live-in nanny. I know of other Latvian women who do this kind of job. I was happy to help, and I look after the little ones who often came to sleep with me in my bed in those early days when they missed their mama.

I was glad to leave my nurse accommodation where I had to share a kitchen with five others. With everyone working different shifts, we had to creep around the place, so we did not wake up those who sleep in the day. I was very lonely there, and I was glad to move to Neil's family house.

It is true that God works in mysterious ways. We slowly became our own little family and I help with settling Grace into school then later Theo into nursery. With my shifts at St Ann's and with being so busy helping Neil and the children I did not see anyone else for maybe best part of a year. Well, apart from my work colleagues and my dance friends.

I know now, this was all part of God's plan, to get to know Neil and his children in and out... no, that is not the correct English term... Ah yes, inside out. And while I was full of sadness, Neil had lost his beautiful wife, I found myself becoming very fond of him. When I was not working at the hospital, we stayed up talking every evening, late into the night. Of course, I did not say anything about my feelings – I was only there to help him – but then one night, not so long ago, he tell me I had make big difference to his life and he held my hand.

'Ingrida, you've been my saving grace. I need to ask you, are you happy here?'

'Yes, I am very happy.'

'But one day, maybe a while away, you'll leave?'

'I... I do not want to leave. Unless you wish me to...'

'No. No, I don't. Ingrida, I want you to stay.'

He then put his other hand over mine.

'I want you to stay. Always.'

My heart, it was pounding, and I could not find the words to answer. But then Neil, he kiss me, and I just knew, there and then, I belong there.

After this, I was surprised we did not make our union together. I began to think Neil, he want a relationship that is... *platoniski* is the word in Latvian. But I was happier than I had ever been, so I did not mind if we did not have full relationship. Besides, I gave up any idea of being married years ago, when I nearly die from cancer. When I survive,

I vow to work as specialist nurse to help others facing such terrible times. Neil and I, we kiss many times but I feel much frustration he and I did not get closer. Reverend Prudence from our church offered for me to go and live with her family – she say something about what she call idle gossip which I did not understand so I looked it up and see it mean conversations about other people's private lives – and I suggest to Neil perhaps moving would be a good idea.

But then, out of the blue, he proposed me.

It was such a happy shock; truly a dream come true. I thank God – *Paldies Dievam* we say in Latvia – he fall in love with me.

I look at the children sitting around the table. They close their eyes and put their hands together. We all say a simple prayer, 'Thank you for our daily bread. *Paldies Dievam.*'

Neil serves the stew and I hand the bowls to each child, happy to see their hungry smiling faces.

'Guy-da?'

It sends a thrill to my heart whenever Grace address me so. I did not think I would ever be a mama, not after my womb was removed. But here I am with three beautiful stepchildren.

'What's this called? I can't remember.' Grace takes a large mouthful and then helps Lizzy to load her spoon.

'*Sipolu Sipenis,*' I tell her. 'Is Latvian stew. My mama used to make it for me when I was little girl.'

'Where's your mama now?'

'She is in heaven like your mama. Perhaps they are friends there?'

Theo pulls a face. 'What are these funny lumps?'

'Onions.'

Theo pushes the onions on one side with his spoon before he eats the rest and I sit back and watch. Now and then I help Grace to feed Lizzy who, I am sure, will one day make decision to feed herself. She is still just baby at only three years old. In Latvia, I grew up too quickly. Here it is good to be children for as long as possible.

'Why aren't you eating, Guy-da?'

'I have dance tonight, Theo. I will eat when I get home. Is not good idea to dance with full stomach.'

'It can't be long until the competition.' Neil reaches for a second piece of my homemade black bread. 'Less than two weeks, yes? I'm just sorry we can't come and watch you dance.'

'Why can't we?'

'It's in Paris,' Grace tells Theo. 'Paris is in France.'

'Why can't we go to France?'

Neil look with kind eyes at his son. 'Paris is just a bit too far and anyway Nanna and Gramps are coming to stay that weekend.'

Theo groans loudly and Neil gives me a look full of meaning.

I nod. I fix a smile onto my face, but inside I am making a frown. While I am gone, Neil will tell Maya's parents we are married.

'We need to keep this to ourselves for now,' he say to me after our short registry office service. 'We can't even tell the children yet, not until I have told Rita and Terry.'

'They will not be happy?'

'It's hard for them, Ingrida. They still haven't come to terms with what happened to Maya.'

'But, Neil, I wish to tell everyone.'

'And we will. We just need to keep it quiet for now.' He kiss me and held me close. 'I'm waiting for the right moment.'

'And right moment is when I am not here?'

'I think it's best to break it to them gently. They'll be staying while you're in Paris and with it being the same weekend as the anniversary of Maya's death, I think it'll go better if I do it alone.'

I have only met Rita and Terry a couple of times – they live in Devon – but I do not think Rita likes me. Also, she is not very good with the children. Grace say to me she is frightened when her nanna claps her hands together loudly many times when she wants the children to be quiet.

'Theo, Nanna and Gramps can't wait to see you again. They're bringing up your birthday presents.' Neil tells his son.

Theo shrugs. 'What's for pudding?'

Grace taps my arm. 'I want to dance like you, Guy-da.'

'Well, you must practise your ballet steps, Grace. I did very much practise when I was a little girl in Latvia.'

'And I want to see you dance in your costumes.'

'One day, sweetie,' I reply.

I have not told Neil I am not in actual fact dancing in the Expression competition. I am only the reserve. I make terrible mistake in the last competition and all my steps went wrong. Clarissa could not hide her disappointment.

The other dancers were really kind, especially Asha and Ruby. But I felt awful. I think it was my fault we did not come first in the North West heats. When Clarissa ask me to dance in Paris, I said no. But Ruby say they needed a reserve and Asha spoke to me so sweetly, in the end I said yes.

I think back to when I first joined Clarissa's class around four years ago. I had met Hazel, Clarissa's close friend, when I show her around St Ann's Hospice, and we started to talk about dance.

'Dance has been my life,' she told me. 'Nothing else compares to that amazing feeling of euphoria that comes with a wonderful dance routine.'

'I also love dance. In actual fact, I dance with Latvian theatre company for few years.'

'Did you? Goodness. Why did you stop?'

'I had my diagnosis and was very poorly. It was not possible to continue. Then, when I recover, I make up my mind to train as nurse and I did not have time, but I miss it very much.'

'Perhaps you would like to come and try out our dance group? All ladies. It is run by my dear friend, Clarissa. We do all sorts of dance styles; theatrical, jazz, American smooth, balletic numbers… a huge variety. You would be most welcome.'

I instantly agreed. Back then, I was a little lonely and had not met Neil.

Hazel gave me the details of the next class and arranged to pick me up. 'There is one condition, however.'

'Yes?'

'You must not tell anyone we met here, at the hospice. I have not mentioned my… my condition to anyone and I do not want Clarissa finding out. Not yet.'

'Of course, I am professional nurse who keeps confidence.'

'Thank you, Ingrida.'

When she left, I looked at her notes and shook my head. *Paldies Dievam*, I recover from my terrible cancer but Hazel's prognosis, it is very bad. I vow then to keep Hazel in my prayers every day.

Clarissa's dance ladies, they were very friendly and soon make me feel at home. Clarissa compliment me on – how did she say it? – my lyrical balletic style. I could not go to every class as some clash with my hospital shifts, but I went whenever I could.

But I have made big decision. Tonight, I will tell my dance friends about our marriage. I know Neil, he say we must keep it quiet but I want to share my happy news. After all, we must only keep this secret from Rita and Terry.

I imagine myself saying to Clarissa, *can you please change the words on the Paris programme from Reserve: Ingrida Valenko to Reserve: Ingrida Goodman. Yes, that is right. I am now a married lady; Mrs Goodman. I got married two weeks ago. It was only a very small wedding…* I will not say we got cancellation at the registry office.

Clarissa and all the ladies will clap their hands with delight and rush to congratulation me.

Now it is the end of the class, and I do not feel so enthusiastic. The dancing has been full of energy but there is not the usual happy talking.

'What on earth is up between Monica and Ruby?' Bonnie says in a quiet voice to Cath and me.

'There is a terrible atmosphere.' Asha joins us as we change out of our jazz shoes.

'Ruby was so late, and so flustered.' Cath shakes her head.

'Monica did not pick her up,' Asha tells us in hushed tones so Ruby – sitting a few benches away – could not hear.

'Why ever not?'

'I have no idea.' Asha, she glance over at Ruby. 'I heard her trying to ask Monica why she had not replied to her messages, but Monica would not answer her. In fact, she would not even look at her. She seemed so angry…'

It is true and I think Monica, she put her anger into her solo number. She dance with a big passion. Clarissa said it was scintillating – I like this word. We all applaud her at the end, but she did not even smile. She left as soon as the last dance finish without changing her shoes. She did not even stay for the stretch out.

Ruby stands to leave and Asha crosses to her.

'Ruby, what has happened with you and Monica?'

Ruby shrugs and looks a bit tearful, so I offer her a tissue.

'Maybe there has been misunderstanding?' I suggest.

Ruby, her lips tight, refuses the tissue.

'If you ask me, Monica was downright rude.' Fay joins us. 'She did not even acknowledge Clarissa's accolade. I mean a gracious response was all that was needed, or perhaps she is veering towards immodesty, having received this kind of tribute on numerous occasions…'

'Oh, shut the fuck up, Fay.' Ruby pushes past us and rushes out of the studio.

'Well.' Fay's eyebrows are knitted tight, and she puts her hands on her hips. 'That just about sums up Ruby's proficiency with the English language…'

We quietly turn away and pack up our things.

'…It is a well-known fact that swearing is the laziest form of verbal expression…'

Fay peters out when she realise no one pay to her any attention.

I know Fay, she read many books – her work, it is in a library – and she is very precise. I listen to her English to make mine improved. I think, however, it would be better if she did not seem to be so cross when others do not speak as she would wish.

Sometimes I wonder if it was wise idea to ask Fay to join in our dance group, but I feel sorry for her. I bump into her in the library and recognise her from Neil's church – I join soon after I became his live-in nanny – but I know she stopped going when she and her husband divorced. Neil told me Andrew had married another lady in the congregation and there was a big scandal over what did happen. I decide I would not mention the church when I spoke to her at the library desk.

'Hello, can you help me please? I am looking for a book with ballet steps?'

'Fiction or non-fiction?'

'I want to study advanced ballet movements, to make mine better.'

'Non-fiction then. Follow me. As it happens, I love ballet. So, you are a dancer?'

'*Ja*, I went to ballet in Latvia when I was little girl and once danced with a theatre company.'

'How delightful. I used to dance in my university days. Are you in a dance troupe here?'

Before I know it, I tell her about our classes and invite her to Clarissa's group. I expect her to say no as I thought she was just showing polite interest, so it was big surprise when she say yes.

Fay has good musicality. Her steps, they are very exact but she is sometimes, how-you-say, a little stiff in her movements. I think it is reason Clarissa put Fay at the back, behind Monica or Asha. I thought I would get to know Fay much better once she joined the class but she does not really speak with me. I am sorry the dance does not seem to make her a happier person, unless she is a happier person inside and does not show it?

I watch Fay as she marches across the dance studio towards Janine, who is sitting with the money tin. Fay has a big purpose in her step.

Clarissa, who I do not think has noticed the falling out with Ruby and Monica, claps her hands to get our attention.

'Ladies, please remember to check you have your passports ready and completed the paperwork required for the Paris trip. Yes, Ingrida? Do you want to say something?'

I open my mouth to announce I am now married and will soon have to get a new passport with my new name,

Ingrida Goodman, but I do not get a chance to speak as we turn to look at Fay, who has started to shout.

'Your bookkeeping is all wrong, Janine. First, I do not owe any more money and second, I need a refund of six pounds and thirty pence.'

Janine looks as if she is going to cry, and Clarissa holds up her hands in air.

'Ladies.' She does not look at Fay. 'We are lucky to have Janine's help after she kindly stepped in to sort the finances when Hazel became ill. We all know Janine is doing her best and we are grateful for her efforts.'

I thought Janine would look at Clarissa with grateful eyes, but instead she has turned bright red and she mumbles an apology to Fay before she rummages in her bag for change.

I see Janine's bag is very messy. It is filled with bits of paper. Some fly out onto the floor. I try to help her to pick them up, but she hurriedly snatches a bent piece of card from my hand, and I am a bit confusion at her response. Janine drops down to the floor and she quickly pick up all the scrunched-up papers before anyone else can get them. She does not seem to know we are only trying to help, and I wonder why so many people at dance are on edge tonight.

I do not mention my marriage or my new name as everyone hurries to go home. Perhaps I will tell them at the next lesson?

Outside it is pouring down with rain and we dash to the car. Asha, who is Neil's dentist and lives just down the road from us, regularly gives me a lift. She grumbles – I think this is the right word? It is word Neil uses when he says Theo grumbles about everything – and she sighs as she drives.

'What terrible weather and what a terrible class. I hope Monica and Ruby can sort out their issues before Paris. It spoilt the whole evening. You could almost feel Monica's animosity and poor Ruby looked so miserable.'

I nod and see my wedding ring finger, it throb very badly as Asha continues.

'And what is it with Fay that she has to have a go at Janine every week? I tell you if the class had this sort of toxicity when I first came for a trial lesson, I would never have joined. And to think we are going to spend three nights with each other in Paris in just over a week. I am not so sure I am looking forward to it anymore.'

I nod agreement and try to twist my wedding ring loose, but it is stuck tight on my finger which, after dancing, has... *uxbriest*? I cannot think of this word in English. The ring was left to Neil by his grandmother and was a little small when Neil gave it to me. He say there was no point in buying a new one, 'It is the same symbol of marriage after all.'

I do not mind. I am happy to wear a simple plain ring. I do not like fancy jewellery, but I wish it was not so tight. I will have to get it make larger if I cannot lose some weight.

We stop at traffic lights and Asha glances across to my hand and gives me an incredulous look. 'Is that what I think it is? Ingrida, you dark horse. You got married.'

I smile back. '*Ja*, I am no longer Ingrida Valenko. I am Mrs Goodman.'

'Congratulations.' Asha waits expectantly and I remember she suppose to have married some years ago, but the pandemic then a family death put stop to her large Indian wedding. We were all invited to go and dance there, Bollywood style. In actual fact, we are going to be dancing this number in Paris. We all have beautiful saris Asha has shown us how to wear. In secret I am sorry to be only reserve for this particular routine in the competition as it is my favourite, but all being well, I will still dance for her wedding this summer.

Will she mind to see I have married before she has? I am nervous when I glance at her as the light changes to green and she drives off, but she flash me such a happy smile I find myself telling her more.

'It was two weeks ago. It was very quiet. Neil did not want big fuss. We went to the local registry office, found two witnesses outside but we did not have wedding party. We need to get back for children. Neil's neighbour look after them. So now I am stepmama to his three beautiful little ones, and I am very, very happy.'

'Ingrida, that's wonderful news. Did you not want a big white wedding?'

'*Ne*. In white, I look *neglīts*.'

'*Neglīts*?'

'It mean ugly… and anyway, weddings very crazy in Latvia with many strange and out-of-date traditions. I did not want Latvian wedding and Neil, he also did not want traditional wedding. I would have liked to marry in church but Neil, he say this is a lot of fuss. Maybe we will have a blessing in church sometime? I would like that…'

'Well, we must tell everyone you are married next week. It will put the whole class in a better frame of mind.'

'Do you think so?'

'I know so.'

Asha then tells me all about her wedding plans as we drive through the pouring rain before she eventually stop outside Neil's house. No, I can call this *our* house now. I smile to myself. I get out of car, putting up my umbrella and before I close door I say, 'Asha, thank you for being so kind to me. It make me feel so much better to tell you and have your happy response.'

'Well, it has made my night. Goodnight, Mrs Goodman. See you next week.'

Inside, Neil is working at his computer and Grace and Theo are waiting in bed for me to tell them a story.

When I have them settled to sleep and have make a check on Lizzy, I eat my stew at the same time as I do the wash up of the dishes and straighten up the kitchen. I lay the table and make it ready for the morning. Then I take a cup of sweet cocoa into Neil who closes his laptop and pulls me into his arms as soon as I sit next to him on the settee. We cuddle and kiss. He is a very loving man and he want me even if I am hot and sweaty after my dance class and rushing about the house. I am feeling a little tired, but I am so happy Neil want to make love with me and does not care if I have a little more weight than before.

To have this beautiful family is more than my best dreams; I think God, he had this plan for me all along.

4

FAY LANGRIDGE

It is pouring with rain and I returned from the dance class drenched despite it only being a short walk from the studio to my flat. My wet coat and shoes – packed with newspaper – are drying by the small radiator. I close the curtains and once changed into my nightdress and dressing gown, I pour myself the tot of brandy I allow myself each night and sit in my armchair. My jaw is tense so I open my mouth and move my chin from side to side to relax the muscles. Rain pounds at the window, but it is not the weather that is playing on my mind. I am seething over the finances.

Janine is totally incompetent and clearly does not know what she is doing. I used to watch her when she only had the lottery money to look after, long before she took on the Paris payments. She was hopeless. Never seemed to know who owed what, and it was impossible to find out which numbers our money had been gambled on. I know we all agreed on lucky dips and they change each week, but she could easily have photographed the ticket and downloaded it to our chat group. I mean, it is not exactly rocket science.

But no, when I repeated this request Asha drew me to one side and told me not to be so hard on the girl. You would have thought a dentist would not be so sentimental.

'Fay, Janine is having a terrible time of it,' Asha said.

'Yes, well, that is not the concern here.'

'Her mother has early dementia and Janine is her main carer.'

I almost replied that surely any dutiful child – should one be lucky enough to have a dutiful child – would be happy to take on the care of an infirm parent? But I did not wish to come across as unsympathetic.

'This is, of course, most regrettable, Asha. But when it comes to finances, the only consideration should be a person's competence. In my opinion, if you take on a job you should do it properly or not at all.'

Asha shook her head. But I am sure she would be the first to complain if she was not paid correctly or short-changed at the supermarket.

We have been paying into the lottery for years now. It goes against my better nature to take part; I have always thought of it as a tax on the stupid. However, if I withdraw, it would be just my luck if the numbers came up. I would be the only one not to share in the winnings; it would be insufferable.

The others all say it is only two pounds a week, but they must realise this soon adds up – one hundred and four pounds a year, no less. And the odds of winning are ridiculously low. We have been led to believe we have won on just two occasions, a good nine months apart. Janine said it was around four pounds each. However, we only had her word for it as the girl did not show us any proof. The others did not seem to care a jot if they did not get their winnings.

'Put it towards extra lines, for luck,' Cath told her before starting to sing Kylie's song about being lucky in her somewhat annoying habit of singing at every available opportunity.

'Yes, good idea. Get a few more lucky dips,' Bonnie added. 'You know what they say, nothing dentured, nothing gained.'

'No, Bonnie. They do not say that.' I find myself constantly irritated with Bonnie's propensity to butcher the English language. 'If there were such a saying it would only be suitable as a poster in Asha's dental practice.'

Bonnie looked at me blankly.

Cath dug her elbow into Bonnie's ribs. 'You daft eejit. You said dentured…'

'Did I? I must have been thinking of having veneers if we were lucky enough to win all that money.'

They had then both squealed with laughter and while the volume was hard on the ears, I confess to feeling a tad envious these women can so easily migrate to mirth.

I lean forward to rub my sore feet before putting them up on my footstool and regard my tiny flat. I spend as much time as I can out and about after it became such an awful prison for the long, long months of lockdown when all the libraries closed. People appear to have forgotten all about his now, but I still shudder nightly when I remember my utter loneliness. I rarely do holidays – well it is no fun on your own – so our dance trip will be a most welcome change of scene.

Paris.

I reach to the side table next to me for the guidebook and unfold the inner map of the city. It lists ten key sights. I hope we will have time to explore some of them in between the dancing heats. At least our hotel is relatively central so I can hopefully slip out when we are not rehearsing or performing.

It is frustrating not to have a single room – the cost of which is prohibitive – but I expect we will be spending most of our time in the theatre.

The annoyance of the spiralling costs of the competition hits me afresh. The trip is costing a small fortune what with costumes, airfares, hotel and then we must find all our meals other than breakfast. And why do we have to pay in cash? Everyone does bank transfers now. Besides, money should not be handled when it is known to carry viruses.

Mental note, I must buy hand gel to take to Paris.

I have informed Janine I am prepared to share a room with Ingrida. As Clarissa is sharing with Hazel – providing she is well enough to travel – Ingrida is the only other one I could tolerate overnight. I am a private person, and it will not be possible to hide my disfigurement from whoever I share with; I need someone who is discreet. Besides, Ingrida is a nurse.

I have not spoken much to her; despite the fact she

was the one to introduce me to Clarissa's class. I decided to keep Ingrida at arm's length, concerned she might tell the others about the details leading to my divorce – I am fully aware she attends my old church where my ex-husband, Andrew, and his floozie are still masquerading as Christians. I am under no illusion Ingrida will not know about what happened. However, to be fair to her, it has now been over two years and there is no sign she has trespassed on my privacy.

I shudder with irritation that I have allowed my divorce to enter my thoughts.

The vicar of Andrew's church had the temerity to telephone – yet again – the other week.

'Hello, Fay. Prudence here. From St Mary's. I was wondering how you are keeping?'

'Perfectly fine, thank you, Reverend. But if you are calling to ask if I am returning to church, I can only reply in the negative.'

'No, I just like to check in on you now and then to see if you are OK. Did you get my previous messages?'

'I have been rather busy with work and my dance group. We are going to Paris for the finals of a large amateur dance competition.'

'How marvellous. Would that be the same competition one of our congregation is dancing in? Her name is Ingrida.'

I chose not to say anything.

'She is a nanny... to Neil Goodman. You may remember his wife, Maya. She sadly...'

'Oh yes.' I decided to engage with the vicar on

this subject as it could throw more light on Ingrida's circumstances. 'There is an Ingrida in our group. A Latvian lady. She is also a nurse.'

'Yes. That's her. She is an absolute treasure.'

I say nothing. Ingrida tells everyone and anyone she is a live-in nanny – as if this were a badge of honour – but I suspect there is more to it than that. She and Neil attend the very same church where my Andrew felt quite at liberty to commit adultery with a foodbank volunteer, despite the teachings of the bible. If the sacrament of marriage is not taken seriously, I would not put it past another congregant to replace his deceased wife before she was cold in her grave. The basic commandments appear to have gone right out of the window at this so-say church.

'Actually, Fay, I have asked Ingrida if she wants to come and live with my family. We have plenty of spare rooms at the vicarage.'

'I see. Are you concerned for her reputation? Living with someone recently widowed?'

'Goodness, no. It is just that she has no gap between nursing and nannying and it must be exhausting for her... Well anyway, Ingrida is a lovely soul, and we just want what is best for her. I know she adores dancing, and I can thoroughly recommend her to you as a friend, Fay. When you next see her, do say to her she is welcome to move in with us.'

I will certainly do no such thing; I do not intrude on other people's privacy.

'Yes, well, I must get on. Thank you for calling again, Reverend, but I must stress there really is no need. Goodbye.'

I contemplate what I know of Ingrida. She is polite and courteous. She even pays heed to me when I correct her English. Indeed, she seems extremely grateful to know the proper pronunciation, which is more than you can say for Bonnie, who is a language hoodlum.

Ingrida's dancing – as Clarissa will keep saying – is wonderfully fluid and elegant. It is down to her balletic training, I am sure. She appears to be a kind enough person and I suppose it takes someone with real empathy to nurse the dying. But what if we have her all wrong? I have read enough articles about those from East European countries cajoling unsuspecting Brits into marriage, no doubt hoping to gain British Citizenship and, after all, what better opportunity than nannying for a grief-stricken widower?

I think of Ingrida's round, smiling face and how she always makes a point of saying hello to me at dance and I feel a little ashamed. As a well-read, sensible woman I should know better than to stereotype an immigrant. I resolve to cautiously extend the hand of friendship to Ingrida. As we will need to talk on subjects other than our domestic situations, I have borrowed a library book on Latvia. I read a few pages each day. Life appears hard there with a shockingly low birth rate and high emigration. The country, adjacent to Russia, is wet, flat, and full of forests.

Yes, I will converse with Ingrida about her home country. I have even learnt a few key words in her native Baltic tongue. *Ja* is yes, *ne* is no, *labrit* is good morning and please and thank you are *ludzu* and *paldies*. She could teach me a few more phrases while we are away. I congratulate myself that this will be a good occupation of our time together when we are not dancing.

Ah, the dancing.

I find it hard to express the joy it brings me. I had forgotten how exhilarating it was to learn the discipline of a new routine and perform with other competent women. I joined a dance troupe at college having learnt as a child at St Eulalia's. Sister Josephine discovered I had an innate musicality when I was just a few years of age. Perhaps my parents were musical? Who knows? But I do know Sister Josephine would be immensely proud of me dancing on stage without a single person knowing about my deformities. She was the closest I had to a mother and showed me how to walk correctly and adjust my balance. She is one of the few nuns I truly miss.

I glance at the photograph of Edith and Bethan on the mantelpiece. Dressed in pink ballet costumes, they were only eight and seven years of age when they took part in the showcase. They were such sweet little girls, back then. So alike. They had been my pride and joy. Edith, in particular, excelled in ballet. She persisted with dance when Bethan began to take an unhealthy interest in skateboarding, of all things. I had high hopes for Edith – perhaps the West End? But that was before everything went horribly wrong… A deluge of distressing memories flood my mind.

It was high school that turned out to be unbelievably bad for them. My girls were polite and fairly obedient up until they got to Queensway High. I told Andrew we should have paid for the girls to go to St Clements. But no, despite being able to afford the fees, he sided with them when they refused to go to a secondary school without their primary school friends.

As the years went on, they rebelled, becoming rude and uncooperative in every aspect of life. Nothing I did helped. I stopped their pocket money, forbade them to go out and sent them to their rooms more often than not. I should have realised they would run to their father who was weak and did nothing. I think back to the row that changed everything.

'Your father will agree, you cannot go out without telling us who you will be with…'

'We don't know who we'll be with!' Bethan had shouted.

'Fay, my dear, look it's a party at a friend's house. At least we know where they are going…' Andrew, as always, sidestepped the issue.

'Well, they cannot go out dressed like that. The Spice Girls wear more.'

Edith swore at me, so I told her she was grounded. She glared at me, grabbed her sister's arm and headed for the door.

'Young lady, if you disobey me and walk out I will never…'

Edith turned sharply. 'What? Never speak to me again? Good. Fine by me.'

'And by me,' Bethan added.

'Now look here…'

'Dad, just tell her. We're not in a bloody convent.'

'It did not do me any harm.' I had responded.

'No? All you ever go on about is your immaculate upbringing. Oh, and your precious four P's. We're sick of it.'

'There is nothing wrong with prayer, practice, punctuality and perseverance. The teachings are an important life lesson…'

'Dad, tell her to give it a rest.' Edith, Bethan in tow, headed for the door.

'Andrew, are you not going to stop them?'

He just stood there, raking his hair with his hand.

The front door slammed.

Andrew turned to me, hands open in supplication. 'Fay, you are too harsh.'

'And you are too indulgent. This defiance will escalate if we do not give the girls a clear message that they cannot continue to act outlandishly.'

'Can't you go a bit easier on them, Fay?'

'I beg your pardon? Easy? Fine. From now on, you do the parenting. You do the cooking, washing, homework duty. In fact you can do everything if you can do it so much easier. I wash my hands of them.'

It was the first – and last – time I had completely lost my temper with Andrew. The memory of him shrugging and walking away is crystal clear, even all these years on.

I blink back a tear and tighten my grip on the arms of my chair.

From that evening, Andrew did take over, in his own haphazard way. He did everything I used to do and – as a woman of my word – I stopped. I resolved not to speak to Edith and Bethan until they were prepared to apologise and reform. Why should I put up with their insolence after my years of devoted motherhood?

Determined to make my stand, I would read in my room and cook for myself when they had all eaten and left the kitchen. Andrew completely sided with the girls and even had the audacity to suggest I alter my approach. Outrageous. It was not I who was behaving badly.

Those years were fraught with tension and unpleasant incidents. It was a relief when the girls both went to university and did not return home. I wanted nothing more than to get back to the former footing I had enjoyed with Andrew. I longed for a sense of peace and harmony to return to our house. But Andrew clearly did not share these desires.

I feel a tug on my heart, and I purse my lips in annoyance. I will not allow these memories to intrude. It was all Andrew's fault our girls turned out badly and then he followed suit. If I never set eyes on him again it will be too soon.

I used to wonder when Edith or Bethan would get in contact with me but of late, I have started wondering if they will ever do so. I have not spoken to Bethan since Andrew and I divorced and only to Edith on two occasions.

'You do realise, Edith, your father is the one who committed adultery,' I had told her as I moved out of the family home.

'If you want me to blame him, you will be sorely disappointed,' she responded.

'Will you stay here with him and that… that woman?'

'Her name is Rachel and no, I am not staying here but

only because I'm going to travel Europe. And before you ask about Bethan, she is backpacking around the world.'

'How ridiculous. You are both going to waste three years of study at university on hippy trips…'

'There you go again.' Edith retreated behind the front door and as she shut it, said, 'Have a nice life, Fay.'

I tear my eyes away from the photograph and force down a surge of emotion, wrenching my mind back to the present. To banish the past, I reflect on our dance practice this evening.

I summon the music of Adele's "Rolling in the Deep" and my feet twitch as I mentally run through the dance.

My toes point and lift.

I confess I am a little irritated Clarissa has barely complimented me on my steps, which I know to be accurate and in time to the music. The only comments she has ever made to me have been to suggest I feel the dance or put my soul into it.

'Ladies, dance with your heart and your feet will follow.'

This is typical of the sort of sentimental advice Clarissa frequently dishes out. I rarely challenge her but when I pressed her to explain herself further, she merely smiled as if I should mind-read her answer.

I once plucked up courage to ask her if I was executing the dance correctly and was rewarded with only a perfunctory nod. I refuse to tell her I have overcome many issues regarding my brachymetatarsia to dance. I had to exercise relentlessly – I walk at least three miles every day – wear modified shoes and endure no small degree of pain to dance even the most basic steps. But I do not want Clarissa's sympathy. I crave only a little of her praise. She tells Monica and Ingrida quite openly they are her best dancers. Of course, it is because they studied ballet in their childhood, so the movements have been instilled in them from an early age. However, most of our routines are not balletic and Clarissa's praise for these two women is not always deserved.

I have seen Ingrida make many mistakes. In the North West Expression heats, she stepped into her fouetté turn on the wrong leg and furthermore her angle was not the correct arabesque position. That is what cost us the first place that day, without a doubt. It is as well Ingrida is only a reserve in Paris, we cannot afford any mistakes there.

My legs lift from the stool as I pantomime the balance steps and half leaps to the track in my head.

When I think of it, the winning group, led by that dreadful woman Sheila, had a ridiculously easy routine unworthy of their first place. Of course, I know all about Sheila Bold and the animosity between her and Clarissa. Hazel regaled me with the details.

'Sheila was one of Clarissa's dancers for years. Pretty good, too. But Clarissa and she had a blazing row about a jazz sequence they were doing to "Sweet Dreams (Are Made of This)" by the Eurythmics.'

'Really?'

'Yes. Sheila wanted to elaborate on Clarissa's choreography, but Clarissa deemed her moves to be coarse and lewd. Sheila walked out taking three of her friends with her and then she set up an alternative dance group.'

'What disgraceful behaviour.'

'Now Bold as Brass are our bitter rivals and Clarissa is desperate we should beat them in the French competition, especially as they got a higher placing in the North West heats.'

'I agree. I have only seen Sheila Bold once. Everything about her is tacky from her ridiculously short skirts to the dreadful name she has given her troupe.'

I reach for my sewing box and, in my head, I pause at the point in the routine where Monica dances her solo. Her performance tonight was, I have to say, dazzling. She did, however, make one error. I will perhaps have to tell her she is setting off with a toe lead in the opening phrase when it is in fact a heel lead that is required. I fear Clarissa has not noticed due to her bias, but I will be careful not to mention it to Monica within Clarissa's hearing. Our dance teacher is an intelligent lady and extremely good at choreography. I would not like her to think I am undermining her teaching.

I finish the dance with an imaginary flourish and smile.

Since my divorce, dance has become one of the few activities I look forward to. The ladies are very friendly.

I am particularly fond of Hazel, Clarissa's dear friend. I am sorry she is no longer attending class, as she is my kind of woman. She is well-read and has great poise and decorum, unlike Ruby who, to be quite honest, is what some would call trashy. Ruby swears continuously and is known to cavort with many men. I have heard her talking to Monica, not that they realise it. Working in the quiet of a library, I have developed a sharp ear.

I know Ruby has given some of our group supposedly comical names, like Batty Bonnie and Lady C. Dear, oh dear, the level of her sense of humour is not just juvenile but borders on the infantile. I suspect she has also given me some derogatory name. Well, I refuse to stoop to her level; she is not worth my contempt, especially after her rudeness towards me this evening. Up until that point, it had made a pleasant change to concentrate solely on the dance and not the disruptive undercurrent Ruby usually creates. She was clearly too wound-up with some disagreement she has had with Monica.

I start to sew my new badge onto my top. The top is not to my taste. It has been designed and made by Monica and errs on the side of being rather ornate in cut. However, I have to concede it does suit all sizes, which is just as well as Ingrida has become rather hefty in the last year or two.

I prick my finger on the needle and force down an automatic panic response. I have always hated needles. Had I not been sitting down, I might have fainted. As it is, I feel light-headed, and I take a couple of deep breaths. I shiver and pull my finger away from the patch so as not to stain it with blood. I place a folded tissue over the puncture and slowly recover. I must find my thimble before I finish the sewing.

I regard the insignia and shake my head. Clarissa has made a dreadful mistake renaming our group. How could she have chosen that awful font for the embossed letters under the figure's raised leg. She has utterly botched Hazel's lovely design. Anyone glancing at the badge will assume it says that vulgar slang word for the male appendage. Dear, oh dear. None of us had the heart to point this out to Clarrisa. After all, she is having such a hard time with Hazel only a few months out of chemotherapy. Poor, poor Hazel. I do hope the dear lady is able to join us in Paris.

5

ASHA GUPTA

My dental nurse quickly disinfects the room before my next patient. I am relieved to see it is a short slot for a simple check-up. It will make a pleasant change after a morning of emergency fillings and the most awful root canal procedure with an annoyingly jumpy patient. Anyone would think I was trying to torture him, not repair his rotten tooth. It took forever.

I remove my mask and disposable gloves and sip my herbal tea. Adele's song, "Rolling in the Deep" is being piped through the speakers from the radio in reception and I smile as my feet start to tap out the dance moves. Clarissa's choreography to this number is inspired.

Monica danced her solo part with such conviction at last night's rehearsal. Her moves – one flowing into the next – were mesmerising. Her dancing embodied the spirit of the lyrics in what appeared to be a completely natural and unrehearsed manner.

Having a performer as good as Monica raises the

standard of the entire class; I said as much to Janine who was watching her just as avidly.

'I wish I could dance that well,' Janine had whispered reverentially as we slowly extended our hands into jazz reaches behind Monica.

'Clarissa says we are all capable of reaching her standard,' I responded. 'Watch Monica in the mirrors. I do. Then try to copy her technique.'

Janine did not answer and on cue we all joined with Monica's steps for the final part of the routine. I have to say Janine no longer seems to be putting her heart into it. I have been wondering if it would be better if she was the reserve rather than Ingrida, who – let us face it – is almost as good as Monica. If it was not for the unfortunate mistake in the North West heats I am sure Ingrida would not have felt compelled to back off from taking part in the finals. I feel extremely pleased I persuaded her to come with us as a reserve. Clarissa may switch her for Janine yet.

Adele's final words abruptly finish the number, and I sigh. It was a pity that in contrast to the wonderful dancing, there had been such an awful atmosphere in the studio. I have no idea what happened between Monica and Ruby. Neither of them – annoyingly – have given anything away. I plan to get to the bottom of their acrimonious split when we go to Paris.

My engagement ring catches my eye, and I polish it against the sleeve of my top. It has now been there for over four years without the gold band to accompany it.

The image of Ingrida's ring, stuck on her chubby hand, flashes across my mind along with her revelation as we drove home yesterday. It is hard to believe she has married her man and now has a ready-made family in no time at all. What a contrast to me being forced to wait so long to organise then reorganise my cancelled weddings. Finding a date when all my family in India could attend took literally years. At least it is now only six weeks away. Thinking about it, Ingrida took less than six weeks to get hitched. Incredible.

She must realise I have known her husband, Neil, for years. He is one of my patients. I will never forget the first time I treated him.

'Are you OK, Mr Goodman? I am Asha Gupta, your new dentist.'

'What happened to Mr Hollow?'

'He retired a few weeks ago. Is there anything wrong, Mr Goodman?'

He mumbled something and did not make eye contact with me once. In fact, he has avoided looking at me at every visit since. I suspect he does not like female dentists. He probably has incredibly old-fashioned views about women working in a professional capacity. Those outdated attitudes should be consigned to history.

I picture Neil Goodman with his balding head and corpulent figure. He has a terrible crossbite and should have had corrective braces, but he refused point-blank to even discuss any treatment. I seem to recall someone telling me he has a dodgy job selling old medical supplies to other countries. But in all honesty, I do not know for sure. It would not surprise me. I have put him down as a lazy type who would rather trade surplus or second-hand goods instead of making anything or providing a service for others, like those of us in the medical profession.

I was surprised Ingrida did not have an engagement ring, just some thin, plain, gold band which – in my opinion – could pass for a curtain ring. Mind, I already had the impression Neil was a penny-pincher. I once tried to send him home with an interdental brush, but as soon as he found out he would be charged for it, he refused to take it. As if seven pounds ninety-nine would break the bank.

Well, whatever I think, Ingrida seems happy with her new status. She seems to make the best of everything and is an incredibly positive person, always looking on the bright side – although she never smiles with her teeth. I suspect, from a quick glance at her mouth when she talks, they are not in good condition. It always surprises me that even with their medical knowledge, doctors and nurses can pay so little attention to oral care.

I expect some people would frown to see Neil has remarried within two years of being made a widower. Not me. I am more intrigued as to how they arranged a wedding so quickly. I can only feel envy at the speed of it all. How simple and straightforward to have only two witnesses plucked off the street. It sounds bliss when I think of my crazily huge guest list and how long my wedding arrangements have taken.

My feet tap to the next radio track, and I smile at the eminently suitable lyrics to "At Last" sung by Etta James.

The words speak directly to me. Like you, Etta, I have my one love and at last we will be married…

I contemplate what it would be like to have a simple

registry office ceremony... No. It would never do. It would be over far too quickly. If you are only going to marry once, you may as well do it in style.

My mind drifts with the lilting melody as I picture Ingrida's reaction to my wedding plans.

'How many guests?'

'Almost a thousand. I do not even know the exact number.'

'*Ne*. They are your family?'

'A few, but most of them I do not know, and I will probably never meet again.'

'And you feed all these peoples?'

'Yes. The wedding, ceremony and celebrations go on for a full weekend. Ma and all my aunts have not stopped cooking for months.'

Ingrida had whistled. 'It must cost much money, Asha?'

'Ah, my parents will be paying for the whole event. Ma and Baba insisted, but it means they get to have it their way – well mostly their way – with all the tradition, fanfare, and rigmarole.'

'Will you wear traditional Indian dress?'

'Yes. In fact, I have two Lehenga dresses – one red, one tangerine and gold – and I am also looking for a white wedding dress, but Baba does not know about this yet.'

'You mind if I ask... your fiancé... was meeting with him arranged?'

'No. I met Jay at university. I refused point-bank to let Baba choose my husband. He did not do a particularly good job with my younger sister, Rashmi.'

Ingrida had smiled and as she pulled at her tight ring she asked, 'And your parents, they approve of Jay?'

'They most certainly do. It helps he is from a good Indian family, and I do not correct Baba when he proudly tells everyone it was he who introduced us. I let him keep up this pretence. It makes him happy, and all my older relatives will approve of our match. Like your Latvian weddings, some of our traditions are outdated but it pleases my family to adhere to them.'

'But you say, your sister, she was not so lucky with her husband?'

I nodded but did not say more.

I am quite sure it is thanks to Rashmi I was not forced down the arranged route. I went to university to study dentistry, so Baba turned his focus on my sister, much to her annoyance. It is not my fault if she did not want to study and did not stand up to my parents, even when they chose a man sixteen years older. I told Ma it was a big mistake. To be fair, if Rashmi's marriage had not been so disastrous, I am sure Baba would have insisted I marry this way. But Rashmi was so unhappy and fled from her disgustingly old, buck-toothed husband the moment she could, bringing her toddler and small baby with her.

Rashmi is cross my marriage has not been arranged like hers. She is always complaining about me getting my own way, saying I can wrap Baba around my little finger. She seems to forget I stuck up for her. Jay says she is just jealous.

I was surprised Baba did not stop me moving in with Jay but again, I should be grateful to Rashmi. They needed my bedroom for Rashmi's two boys. In fact, her return to the family home with the little ones has provided a much greater diversion for Ma and Baba's attention than anything I could have contrived.

The song fades with words about being in heaven. I imagine Jay as he will look on our wedding day, dressed in his Sherwani, which matches the colour of my red Lehenga. I am so glad I moved in with him; I could not have stayed in my parents' house for a day longer. I had to escape from all the dreadful noise and mess my nephews make. I cannot believe the disorder caused by two small people.

I replace my mask with a new one as the next patient, an older lady with a crowded mouth of teeth, enters and settles into the chair.

'Hello, Asha.' She points at my left hand. 'Oh, deary me. I see you have still not managed to get married then. How long has it been since the original date?'

She does not wait for me to answer, babbling on as I snap on a new pair of gloves.

'You've had to postpone it twice, or is it three times now? First the pandemic and then – what was it? A death in India was it? Poor dear. Well, you need to ensure it happens this time. I know of several young people who split up before their weddings could be rearranged. It would be so tragic if that happened to you…'

I smile with my eyes but – unseen behind my mask – bob my tongue out at the irritating woman.

'Good afternoon, Mrs Little. Lie back. Now, open wide please.'

The music from the radio changes to a well-known Indian song. The track is similar to my special wedding dance. It is one of our entries in the Paris competition and I am very proud Clarissa let me assist her with the choreography. Rashmi and I used to do Bollywood dancing when we were teenagers.

My mind is solely on the music as I mechanically check the teeth in the gaping mouth beneath me and attend to the brush and scale.

I have to say, Clarissa's ladies all look beautiful as we dance in our blue and green saris with matching scarves floating in the air. Ma helped Monica make the costumes at our Rusholme family sari shop. She said Monica was a very good seamstress, but I had to be very firm with Ma when the job was done. 'Do not dare to ask Monica to work in the family business. It would be a complete insult and so embarrassing.' I told her. 'Monica is a very well-to-do lady of a very high class in Britain. She works for a well-known wedding dress designer. So please, Ma, she is not a lady to sew saris for a living.'

Poor Ma, now every time she sees Monica, she bows as if she is royalty.

I think of my wedding dance. None of my family have an inkling about it and Paris will be the perfect opportunity to ensure it is performed to a high standard. I want my guests to be utterly blown away with our performance.

My patient swats my metal probe away with her hand to quickly gulp down a swallow of saliva before gingerly opening her mouth again.

'Almost done, Mrs Little. Now, wider please.'

Paris will be the first of a long line of trips for me. I have only told a few of my patients, but I will be taking a six-month break when Jay and I go around the world on our extended honeymoon. With a bit of luck, Mrs Little will be seen by one of my colleagues on her next check-up, which will be due before I am back.

Rashmi was furious when Jay and I announced our plans.

'Why is Asha allowed to go gallivanting around the world?'

'She will be with her husband,' Ma explained. 'Besides, you have responsibilities now. You have two children to look after.'

'It is not fair,' she had cried.

'Of course it is fair,' I said, watching her plump baby guzzle from her breast and wincing at the thought of a child latched onto my nipple. 'I am in a professional job where staff frequently take sabbaticals. It is not my fault you are not in a similar position…'

'It is nothing to do with your job. You always do just as you please.' The baby started to cry, and Rashmi sat him up to wind him, when he proceeded to vomit out almost all of his feed.

'Now look what has happened.' She burst into tears as Ma tried to mop up both mother and baby.

'Here, take Nikhil for a minute.' She dumped the wet child on my lap and when the fumes of his soiled nappy hit me, I was overcome with nausea. I managed to hold him at arm's length until Ma took him from me.

'Can you not see you are being unreasonable, Rashmi…' I started.

'Unreasonable? You get to choose your husband, to choose your job, to dance in competitions, to go to Paris. I always wanted to go to Paris…' Rashmi is now crying uncontrollably.

'And I studied hard at university for several years to…'

'Leave her be.' Ma gave me a warning look. 'Rashmi has not slept properly in weeks.'

I thought then that if this is what having children does to you, I would rather not bother…

I spot an inflamed area in the gums in front of me and test it with the probe. Mrs Little pushes her head back into the seat and I pull the instrument away.

What is it with jumpy patients this morning?

'Ah, a sore area. Yes, Mrs Little, you need to get your brush right into this part of the gum. There is an unfortunate build-up of plaque…'

Mrs Little gargles something incomprehensible as I pick up the metal scaler to remove the hardened plaque.

My mind freewheels as I systematically scrape between the teeth.

I was over the moon when Clarissa picked me for the Expression competition. She has only allowed a fraction of her ladies to represent the group in Paris. I have asked the exact same ladies to dance at my wedding. After all, we move intuitively, checking our spacing and dancing as a unified whole. Hazel came to watch a recent rehearsal and said we oozed talent, our combined force giving a stage presence that would be hard to beat.

Mrs Little below me winces as I hook and wiggle at a resistant lump of plaque and I am brought back to the present.

'Sensitive there, is it? Make a note,' I call to my nurse. 'We need to watch lower right three. No need to look so worried, Mrs Little. It is common for people of advanced years to develop sensitivity in their teeth.'

Mrs Little frowns and starts to mumble a reply but I insist she opens her mouth wider so I can reach around the back of her molars.

It will be hard to be away from Jay for three nights.

I glance at the small mirror in Mrs Little's mouth and smile as I catch a brief reflection of my kohl-rimmed eyes. I have started using a new type of make-up and love the effect. With this and my efforts in the gym every evening, I am sure to look my absolute best for Paris and for my wedding. It has been worth all the hard work.

Of course, most of Clarissa's select ladies are very fit. Bonnie and Cath appear to do a different class every day, including belly dancing of all things. Monica runs, Ruby swims and Fay walks and does several yoga and Pilates classes at the library where she works. I think Ingrida is possibly the least fit of our number, but she tells me she has no time for other classes and to be fair to her, she must be on her feet all day with her nursing job and looking after Neil Goodman's exhausting children. Perhaps her extra weight is a sign of nervous eating? I know Rashmi's figure has exploded with exactly this since she had her children. She is always in the kitchen stuffing her face... I guess I should feel sorry for my sister. She has lost her husband – not that he was any great loss – her freedom, and her figure. If only she were not so annoying, I would pity her.

'All finished, Mrs Little. Do swill out your mouth and we will see you again in six months.'

As Mrs Little almost runs from the room, I wonder about Janine. I have no idea if she does any other fitness classes. In contrast to Ingrida, she has lost a lot of weight in the last year; she is quite skinny now. Janine has been a good dancer, and she is pretty enough, although her teeth could do with whitening. I am not that close to her, so I have not suggested this as yet. She is probably self-conscious about her height; she is very short and would look so much better if she styled her hair. It is all lank and mousy but with a good cut it would look so much better. I guess if her mother is that poorly, she probably has no one who can give her a little encouragement with her appearance. I wonder what her life is like. Janine used to light up when she danced, but in the last few months her moves have become almost mechanical. I heard Clarissa urge her to elevate her performance and wondered if she regretted adding Janine to our competition group. Perhaps I will try to talk to Janine more in Paris. I could always offer to whiten her teeth for free to give her a boost.

6

MONICA

My case is open on the bed and I begin to pack. We set off for Paris tomorrow morning and I'm in two minds about the trip. I don't want to be within stabbing distance of Ruby, but I do feel desperate to get away.

I haven't yet had it out with Vince; biding my time until all my plans are in place.

Last weekend was the only time he had been at home since I uncovered the truth. He appeared in the kitchen, shirt sleeves rolled up and perspiration beading on his brow.

'Monica, I left a device… a tablet… it's here somewhere. Have you seen it? It's a bit like James's one.'

'A tablet?'

'It was in the lounge, I'm sure. There's a lot of work stuff on it…'

I continued to clear the kitchen.

'Or I could have left it in the bedroom? Monica?'

'I need to get ready for Aerial Yoga.'

'You don't usually do classes on Friday evenings?'

'I have just signed up to this one.'

'Right... Well, if you come across it, I need to give it back to a colleague. It's not mine, we... er... we switched them in error...'

I said nothing as I turned my back on him and left the room.

'So... See you later?' he shouted into the hall.

'No,' I call from the top of the stairs, where he cannot see my clenched fists mock-punching the banister. 'I am calling in to see Clarissa afterwards. Do not wait up.'

'Right. Er... have a good time.'

I turned up at my new class still seething but, just like with dance, the yoga proved amazingly therapeutic. Soft music, yoga moves mid-air wrapped in a silky hammock. My first reaction was almost, *Ruby would love this*, but I'm getting better at banishing any reference to my ex-friend from my mind.

After the yoga, I had a good heart-to-heart with Clarissa about Hazel – who now has to spend many of her evenings in bed – and I realised how, in the whole scheme of things, my problems were minor compared to hers. Plus, unlike Clarissa and Hazel, I have the power to change things. And change things I will.

The next morning, Vince found me working at my sewing machine.

'You got up early?'

I changed the thread on the bobbin without looking up.

'You slept in the guest room?'

MONICA

I rummaged for the scissors, picked up the bobbin thread with the needle cotton and pulled both ends through. Snip.

'Was I snoring again?'

Placing the edges of the first top under the needle, I dropped the foot and started to stitch.

'Monica, are you OK... you seem...'

'I need to finish these costumes for Paris.'

'Oh yes, next weekend. Look, I'm sorry I can't be here to look after the twins. This conference is bad timing, but it was sprung on me last minute, so I have to show my face...'

I increased the speed of the machine.

Conference – Ha. And he even has the audacity to use the word sorry – not usually anywhere in his vocabulary.

'Anyhow, I'm off to take James to his match. We could get a takeaway later? Maybe?'

I studiously ignored him as I clipped the thread and started to hem a pair of trousers.

'Well, we can decide when we get home. Bye then.'

When I did not look up, he pecked the top of my head. As soon as I heard the front door close, I took my foot off the electric pedal. Damn. That will need to be unpicked.

I now hold up the trousers and examine the hem – satisfied with my invisible repair – before carefully folding the garment and placing it in the case.

In terms of my marriage, I've decided there is nothing left to unpick. It's time to move on.

Yesterday, I opened two new bank accounts in my name and transferred lump sums from our joint accounts, taking half of each balance. My salary – for what it is – will now be paid into my new current account, so I'm making progress. Vince only checks the statements monthly. By the time he realises what I've done, he'll be packing his own bags.

My pink bowler hat beckons so I place it on my head and run my finger and thumb along the rim with the other fingers raised and my elbow high, checking the angles in the wardrobe mirror and giving a little shudder of excitement. "Dancin' Fool" is one of Clarissa's quirkiest dances and the precision needed for each and every move is exacting. When we are all in sync, the routine is fast and slick. I lift my hat high into the air with a majestic sweep, Clarissa's words echoing in my head, *full circle up and pull back to the chest – elbows out – with a pulse*. Routines like this have to be spot on; the reason only Clarissa's best dancers have been entered into the competition.

I pack my pyjamas into the centre of the hat to stop it getting crushed and make room to cushion it among the other clothes. My hand glances smooth metal. I smile. Vince's tablet fits very neatly in between the layers.

My mobile rings and Annabelle's name flashes up. A groan escapes my mouth before I reluctantly answer.

Annabelle doesn't give me a chance to speak and I know I'm not going to like what she says as she's using her best BBC voice, 'Monica, thank goodness I have caught you. We have a last-minute alteration, my dear.'

I know what's coming, so I say nothing.

'A wedding that is only a week away. The bride has been given a cancellation, so she needs her dress altering this weekend.'

I shake my head, glaring at the phone.

'Monica, are you there?'

'Yes.'

'Super. So when can you come in?'

'Annabelle, I can't do it. Remember? I'm off to Paris for three nights.'

'Monica, we cannot let a bride down…'

'Someone else will have to do it.'

'But, Monica, you are my best seamstress…'

Seamstress – Ha. How about dress designer? I count to ten.

'… So, I'm afraid you will have to cancel your trip.'

'Sorry. Try Stitch in Time, the place on the high street.'

'But… but they charge a fortune. And we pride ourselves on doing all our own alterations at A-Belle-Bride…'

'No can-do, Annabelle.'

'Really, Monica. After all I have done for you, I had hoped you would prioritise your job over this Paris jaunt.'

I slow my speech to make myself absolutely clear, 'Annabelle, I have had this trip arranged for over four months. It is not a jaunt, but a dance competition and I have not taken any holiday in two years.'

'My dear girl, barely any of the staff have had a holiday since the wedding business finally picked up. We're still making up for our huge loss of sales during the pandemic. And on that point, you must remember I did pay you throughout the crisis when no one was ordering gowns.'

Annabelle waited for me to back down and thank her

for everything she had done, but that was the old Monica. Today I wasn't backing down for anyone.

'Annabelle, can I remind you I worked throughout the pandemic not taking a day off. I worked from home when we had to close. I designed three new dresses for the business, sourced the materials, did the mock-ups and all three designs are now in high demand. The profits on a couple of these alone would cover my paltry salary.'

Silence.

'Can I also remind you I have only been paid as a seamstress not a designer and for only half of the hours I have worked. Your name is on every one of my creations and my name has never been mentioned, not even in the awards article.'

'Well, I cannot help what others write...'

'No? I saw your interview in *Wedding Cuts* magazine. You were quoted as saying, "the whole idea for the floaty, festival Freedom dress came to me when I took a trip to the Peak District... " Ring any bells?'

'Well yes, but—'

'It was *my* Freedom dress that won Bridal Dress of the Year. *My* trip to the Peak District. *My* inspiration. Annabelle, it is crystal clear you are passing off *my* designs as your own.'

'My dear girl, the credit goes to the business.'

'No, it goes to you.'

'Monica, my dear... let us not get carried away...'

'The recent success of A-Belle-Bride is almost entirely down to my skills. And quite frankly, I have had enough.'

Silence.

I can picture Annabelle's mouth flapping as I clearly enunciate my final words, 'So, no Annabelle. I will not be cancelling my trip. On my return from Paris, we can talk about the basis on which I might be persuaded to stay with A-Belle-Bride. If at all. But be assured, if there is the remotest chance I might stay with you, it will be on a new footing, or I will be taking my designs and my work elsewhere.'

Annabelle gives a sharp intake of breath and I end the call.

I look in the mirror. My face is glowing. I feel as energised as I do when I have performed a complex dance. I regard my reflection. Am I standing taller?

I bite back a grin, slightly in awe of this new me. It is like putting on an outfit of a style I have never worn. Surprisingly smart and sharply cut. It feels strangely new but a wonderfully flattering fit.

Joanne appears at the bedroom door and puts her hands on her hips.

'What's going on, Mum?'

'Nothing, it was just Annabelle trying to get me to—'

'No. I mean, what's going on? James said you told him he can only have Will around to ours if he comes by himself. Why don't you want Ruby coming here?'

'It's complicated.'

'What's happened?'

'Nothing to concern you. I just need some time away from Ruby. It's not good to be in one another's pockets.'

'Right. I feel that way about some of my friends now

and then. But she must have done something to upset you?'

'Look, we've fallen out. That is all you need to know.'

'It won't stop us going to Glastonbury again, will it?'

'Of course not. We can go with or without Ruby.'

'And Will can come with us too, can't he?'

'I… I'm not sure. Look, I've got a lot on my mind at the moment…'

'That's bloody obvious.'

'Do not swear.'

I close the case and sit on the bed with a sigh. 'Look, Joanne, I will tell you and your brother all about it, but not now. I need to get ready for Paris. Come here.' She reluctantly sits next to me, and I give her a brief hug.

'I wish I was in Paris this weekend.' Joanne kicks at the bedroom carpet. 'Anything would be better than having Grandma here. She's so strict. I mean, honestly, we're old enough to look after ourselves.'

'There's no way I am leaving the two of you in the house alone.'

'Well, I plan to be out most of the time.'

'Fine, but only if you do all your schoolwork. Do not pull a face. And be kind to Grandma…'

'Because she pays our school fees…'

'No. Because she's your grandmother.'

Joanne rolls her eyes and heads out of the bedroom, leaving me to my thoughts.

How will she and James react when they find out what their father has done? James, in particular, has always been very close to him.

MONICA

They'll be fine, kids always are. They adapt. I instantly eject Ruby's would-be advice, annoyed her voice has yet again jumped into my head.

Her number and emails are now consigned to trash. I never go to the door when she picks up the twins on her lift days and when I collect Will, I wait in the car around the corner and send James to knock on.

I've also stopped answering the house phone after Ruby tried me three times. I stood there barely able to contain my anger as I listened to her recording her pathetic messages before hitting delete.

The first was almost two weeks ago, the day I sent her the text telling her to keep away.

Monica, we need to speak. I'm so sorry. Please forgive me. Let's talk on the way to dance tomorrow. I need to explain.

Forgive her? Like hell.

The second message – a few days later – was close to tearful.

Monica, please pick up. I know you're there. We need to speak. Come on, we're best mates…

The final message was late last Thursday evening. Thankfully Vince was away and the twins in bed. Ruby had clearly been drinking, and her slurred words were no longer beseeching but accusatory.

What do I have to do, Monica? You want... want me to what? Postray... pro... prostrate myself on the floor? Tear out my hair or flay myself with birch branches? I mean, it was a frigging mistake. I never intended for you to... oh, what's the bloody point? Don't worry, I'll stay away. I can be just as stubbing... stubborn as... as... Oh piss off.

I made a rude sign to the answer machine, stabbed delete, and I haven't seen or heard from her since.

Ruby didn't make the final dance rehearsal a few nights ago.

'Dear, oh dear, this is no time to miss class.' Clarissa had wrung her hands. 'This competition has to be the priority for everyone if we are to be in with a chance of winning. You all know Sheila's dreadful group will be our main competitors. We cannot possibly allow them a higher ranking than us. Ingrida you will have to stand in for Ruby. Now places please...'

Ingrida danced beautifully; her arm and hand movements are so graceful. It is obvious she has trained in ballet. Without being mean, she's a far better dancer than Ruby.

Clarissa put us through our paces and the excitement in the studio was electric.

'Well done, Ingrida. It's not easy to step into another position with all the changes in spacing and direction.'

'It is very kind of you to say so, Monica. But I do hope Ruby will be there for the competition.'

I absolutely hope she is not. I find my jaw tensing as I bend to take off my jazz shoes. If Ruby does come, I'll be civil with her, but I've already told Janine I will not share a room with her under any circumstance.

Poor Janine, she seemed a little overwhelmed with the rehearsal.

'What time do we have to be at Manchester Airport?' I asked her.

'Oh… er… I'll check.'

'Is it Terminal one or two?'

Fay picked that moment to interrupt, and I didn't catch Janine's mumbled answer before Fay started on her latest diatribe. I pity poor Ingrida having to share a room with Fay.

The house phone interrupts my thoughts, and I wait for Joanne to answer it to ensure it's not Ruby.

'Mum – Clarissa.' She throws the phone onto the bed from the doorway.

'Clarissa, how are you? I was going to give you a ring to check which terminal we fly from. It is so exciting to think we'll be in Paris this time tomorrow.'

'Yes, the time has finally arrived. And Hazel will be coming too.'

'Amazing news.'

'Of course, it is going against the advice of her doctors, and we will not be able to get travel insurance for her, but this could be her last…' Clarissa's voice catches and my heart goes out to her.

'It is her dearest wish to see us perform in the competition and I am willing to do everything in my power to make it happen.'

'It's wonderful Hazel's going to join us,' I respond.

'She will need plenty of rest at the hotel. Her energy levels are so low.'

'We can all help look after her.'

'Thank you, Monica. Knowing Hazel, I am sure she would climb a mountain – on her knees if she had to – in order to watch us. She is a most determined lady, despite her poor health.'

I have often wondered about their relationship. No one has ever questioned if they are together as a couple or just close friends, but Clarissa told me they met in the West End of London where they were both teenage dancers. When Clarissa turned to choreography, Hazel – who appears to have come from a well-off family – funded her career and encouraged her to open dance schools up and down the country. She was the brains behind both starting and eventually selling off the Kirkland franchise. When she found Clarissa was bereft without her own dance classes, it was Hazel who encouraged her to start a new amateur dance group. It has now been running for over fifteen years. I can't imagine Clarissa without Hazel, or vice versa. They've been together for forty-plus years, and I feel a stab of envy at their obvious closeness and mutual support.

'Now the reason I called is I am more than a little worried about the flight.'

'I'm sure it'll be fine. By the way, do you have our boarding passes?'

'Those? Oh, no. Janine advised me that as we are a large group booking, we must check-in together and the passes are issued at the airport. No, Monica, my troubling thought is about Sheila.'

'Sheila?'

'Yes? What if Sheila's group is on the same flight as us?'

'Erm… I hadn't thought about that. Well, if her group appears, Clarissa, we'll just smile politely, hold our heads high and keep ourselves to ourselves.'

'Yes, of course we will. Thank you, Monica. Oh, you must think me paranoid, but you know I cannot stand that woman after what she did to me. The only reason Sheila Bold won the Expression North West heats was because she used my choreographic techniques. It is dance plagiarism. After all those years under my tutelage. I feel utterly betrayed. I hope you never have to experience such hurtful behaviour.'

I think to myself I could tell her quite a bit about hurtful behaviour, but I say something supportive and once I've checked which terminal we are meeting in, we say goodbye.

Once I've dropped the twins at school in the morning, I'll pick up Bonnie, Cath, Asha and Ingrida then park at the airport. Ruby can make her own arrangements – that's if she comes.

As for Vince, he has no idea what's coming to him.

I zip up the suitcase and pat the top, his tablet safely nestling inside.

No idea whatsoever.

7

RUBY

The meal has been ready for twenty minutes and is beginning to dry out. It's an hour after Will should've been home, but I resist texting. He's got out of the habit of letting me know where he is, but the last thing he needs is an overbearing mother checking up on his every move. Besides, I know he's been at a rugger practice and it's no doubt overrun.

I decide to dish mine up – shoving his in the microwave – and sit in the kitchen with my laptop as I eat.

Sighing, I think of Max. It's too bad he's so far away. I could've done with him here to completely take my mind off things.

He was really supportive about Monica-gate. We've spoken by phone most days; morning-time for me – night-time for him.

'Look, if you were true friends, Monica would surely laugh it off?'

'That's what I thought. That she'd come round once

she'd calmed down. But she's jumped right up on her high horse, and I can't reach her.'

Of course, Max hadn't heard the exact message as I deleted it the minute I realised what I'd done. I regret not copying it before trashing it.

'Give me the gist of what you said again.'

'In all honesty, I can't remember my exact words. But I know the *practically-perfect-never-had-an-orgasm* bit will have grated...'

'Ouch.'

'I know, I know... but Monica's reaction is ridiculously extreme. To cut me off without a word. I mean, seriously? She knows what I'm like.'

'Well, you've tried to explain. If she really doesn't want to listen, you can do no more. After all, you've left her messages and made it clear you're sorry.'

I didn't tell Max about the last message. I realise it'd been a mistake to phone after I'd had a drink or two. It was last Thursday when Max was supposed to have come home, but his return was pushed back by over a week, and now I won't see him before I go to Paris. My voice message to Monica may've been a bit belligerent... OK, if I'm honest it was downright abusive, but who can blame me when she's turned colder than a frigging iceberg?

In truth, I miss her. I have loads of girlfriends, but I can confide in Monica like no other. We shop for clothes together – she has amazing dress sense. We chat about our kids over coffee and talk all the way to dance and back. She knows my hopes and desires and she was beginning to open up about what she really wants in life. Heck, we even like the same books and on top of that, we have Glastonbury; it was epic. If I have a problem, it's more often than not Monica I'll call, and vice versa. *Would* have called – past tense now.

I went swimming the other night to get it out of my system. Did fifty lengths of the pool and then realised I'd missed the final dance rehearsal. Normally, Monica would've reminded me – she is uber-organised compared to me – but it just fell out of my brain.

Clarissa was unimpressed. I called her the next day.

'Ruby, I cannot emphasise enough the necessity of rehearsal.'

'Yes, I know, sorry, Clarissa. Something came up…'

'Ingrida had to step in for you… and before I forget, I need to advise you I have made a change to the final sequence of the Adele number. The syncopated turn is now a turning développé kick.'

'Oh fuc—er, fine. Right.'

Frigging hell, why does she always make last-minute changes when we have consigned the moves to our muscle memory?

'Yes, one knee lifts into the other leg, toe pointed, and the leg gently unfolds as it extends away…'

As Clarissa explained, I rolled my eyes to heaven. I couldn't for the life of me picture what she meant. The new step is no doubt some sort of balletic move my former exotic and pole dance classes definitely wouldn't have included.

'…and so we dip down on the leg lift and rise with the extension. It is quite simple. Monica will show you.'

Jeez, Lady C must be the only one not to have noticed our fall out.

'Right. Thanks. See you at the airport then, Clarissa.'

I'll have to get Ingrida to show me the step. We can practise in the departures lounge or even on the flight. I smile at the thought of rehearsing ballet moves in the aisle amid a planeload of passengers.

Will saunters into the house as I finish my meal.

'Hi. All good?' I fix a bright smile on my face.

Will's been funny with me on and off for months now, being generally moody and uncommunicative. So, it's a surprise when he pulls out the chair next to mine and drops down onto it sideways, leaning forward until we are face-to-face.

'Are you OK? Your dinner's in the microwave. It's your favourite, jerk chicken…'

'What have you done to piss off James's mum?'

'O-K…' I should've known he'd be hangry after rugby.

'Well, you have, haven't you?'

'Will, I—'

'Wasn't she having a hard enough time without you making matters worse?'

'What do you mean? About her having a hard time?' Have James and Joanne found out about their father's extra-marital affairs?

Will mumbles something incomprehensible before adding, 'All I know is you must have really upset Monica if it's so bad she won't even speak to you.'

There's no point responding to him when he's like this, so I say nothing.

He rises, heats up his meal for a minute or so, and grabs his fork to take the plate up to his room.

'And, by the way...' he adds from the doorway, pointing his fork at me. 'Don't you dare say anything to James when he comes here. Whatever's happened, it's your problem, so don't make it mine.' The door slams on his way out.

I shake my head. Frigging teenagers.

I can imagine the discussion I'd normally have had with Monica. We'd have started by normalising Will's behaviour, saying Joanne and James were exactly the same and that these teenage strops were a rite of passage and then we'd have sympathised with each other before finally ending up laughing as we always did...

Annoyed I'm thinking of Monica again, I throw the dirty pans and plates into the dishwasher and pick up the filthy rugby kit Will has dumped in the hall.

Well, at least Will didn't bring up the subject of his biological father again.

I sigh. My once little lad now towers over me and, disconcertingly, he's grown to look just like his dad. I sometimes catch my breath when I see him; he has Dev's startlingly good looks.

Fobbing off my son is becoming increasingly difficult, but I stick to the same story. 'I decided to be a single mum, went to a sperm bank and asked for a donor from the same ethnic group. End of.'

Yesterday he started a whole new tack.

'There's no such thing as remaining anonymous if you donate sperm. I looked it up. They have to give you a name and I have a right to know.'

I'm in a dilemma. I mean, the truth isn't so bad, but it's bound to change how Will thinks of me. Where would I begin?

Will, you were a complete miracle; a one-in-a-million chance. It's true. I was told I was infertile.

What I won't say is how I laughed it off in front of others – why would I want children? – while shrinking inside. It completely sucked. As my mates got pregnant, one by one, I decided to stick with my single friends and then I discovered the dating apps and the freedom of never having to take precautions. I soon convinced myself that having kids didn't matter one jot.

So, I went to a wedding. Penelope's wedding. It was the same day as my thirtieth birthday – a double celebration. And…

And there was Dev. Dressed in his usher garb looking completely edible; what a hunk.

…I met someone. I'm sure you don't want the detail.

He came into the posh ladies' powder room claiming he'd made a mistake, but I knew he'd followed me in. We ended up in one of the cubicles, stifling our giggles every time someone came in to use the loos. I honestly hadn't known he was married with children. I mean, he didn't wear a ring and there was no sign of any wife at the reception.

Several weeks later, when I found out I was pregnant, I wasn't so much filled with dismay as utter disbelief. It only took the space of a few hours to know with absolute certainty I wanted to have this child.

And you were the result. A wonderful result. Your father is called Dev, but I found out he was already in a relationship, and I decided to go it alone.

I got Dev's number from Penelope – told her I had a work-related question. He was horrified to hear from me.

'Calm down, Dev. You need to know this pregnancy was a complete fluke.'

'Right.'

'I was told I'd never have children. I have a severe type of Polycystic ovary syndrome. Found out in my early twenties. Look, Dev, I know it was just a fling. I know that. But this is my one and only chance to be a mother, so I'm going through with it.'

'Right.'

'I just thought you should know.'

'I don't know what to say to you, Ruby. I'm married. Our second baby is due next month. I can't... I can't...'

'Dev, it's fine. I neither want nor need your permission, and given that you're a bit of a shit, I certainly don't want your involvement. I've told you. Now we're done.'

We didn't discuss anything else. It was the first and last conversation I had with him, and it suited me down to the ground. My decision, my baby, my call.

I can't tell you much about him other than he has his own family, so I never got in contact with him.

Do I tell Will Dev was one of a long line of one-night stands? That'd go down well – not. Or that Dev knew full well he was going to be a father but opted out? I don't want Will to view himself as some sort of reject when nothing could be further from the truth.

Oh, it's so frigging difficult to know what to do for the best. Fourteen is a delicate age. His emotions are on a knife-edge as it is. One of my ex-workmates told me –

in his thick Bristolian accent – '*Neither man nor boy, but hobbledehoy.*' So frigging true.

I go to the hall and shout up the stairs, 'Will, don't forget I'm off to Paris tomorrow. Your grandpa is coming to stay, remember? Will?'

A distant grunt is all the reply I get and on hearing the ping of an email I return to my computer.

Here it is. Gobby Giles's response to my three-hundred-and-sixty-degree appraisal report awaits me. The subject line is, *Hugely Disappointing.* I open it, prickling with each word.

> *Ruby's heart no longer seems to be in her job. Her presentation was ill-prepared, and she did not appear to take the task seriously. Comparing herself to a new variety of laxative, ready to increase productivity from the basement out appeared, at best, ill thought out and at worst, fatuous. It was as if the idea just popped into her head without planning or forethought. I am of the opinion Ruby needs to re-think her role with First Bite. Unfortunately, her peers – on the basis of this exercise – would appear to agree.*

Bloody cheek. I swear out loud and bang my fist on the table. I've worked my socks off for this recruitment firm for over eight years. I was their best agent for most of those. Hell, I even thought up the company's new name.

Fingers stabbing the keyboard, I start to write an angry response, then notice Gobby had included an attachment with his negative missive. I double-click the paperclip and scan the spreadsheet.

My heart sinks. My figures for placing people in the last few months have plummeted. I press my hands into my forehead and force myself to think objectively.

It's true, I no longer feel the same way about my job and recently I've begun to hate it. I think the rot started when we were forced to work away from the office during the pandemic. I'd always loved the office banter. Then the job market dried up for months, and they got rid of several employees. Most of those they 'let go' had been good friends of mine, and it's just not the same without them.

And then Max walked into my life. Hearing him talk of his engineering job with such passion, I began to realise I'd never felt the same about my employment. I know I can do better; my IT skills are up there. Hours spent hunting for new opportunities haven't yet thrown up anything, but I'm resolved to keep looking until I find something. Sadly, I can't afford to take an employment break. Will's school fees may be paid through his scholarship, but a mortgage on one wage is no joke, even in our small, terraced house.

No, for the time being I must ingratiate myself to the board of First Bite and hold on to this job so I can leave of my own volition before I am… well, to put it bluntly, evacuated.

I delete my email and start again. This time it's closer to contrite, reminding them I have been a great asset to the firm. I hit *send* imagining the pleasure of mailing a resignation at a future date.

At least the Paris trip will give me time to fathom out where to go from here.

Paris.

The dancing's been a lifesaver; a wonderful way of

releasing tension with exercise thrown in. Apart from the spat with Monica, I'm as excited as a small child at the prospect of dancing on stage in a professional Paris theatre. If I never speak to Monica again, I'll be forever grateful for her introducing me to Lady C's class.

I grin when I think of Clarissa's exclamation after my first session.

'Ruby, you have real potential, but you are a little too flamboyant in your moves. And my dear, I will need to take the bounce out of you if you are to be a true jazz dancer.'

It took practice, but once I appreciated exactly what she meant, I put all my energies into curtailing my so-called effusive moves to meet her high standards. I was determined to make the competition team.

My neck muscles ache and I lift and roll back my shoulders. Time to relax. I flick my phone to play the "Dancin' Fool" music through the Bluetooth speaker and grab my red bowler hat to start the routine. My hands click, Fosse style, and I freeze – all angular with one knee bent into a jazz position. When the routine launches, I skid around the small kitchen in my socks. In seconds I'm transported to the studio and ignore knocking a tumbler to the floor when I sweep my hat behind my back to change hands. I sing the lyrics aloud and dart from one side of the kitchen to the other.

My legs keep low, dancing *into* the ground – as Lady C insists – my isolations are slick and concise. When the dance speeds up, I race to and from the cooker and when I throw my hat into the air at the end, I shout 'Yeah!' and gasp for breath.

Applause. Will is at the kitchen door, smiling as he claps. 'Bravo.'

I bow.

'You're not half bad.'

'So, not half good?'

He laughs and points to the tumbler. 'Hey, when I heard that clatter, I thought we were being burgled.'

'What? By the all-singing-all-dancing jazz thief?'

'...In a bowler hat. That's the one.'

Will punches me playfully in the arm as I catch my breath. I knew he'd come round once he'd eaten.

'So, how are you getting to the airport tomorrow?'

'Uber. Seems everyone else has a lift.' I tried them all, well, except Monica and Frosty. Lady C and Hazel were making their own way in a disability taxi, and there was no answer from Little Janine Young.

'Are you sharing a room with Monica?'

'No idea. We're supposed to.'

'Hey, if you're forced together you can sort out this shit. It's only a daft row isn't it?'

'Yeah. Daft. In the whole scheme of things, it's ridiculously petty and insignificant.'

'Well then, you'll make it up and come back friends.' He slapped me on the back and grabbed a huge wedge of cake from the fridge.

'Oi. That was supposed to be for sharing.'

'I'm a growing lad,' he said, winking and taking a massive bite from the block of cake.

I watch him disappear upstairs again and sigh.

Monica and me, friends again? If only I shared Will's optimism.

8

INGRIDA

Monica parks her big smart vehicle in the vast airport car park.

'How's Ruby getting here?' Cath quietly asks as we retrieve our cases from the boot.

'I would have thought Monica had bags of room for Ruby,' Bonnie starts to say. 'It's an enormous car…'

'Keep your voice down.' Cath urges as Monica puts a crook lock on the steering wheel.

I do not say I know Monica did not offer a lift to Ruby, as Ruby had called me to see how I was getting to the airport. I make it sound as if Neil was dropping me off. I felt bad not to be honest with Ruby, but to say I was going with Monica did not feel right.

'Oh of course, I forgot. Have they still not sorted out their argument?' Bonnie asks in a stage whisper.

'No.' Asha pulls her case from the boot as she hisses. 'I hope they do soon. It must not be allowed to interfere with our performances in Paris.'

Overhead, an aeroplane comes in to land and I give a small shiver of excitement. It has been a long time since I have been in an aircraft. Not since I first came to England six years ago. I smile to think how bad my English was then.

I think of all the things that have happened to me since I moved here. My mama would be very proud to see how I have made good. She would be proud to see I have become a specialist nurse and to know I am dancing again; she loved to watch me dance. I think too, she would be very surprised to see I am now a married lady and stepmama to three children. She thought I would never have children after my cancer, but I think she is up there watching me from heaven, and I can see her face smiling. Her last words to me repeat in my mind.

Ingrida, we have had a very unhappy time here in Latvia. First your father die in that terrible accident, then your uncle – Papa always said he would come to no good – brought shame on all our family, then your bad illness… and now God has decided to take me from you before my time… Do not cry, Ingrida, you must go and make a beautiful life away from all this sadness. Trust in God and always be kind to others.

I have done as you said, Mama. I have left Latvia and made a good life for myself here in the United Kingdom, *Paldies Dievam.*

'All OK, Ingrida?' Asha asks.

I stop staring at sky and – how you say? – ah yes, snap out of my memory. I realise my eyes are a little wet, so I dab them with a tissue.

'*Ja*, thank you. I was just thinking how I am very happy

to be here and also how much I look forward to Paris.'

Monica locks the car and smiles at me. 'Ingrida, you're always happy. It makes a refreshing change to have such a positive person on the team.'

Asha, she frowns at Monica and say under her breath, 'There are plenty of positive people here,' before she pat me on my arm in a kind way.

Monica's words, when she say I am part of the team and positive give to me a warm glow, even if I am only the reserve.

'I checked our flight on the airport departures site and it was looking to be on time.' Asha inform to us as we walk to the bus stop and wait for the coach transfer to the terminal.

Cath, she sings a line from John Denver's song "Leaving on a Jet Plane".

I love to listen to Cath sing – and to her happy chatter with Bonnie.

'Oh, did I tell you? I nearly forgot my passport this morning,' Bonnie announces.

'You have got it haven't you?' Asha asks.

'Yes, but I got so distracted looking for it, I actually opened the fridge door to get my jacket.'

'You never did?' Cath laughs out loud.

'You are a bit on the young side to be having senior moments, Bonnie,' Monica laughs.

Cath then adds, 'I'm not so sure about that. Bonnie, do you remember the time you got to dance and found that instead of your jazz shoes, you had put your slippers in your bag by mistake.'

Cath's Irish accent sounds musical to my ears.

'Oh heavens. I'd forgotten that. Goodness, don't tell my kids. They'll start planning when to put me in a home. Oh ladies, did I tell you I have become an auntie again?'

'Oh, Bonnie. That's wonderful news. Is that Ryan and his wife?'

'Yes, they've had a little girl. She was born yesterday.'

We all congratulation Bonnie and Asha asks, 'What have they called her?'

'Freesia.'

'Oh, how lovely. After the flower?'

'No, the cow.'

Asha, Monica, and Cath all stare at Bonnie, who shrugs and says, 'They spent a lot of time in Holland. Well, I think it was Holland…'

Then everyone breaks out laughing. I join in, but I am not quite sure what the joke is.

'Bonnie, you crease me up,' Asha says just as the bus arrives and we set off to our terminal.

I will remember this expression, crease me up. The creases of laughter like the creases in one of Neil's un-ironed shirts. It is good term. It make me giggle inside.

'I wish we didn't have to be at the airport so early.' Monica frowns.

'It'll be all the security checks,' Cath replies. 'But it means I'll get time to buy some perfume and I love looking in the wee shops in the forecourt.'

'Will you be buying anything, Ingrida?' Bonnie asks.

'I am going to look for gifts for Grace, Theo, and Lizzy.'

'Oh yes, your new stepchildren. How lovely. And don't

forget your new husband. But perhaps you should wait until we're in Paris and get them something French?'

I think to myself what Neil tell me, that Paris is expensive place to buy souvenirs and I have only small amount to spend. I did have a credit card but Neil, he does not like them and he tell me many people get into bad debt with these cards so he tell me it would be good idea to cut mine up.

Now we are married, I want us to do everything together and we are to have new joint bank account. Neil says my nurse salary can be paid in there and he will give me money every week. He say this is a tradition in the United Kingdom for a husband to give his wife – what did he call it? – *ja*, I remember, the money for keeping the house. My nursing friends they say to me this is not tradition any more, but I do not mind if Neil is old-fashioned. I like being a traditional United Kingdom housewife and I think it is good to share everything.

I am surprised at how much is the cost of the shopping for a family with three children. This cash, it does not go very far but I am very good at making budget. I use less expensive cuts of the meat, bake my own bread and always use leftovers. When my poor mama had to manage on her own, she show me how to make a little go a long way, God rest her soul.

*

We arrive inside the busy terminal and Clarissa and Hazel wave us across to the area near the check-in desks. Hazel is sitting in her wheelchair. I think she look pale, but I can see she is content to be here.

'Good to see you, ladies.' Clarissa smiles at us. 'I managed to book assistance for Hazel to get onto the flight and they will come across as soon as we are all here.'

'Who are we waiting for?' Monica asks.

'Ruby and Fay. We all need to check-in together. Has everyone got their passports ready?'

Clarissa anxiously scans the busy area for the others.

My Latvian passport is at the top of my bag. I smile when I look at the name: Valenko. I will soon be getting a British passport with my new name, Mrs Ingrida Goodman.

Clarissa suddenly gasps and we all look up. Her expression, it has changed to one of horror.

We turn to see what she is looking at.

A big group of about twelve ladies, all dressed in fluorescent pink leggings and tight matching tops – which are so low cut you can see their black bras – head towards us. They are giggling and speak very loudly. Many passengers have turned to look at them. As they get closer, I recognition them. They are the group who won the heats in the North West Expression dance competition. I do not know them in person, but I know Clarissa she does not like them at all.

The woman at the front of the group – I think she is call Sheila – is wearing a lot of make-up. She stops when she see Clarissa and clicks her fingers. All the other pink ladies suddenly shuffle into different places behind her, dragging their suitcases behind them.

'Clarissa. Pleasure to see you...' She wink to her group who form a semicircle behind her.

'The pleasure is all yours.' Hazel folds her arms.

Sheila turns her back on Clarissa and she make some kind of signal to the other ladies. They instantly start to click their fingers at the same time. Sheila turns sharply back to face us and she and the women dance, in unison, towards us using what Clarissa calls exaggerated crossover steps. They are all singing a chorus from a well-known Tina Turner song, "Simply the Best", as they advance.

Clarissa takes a step back, closer to Hazel, and the passengers nearby get out their phones to film.

'It's a flash dance,' someone shouts.

The pink women spread out and surround our group, each one coming right up close to each of us, clicking their fingers in our faces.

I do not like this. It is what Fay say is intimidating.

They then stop – Sheila bang in front of Clarissa – and do a front twist turn. I briefly see the rhinestone letters 'BAB' emblazon across the back of each top. The women face back to us again and each one extends an arm and then sticks a single finger in air. I pull back so the woman's finger right next to me does not touch my face. I know this is a rude sign in England. It is also a rude sign in Latvia.

'See you in Paris, Clarissa, but don't expect to beat us,' Sheila shouts at Clarissa who has almost turned the very same colour of their pink tops.

'Expression Paris winners, this way,' Sheila calls to her group. They scream with laughing as they get their bags and head off to the check-in desk.

Monica puts her arm through Clarissa's. 'Take no notice of them. They're dreadful.'

'They have definitely been drinking. Sheila stank of booze.' Asha looks most annoyed.

'Let's hope they don't let them on the flight,' Hazel murmurs as she pats Clarissa's free arm.

'What was it they were singing?' Bonnie asks.

'Sure you know it. Tina Turner, "Simply the Best". Bold as Brass is as apt a name as any for that brassy pack. And Sheila's dancers are no way better than us…'

'Only in their dreams.' A loud voice joins in.

I turn and see Ruby glare at Sheila's group. Fay is behind her.

'Stuff those tarty flamingos. We can beat them hands down.' Ruby smiles at Clarissa and Monica looks away.

'Ruby, Fay, thank goodness you've arrived.' Clarissa quickly switches her attention away from the shrieking pink women. 'Now everyone is here we need to get checked in. Get your cases and we will demonstrate what it is to have decorum.'

I suddenly feel a little sad. I am only a reserve and now everyone is here I will not be required to dance in the competition. I think maybe in secret I did want to perform on a big Paris stage? It is no good thinking this way, Ingrida. It will be wonderful just to be back in Paris.

I follow the others to the end of the check-in queue. I will concentrate on buying gifts for the children. I look at my watch and see we will not have long once we are through security.

'Wait a minute.' Fay has been counting us. 'Where's Janine?'

We all look around, but there is no sign of her.

'Has anyone seen her?' Ruby asks.

'Hasn't she got the flight thingies?'

'Boarding passes, Bonnie,' Fay corrects. 'Yes, I believe she has. And she is leaving it very last minute. The latest time we can check-in is only an hour away. Punctuality is sadly lacking here.'

We all look around again and a security person asks us to move out of the way of the check-in queue as we are blocking it.

We move to the wall nearby and I begin to get very bad feeling about this.

Monica, Ruby, Clarissa, and Asha all try to call Janine from their phones, but none of them gets an answer.

'I spoke to her last night,' Monica says. 'She said she would see us at the airport…'

'I tried to call her last night, too. To see how she was getting here, but it just rang out. I called about 9 p.m. What time did you call?' Ruby looks directly at Monica, but she looks away as she mumbles it was around 8 p.m.

'Has anyone else spoken to her since then?' Hazel asks.

We all shake our heads.

'What if something has happened to her mother?' Asha opens her hands. 'I mean, I understand she has been ill for some time. I know people with dementia can sometimes go missing…'

'That is pure speculation, Asha. The facts as we have

them are that Janine is not here, and she is not answering her phone.' Fay looks very angry.

'Something must surely have happened,' Cath adds. 'I mean, if she knew she was going to be delayed, the wee girl would have got in contact with one of us, would she not?'

For the next fifteen minutes Monica and Clarissa try Janine's house phone and her mobile phone non-stop. The rest of us split up to look around the terminal just in case Janine has been waiting in the wrong place.

We are all now with much worry and there is not so much time left to get on the flight. My phone pings with a notification and I click on the chat group.

'*Ne.* Ruby, look...' I show the screen to Ruby as her phone pings with the same notification.

Janine Young left.

Ruby's brows furrow as she shakes her head and clenches her fist.

'We need to check-in without her,' Ruby announces to us all. She marches across to a free desk, ahead of the queue where many people look annoyed as she jumps in front.

I watch with the others from a distance, and we see Ruby as she gesticulate and throw her hands in the air. A supervisor crosses to join the clerk at the desk and they look intently at a screen. Ruby motions for Clarissa to go and join her.

My stomach now has got what I think are called butterflies and I feel a little sick.

'This is not looking good,' Asha says aloud.

We wait for another five minutes and then Ruby and Clarissa walk back to us. Clarissa's face is as white as a sheet and Ruby has her lips pressed tightly together.

'What is going on?' Monica asks Clarissa but when Clarissa says nothing, Monica looks directly at Ruby for the first time.

'We're not even booked onto the frigging flight,' Ruby replies. 'There's no record of any group booking other than Sheila Bold's group.'

'Oh my God.' Bonnie looks aghast. 'What does that mean?'

'It means we're fuc—'

'What it means, Bonnie…' Fay steps forward and interrupts Ruby. 'Is that despite all our payments over all these months, we do not have flight tickets. It means… we are not going to Paris.'

'You are joking,' Asha mumbles, but I can see from her face she does not think this is joke.

'Not going to Paris…' Clarissa does not seem able to take it in. She leans into Hazel who puts a comfort arm around her.

I cannot speak.

'No. We are not going to Paris unless…'

We all look with expectant eyes at Fay.

9

FAY

When Ruby starts to swear aloud in a most unladylike fashion, I put my foot down. The last thing Clarissa needs is for our group to make a spectacle of themselves like that abominable Sheila Bold and her women. I glance at Clarissa and can see the poor lady is pale from the shock.

'We are not going to Paris unless… unless we can make new travel arrangements.'

'How could Janine do this to us?' Monica starts to fret.

'I cannot believe it,' Asha adds.

'Indeed, and what has she done with all our money?' I add. 'I have my suspicions. But as she has left us completely in the lurch we must, for now, put all our efforts into getting to Paris.' I clap my hands together.

'How?' Bonnie stares at me.

Taking my notebook and pen from my bag, the plan of action forms as I speak. 'We need to see if we can obtain any aircraft tickets on either this or a subsequent flight. Monica, perhaps you, Hazel and Clarissa can go and enquire with the airline? I will look after the cases here.'

Monica nods and hurriedly pushes Hazel's wheelchair to the airline desks, Clarissa walking ghost-like behind.

'Bonnie and Cath, I can see from the departures board that there are two other airlines with flights to Paris today. Go and see if you can find out if any tickets are available from the desks over there.'

'Right you are.' Cath and Bonnie make a beeline for the desks I have indicated.

Ruby is shaking her head. 'There's no way there'll be seats for all of us. Frigging hell...'

'Ruby, you and Asha make a search for Eurostar train tickets on the internet.'

'Yes. Good idea, Fay.' Asha pulls out her phone, nodding respectfully to me while Ruby is already using her phone without any glimpse of acknowledgment of my leadership. Typical.

'The new tickets, they will cost much money?' Ingrida is chewing her lip.

'Let us worry about that if we can actually procure any,' I reply, but I am also concerned as to how we will fund the extra expense.

'Ingrida, can you check on the train times from Wilmslow to London, or even Stockport or Manchester to London? See if there are any late deals on services today.'

'Ja.'

I search on my phone for travel times to London, the time it will take to get from Euston to St Pancras Station, the time it takes the Eurostar to get to Paris and note these all down in my book.

'There is train from Wilmslow, it is in just over one hour, but best price tickets, they are expensive…' Ingrida shows me the screen and the cost.

'I am afraid there will be an inevitable outlay for us all to get to Paris, but rest assured, Ingrida, we will be getting our money back from Janine. On that I am determined. Hold that screen until we know more about the Eurostar…'

Bonnie and Cath wave at me from across the terminal with a thumbs down and a shake of the head before moving to another counter.

My biggest fear is that there will be no flight tickets. I know Hazel would not be capable of making the journey by train, and I am sure Clarissa would not want to go without her.

Monica waves wildly from her desk and I leave Ingrida in charge of the cases to cross to her.

'There are two remaining seats for the next flight to Paris in just a couple of hours. Hazel and Clarissa are going to take them. They have to use their special assistance to get to the gate immediately as it is not available later, so they need to check-in straight away.'

Hazel purchases the remaining two air tickets so they can be fast tracked to the departure gate. I cannot help thinking to myself that it was sloppy work of the airport to allow assisted travel to be booked without evidence of documents confirming the flight, however this has worked in our favour on this occasion.

'I am sure we will find a way to join you there,' I say to them with as much confidence as I can muster, fighting a terrible urge to cross my fingers.

An escort arrives to push Hazel.

'Thank you, Fay.' Clarissa dabs a tear from her eye.

'Yes, thank you,' Hazel adds. 'Has anyone ever told you, you're simply marvellous in a crisis?'

'I think it helps if one remains calm and analytical.' I smile, aglow inside. 'It was drilled into me at school.'

Monica hugs Clarissa and I take the opportunity to lean into Hazel to whisper to her so Clarissa cannot hear. 'Hazel, I fear we may not have hotel bookings either.'

'Yes, that thought's occurred to me.'

'Still, Paris will be full of hotels. I am sure we will be able to find something even if we have to spread out at different places.'

'Precisely. I'll sort out accommodation for the two of us if you can sort the dancers?'

'Of course, safe travels.'

Ruby rushes up to us as we wave Clarissa and Hazel off to the check-in.

'I've managed to get a group booking on the Eurostar this evening. It's a bargain deal for that route.'

'Really?' Monica starts to smile but then seems to think better of it and looks down at her shoes.

'Excellent work, Ruby. Let us get back to the others and get the seats booked.'

'Yes, Miss.'

I regard Ruby with a stern stare, but she winks at me, and I have to confess feeling a similar flush of excitement as is evident on her face. Now is not the time to get churlish, so I hold my head in the air as we return to our suitcases.

Ruby outlines the costs, and I get everyone to queue up and open their passports. I ignore Ruby's sarcasm as she starts to make remarks about it being like they were back in school. Instead, I direct her to transcribe each person's details onto the online application form in a methodical and ordered fashion as I read aloud.

'OK.' Ruby looks up. 'I need to make the payment. Afraid my credit card won't take a hit like this.' She shows us the phone screen and Ingrida gasps at the total.

'Put it on my card.' Monica passes her card to me rather than Ruby. 'We can sort it out when we get home.'

'That is very generous of you, Monica.' Asha beams at her.

'Indeed, thank you,' I say, passing the card to Ruby.

'Are you sure?' Cath asks.

'Yes. There is plenty of credit. It is my husband's card.'

Ruby looks up sharply. There is a hint of a smile on her face, but Monica steadfastly ignores her. Ruby shrugs and enters the details, her fingers flying over the phone keys at impressive speed.

'We're booked.' Ruby screams in an unnecessarily loud voice. 'Whoop!'

'Marvellous.' Bonnie and Cath high five each other.

Monica takes back the card Ruby hands her without making eye contact.

'Good. Now, Ingrida, you need to book the London train tickets?'

'*Ja*... I mean *ne*, the tickets, they cost big sum...'

'It is OK, put it on the card too.' Monica hands it to Ingrida.

Ruby appears to chuckle quietly. I think she is overexcited.

Monica keeps her eyes on Ingrida's screen as she enters the card details.

'The train tickets. They are all booked for us.'

'Now we are making headway. Ingrida, please share the reference to everyone on the chat group so we can all show we have paid. I think it most unlikely we will be able to sit together.' I return the card to Monica. 'This has been most helpful, Monica. Thank you. Be assured, I shall keep a note of everything we spend, and we can sort out who owes what on our return. You must thank your husband for us.'

Ruby makes some strange guttural noise, which I ignore as I turn to Ingrida.

'Now, what time is the next train to London?'

'We do not have long. It is in forty-five minutes.'

'Right, we must hurry to the taxi rank. It will take at least fifteen minutes to get to Wilmslow station…'

I look around to do a head count and find there are two women missing.

'Where on earth are Cath and Bonnie?'

We scan the area and I begin to feel peeved those two have disappeared just as we need to get going.

'For goodness' sake. Where are they?'

'They have taken their cases.' Asha points out.

'Well, this is a travesty,' I say to Monica. 'I manage to sort out this terrible mess and two of our party go missing—'

'Keep your frigging hair on, Fay,' Ruby cuts in. 'They're over there, waving to us by the minibus bookings office. Looks like they've got us a ride. Whoop again.'

I glare at Ruby – she has such a common tongue – but I soon find myself at the back of our group as they race with their cases to join Cath and Bonnie as they set out for the taxi rank.

I rush to catch them up, irritated they appear to have instantly forgotten my part in getting us organised.

For some ridiculous reason, I am reminded of Edith and Bethan turning their backs on me. I know this will not do at all, so I hurriedly squash these thoughts, refusing to indulge them.

*

The traffic between the airport and the station is murderous.

'I don't believe it. Another frigging red light.'

'Are our tickets valid for any other train?' Asha asks.

'*Ne*, only this one.'

'Wait until I get my hands on Janine...' Bonnie starts to say as we inch forwards in a long line of vehicles.

'I still can't believe she has done this to us.' Cath starts to drum her fingers on her bag. 'Alleluia. We're moving at last.'

'She must have known for weeks that we had no flights booked.' Asha shakes her head, then suddenly starts. 'Wait, she probably has not reserved the hotel either...'

'No.' Bonnie puts her hand to her mouth.

'Fuck. You're right.' Ruby makes a fist.

'Ahem. I have already considered this, ladies, and we will sort this out en route, as they say in France. Paris is a vast tourist city. There is bound to be lots of accommodation, I am sure.'

Monica gives a loud moan.

'Monica, I am quite sure—'

'No, not the hotel issue, look. A massive queue and roadworks ahead.'

We all groan, and I look anxiously at my watch. I find my heart is racing rather too fast and concentrate on doing some deep breathing.

We arrive on the platform, completely out of breath, just as the train is pulling into the station. The carriages are full, people standing in the aisles and at the end of each coach.

'It's packed.' Bonnie shakes her head.

'Well, at least we made it,' counters Cath. 'I'm for getting as close to the buffet car as we can.'

'Good move, Cath,' Ruby shouts and Asha laughs with them as they rush towards the buffet car to get on.

'Remember, we will all meet up at the M&S food store outside the station.' I try to make myself heard over the hubbub.

I cannot be sure if they heard me; they are all on what I can only describe as a high, their emotions completely unchecked as they shout and laugh to each other.

Well, I am certainly not standing all the way to London. My foot problem is exacerbated if I stand for long periods of time, and I need them to be in top form to dance in Paris. Besides, I have a book I wish to read.

I set off down the crowded corridors, ignoring those who tut when I repeatedly say, 'Excuse me.' I will find a seat if I have to walk the length of the train, mark my words.

10

ASHA

Once we have got over the euphoria of making the London train, I lean against the corridor wall of the buffet car next to Ruby and Ingrida and send Jay a message.

> *You are not going to believe this. I can barely believe it myself. Janine did not book our flights. Seriously. We did not find out until we got to the check-in desks. She has disappeared off the face of the Earth and we have no idea what she has done with our money. Anyway, we are still going. We managed to get Eurostar tickets and I am currently on the train to London. What a crazy rollercoaster. We still do not know if we have hotel reservations. I will call you when we get to Paris. Let Ma and Baba know what happened. Love you XX*

'Well, what a terrible turn of events,' I say to the others.
'I am still a little in shock,' Ingrida replies.

'You couldn't make it up.' Ruby shakes her head.

'Where are the others?'

'I think Bonnie and Cath, they are in next carriage, sitting in the aisle. I do not know where Monica and Fay have gone.'

'What was Janine thinking?'

'Probably what a bunch of frigging idiots we are.' Ruby snorts.

'She was always so quiet. Barely said a word. Jay is always saying to me, you cannot judge a book by its cover and in this case, it has proved true.'

'I very much like this saying. I have picked up some awful books in the library, when I think they would be as good as cover.' Ingrida smiles.

'Who would have thought Janine was capable of doing such a terrible thing?'

'But who knows anyone?' Ruby purses her lips. 'I mean for real?'

Ruby's eyes are far away but then come back into focus as she adds, 'I never really spoke to Janine. She was as quiet as a mouse.'

Ruby then perches on top of her upright case and turns her attention to her phone as she half listens, looking up every few minutes.

'I spoke to her quite a bit – when she and I stayed to help Clarissa tidy the studio – although she did not tell me much,' I tell Ingrida. 'I mean, I was completely sympathetic when she told me about her mother the other year. It must have been just before the pandemic started.'

'I hear she need full-time care, *ja?*'

'Yes. Janine said it was early Alzheimer's. She told me she had to give up her job in the ticket office of a Manchester theatre when her mother got worse.'

'She has no father?'

'She did not say.'

'Does she have brother or sister?'

'One sister who had left home years ago. Apparently, she is not in contact with Janine. I was itching to know why this was, but it was so difficult to get Janine to open up.'

'Still, you managed to find out a fair amount, Asha,' Ruby comments while looking at her phone screen.

I cannot decide if she is being funny, so I let it go.

'I was trying to help her. I told her she should contact this sister of hers and get her to come home and help her to care for their mother, but Janine put on her coat and started for the door. I even said to her, it is a good thing that you are doing, looking after your mother. We should all look after our families, but with no job it must be hard for you. I said, I hope you are able to claim some financial help. It must be very worrying. She mumbled something about claiming benefits and being OK for money. But that is all she would say.'

'Is that all?' Ruby sniggers and I am not sure why. Perhaps it is something on her phone?

'Maybe that is reason Janine take our money?' Ingrida frowns. 'But I still do not believe it. Janine is sweet girl…'

'Did you know she is only twenty-three?'

'*Ja*, it is very young to be carer.'

'I must admit, I wondered how she was coping by

herself. Can you imagine only having a demented mother for company?'

'*Ja*. It is very sad.'

'It was not the sort of thing I could ask Janine when we moved to online rehearsals. Let's face it, there was very little time for conversation. But once we resumed live classes, I tried to be caring and compassionate whenever I spoke to her. I did tell her she could always call on me for help. But now look. She has left us high and dry.'

We go quiet for a while, moving with the motion of the train and listening to the hum of chatter in the buffet car.

Jay sends me a message asking if we have called the police. I reply we have not but turn to the other two. 'Should we report it to the police? I mean, she must have known what she was doing.'

'*Ne*, it would not be good to go to the police until we know more.'

'But it does look like theft…'

The more I think about it, the more annoyed I feel with Janine. I cannot believe I was ready to whiten her teeth for free.

My phone buzzes again and I read Fay's message.

Asha, the battery on my phone is about to die and I cannot access my charger in this crowded space. Can you check the situation with the hotel and let me know where we stand? We may need to use your phone to find an alternative if we do not have reservations. I am in carriage C.

It does not take me long to get through.

'*Allô, Ibis Paris Bastille Opéra. Puis-je vous aider?*'

'*Bonjour*, do you speak English?'

'*Mais oui*. Can I 'elp?'

'I wish to check if you have reservations at your hotel for our party?'

'What name?'

'It could be under Janine Young?' When she says no, I give the receptionist all our names, including Clarissa and Hazel's.

'No, I am sorry. No one with zose names iz staying 'ere.'

'So, do you have any spare rooms for the next three nights?'

Ingrida scans my face hopefully as I listen to the reply and say a brief, '*Merci. Au revoir*,' before ending the call.

I shake my head. 'Fully booked. Oh, and get this, the receptionist explained it was due to the large dancing competition taking place at the *Opéra Bastille* this weekend...'

'No shit.' Ruby snaps her phone away and stands up. 'I reckon we need a stiff drink.'

'I need to go and tell Fay. Her phone is on the blink, but I have my charger here.' I reach for it from inside my handbag. 'I am sure she would rather book the hotel. Watch my case. I will go and give this to her.'

I squeeze my way down the moving train past all the standing passengers. Amazingly, Fay has managed to find probably the only empty seat in the furthest compartment. I sense from the glare on the face of the young man next to her that Fay had made him move all his belongings in order to free up the seat. He has a huge number of bags now both on his lap, on and under the table and spilling into the corridor. Fay steadfastly ignores him as I quietly report my findings.

'Thank you, Asha. I am not surprised. Why would Janine book our hotel if she had no intention of booking our flights? I will look for somewhere. Now that I have managed to procure a seat,' – she pauses to throw the young man a disdainful sneer – 'and now I have the charger,' – she leans across the man to plug it into the table socket – 'I will make it my mission to get us accommodated. Thankfully, you can usually reserve hotels without having to pay up front.'

'I hope we can find somewhere.'

'Oh, Paris is a big place. There will be a hotel with space for us all, I am sure.'

I hope she is right; I do not fancy spending the night on the streets of Paris.

'Thanks, Fay. Let us know how you get on via the chat group and hang onto the charger. I do not think I will be able to make my way back up the train a second time.'

There had been no sign of Monica in any of the carriages I have traversed, so I glance through the glass of the door into first-class beyond Fay's coach and spot Monica sitting in a large, almost empty area. I wave, but she does not see me. She is using what looks like her husband's card to pay her upgrade to the ticket inspector.

All right for some.

As I battle my way back to the buffet car, I think about Monica. She has very symmetrical features and, I have to say, perfect teeth – I wonder who her dentist is – but she is quite distant and aloof. I thought we would get to know one another better when she helped Ma make the saris for our costumes, but she remained quiet and completely wrapped up in the sewing. It is hard to see how she and Ruby, seemingly so different, had such a close relationship – I guess what Ma would call chalk and cheese. I wonder who has caused the fall out, Monica or Ruby? Perhaps Ruby will tell us.

Cath and Bonnie are sitting cross-legged next to each other in the aisle of the crowded car next to the buffet car and have to stand to let me pass. They are laughing aloud and Cath bursts into song on and off. I can see they are getting annoyed looks from the weary passengers who are either putting on their headphones to block out the noise or shaking their heads in an irritated manner.

When I finally get back, Ruby presents me with a can of gin and tonic. Ingrida tentatively raises her can to me and Ruby raises a plastic cup filled with red wine.

'Sorry, I do not drink.' I hand back the can.

'Would you like a tea or coffee?'

'No, thank you. To be honest, I feel a little nauseous.'

'It's the motion of the train. Renowned for it.' Ruby hands me a bottle of water instead. 'I got you this too.'

'Thanks.'

She opens the can of gin and tonic, saying, 'Shame to waste this.'

To my surprise, she continues to sip both her red wine, which she must know is very bad for staining teeth, and the gin.

Ingrida only has the odd sip from her tin. From the

grimace on her face, I am not sure she likes it and I think she has only accepted it so as not to offend Ruby.

'Tell us more about your fiancé, Asha?'

'I have been with Jay for almost six years. I cannot imagine being with anyone else.'

'You find love at first sight?' Ingrida asks.

'Wow, you're a romantic, Ingrida.' Ruby smiles.

'Jay and I were in the same classes at university and became good friends first. It was more a gradual realisation we were meant for each other.'

'Was it love at first sight with you, Ingrida?' Ruby asks.

'*Ne*. Neil, he was married when I first met him. And then, after Maya passed away, I became live-in nanny and got to know him better.'

'When did he propose?'

'It was only six weeks ago. I know, I get married very quickly. We will tell children next week.'

'What? You mean they don't know?'

'It had to be secret until Neil tell Maya's parents. He is kind man who does not want to upset them.'

'That must be awkward for you?' I ask.

'How old are the kids?' Ruby asks.

'Between three and seven.'

'They'll know.' Ruby shakes her head. 'Kids always do. I mean you're sleeping in the same frigging bed, aren't you?'

'*Ja*, but I get up very early to get breakfast…'

'Don't they come in during the night?'

'Sometimes, if they wake. But they are very tired… And they are still only small.'

Ruby pulls an 'if-you-say-so' face and closes her mouth as if she thinks better of saying anything else.

'How about you, Ruby? You mentioned you were in a relationship.'

'Yes. Max. We've been together over a year now. To be honest, I never intended settling down, but Max is the first bloke I've met who could possibly change that.'

'What does he do?'

'He's an engineer. Learnt his trade in the army. Only problem is he travels a lot, so I don't get to see that much of him. He's in India at the moment, or is it Thailand? I lose track.'

'How wonderful to travel the world and at someone else's expense. Jay and I have planned a six-month honeymoon to go and see India and as much of the world as we can.'

'Lucky you. Six months off work sounds idyllic.'

'I would like honeymoon…' Ingrida looks slightly sad. 'But it is not easy with small children.'

'It doesn't get much better with teenagers.' Ruby laughs.

'Your son, does he like Max?' Ingrida asks.

'Yes, they get on great. Will was a bit wary about him at first, but once he realised Max was as passionate about cricket and rugby as he was, there was no stopping them talking. I hardly get a word in edgeways.'

'Does Max see his father?'

Ruby shakes her head and sips her drink.

'Maybe Max will be a father figure for your son?' I widen my eyes for her response, but Ruby goes quiet and her expression is unreadable when she eventually says,

'Maybe,' before changing the subject.

'What're our chances of winning this competition, then? Hey, Ingrida, you'll be dancing now Janine isn't with us.'

Ingrida puts her hand up to her mouth. '*Ja*, you are right. I had not thought about this. I will have to dance in Janine's place. I hope I do not make mistake again.'

'You will be brilliant, Ingrida,' I say. 'You are a fabulous dancer. You and Monica are Clarissa's star performers.'

Ingrida smiles and I turn to Ruby and risk asking, 'Whatever happened between Monica and you?'

Ruby shakes her head and instead asks Ingrida to show her the dance step she missed.

I watch them attempt the new step in the limited space next to our cases, smiling as other passengers crane their necks to watch Ruby copying Ingrida's développé kick.

I still feel a bit rough – the motion of the train is worse when you are standing – so I perch on my case, sipping my water as I contemplate if I have ever had such a bad fall out as Monica and Ruby. The only ones I can recall were with my sister, Rashmi. Before I moved in with Jay, we had many heated arguments.

'You never help around the house,' she would shout at me.

'I am at work all day.'

'And you never lift a hand to cook or clear up…'

'You are being ridiculous. I am in a responsible clinical job, attending to patients. All you do all day is feed and change your babies.'

She then screamed at the top of her voice, 'You are

nothing but a spoilt brat and you never do anything for anyone other than yourself.'

Ma came to break it up, but I was so furious, I could not help but say, 'And you are nothing but ungrateful. You have clearly forgotten it was only down to my support for you that you were able to flee from your dreadful marriage and move back home, and now we all have to put up with the noise and the mess.'

It is a relief to be living with Jay away from it all. I will not make the same mistakes as Rashmi.

As we approach London, Ruby, who has had two further tins of gin and tonic, leans in to both Ingrida and me. 'You know you're both very lucky. You with Neil,' – she lifts her can to Ingrida – 'and you with Jay.' She lifts it to me. 'Maybe I should settle down? And well, I think Max's probably the one...'

Ingrida clasps her hands together and says, 'This is wonderful, Ruby.' And they chink tins as I raise my empty bottle of water.

We all say, 'To Max, Neil and Jay.'

Ingrida adds, 'And true love.'

We giggle as we disembark the train and go to meet up outside the M&S food store outside Euston Station.

The air is cool and fresh, and I feel better to be outside on solid ground. As we set off for St Pancras station, Fay in the lead, I get another shiver of excitement. Despite everything that has happened, we are on our way to Paris.

11

MONICA

It is late evening by the time we arrive at our hotel, the only one Fay could find that had vacancies for our number. I look up at the grimy name, barely legible, above the entrance; the Charbon Hotel. The cold, grey concrete exterior could not look any less inviting.

'What a dive.' I hear Ruby announce as Fay marches to the desk with Vince's card to check us in and we crowd into the small foyer.

'What does it mean, Charbon?' Bonnie asks Ingrida.

'I think it is name like carbon. It mean coal or smut...'

'Frigging brilliant. The Smut Hotel.' Ruby shakes her head.

'First impressions are not good and it is such a terribly long way from the *Gare du Nord* Station.' Asha also shakes her head, adding, 'How long will it take us to get to the theatre tomorrow? I dread to think.'

'I do not feel as if I am in Paris.' Ingrida sighs.

'Me neither,' Asha adds. 'This is not at all how I pictured it.'

No one wants to sit on the grubby green plastic seats in the cramped entrance way, so we clump together next to our cases and wait.

After several minutes, Fay starts to raise her voice.

'No really, this will not do. Is there anyone here who can speak English? *Avez vous receptioniste avec parlay beaucoup de Englais?*'

Ingrida – who, as it turns out, speaks fluent French and was brilliant getting us taxis at the station – crosses to assist Fay. The young man on duty converses with her before shrugging and handing her a single key.

Ingrida talks quietly to Fay, pats her arm gently and then holds the key up in the air as she returns to the group. 'We are to share this room.'

'What, all of us?' I ask.

Ingrida nods.

'All seven of us?' Asha's eyes could not go any wider.

'You're frigging joking?' Ruby says.

Fay joins us, shaking her head. 'I am afraid so. The concierge has told Ingrida all the rooms are multiple occupancy. No wonder the hotel was so affordable. Still, it cannot be helped, and I doubt we will be spending much time here… At least we have arrived safely and in time for the competition tomorrow.'

From the corner of my eye, I see Ruby pulling a face, but Bonnie and Cath are giggling.

'Oh, come on now. It'll be a right laugh to share a dormitory,' Cath digs Bonnie with her elbow. 'We went backpacking around Europe not so long ago. Stayed in every grade of hostel imaginable. This isn't so bad.'

'If this isn't so bad, I'm dying to hear what's worse,' Ruby sniggers.

'Our room it is on the fourth floor.' Ingrida presses the lift button but then exclaims, '*Ne. Jāšanās…*'

'*Jāšanās?*' Bonnie asks.

'It mean—'

'Oh frigging hell…' Ruby stamps her foot.

'*Ja* something like that…'

Ruby points to a small hand-written notice on the lift door. '*Hors de service.* It's out of bloody service.'

'We'll have to use the stairs.' Cath groans. 'I think we'll all feel *hors de service* by the fourth floor.'

We grab our suitcases and begin to mount the metal stairs, a bare bulb lighting the way on each floor. The walls have a thin coat of whitewash, which fails to cover up the graffiti underneath. I avoid touching the banister or the wall.

I am more shattered than I care to admit. We have spent the entire day travelling, much of it on our feet hanging around at stations. At least I managed to get a first-class seat on the train to London.

As it turns out, it proved to be a huge bonus to travel by train. I was able to put my plan into action on Vince's tablet – I doubt I could have done this on a flight – and now everything is set up. It just needs to play out. I would have rewarded myself with a glass of wine, however, having had my head down looking at the screen combined with sitting in a chair that faced backwards I was left feeling really sick.

I pushed the device back into my case and asked the lady serving refreshments if she had any paracetamol. She was unable to help, saying, 'Sorry love. It's these Pendolino trains. They cause a lot of trouble.'

Once in London, we had to battle through the crowds to get to St Pancras. Then we almost missed our train to Paris after the hold up over Ingrida's passport.

At least we have eaten. I gave Fay the credit card to purchase a large batch of sandwiches, biscuits, and water for our journey to France. It was just as well as the buffet trolley on the Eurostar turned out to have sold out of everything but alcohol and crisps.

Ingrida, who is in front of me, pushes the heavy door to the fourth floor open and we trail after her down a narrow corridor to our room.

She opens the door and I follow her in.

The room is full of beds – two doubles and four singles – with barely any space in between. One wall is lined with a few kitchen units next to a single bed in the corner and the other beds are criss-crossed in the main area of the room with just enough space to close the blinds of the large windows that face the brick façade of an adjacent building.

'Woah. Look at all these beds.' Bonnie shakes her head.

'Someone is going to have to share a double.' Asha puts her case on top of a single bed, and I quickly follow suit, putting mine on the single bed in the corner.

'Oh, we'll share, no problem.' Cath throws her case onto the double, as does Bonnie.

'At least the bedding looks clean.' Fay inspects the pillowcase of the single she has chosen.

'And there is a fresh towel on each bed,' I add.

'Ruby, you have double, I am OK in single.' Ingrida points a hand to the second double bed, up against the window.

'Thanks, Ingrida,' Ruby replies. 'This is so nuts. But I guess we only have to sleep here. By the way, Fay, whatever you paid, you were frigging robbed.'

'We have paid nothing yet…' Fay tuts but continues to inspect the amenities. 'I see there is no storage space whatsoever. Not a wardrobe or chest of drawers in sight. We shall have to put our cases under the beds once we have retrieved the few things we need, otherwise we will trip over them.'

'Let's hope we can iron our costumes at the theatre.' Bonnie holds up a crushed top from her case.

Ingrida flops down onto her bed. 'I cannot believe we have made it to Paris. Thank you, Fay, for organising it all and you, Monica, for putting cost on your card.' Ingrida gives a little smile, but her brows are furrowed when she adds, 'I hope there will not be too much more expense.'

When I paid the taxi – a ridiculously large sum but unfortunately the only option after arriving so late – I noticed she was biting her nails. For the first time she is not living up to the name Ruby gave her, 'Happy-To-Be-Here-Ingrida'. I guess nurses do not earn that much, although come to think of it, she announced she has just married a widower at the last rehearsal. So surely, she'll be better off? When my dad died, he left a fortune to my mum. A flash of Vince's face when he discovered how wealthy she was crosses my mind. I always suspected it was not just my pregnancy that convinced him to propose.

MONICA

Ingrida's phone rings, and she disappears into the bathroom to answer it.

'Yes, thanks again, Monica, and well done, Fay. You certainly got us all organised.' Asha pulls out her pyjamas and starts to undress.

We all unpack our overnight items. Fay meticulously places everything in an ordered line across her bed before selecting what she needs and then neatly repacking her suitcase.

I must say, Fay has been quite a revelation, the way she took control and made a plan of action. It's a pity she has such an unfortunate manner; she reminds me of my old headmistress.

I sigh inwardly as I scan our crammed room.

'Where did you say Clarissa and Hazel were staying, Monica?' Asha asks me.

'They checked into a four-star hotel in an area close to the competition hall.'

'Four stars. Lucky them.' Bonnie's bed is strewn with her costumes, make-up, curlers and heaven knows what else.

'If I could give our hotel one star, it'd be one too many.' Cath laughs.

'And we will probably have to be up at the crack of dawn to get back into Paris to our theatre in time for the run-throughs.' Asha yawns before adding, 'I have never felt so tired. It feels way later than eleven-thirty.'

I start to yawn too and putting my hand to my mouth, I realise I'm still holding Vince's credit card. Smiling to myself, I tuck it back in my bag.

Vince, you have no idea how handy this has been… No idea. Still, the way you brag about your creditworthiness, our expenses should hardly have made a dent in your so-say vast credit limit. I vaguely wonder if I will be able to get a room in Clarissa's hotel tomorrow.

My fingers glance the new business card inside my bag, which I pull out with an involuntary shiver of delight before putting it back and getting changed.

The journey to Paris was the only part of the day to go too quickly. I found a seat well away from all the others, in particular Ruby, where a smart, well-dressed man helped me put my case in the luggage rack.

'Thank you.' His eyes were a piercing green and twinkled when he spoke.

'Jean-Claude at your service, may I sit 'ere, opposite you?'

I had nodded, determined not to blush.

Jean-Claude began talking and his enchanting French accent drew me in.

'I visit London to see my sons. Zey are at university there. You live in London?'

'No. I live in the north of the England.'

'I know Manchester.'

'Yes, I live close to Manchester.'

'My sons, zey love Manchester.'

'Are they both at the same university?'

'Yes. Zey do everything together. Zey are identical twins…'

'Really. I have twins. A girl and a boy. They are fourteen.'

'*Quelle chance*. Pardon, I mean what a coincidence.'

He then showed me photos of his sons and I showed him my screensaver shot of James and Joanne. Talking to him came naturally, and our conversation flowed.

Jean-Claude told me he was divorced; his sons lived with his ex-wife in London. A little white lie, I said I was also divorced, but I was picturing myself in just a few months' time when my marriage to Vince is forever behind me.

'Tell me, Monica, what do you do for a living?'

'I am a wedding dress designer.' This does not count as a lie, as I am the unnamed designer of A-Belle-Brides.

'*Je ne le crois pas!* I too am in haute couture. I have a chain of boutiques in France, including ze bridal wear.'

It was no surprise. I mean, he was so well dressed; his suit beautifully cut. There was no stopping us after that. We talked fashion shows, catwalks, and seasonal changes. He wanted to see my latest designs, so I showed him the award article on my phone. I was almost dumbstruck when he said he was sure he had already seen my floaty festival winning gown in a French magazine, telling me how much he admired it. Delighting in his compliment I was also tinged with annoyance at Annabelle. Typical of her not to tell me about the French magazine.

Jean-Claude had then shown me a couple of pictures of his favourite creations and the journey flashed past. I could have gone on talking to him for hours. He was fascinated I was dancing in an amateur competition and wanted to know all about what dances we performed.

'A mix of jazz, Fosse, Bollywood...'

'Where is zis being held?'

'The *Opéra Bastille*.'

'I know it well.'

'The finalists perform in front of the public on Sunday, so we are hoping to qualify tomorrow.'

'*Bonne chance*.'

Arriving at the *Gare du Nord*, he asked for my number, but I decided I should exercise some caution, so I hurriedly mumbled how nice it had been to meet him and he quickly pressed his card into my hand before I made a dash for the exit with my case.

Loud giggling from Bonnie and Cath brings me back to the present. They are in their element, laughing away on their large king-size bed.

'Well, this'll give us something to talk about when we get home.' Bonnie beams and smiles as if we were a party of schoolgirls on a sleepover.

'To be sure, I can't remember when I last bunked up with a bunch of girlfriends.' Cath is in an equally good mood as they start to put each other's hair in rollers.

'Reminds me of that programme where everyone has to sleep in the same house.'

'You mean *Big Brother*?'

'No, that I'm A Celebrity Get Out of It.'

'*I'm a Celebrity Get Me Out of Here?*' Ruby suggests.

'Yes, that's the one.'

'Oh, it's just like that,' Ruby winks at Asha. 'Except there're no celebrities, no edible insects – although hold that thought until we've seen the breakfast – and definitely no Ant and Dec. Other than that, it's just the ruddy same.'

'Oh, Ruby, you are a scream.' Bonnie snorts with laughter.

They must have had a good few drinks on the journey, including Ruby. They all seem far from tired.

Cath calls out, 'Shh – ladies, listen. What's that noise?'

The room goes quiet, and a buzzing can be heard coming from under the beds. Ruby grabs her case, throws it on the bed and lifts the lid. The buzzing noise gets louder.

'What the?' Ruby starts to rummage in the case.

'It's not one of those sex toys you showed us at your party the other year, is it?' Bonnie peers across from her bed to see if she is right.

'No, look.' Ruby pulls out her electric toothbrush, which has switched itself on in the case. All the other ladies, well apart from Fay, squeal with laughter.

Bonnie, looking rather glassy-eyed, turns to Asha. 'You came to that party, Asha. As an upright Indian lady, were you not shocked to see all those naughty sex aids?'

'You forget, Bonnie, the *Kama Sutra* was written by an Indian.'

'Was it? Who wrote that then?'

'Vātsyāyana.'

'Ha ha. Don't expect me to remember that. I couldn't pronounce it, let alone spell it.' Bonnie howls with laughter bordering on hysterics.

I keep my head down and quietly check my phone for messages as the others gleefully chatter away.

Ruby is on the other side of the room and nowhere near me, thank heavens. We have barely spoken although she tried to engage with me while we waited for Ingrida at Passport Control in St Pancras.

'Monica, please talk to me,' she had begun.

I had merely stared at her.

'You have to know we can't go on like this. We're mates, best friends. Six years have to count for something.'

I had maintained a stony silence.

'Look, friends stick together through thick and thin. I get that you're annoyed with me, I get that I hurt you, but you know it was unintentional and anyway, if we're true friends we should forgive each other our silly mistakes...' Her speech was slightly slurred. 'And also, in the whole sch... scheme of things, this was a ridiculously petty frigging reason to fall out...'

When I said nothing, she looked as if she was going to cry and then suddenly stamped her foot on the ground and shouted, 'Fine. Have it your way. I'm sorry I'm not frigging perfect like you. I'm sorry I mess up all the time, and I'm really sorry you don't appear to value our friendship...'

She had then stormed off to wait at the Eurostar gates and we've not so much as looked at each other since.

Ridiculously petty. The words sting. She really does have what my mother would call low morals if she thinks petty is an adequate word to describe her behaviour.

'Ta da,' Bonnie shouts, and my mind lurches back to the present.

Bonnie produces a large bottle of brandy from her case and suggests we all have a night cap.

Given the circumstances, I readily accept. Anything to send me to sleep quickly.

'Have you had that wee bottle with you all the time?' Cath asks before singing something about Brandy.

'Oh, I don't think I've heard of that song.' Bonnie pulls a number of plastic shot glasses onto the bed.

'"Brandy"… O-Jays.'

'Well, there's no need to be rude.'

'What? It's the name of the group, Bonnie. The O-Jays.'

Bonnie snorts with laughter. 'Ha ha. And I thought you were blaspheming.'

Ruby laughs and glances at me, but I turn my head away.

Bonnie pours us each a measure.

'The authorities would have confiscated that bottle at Manchester Airport you know.' Fay waggles her finger. 'You are not allowed liquids over one hundred mils in your hand luggage.'

'Really? Oh, it's a good job we came by train then. Here we are, Fay, one for you too. You deserve it as you managed to save the way.'

Fay opens her mouth but Ruby interrupts as she mimics Fay's voice and says, 'Save the *day*, Bonnie, not the way.'

Bonnie and Cath guffaw loudly and Fay looks taken aback.

I half expect Fay to turn on Ruby, but she appears to think better of it and accepts a shot of brandy with a curt 'thank you.'

'A toast, ladies,' Cath raises her glass. 'To dancing our best and beating Bold as Brass hands down.'

Asha lifts her bottle of water as the rest of us raise our glasses. 'Or would that be feet down?'

'Feet down. Cheers.'

I suddenly notice Ingrida's bed is vacant. 'Wait, where's Ingrida?' No one has seen her for a good ten minutes. I go and listen at the bathroom door, and I hear her voice speaking in what must be Latvian. I have no idea what she is saying, but even in this foreign language she sounds upset with whomever she is speaking to. I hesitate but eventually knock on the bathroom door when the conversation has gone quiet.

'Ingrida, are you OK?'

I open the door a chink and slowly push it wide to see her blinking back tears and staring at her phone.

'Have you had bad news?' I look at her phone. She hurriedly puts it in her dressing gown pocket.

'*Ne*, I... no, I have just realised I may not remember all the dance for Janine. I have not practise her position very much...'

I feel sure the problem is something connected to the phone call, but who am I to intrude? 'Ingrida, you're a lovely dancer, you'll be fine. Please don't worry about it.'

'I need to practise more but it is too late...'

Asha, who must have been listening in at the door, pushes her way in the bathroom and immediately says, 'It is never too late. Come on.'

She pulls Ingrida into the bedroom and pulls out her phone to select the music for our numbers.

'Everyone on your feet or your beds. We are going to run through our numbers before bed so Ingrida can take Janine's place.'

'Oh Lor, we'd better have another drink first.' Bonnie sloshes more brandy into each glass and we all knock it back.

The brandy has a welcome warming effect, and the comedy of our situation doesn't escape me as I look around at us all dressed in an assortment of nighties and pyjamas, Bonnie and Cath with their hair in curlers.

The room is so full of beds there is really nowhere to dance other than on the beds. As soon as the introduction starts, our feet begin to tap. Even Fay smiles as she finds a small patch of floor and the rest of us hurriedly assume our starting positions on top of each mattress, where we all dance on the spot.

Our dance training takes over and we all move as one, albeit without crossing the room. At the end of our three numbers, we all flop onto our beds laughing.

The dance is cathartic and as I settle to sleep, I am full of hope. Not only will I soon be free of Vince, tomorrow we dance on a professional stage.

12

RUBY

Wow. My head hurts. Drinking copious quantities of gin and wine on the Eurostar and then brandy on an empty stomach the night before a dance competition is definitely not recommended. I couldn't have gone to sleep until well after 2 a.m. I'd pushed my head under the covers to have a silent text exchange with Max for over an hour.

He was outraged about Janine and wonderfully supportive about Monica. He told me I'd tried my best and could do no more. He agreed that if she was so determined not to make up there was nothing I could do about it.

I can't wait to see Max again, and not just to release my pent-up sexual frustration. No, I realise I want to share a lot more with him and while this is an unprecedented situation for me, it's not an unpleasant one.

Max wanted to know all about the competition and our hotel and when I told him about the sleeping arrangements and our impromptu dance rehearsal, he messaged:

RUBY

I can just picture the scene. Sounds like an adult version of the musical, Annie.
Just like it, I replied, but without the cute factor.

Ouch – my head. I must buy some paracetamol before our rehearsal.

Talking of *Annie*, I have seen a new side to Frosty Fay. She had a few too many brandies last night and became quite relaxed. She was more talkative than I have ever seen her. She said the room full of beds reminded her of growing up in St Eulalia's and the dormitories there. I'm not sure the others realised St Eulalia's was the local orphanage back then. I only knew because my dad used to talk about what he called the *forgotten kids* there when he helped to re-wire the place.

I couldn't help noticing there was something wrong with Fay's feet. Looked as if she was missing at least one toe on each foot, but I was careful to look away as she hurriedly put on bed socks. That must make dancing quite a challenge.

Still, she's back to her usual irritating frosty self this morning. First, she ticked me off. 'Please, Ruby, ladies perspire – they do not sweat.' And then she corrected Batty Bonnie two or three times in the space of half an hour as we ate breakfast in a small café near our grotty hotel.

'That is not how you pronounce croissant… The Eiffel Tower is *either* an eyesore *or* sticks out like a sore thumb, but it is not, I repeat, not a thumb sore.'

And when Ingrida asked what would we do if Sheila's group tried to intimidate us again and Bonnie responded,

'We'll cross that ridge when we come to it.' Fay nearly exploded with irritation.

I told Fay to cut Bonnie some *sack*, but I also winked at her so she knew I was only teasing. Fay did a double take but didn't give me her usual glare and as far as I know she hasn't said another critical word to Bonnie.

Time was moving on, so I suggested we grab our cases with our costumes, props and make-up and head for the dance venue.

'Just look at us dressed identically in our DICK/DECK outfits.' I wink at Ingrida. 'With Fay at the front, I feel as if I'm back on a school trip.'

'I think we look very smart in our matched tops,' Ingrida replies as we hurry after Fay.

I do a double take before realising Ingrida is being serious. Well, I, for one, don't want anyone looking at the awful insignia stuck on my chest, so despite the warm morning, I throw my jacket over one shoulder to hide the damn thing.

Now we are on the packed Metro in the French rush hour. We are still on the outskirts of Paris and the line is overground, but with little to see as we travel through suburbs and industrial areas. As passengers stand to leave, Bonnie, Cath, Ingrida, and I manage to grab a seat. Monica continues to keep a good distance from me. Well, stuff her. If she wants to hold a grudge, that's her lookout.

As the Tube nears the centre of Paris and goes underground, we lean into each other to talk about the forthcoming competition and the venue.

'I've never heard of the opera theatre at the Bastille,' Bonnie comments.

I look it up online and show her the images.

'Hey, it's huge.'

'And very contemporary. Get this, the amphitheatre seats five hundred and the main theatre, a couple of thousand.'

Cath whistles. 'That's bigger than any of our previous audiences. I hope my nerves don't get the better of me.'

'I always dance better in front of an audience.'

'Bit of an exhibitionist, eh, Ruby?' Bonnie nudges me in the ribs.

'Yes, if you like. But Clarissa's right, we all perform better when watched.'

The seat next to me becomes free and Monica makes to sit down but then thinks better of it and tightens her hand on the rail next to her, studiously looking away. Pathetic.

I survey the other dancers dotted around the carriage. Perhaps I can cultivate a new close friend?

Asha is a positive, friendly type, if a little over-interested in the latest gossip. Plus, when you talk to her she looks at your mouth not your eyes which is a bit off-putting. My hands always go to my teeth in case there's a piece of food stuck in them or a smear of lipstick. So, maybe not Gnasher-Asha.

Celtic Cath and Batty Bonnie are completely wrapped up in each other.

I'm really warming to Happy-To-Be-Here-Ingrida; she's a good laugh. I remember her coming to my Ann Summers party and telling us about her unusual sex education in a Latvian dance company. Come to think of it, she was one of the few dance ladies who didn't bat an eyelid at the erotic goods for sale. Mind, she's dead busy now she's taken on all those stepkids…

Frosty Fay's a definite no, although it turns out she's pretty amazing at navigating the Metro and getting us on the right lines to ensure we get to our destination. She's a much nicer person when she's in charge. She even smiles more, which is a pleasant change to her usual icy frown.

I glance at Monica at the other end of the compartment, studiously ignoring me and I feel a pang deep in my gut. Oh, why's she being so frigging unreasonable?

As the Metro nears our station, the conversation turns to Janine.

'She seemed the least likely member of the group to cause upset,' Bonnie comments.

'Thanks for that, Bonnie.' Cath pokes her in the arm.

'Oh, you know what I mean. Actually, I know her neighbour, Maureen.' Bonnie reflects. 'I could text her to see if she knows anything about Janine's situation?'

'Yes, do that, Bonnie,' I say. 'See if she can find out what's happened.'

'I feel guilty we didn't ask the wee girl more about herself and offer her some help,' Cath adds. 'She must have been having financial problems if she needed to take our Paris money. Maybe one of us should have befriended her?'

'She wasn't exactly friendly,' I remind Cath. 'She wouldn't share lifts with anyone or join in conversations.'

'That's true,' Cath agrees. 'I asked her to come to our *Strictly* evenings, but she wasn't a bit interested. She kept her distance with all of us…'

'Well, I hope Janine's found something good to spend our money on.'

'Ruby.' Bonnie looks shocked.

'I mean, if you're going to be robbed it might as well be for a good reason,' I say.

'Like what?' Cath is smiling.

'An exotic holiday, champagne by the crateful, luxury underwear...'

'Oh, Ruby, you are awful.' Bonnie laughs.

Cath starts to sing about spending money on whisky and beer, but she trails off when Fay carefully edges her way over to us as the Metro wobbles along.

I quickly appreciate Fay's hearing is much better than I realised.

She leans into our group and says in a low authoritative voice, 'We will be getting our money back whether Janine has squandered it on any such items. I have already reported the matter to the police.'

'What? Without knowing anything about her circumstances?' I stare at Fay.

'It is a criminal offence. She has stolen thousands of pounds.'

'Thousands?' Bonnie looks aghast.

'Yes, thousands. Our Paris payments add up to four thousand and thirty-five pounds, and my guess is she has not been using our money for the lottery. The entire class paid two pounds a week for the last two years. That amounts to another five thousand two hundred pounds. So, you can see she has embezzled over nine thousand pounds from us.'

We are all stunned and say nothing until Cath gives a loud whistle.

'Bless my soul. What in heaven's name did she spend it on?'

'Hang on,' I say, unsure why I feel a sudden need to protect Janine. 'We've no proof she misappropriated the lottery money or for that matter deliberately stole the Paris money. She may have borrowed it if she was in debt, or perhaps she was being blackmailed… OK, maybe far-fetched, but what I'm trying to say is we just don't know.'

'*Ja*, it does not seem possible Janine steal from dance ladies—'

'Well, it is a police issue now. They will get to the bottom of it.' Fay has never looked so frosty as she consults her map and indicates we need to get off as the Metro lurches towards a stop. She pushes through the other passengers, and we all follow.

She calls back in a loud voice, 'As far as I am concerned, Janine has betrayed us all and deserves everything she gets.'

Feeling somewhat subdued, we all silently follow Fay up the escalators and group together on the busy French street.

Ingrida taps me on the shoulder, her face pale and anxious. 'Janine will be in trouble with police, *ja*? I am so sorry for her. Maybe this is all big mistake?'

Before I can answer, Fay orders us all to jump onto the nearest bus for the last leg of the journey. There are no spare seats, so we cram into the vehicle and hold onto the straps that hang down from the ceiling. I end up squashed between Monica and Ingrida. Monica turns away, so I am looking at her back. I am tempted to hiss an insult at her, but Ingrida tugs my jacket, so I turn to her.

'Will she go to prison? Janine?'

'I've no idea,' I reply truthfully.

'Prison is a terrible place.' Ingrida bites her lip and says no more.

'Clarissa's ladies.' Fay's voice booms from the front of the bus. 'Our stop is the next one. The Bastille.' She adds in a quieter voice her apology – '*Excusez-moi*' – to the driver who has one finger in his ear having exclaimed, '*Sacré bleu.*'

Fay motions for us all to make our way down the bus to get off.

The driver mutters something in French.

I whisper to Ingrida. 'The Bastille. It looks like we're the ones getting to prison first.'

Ingrida is smiling. 'With *la grande gueule*,' she repeats the driver's insult.

'*Grande gueule?*'

'It mean loud mouth,' Ingrida replies, a small grin on her face.

We edge our way off the bus, and I have to stifle a laugh to see Fay's *grande gueule* is set in a glacial clamp as she glares at the bus driver before he drives off.

Traffic is moving in every direction around the busy multi-lane junction where we have alighted, and pigeons fly in the air. We turn full circle to look at our surroundings.

'Now I feel I am in Paris.' Ingrida points to the tall column at the centre of the *Place de la Bastille*. A golden-winged figure is poised on a gold sphere right at the top.

'It is the *Colonne de Juillet*. The July Column. And the statue, it is *Le Génie de la Liberté*; to remember French Revolution.'

'You should be a tour guide, Ingrida.'

'I spend few months in Paris, long time ago now—'

'Ah, look. The *Opéra Bastille*.' I point at the large circular glass-clad front of the theatre skirted by a cascade of concrete steps. Above the doors, two large banners with the word *Expression* flutter in the mild breeze. Groups of people are heading up the steps towards the main entrance, bags and brightly coloured costumes in every hand.

We all stand for a few minutes to take it all in.

'This is it.' I squeeze Ingrida's arm, forgetting for a split second she's not Monica. 'Happy to be here, Ingrida?'

Ingrida, who had glazed over, gives a jump. 'Oh, *ja*. Of course.'

I look at Ingrida's face. She does not seem that happy or excited. I give her a quizzical 'what's up?' look. She shakes her head and lightly squeezes my arm as we cross to the entrance together. Monica, face like a poker, sweeps past us without turning her head.

13

INGRIDA

Once we are checked in with the organisers of Expression Paris, we walk down many long corridors to the dressing rooms. There are people everywhere carrying holdalls and costumes draped on hangers. As we pass dozens of rooms, we see dancers limbering up and stretching out. Some are in leotards, others in baggy training tops and leggings. I feel a bubble of nerves in my stomach, but it is not a frightened bubble, more one of anticipation.

'Which room is ours?'

'Number twelve,' Fay calls as she leads the way. 'Here we are.'

We all step into the spacious room and exchange with each other smiles.

'Wowzers.'

'Will you look at this?'

Asha pushes her case to one side and twirls in the middle of the room. 'Well, this is something else. Nothing like the dressing rooms we have had to put up with in the past.'

'Is this all for us? I mean, now you're talking.' Bonnie gives Cath a high five.

We spread out, open our cases and hang up our costumes on a long central rail. Beautiful dressing tables run the length of the room on both sides under a continuous run of mirrors. The mirrors are surrounded by large bright bulb lights and have comfortable swivel chairs for seating.

'This is incredible.' Monica smiles.

'There's even an iron and ironing board in the corner. Better get my stuff pressed.' Bonnie switches on the iron.

I cannot move for a minute; I just stand there taking it all in.

'What're you thinking, Ingrida?' Ruby, she ask me with a smile.

'That we are here in actual professional theatre.'

'Amazing, isn't it? Look they've put bottles of water and a box of tissues at every place.'

'Very nice.' Asha takes the chair nearest the door, and we all claim a chair each – Monica quickly putting her bag on the chair between Bonnie and me.

'This is extremely luxurious.' Fay points to a television fixed high up on the wall. It is showing the full theatre stage where a handful of people are setting up. One person is climbing a tall stepladder to adjust lights.

'What a wonderful touch to have a linked screen to the theatre. We will be able to see what is happening on stage throughout. It is a pity there is no sound but at least we can see all the other dances.'

'Oh look,' – Asha points – 'there is a programme and timetable stuck to the mirror here.'

'I feel like a proper film star.' Cath sinks into her chair.

'Do the lights have to be this bright?' Bonnie asks, bending to look at herself.

Cath sings something about being blinded by light, and Bonnie says, 'It is blinding. Look, I can see wrinkles.' She put her hands either side of her cheeks and pulls the skin taut. 'I can't iron these out.'

'Wrinkles, never. Those are smile lines and they're evidence you've had a happy life.'

'Less of the *had*, my dear Catherine,' Bonnie retorted with a mock insult in her voice.

'These lights, they are very bright,' I say, thinking my skin, it look very pale in the mirror.

'Well, Ingrida, we need to ensure we have adequate make-up for under the stage lighting...'

Fay, she sounds like a teacher, and I do not like to say I work in Latvian theatre and know this already.

'It can completely wash out your complexion. That's why we accentuate the eyes and mouth, so we are not blanked out. I used to do the stage make-up for the girls' ballet shows...'

Fay pauses, shakes her head and smiles before saying, 'Anyway, I have to agree. This is a lovely dressing room. You are right, Asha, far better than the last one at that Manchester venue.'

I remember this horrible room in Manchester, when we competed in the North West heats and when I make a bad mistake in the dance number. It did not look like a dressing room at all. It was very small and to me it look more like Neil's attic room – which I only see briefly –

cluttered and messy. I think to myself one day he will let me tidy up in there, but he say it is what he call his manhole, and I am not to go in. English men are funny.

We use the very nice ladies' toilets close to our room and we all fresh ourselves up. The corridor is busy, and we hear people speaking many different languages.

'Ooh, this is exciting.' Bonnie claps her hands together. 'There are Spanish dancers in the next dressing room. Their costumes are all neon colours.'

'I heard someone speak in Russian tongue,' I add.

'You speak Russian too, Ingrida? Is there no end to your talents?' Cath smiles as we return to our room.

'Latvian, Russian and French, they are the languages I know best, but I am getting better at English.'

'Respect, Ingrida.' Ruby bows her head to me. 'With all those languages, you should be a translator.'

'Let us go and explore.' Asha grabs her handbag.

'Clarissa told me she would see us in the dressing room. Where's she got to? Let me text her.' Monica gets out her phone and it remind me; I must call Neil soon.

Asha looks at the schedule on the mirror. 'Hey, the programme gives a brief description of our dances. Our Adele number is described as contemporary jazz. And "Dancin' Fool" – which, by the way, is very close to the first number – as an "upbeat jazz fusion". I like that.'

'Jazz fusion. Sounds excellent.' Bonnie puts a thumb up in the air. 'How about our last dance?'

'A Bollywood spectacular.' Asha beams and smiles proudly.

'How many numbers are Sheila's group performing?'

Asha runs her finger down the list. 'Looks like they are doing two.'

'Talking of Sheila, has anyone seen Bold as Brass?' Cath asks.

'No. Maybe they did get chucked off the flight in Manchester?' Asha grins. 'What time is it?'

'Ten.'

'Oh good. It says here we will be getting a tour of the theatre in half an hour. Excellent.'

'Clarissa is running late.' Monica looks up from her phone. 'She said continue without her as best we can, and she will join us as soon as possible.'

'Is she OK?' Ruby asks, but Monica only shrugs without looking at Ruby.

'Oh, for God's sake...' Ruby steps towards Monica but her phone buzzes and Ruby stops to look at her message.

Asha hurriedly throws her bag on her chair. 'Come on, everyone. Let's make good use of the time and warm-up and run through the dances.' She calls to Ruby, 'Ruby, get off your phone. I know you have a new love in life but right now Dance Excellence – Clarissa Kirkland needs you.'

We all smile apart from Monica.

Ruby, she sees Monica look away, so she turns to me and rolls her eyes up to heaven – I love this expression. I have only learnt it in the last few weeks, and I often roll up my eyes to heaven when Neil is not looking if he says something I disagree with, but I do not want to be in argument with him. After all, we are newlywed. Fay tells me this, another expression I am liking very much. So, when Ruby rolls up her eyes, I give her a smile to say to her, 'it is better we do not have any arguments'.

There is a wider empty area, a vestibule – a good French word – at the opening of the room. Asha suggest we can practise our steps in this vestibule even if we have to make them a bit smaller.

We spread out and follow Asha. First, we march on the spot, roll out our shoulders, swing our arms, and then we do plié squats to get our muscles ready to dance. My mind, it go to thinking of the telephone call last night and I must be frowning as Asha tell me in a joking way to cheer up. I quickly fix a dancer's smile on my face, but my thoughts are elsewhere.

At first, I was very relieved to be back in Paris. At Manchester Airport, when we found we had no flight tickets, I thought we would have to go home. I know Neil, he would not have been pleased to see me – not until he has spoken to Rita and Terry. Then I thought the French authorities would stop me getting on the Eurostar in London. They wanted to know where Kazimieras Valenko was. I told them I had not seen my uncle in years, which is true, but they say he was wanted in connection with a number of criminal offences and had left France saying he was staying with his niece, Ingrida Valenko. They also told me my visa will soon run out and I will have to go back to Latvia or get a new visa. So, I explain to them how I am a specialist nurse in the NHS, and how I am also now Ingrida Goodman, but I did not have time to get a new passport to show this. I show them my wedding ring and photographs of Neil and the children on my telephone. It was a big relief when they let me go so I could get onto the train with the other ladies. I had not done anything wrong but it make me feel like a criminal.

At the hotel, when I get the call from *unknown number*, I knew it was going to be Kazimieras before he spoke in our native language.

'Ingrida. At last, I have found you.'

'How did you get my number?'

'That is no way to greet your uncle. You have been very elusive these last five years.'

'Kazimieras, what do you want?'

'What? You do not ask me how I am? You do not ask your uncle how he has been doing, how he has been managing with no home when he comes out of prison to find his sister's flat is gone? How he has lived when he realised the money his sister held for him has also gone? When he finds his only niece has left for Paris without leaving her phone number…'

I could not speak. My stomach did a knot twist.

'…And when I find you in Paris where you promise to pay me back before, you disappear without giving me a single euro? I have spent five long years looking for you.'

I hover my finger over the *end call* symbol, but pull it back sharply when he adds, 'I know where you live. Yes, Ingrida, I do. I know you are in England, and I know you work as a nurse and where you work – your friends in Latvia. They tell your loving uncle how to contact you. I think you are earning very good money, yes?'

I felt sick. 'You are wrong.'

'I think now you will pay back what you owe?'

'I do not owe you anything. Mama left only a few

hundred euros, and it was not yours. Besides, it is gone. I used it to fund my training as a nurse.'

'You are not taking me seriously, Ingrida. Perhaps I should tell you I am in England on business? Perhaps I should tell you I am going to Manchester...'

'I am not in Manchester. I am in Paris.'

'Why are you in Paris?'

'It is none of your business. Kazimieras, I have no money to give you. Nothing.'

'Oh, I think you have, Ingrida. I hope you are back from Paris soon as I will be here waiting. In the meantime, maybe I will check out your English home... We will speak again, Ingrida.'

He cut the call, and I had no time to think as Monica and Asha appeared in the bathroom. I make up an excuse why I was upset. I tell them it was because I did not know the dance numbers well – I could not tell them about Kazimieras.

Our practice, it help to calm me before I go to sleep and I say a prayer. 'Please God, do not let Kazimieras find Neil and the children while I am here.' God, I know he answers me as I feel his sense of peace lying in the hotel bed. I put my trust in Him as I always have. I must warn Neil about Kazimieras when we next speak.

'Good, we are now warmed up.' Asha's voice brings my thoughts back to our rehearsal, and she directs us to our positions for the first dance.

I stand in Janine's place and put my concentration to the dancing. It is like when I am professional nurse and cannot let worries distract from doing my job and must put them aside when I am with patients. In same way, I cannot do anything about Kazimieras while I am here and I must not let my dance friends down again. I have put the matter into God's hands and I will not think about it anymore until the dance competition is over.

When the music starts, I concentrate on the steps and I am soon absorbed by the movement, even though we have little space, and I put my deep feelings into every move.

At the end, Asha is smiling at me and clapping. 'Ingrida, you danced that with such expression.'

We all sip at the water, and I try to call Neil but there is no reply. I leave a message.

Hello, Neil. We are at the Paris theatre. It has wonderful Wi-Fi, so I can make call to you from here without it costing much money. Please ring me when you can. I miss you. Give the children my love.

14

FAY

I am not used to drinking. Even though I only had a couple of small brandies, they have upset my stomach and it has taken most of the morning for it to settle.

The breakfast in the café near our hotel was cheap and not a good example of French cuisine. It is a sorry discovery to find a dry, almost inedible croissant in Paris, the culinary capital of the world. I know we are close to the outskirts of the city, but I had expected this basic food would be excellent wherever we ate. I suppose standards here are slipping as much as they are in the rest of the world.

To my surprise, I have found I am enjoying being with the other women in our shared room. I am a little cross with myself for letting slip I had gone to Saint Eulalia's, but I doubt if any of them realise it was an orphanage back then. It is, after all, a boarding school now.

Ingrida is turning out to be as kind-hearted as I had hoped. At first, I had been rather taken aback when I learnt she had married her employer, apparently within weeks of his proposal. Did this confirm my suspicions that she was using him to get British Citizenship? However, there is no indication this is the case. And with a bit of research, I discovered she does not need this in order to work in the UK. She is counted as a skilled NHS worker with or without a British passport, although why she had to explain this to the French customs officers at St Pancras, I have no idea.

My concerns regarding Neil replacing his wife so quickly have also diminished. Apparently, two whole years have elapsed since the poor woman died. I had thought it was less. Some men just cannot manage without a partner – look at Andrew installing a substitute for me in a scandalously short time. No, I did Ingrida an injustice, and I am sorry I did.

I also find, somewhat to my surprise, that I am warming to Ruby. I am sure she noticed my deformed toes, but she did not say a word. I am grateful for that; it means she can show a little discretion. I have observed her being kind to Ingrida and I believe there is a little camaraderie growing between us as she also notices every incorrect saying Bonnie utters.

Sadly, I cannot say I have connected with Monica. I had hoped to converse with her more during the trip. She is, after all, better spoken than all the other dancers and has great poise and decorum. However, she has stayed aloof so far, and her demeanour is often one of total abstraction. Aside from one moment when she comforted Ingrida with Asha and then joined in our impromptu rehearsal in our nightwear, Monica has a permanent faraway look etched on her face.

As Monica and I waited to check-in at the front desk of the theatre, a group of young adults dressed in shorts, crop tops, and trainers joined the queue behind us. They were chattering loudly in French and pushing each other in some sort of childish game. One pushed me – thankfully lightly – into Monica, so I turned to admonish the individual, but she quickly held up her hand and said, '*Pardon. Désolée, Madame…*' She did look genuinely sorry, so I let it go.

I leant into Monica to say, 'These entrants look young. Clarissa said all those participating had to be over eighteen.'

'They do, but at eighteen they are still teenagers.' Monica shrugged, and I recalled her twins are aged fourteen.

'They are clearly in high spirits. Are your twins well-behaved?'

Monica cocked her head to one side and answered, 'They have their moments.'

This would have been an opportune moment to talk about Edith and Bethan and the difficulties I had experienced with them during adolescence, but Monica turned away.

It is good to go on the tour of the premises of the *Opéra Bastille*, a diverting occupation for my mind. While the building is not to my taste, with its modernistic architecture and vast airport-like foyers and walkways, one cannot deny it is impressive. Our tour guide is speaking in rapid French, and I do not have the patience to await Ingrida's translation, so I wander around the spaces a short distance from the group.

I have read up on the history of the building and was amused to learn of all the issues. There was controversy and scandal between the various directors, which could have constituted the plot of an opera in itself. Then the building construction was fraught with difficulties, not least being when the limestone cladding on the facade began to drop off. In the early 1990s, safety nets had to be put into place to catch the panels as they fell. The director made a widely praised joke when he dubbed them 'condoms with holes'. I can only think this is comical to the French humour, as I do not find it remotely funny. Anyway, the entire cladding was eventually replaced in 2009.

We are shown into the main theatre, where the finals will be held, and I have to say it is extraordinary with its vast hanging balconies. I am not surprised it has been dubbed a vessel as each balcony is reminiscent of a ship – although I have read that in French the term vessel is intended as an insult when compared to the praise given to traditional opera houses. I have to say the place is somewhat soulless, not a patch on period theatres.

I am slightly daunted at the prospect of dancing on the main stage, but this may as yet not happen. We would have to win through the semi-finals today, and there is no guarantee of this. I just hope we can get a respectable placing above Sheila Bold's group.

I have craned my neck to look for any sign of Sheila and her band of women, quite sure we would hear them before we see them. It is a relief there has been no hint of them so far. Clarissa's ladies are far superior in both presentation and manner.

Our tour over, we all sit in the smaller and preferable amphitheatre. The warm wooden flooring gives it a cosy feel and we commandeer a section of the black, padded circular benching. We sit and wait for Clarissa, and I quickly calculate our expenses to date.

'Ahem.' I stand in front of our group and wait for them all to give me their undivided attention. 'Before Clarissa arrives, I just thought you should know what we owe Monica so far. I used her card – thank you, Monica – to purchase the three-day Metro tickets for our entire group so with that and the train fares, including the Eurostar, our running total works out to be four-hundred-and-twenty-two pounds each. Of course, we will have the hotel to add to that, but this is, thankfully, a relatively small sum...'

'Hey, there's something good to be said for the Smut Hotel, then?' Ruby mutters, but I ignore her as I notice Ingrida is chewing her lip.

'Please do not worry. I plan to get back everything we have paid to Janine, and I have taken the first steps towards this.'

'You said you'd reported it to the police—'

'Yes, I did, Ruby, and I have no idea why you should look so irritated that I have done so. Someone had to. I went online on the Greater Manchester Police site – I did it first thing when you were all getting dressed. I reported her theft of our Paris money, and I also reported my suspicions that Janine had embezzled our lottery money...'

'You did what?'

'Really, Ruby, you must let me finish. I did add this was only supposition, and I had, as yet, no proof, whereas I made it clear there was plenty of evidence she had stolen our competition trip money.'

'Fay, I wish you'd waited until we got back to England…'

I was surprised to find Monica voicing her objection to my actions.

'It just seems wrong to initiate police involvement before we have found out what happened.'

'Hear, hear.' Ruby crosses her arms, but neither she nor Monica make eye contact with each other.

'I am sorry,' I say with a degree of frustration I cannot keep from my voice. 'But we need to be very clear that regardless of Janine's reasons for stealing from us, she has, plain and simple, committed an offence. She must make restitution for what she has taken and pay the penalty.'

Bonnie and Cath shake their heads and one by one, the ladies turn to each other and talk in low voices about anything other than Janine. When no one responds to me, I sit down, more than a little piqued.

I could have told them that in all probability it will take an age for the authorities to act on my report. One of the questions I had to answer on the website form was whether I was in immediate danger. It made me appreciate there are others who will have been the victims of far worse crimes and that this theft falls more into the category of a scam. But if the other women choose not to listen to me, I will not inform them it is unlikely to have the highest priority for the police.

A short blast of feedback resounds from the overhead speakers, making us jump and the theatre starts to fill up while announcements are made over the sound system.

'*Messieurs dames, attention. Nous allons commencer la répétition détaillée...*'

'He say, we are to start the rehearsal,' Ingrida translates.

'*Afin de déterminer le positionnement et vérifier l'éclairage.*'

'It is for us to check positioning and lighting.'

'*Et nous appellerons chaque groupe à tour de rôle.*'

'Each group will be called in turn.'

'*Veuillez écouter votre nom.*'

'Listen for your name...'

'*Et s'il vous plaît soyez rapide.*'

'He ask us to be prompt.'

'This is it.' Asha claps her hands together and we watch the first group take to the stage. There are further blasts of music and feedback and after ten minutes of eagerly anticipating the first performance, nothing has happened. The dancers, a group of eight women wearing bright leotards overlaid with sarongs, stand talking to each other as they wait. The lights flash on and off in strange combinations and the opening bars of *Dance of the Knights* by Sergei Prokofiev play in repetitive and tedious snatches.

'That's the theme tune to *The Apprentice*.' Cath nudges Bonnie. 'Do you remember Clarissa's skirt dance to this?'

'I certainly do. It was incredible. We did it in the very first Expression contest, when only a few dance groups took part. Do you remember it, Fay?' Bonnie asks.

'Before my time with Clarissa, I am afraid. But Hazel

has shown me a video and I have to say, it was extremely accomplished.'

Eventually, the rehearsal gets underway, and we sit forward to watch the first dancers perform.

There is polite applause at the end as Asha whispers, 'It was nowhere near as good as Clarissa's choreography.'

Thirty minutes later, we are still sitting waiting for Clarissa and only four more groups have run through their acts. The sound of the music stop-starting in loud blasts is beginning to give me a headache. I can also see these run-throughs will take an age, and it is frustrating to think the sights of Paris are only just outside our door and we are stuck here, unable to reach them.

The volume of the music lowers as a classical piece begins to play and a group of six male ballet dancers get into position.

'Now that's what I call tight tights.' Ruby nudges Ingrida who stifles a giggle.

I ignore them and sit forward, eager to see a traditional ballet performance.

Everyone quietens, but as the dancers begin, there is a disturbance at the entrance on the opposite side of the auditorium.

'Uh-oh.' Bonnie shakes her head as shrieks of laughter resound around the theatre and Sheila's group bursts into the space, talking loudly and oblivious to the disruption they are causing.

The audience turn as one to shush Sheila's group who merely giggles before noisily taking over a row of benches opposite us.

'Just like a bad penny,' Cath whispers. 'They were bound to turn up.'

I feel relieved to see Clarissa descending the steps towards us. We all wave quietly in greeting as she puts a finger to her lips, and we turn our attention back to the stage.

The ballet is rather strange. The music is, I think, from *Giselle* but the movements are rather jerky and have rather too many scissor kicks. I expect it would be described as contemporary. It is only part way through when a loud scream of laughter emanates from the direction of Sheila's group and is followed by wolf whistles and more laughter.

The dancers on stage stop and glare, hands on hips or arms folded, and the music is cut short. The lights go back up and an official descends to the Bold as Brass group. We see him remonstrating with Sheila.

'What is she saying?' Asha asks.

'I can't hear, but judging from her body language, Sheila's definitely taking issue,' Ruby comments.

'Ay-up,' – Bonnie points – 'they're going to get slung out.'

The official points to the exit and – as one – Sheila's women grab their bags and head out. When they get to the door, Sheila turns and shouts back to the man, her words crystal clear, 'Stupid arse.'

There is a stunned silence quickly followed by the murmur of spectators and dancers conversing in their groups.

'Well, let us hope that will get them ejected from the competition,' I say to our ladies.

'I rather hope they are not, Fay.' Clarissa surprises us all. 'I would prefer to knock them out of the competition by way of our superior dance numbers.'

She is, of course, right. We must triumph over these ill-mannered roughnecks without a doubt and I for one, want to immerse myself in the competition, the music and the atmosphere. I realise this is a wonderful opportunity to be part of something big and artistic; a new experience.

It dawns on me that Expression Paris has become synonymous with my sense of moving towards a happier future; I do believe I can feel it in my bones.

15

ASHA

The *Opéra Bastille* building is incredible. We were given a short tour and are now waiting in the audience area of the amphitheatre, which seats five hundred people. If we get to the finals, which are presented like a proper show with members of the public paying to watch, we will be in the main theatre. Totally daunting. It looks like something from the space age with hanging seating above the stalls. The seating capacity in there is over two-thousand seven hundred. Can you believe that? Bigger than any other audience we have danced for.

But even this smaller amphitheatre looks huge. A sudden realisation makes me do a double take. This holds just half the number of people due to attend my wedding. That is one heck of a crowd. It is as well our group is dancing my wedding number in front of a large audience in advance. It should help with any nerves on the day. Truthfully, even I am a little anxious about performing to so many, but it is an excited anxiety, not a worried one.

The other entrants are dotted all over the modern auditorium seated on the tiered, curved black benches descending to the wooden dance floor. Some are chatting, some warming up and stretching out, and others just watching.

When Sheila's dreadful group was dismissed from the theatre, I was delighted. I cannot, however, agree with Clarissa. I think Bold as Brass should be ejected from the competition and sent home.

Once Sheila's group has gone, the audience engages in low-level conversation as the rehearsals continue.

Clarissa, who is sitting sideways on the bench in front and below us, has now been addressing us for several minutes. I find it difficult to listen to her as my eyes are constantly drawn to the stage to see what is on next. She is trying to tell us about backstage protocol and costume changes, but it is very hard to concentrate with everything that is going on. Announcements are being made over the sound system to get the artistes to the floor in turn and each dance group leader shouts instructions for their dancers that resound through the acoustically sensitive space. This, and the music for each dance, drowns out Clarissa, who instead of waiting patiently for a gap in the noise, keeps raising her voice until she is almost shouting. More distracting are the many dancers moving on and off the stage area in groups of anything from two to thirty performers. All ages, all races; truly cosmopolitan. No one is in costume for this run-through and the lighting engineer is playing around with the settings for each group, sending random flashes of every colour across the stage.

I try to watch as many dances as I can from the corner of my eye. There is quite a mix here. A few routines look fairly tame, but some of the choreography is fantastic. I am pleased to see the standard of the dancing is variable. Without boasting, I think we are better than most of the ones I manage to watch, so maybe we are in with a chance to reach the finals.

Clarissa clicks her fingers and fixes me with what can only be described as an evil eye. I wish she had arrived earlier so she could have given out these instructions in the dressing room. Then we could have just sat and watched the other groups. We will not be able to see them during the heats. Even if the theatre is not full, performers are not allowed front of stage while the dances are in progress. This is a double disappointment, as I do not want to be stuck in our dressing room for hours on end, no matter how well appointed it is. It will only take a spat between Monica and Ruby, and it will be unbearable. And I can sense this is brewing. As soon as one thinks the other is not looking, they shoot daggers at the other.

'Ladies, after all your efforts to get here, I know you are going to do well.' Clarissa shouts above the rather appropriate Elton John track, 'I'm Still Standing'.

'Look at the obstacles you overcame just to get here. You should be proud of yourselves…'

Clarissa's raised voice fogs as I look past her to the routine, which appears more gymnastic than dance. I am amused to see the dancers are rarely standing for this song; the majority of their movements are made while they lie prone on the floor, kicking out and scissoring their legs, hips high in the air. I find it hard to categorise this as dance.

'Asha, are you listening?'

'Yes, Clarissa. Sorry.'

'Now, to the final order for our numbers. We are one of the few groups who have been entered in three categories and to accommodate this we have little time for one of our costume changes. It is between our first and second performance. We will only have a maximum of ten minutes, including getting to the dressing room and back. I asked them to put the Adele number first, followed by "Dancin' Fool" second, as this is the simplest costume change.'

We all nod.

'Then you can do the Bollywood number at the end, as the saris take the most time to put on. As it happens, this will be the last dance of the competition heats, so it will be good to finish with something completely different. A scintillating showstopper.'

The noise stops suddenly and Clarissa's voice shouting *scintillating showstopper*, resounds through the space and many heads turn to look at her.

Clarissa instantly lowers her voice and proceeds to tell us the dressing room rules. I am only half listening. I am thrilled my wedding dance will be the last number, effectively making it the finale of today's competition before the judges decide who will go through to the show tomorrow for the final. Clarissa has even put my name with hers on the programme as joint choreographers for the routine.

I observe Clarissa critically. She looks drawn. I vaguely

wonder for the umpteenth time if she has dentures. Even for me, it is hard to tell.

Hazel has not come to the run-through as the journey yesterday really took it out of her. I think to myself she would not have survived our long expedition. She is resting in their hotel and hopes to watch the competition later. I reflect on what it would be like to have a member of my family so ill. I shudder when I think of Jay and try to pay more attention to what Clarissa is saying.

'You should all know the drill, but just to remind you. No alcohol is permitted. Snacks must not be eaten in the green room at the end of our corridor. At all times, you must conduct yourselves with the utmost decorum. You are representing the Clarissa Kirkland Group and must show model behaviour at all times. We should be seen as the *crème de la crème* of amateur dance. If you have to leave the theatre for any reason, you must change back into your ordinary clothes. No dance costumes outside. Now about wearing rings and other jewellery…'

I see Ingrida self-consciously touch her wedding ring, which seems to be stuck solid on her finger. I doubt she will be able to remove it without having to have it cut off.

Ruby looks at her ringless fingers and whispers some comment to Bonnie who in turn stifles a laugh.

Well, I will not say anything to Clarissa, but I refuse to take my engagement ring off for any of the numbers. I would not risk leaving it in the dressing room. Clarissa can forget that. Jay spent a good six months' salary on my ornate sapphire, diamond, and platinum ring. It is staying firmly on my finger.

As I place one hand over the other to cover my ring from Clarissa's eyes, Fay, who is sitting next to me, gives a sudden start and leans forward in her seat. She stares as a small group enters the amphitheatre from the stage area.

Clarissa is no longer able to see me, with Fay blocking the way, so I follow Fay's eyes. Two beautiful young women and two svelte young men, all tall, barefoot and wearing loose-fitting warm-up outfits, begin to walk around the space as the lighting around us dims. The stage ceiling lights change to a night-time setting and patterns representing a star scape pepper the floor.

The name of the group is announced over the sound system, *Corps et Ame*, and I hear Ingrida whisper to Ruby that it means 'Body and Soul'. What a suitable name. Clarissa often says to us we should dance with the soul, not just the body.

Fay is tightly gripping the top of the seat in front of us and I can see the whites of her knuckles. I cannot see her face, but as the music starts, two spotlights are trained on the dance floor and follow the two couples. I find myself transfixed by the dance. I know the track well. Clarissa choreographed a ballet solo for Monica to this very version a few years ago, "Fix You" by Coldplay. Even though the dancers are not in costume, they move so beautifully I cannot take my eyes off them. They are completely in time with each other and appear to float on the dance floor. It is a mixture of contemporary dance and ballet, and it is incredible. One by one, everyone in the auditorium stops talking to watch in hushed admiration. This group is way better than anyone else I have seen and way better than us.

When they finish, the entire theatre bursts into spontaneous applause and the dancers smile and bow, a little self-consciously.

Fay sits back in her seat, and I see her eyes are brimming with tears.

'You know them?' I ask.

'Edi…' Is all she can say in a reverential whisper as she stares at the group retreating behind the stage rear curtain.

'Who? Fay, are you OK?'

Fay turns towards me and quickly snaps out of her reverie. She frowns and purses her lips before dabbing her eyes with her linen handkerchief.

'What? Oh, yes, I am perfectly fine. Thank you, Asha. Dust. I had some dust in my eye. I think we will be on next.'

She turns away from me to face Clarissa, who has clasped her hands together and is gushing out rapturous praise for the dance we just watched. She sees we are all now a little daunted at the prospect of competing against such high-quality dancers and hurriedly adds that in her opinion they are the only ones we need to worry about and when we dance our best, we are more than worthy opponents.

I am not so sure about this, but the dance has left us all in awe and I feel a little giddy when we are finally called to go down to the stage to go through our numbers.

An amplified male French voice booms out, '*Messieurs dames, attention, maintenant c'est, "Dance…" C'est qui? Ah oui? Le groupe "DICK",*' and then in English, 'Can ze dance group DICK go to ze stage, please.'

Clarissa jumps to her feet, an outraged expression on her face. She makes a beeline for the organiser who is sitting with the lighting engineer at the top of the tiered seating in a raised box.

She indicates for us to go down to the stage level and I see Ruby is biting her hand to stop herself from laughing as the others giggle to each other. Even Monica, who has been so serious this whole trip, has a grin on her face.

Once Clarissa has clarified our name should be Dance Excellence – Clarissa Kirkland, she is handed the microphone and calls to us. 'Attention, Clarissa's ladies, I will remain here to sort out the lighting with this gentleman. I will leave you to work out your positions and make sure you are well forward on stage. This is just a walk-through to get the lighting and spatial awareness correct. Performance level will not be required until the competition later on. Feel the stage, breathe in the ambience.'

We descend the final steps to the circular stage, and all take a sharp intake of breath as we turn to look around the auditorium. Not for the first time today, I feel a little sick. My nerves are beginning to get to me.

'Wowzers.' Ruby whistles her appreciation.

'This beats Woodford Community Hall,' Cath murmurs.

'It all look very different from down here.' Ingrida sounds nervous as she adds, 'My stomach has just – how you say?'

'Flipped?' I suggest before adding, 'Mine too.'

Monica squeezes Ingrida's arm and says, 'You will be

fine. Just pretend we are in Clarissa's studio. You danced brilliantly in the dressing room today.'

Ruby takes Ingrida's other arm and says, 'It's good to have a few nerves. Keeps it edgy.'

I watch Monica glare at Ruby over Ingrida's head, and Ruby glare back.

I cannot help myself when the words burst from my mouth. 'Monica and Ruby, for goodness' sake, please drop this animosity. If only for the duration of the competition. It is an unnecessary distraction from our dancing.'

Ruby bites her lip and nods. She turns to Monica and gives her a small smile, but Monica merely shrugs and walks away to take her start position for the dance.

Such a disappointment. But at least I tried.

I find my position and the lights begin to flash bright colours in time to the first beats of "Rolling in the Deep" which pounds into the space from the towers of speakers. I feel a flutter of excitement as we begin to move together, and our dance training takes over.

Everyone gets their steps right and Monica gives a solid solo in the middle of the number. Not as good as the other week when she was fuelled by what seemed to be a righteous anger, but she is a glorious dancer even when she is only doing it half-heartedly.

The first routine is over in a flash and to our delight, those watching in the audience give us a round of applause when we finish. We all smile at each other. Our next two dances, our jazz number to Barry Manilow's "Dancin' Fool" and my own Bollywood number also get enthusiastic applause.

As we perform, I watch the others in our group from the corner of my eye. Ingrida is on fire, and even Fay is better than I have ever seen her. Their concentration is palpable. Both ladies completely immerse themselves in the practice.

If I have any criticism, it would be regarding both Monica and Ruby. They are just not up to their normal standards. Monica is usually stunning, but it is obvious her mind is not fully on the dance. Also, I am sure she was grinding her teeth in her bed last night – a sure sign of tension. Perhaps I should recommend a gum shield?

As for Ruby, she normally has an incredibly sexy stage presence but, if I am truthful, she appeared self-conscious in all three dances, which is not like her at all.

If I can bring these two around and get them to resolve their issues, I am sure they will dance better. Not only will it be my good deed for the day, it will elevate all the numbers to something wondrous. I want to be in the finals.

Plus, I need them to dance well at my wedding.

16

MONICA

I find myself getting more and more annoyed with Ruby. She is laughing and joking with everyone as if she hasn't a care in the world. I've been watching her chummying up to Ingrida, Asha and even Fay. She's clearly determined to show me she doesn't care a jot about our break-up, to the point of throwing it in my face.

I know it's affecting my dance and I know I need to pull myself together. We've finished our run-through, so I grab my bag from the dressing room and go to the ladies – thankfully empty – for some peace and quiet.

My reflection in the mirror above the wash basin looks pinched so I fish out my make-up to dab a little concealer on my frown lines. I practise a smile. It does not seem natural. Then again, I've had little reason to smile in the last few weeks.

Staring into my eyes, I recall the other times in my life when I barely smiled. There were several long sad years soon after I rushed into marriage to Vince, having found out I was pregnant. I wondered then if I would ever smile again, but I came through it. I did. And I owe so much to Clarissa for her help. It was Clarissa who saved me after I lost my first baby. I was drowning in the depths of despair until my psychiatrist recommended taking up an open university degree in fashion design and starting dance as a form of therapy. The degree was hard work and took several years to complete, working late into the night, but the dance was sublime. I had, after all, adored ballet in my childhood.

Clarissa's inspiring choreography and gentle encouragement slowly brought purpose back into my life. Nothing could replace the love of the baby I would never hold, but I found a rekindling of my love of music and dance as an art form. Then the twins were born and although I love being their mum, I only feel truly alive when I'm lost in the performance of an amazing dance. It allows me to express my deepest feelings without having to verbalise. To me, it has become as essential as breathing.

Making a fist, I resolve to give the competition my all. It is the least I can do to repay Clarissa.

My phone rings and I retrieve it from my bag. A satisfied smile spreads across my face. Payback time for Vince.

The message from the dating app which I have now transferred to my phone is just what I'd hoped for.

Greta Grinder, who describes herself as a super-size lover – and judging from her picture she's not lying – has responded and has agreed to meet Vince at 9.30 p.m. tonight, providing she can have meatballs with plenty of sauce. Yeuw. Although technically, she'll be expecting Butch Cassidy – the new profile I've constructed for him.

I congratulate myself for working out how to make this hidden from view, so it's not on Vince's homepage. He'd have to hunt to find it as it's not obvious. He's never been great with IT so with a bit of luck, he'll be oblivious to the new correspondence which I've diverted to my phone having added my number to the secret profile.

I quickly tap in Butch's reply, ignoring the fact it is Ruby's voice that enters my head with the phrase,

Can't wait to get grinding with you, Greta. Look for me on the corner table to the right of the bar. I'll be the one ordering the extra-large saveloy sausage with fries.

I know this is Vince's seat of choice as I have seen his previous dates made from his Ben Johnson profile. He will be under the impression he is meeting someone called Venus – set for 9 p.m. – in this Cock and Bull pub. The bastard set this up this date a week ago, so knew full well he would not be around to look after the twins while I was in Paris. All that rubbish about a conference…

Another ping and I grin to see it is a message from Cindy-Just-Cindy – her photo shows a mass of blonde curls and the longest false eyelashes I have ever seen on her air-brushed face. She asks if she can bring her pooch.

I never go anywhere without poochy poochy pie, so I hope you love doggies, Butch.

Not a problem. Bring your adorable doggy, Cindy.
I will be at the corner table waiting to pet you both.

I hit *send* with a flourish of satisfaction.

Pity Vince is allergic to dogs.

I check the other arrangements before smiling at my reflection, aglow with both the exertion of dance and a delicious new sense of gratification.

As Vince meets Venus, he will first be interrupted by Greta Grinder, then Cindy with her lap dog, followed by Titania with her 'hidden talents' – possibly something to do with the handcuffs and whips in her profile picture. And then Bruce – who looks neither male nor female and declares he/she swings both ways – will enter the affray. I'm glad I ticked the option of him/her bringing a few extras along for the ride.

'What are you smiling about, Monica?' Bonnie says as she and a couple of other ladies enter the toilets.

'Oh nothing. I'm missing a bit of a bash back in the UK. Just imagining being a fly on the wall.'

'Wishing you were there?'

'Oh no. I'd much rather be here.'

Asha dashes in and makes a beeline for me.

'Monica, you will never guess what has happened?'

'What?'

'Sheila's group has turned up. They have been assigned to our dressing room. Your face says it all, Monica. I know. It is horrendous. They arrived shouting and swearing. They squashed all our costumes along the rail to fit theirs on. They are loud, rude, and completely disruptive.

Apparently, the officials are deciding if they can still take part after their outburst during rehearsals. I hope they cannot. Sheila is in a foul mood and Clarissa has had to go back to the hotel. She was too upset to be in the same airspace as Sheila.'

Before Asha can say more, Sheila herself and another woman burst into the ladies', shrieking loudly to each other.

'Thank fuck for that. I'm busting for a wee.' Sheila's eyes meet mine momentarily before she completely blanks me and rushes into the only free cubicle, slamming the door shut.

'Hurry up, Sheila. I'm wetting myself here.' Her large-busted friend cries out as she hops from foot to foot.

Sheila calls through the door, 'I knew we shouldn't have downed those bloody beers last night. They always make me pee for days.' They both cackle.

Another cubicle becomes free, and the large-bosomed woman dives in. The pair continue to converse loudly from within their respective cubicles. Asha and I grimace.

'Sheila, do you think they'll let us dance after what happened?'

'They'd bloody better had, Bridget. We didn't come all this way not to compete. Besides, we have to beat those stuck-up bitches in Clarissa's la-di-da group.'

I glare at the door. Sheila knows full well we're here. She was in Clarissa's dance group at the same time as me for a couple of years before she left. She's what my mother would call common. The sort of woman who loves confrontation and only has two volumes, loud and deafening.

MONICA

I begin to say, 'We can hear you, Sheila,' but the toilets flushing drown me out and Asha puts a hand on my arm and pulls me out through the door. Instead of turning towards our dressing room she leads me in the opposite direction down the corridor.

'Where are we going?'

'Monica, I need to have a word.' The corridor widens, and she pulls me into an alcove away from the bustle of competitors going to and fro.

'We have to get to the finals.'

'Yes, that'd be amazing...' I begin to say.

'But, Monica, I have noticed... that is we have all noticed the terrible tension between you and Ruby and... well there is no easy way to say this, so I will just come right out with it. It is spoiling the dynamics. I have to be honest when I say neither of you is dancing your best. You, in particular, have always been the best dancer in the group. We need you to be on top form. So, you and Ruby have to put aside your differences. For the sake of the competition.'

I glaze over and say nothing. Asha has no idea.

'I mean, seriously, Monica, what can Ruby have done that is so bad you won't even look at her?'

Ruby suddenly appears behind Asha and before I can start past them, Ruby holds one hand in the air to stop me and stands the other side of Asha. She addresses Asha while staring at me.

'I'll tell you what I've done, Asha. I made a silly, stupid mistake. I sent Monica a voice message in error. One meant for Max. I would never deliberately hurt Monica's feelings, not for the world, but she heard my stupid jokes, and she's taken what I'd said to Max to heart. She's decided to turn her back on our six years of friendship without even a chance for me to apologise, and I *do* want to apologise. Monica, I'm so, so sorry.'

Ruby looks at me hopefully, her hands spread out.

Asha eagerly turns to me, nods, and awaits my response.

For a minute I'm dumbfounded and before I can open my mouth, Asha adds – with a degree of irritation – 'See. Ruby is sorry. Whatever misunderstanding has happened, you can now put it behind you. We all make mistakes.'

'Mistake?' I clench my fists barely realising I'm shouting straight into Asha's surprised face.

'Misunderstanding? Forgive Ruby? You have no idea. What Ruby has done is unforgivable. I wonder if you'd forgive her if you'd found out she'd slept with your fiancé? Quite deliberately and without a care in the world. Not even a modicum of guilt. How would that make you feel? Except Ruby hasn't slept with your fiancé. She's slept with Vince. She's committed adultery with my husband and has no doubt been gloating over the fact I hadn't the slightest idea…'

My words ring out down the corridors, and I'm vaguely aware of other dancers stopping to listen beyond Ruby's gaping face.

Asha flounders, her mouth open and frozen.

'So, no, Asha. I cannot forgive Ruby. She's the worst kind of person. I cannot put anything behind me because she's already stabbed me right there – in the back. And she can just… just go to hell.'

Pushing past them both, I head down the passages leading to the exit at the front of the theatre.

*

Out in the open air, a barrage of traffic noise from the busy French road hits me. I set off in any direction just to be clear of the building. Breathing deeply, I walk to slow my heart rate and replay snatches of my past friendship with Ruby.

How could she have carried on as if nothing had happened? How could she be so blatant? I really didn't know her at all…

When I think about it, her entire life has been based on deceit. She even lied to her son about who his father was, pretending she used a sperm bank. When she told me this a few years ago, I told her she should tell Will the truth, but I'm not sure Ruby would recognise the truth if it came up and punched her in the face. Will is such a decent kid too.

*

After ten minutes of walking, my mind is easing. I leave the main roads and find myself in a beautiful part of Paris. I check the name: *Place des Vosges*. A wide, tree-filled park spreads out before me. It's bordered by elegant tall townhouses. I take a deep breath of fresh air and wander around the boxed hedges and fountains before finding my way to the arcaded cafés that line the perimeter. Hanging baskets overflow with flowers as I pass boutique cafés and tiny bars where people are seated outside under the arches, drinking coffee or wine, and eating an assortment of French fare.

The smell of fresh bread fills the air and I pass a *boulangerie* displaying a wonderful assortment of savoury delicacies. My stomach rumbles and I realise I'm hungry, having barely touched the awful breakfast at the café near our hotel.

The shop front of a patisserie stops me in my tracks. Beautiful multicoloured cakes, mille-feuilles, éclairs and macaroons fill the window. The shop is rammed with customers ordering cakes by the box full. I catch fragments of their French, '*Puis-je commander une douzaine de macarons...*', '*Très bon...*', '*Deux éclairs s'il vous plaît...*', '*Délicieux, merci.*'

I pull out my phone and text Fay to ask her if she wants me to purchase a light lunch for the ladies. She instantly replies.

'Yes, please, and make sure you keep the receipt.'

The scents of French cooking fill my nostrils. A small sign fixed to the brickwork at the end of the arches catches my eye. The word *Enchanté* is next to an arrow; there is a logo of a long-silhouetted dress next to it. I recognise the brand at once and fumble in my bag to find Jean-Claude's card to double-check the name. *Je ne le crois pas* – his words when he found out we both had twins – one of his fashion shops is just around the corner.

It takes me mere seconds to come to a decision before setting off in the direction of the sign and I soon find myself outside a quirky dress shop displaying off-the-peg high fashion.

I check my hair in the reflection of the shop window and go in to browse. There are some fabulous outfits in here. I am examining the detail on an embroidered day dress displayed in the centre of the shop when a familiar voice calls my name.

'Monica? *C'est vrai. Vous êtes ici.*'

'Jean-Claude. I didn't expect to see you here.' I can feel myself starting to colour.

'I am so glad you come to my boutique. How is ze dancing going?'

'Oh, I have a short time between rehearsals and our main performance, so I just came for a walk to clear my head.'

Jean-Claude looks quizzical, so I elaborate. 'I needed to get some fresh air. Have a break.'

'Ah *oui*, I love to get fresh air. Please come and see our newest garments.'

I accept his invitation to go to a screened area at the back of the shop where there are racks of outfits still in plastic wraps. He uncovers a couple to show me some of his *Enchanté* designs. They're beautifully cut and original. I admire a couple of the long dresses and his mouth spreads into a wide smile. My stomach flutters and I tell myself to stop behaving like a schoolgirl. The way his eyes twinkle is quite disconcerting.

Jean-Claude then reaches for a fabulous knee-length cocktail dress in crisp gold satin overlaid with soft black lace. He studies it for a minute. His eyes ask, 'do I mind?'

and I shake my head, giving him permission to hold it against me. He gently turns me to look in the mirror as he takes the dress off the hanger, stands behind me, and drapes the garment from my shoulders. I catch my breath; he's so close.

He leans into me and fixes his eyes on mine in the mirror. Disconcerted, I quickly look down to the dress.

With his sexy French accent, he says, '*Magnifique*, Monique. It suits you. You should try it on.'

A blush rises as I dramatically look to my watch and hurriedly shake my head and pull away. 'It's a beautiful dress, but sadly, I have no time. I need to get back.'

'Of course. Perhaps I can walk you back to ze Opéra House? I have a little confession to make. I came to zis store today as I was going to see if I could get a ticket for ze dance show tomorrow afternoon. I would love to watch you dance.'

'Oh, that's so sweet. But we may not be in the show. We have to get to the finals first and we have some stiff competition. If we don't make it, we'll be sitting in the audience tomorrow too.'

'Maybe I could join you in the audience if so? But I 'ope not. I mean, I 'ope you do get into ze finals? I would be happy for you to send me a message on my phone to let me know ze outcome. Ze number is right there.'

He leans across to tap the business card still in my hand and brushes my arm. It sends a shiver up my spine. Steady, Monica.

Jean-Claude offers to help me with the shopping and walks with me to the *boulangerie*. He guides my choices and orders the pastries and baguettes in French for me. I end up with two large carriers filled with delicious food. The bill is ridiculously large, but Vince's card is instantly accepted.

'I will 'elp you carry these back to ze theatre, oui?'

'Thank you, Jean-Claude. That'd be lovely.'

He takes my arm and one of the bags and we walk companionably back to the theatre.

At the foyer, Jean-Claude pecks me on each cheek before handing over the bag. I promise to send him a message later as we part. He heads for the ticket office, and I head for the dressing room, a warm glow spreading through my body.

I warn myself not to lose my head but meeting this dreamy Jean-Claude and knowing he will be watching the show tomorrow makes me further determine I will dance my best.

17

RUBY

Everything goes out of focus as Monica barges past. I steady myself against the wall with her words ringing in my head.

What the…? Slept with Vince? How can she think such a thing? Why didn't I just outright deny it? I feel as if I've been punched in the stomach. My breaths come short and shallow. I've never even met Vince, and I never want to meet him, the complete bastard. A small voice in my head prompts, *unless…*

Monica's weeping voice replays in my mind. From in the car, the other week, when she told me about Vince. She found his tablet. The app.

Unless you met him without knowing.

Oh shit. Spontaneous Encounters.

My vision tunnels and with a growing nausea in my stomach, I slide my hands down the wall until I am sitting in a crouch position. I wrack my brains. Which one was he? How long ago? I've no idea. I ball my fists and press them into my eyes. What have I done?

I then realise Asha is staring down at me, horrified.

'It… it is not true, right?' Asha begins.

I shake my head and then shrug. 'I don't know.'

'You do not know? You do not know if you slept with Monica's husband?'

'Asha, leave me alone.' I glare up at the faces of random dancers who stand transfixed. I rise to my feet and shout, 'What're you all staring at? The show's over, so just piss off.'

When they have all melted away and I am completely by myself, I begin to pace the floor. Monica must have looked at the SE App and gone through all Vince's past dates. She said he had many profiles. Which one did she say she had seen when she first told me? Ben something? Ben Johnson. I'm sure I never had a date with anyone of that name. But what were his other names? She must have trawled through his other profiles and found a photograph of me, and she already knew I used the name Scarlet. I'm appalled at the very thought of being intimate with her husband, even if I didn't know it was him at the time. My mind's veering all over the place. I have to know which one Vince was and when it was.

It then dawns on me that I can check, go back to the SE App and scour all those past dates to find out where and when.

I need to get out of the theatre.

I dash back to the dressing room where some of Clarissa's ladies are in a huddle in the far corner away from Sheila's loud, shrieking group.

Gnasher-Asha is talking to the others in hushed tones.

She quickly goes quiet when she sees me. No doubt she was filling them in on all the gory details. All their eyes follow me as I grab my bag and head out of the theatre.

'Don't forget we are dancing in a few hours,' Asha calls after me in a weak voice.

I don't reply. I need fresh air.

Thankfully, there's a roadside café a short walk from the Opéra House. I perch on a metal chair outside and order a coffee and a large slice of cake – Monica always says *take sugar for shock...* I quickly correct myself. That's before she stopped speaking to you.

I finally get onto the app after downloading it afresh and retrieving a new password from my email. I haven't used Spontaneous Encounters for over a year. I sip my coffee and nibble at my cake absent-mindedly. I'd forgotten most of these dates. The numbers really add up. Then I spot it; it must be him. The date was a few years back in Birmingham city centre when I was on a work course. Birmingham. Monica had told me Vince had a flat in the Midlands, but I hadn't known where. And it hadn't even occurred to me her husband would use the same app. I mean, it wouldn't occur to anyone. Would it?

I open the page for the details and stare at his photo as my heart sinks. The memory's blurred, but his name isn't. No. Ruddy Clint Westwood. Bloody hell.

Vince's dark hair – a little too dark so probably dyed – and designer moustache made him a good prospect from just his photo. At the time, I thought he looked like the old film star, Clark Gable. He's as handsome as Monica is beautiful. With such a striking face, I would've remembered if I'd ever met Vince or seen a photo of him, but Monica doesn't damn well do social media so there's nothing online. Thinking about it, there're no pictures to be seen in her house, not even a wedding shot; her walls are covered in tasteful artwork. The only photos I've ever seen are on the pin boards of her workshop and they're of our dance shows and the twins...

I try to recall the date with *Clint*. From what little I remember from my alcohol-fuelled haze, it was an utter let-down. My overriding impression was that he had a sneering condescension and pumped-up opinion of himself. If I hadn't been pissed, I would've walked away, but I was up for almost anything back then.

Bloody frigging hell...

I check the date again and my stomach lurches. Monica. Poor Monica probably looked after Will that very night, as it was a school night. I can hardly believe it. I slept with her husband as she looked after my son.

The bites of cake feel like rock in my belly as I stare at the details and the stark sordid truth hammers home. Of all the people I could have met up with in a huge place like Birmingham, why did it have to be him? The words of that famous line from *Casablanca* repeat in my head, *of all the gin joints in all the towns in all...* Shut up Ruby.

I briefly consider if Vince's other profiles are variations on the likes of Jesse James and John Wayne. Sadly, whereas I would've once howled with laughter, now it's not even remotely funny.

I then realise something worse. I'd actually regaled Monica with details of this particular encounter when she'd asked me about my past dates. I cringe at the memory of her laughing and saying, 'Time to get out of the saddle...'

I had sex with Monica's husband. The words keep going round in my head. No no no. I shut my eyes tight to expel the memory. Why the fuck did this have to happen? It then dawns on me. Monica believes I did it knowingly... what was it she said? Something about me gloating...

No, I'm not having this. A surge of indignation rises. How was I supposed to know it was him? As if I would do that to a friend. Frigging hell. How could she think that of me...

'Are you going to eat the rest of that cake or just hold it mid-air?'

My eyes flick open. I look up and there he is. Max. Right in front of me. There in Paris. What the...

I drop the cake, quickly snap my phone cover shut and stand to greet him, spilling my coffee all over the table.

'Woah. Hold on there.' Max steadies the table. 'You look like I've just discovered you indulging a guilty secret.'

'What?'

'Something you need to hide?' He points to my phone, and I quickly recover myself, throw the phone into my bag as I shake my head.

'Max. What the hell are you doing here?'

'Delighted to see you too,' he leans in to kiss me lightly on the lips.

'Hey, I'm pleased to see you, but it's... well... a bit of a shock.' I wrap my arms around him and breathe in his musky scent.

Max gives me a squeeze then gently disentangles

himself to lower me into my seat. He takes the seat opposite and I try to compose myself.

'Why are you in Paris? I mean, you might've warned me.'

'It was going to be a surprise. I came to watch you dance. I was about to go and get tickets, but then I spotted you in this café and you looked so intent on your phone – and worried – I just had to come over. Is this about Monica-gate still?'

I nod.

'Want to talk about it?'

'No,' I say without hesitation. 'Tell me when you got here. Where you're staying.'

Max gives a comical account of how he organised new flights to divert to Paris and some tale about the hotel he found, but I'm barely listening as I absorb the full implications of what's happened with Vince and the effect this must've had on Monica.

I had nurtured an outside hope we would eventually make it up but now I can see no future for our friendship. Even if I could convince her I had no idea that bloke was Vince, it would be too weird knowing your best friend had had carnal relations with your husband.

I look at Max's animated face as he continues the tale. He's turned up at just the right time.

Then it strikes me. If Max finds out the real reason Monica has ditched me, would it alter his opinion of me? I mean, according to her, I am the world's top superbitch. I wish now I'd told him about my numerous blind dates. Not that he has any right to judge. I refuse to apologise for my past, but I don't want it to affect how we are together…

Max stops talking and leans across the table. 'Hey, want to go for a walk?'

I nod and when I've paid up we set off towards the river.

Max puts his arm around me and we stroll down the boulevard *Henri 1V* towards the *Pont du Sully*.

It is a lovely April day, and the banks of the Seine are less than thirty minutes away.

The traffic noise is somehow different to that in Manchester. There's more sounding of horns and squeals of brakes for starters, and I know I'm in Paris by the skyline opening up in front of us as we get to the bridge. There's *Notre Dame* Cathedral – no longer clad in scaffolding to fix the damage from that awful fire some years back – looming large and dramatic across the river.

We stop on the bridge and take in the vista, leaning on the stone parapet.

I decide to test the waters with Max. 'Can I ask you a question? Did you have many girlfriends before me?'

'A few, why?'

'Just wondered. I mean, don't you wonder about my previous relationships?'

'You're asking me if I'm curious?'

'Yes.'

Max turns and smiles at me. I can't help but smile back and he squeezes my hand affectionately.

'Well, let me see. I believe what's in the past is dead and gone, but I suppose I have occasionally wondered about your previous boyfriends.'

We look down at the flowing river and watch a boat emerge from below and travel upstream.

'Would you mind if there were lots?'

'Are there?'

'Depends what counts as lots.'

'True.'

'Would it bother you if I'd had lots of girlfriends?' he asks.

'No,' I answer a little too quickly. 'As long as there's only me now.'

He kisses my cheek before saying, 'There is only you now. And by the way there weren't lots. Less than five in fact.'

I look at him nervously but can't find the right words.

He cocks his head to one side. 'I'm guessing five would be a small number in comparison to your dates?'

I chew on my lip. If I am contemplating a future with this man, I need to be up front. Not that I need to justify anything to anyone, but I do need to explain about Vince, so he understands what happened with Monica.

'Yep. A lot more than five.'

'Right.'

'I mean, if I'm truthful, I lost count.' I look into his eyes and see they are not judging me, just asking for more.

'I was only about twenty when I was told I could never get pregnant; I mean, not ever.'

Max gives an empathetic nod.

'It kinda sent me into an abandoned frenzy of dates. I knew I couldn't have kids and I was trying to demonstrate I didn't care. It became quite a thing when all my friends got married and started having children. It gave me a bit of kudos when their lives turned into an existence of slave labour and exhaustion. They all said I was lucky to be free and able to... to "kiss more frogs" – that's what Penelope said.'

Why the hell am I laughing nervously? I can hear Monica's voice in reply, *because you care what he thinks.*

Max stays silent, waiting for me to continue. His eyes hold mine and I plough on.

'So, I kissed a number of frogs. Frogs, toads, and other amphibians.' I'm relieved to see him smile; it gives me courage to go on.

'I kinda got into a habit of dating new blokes and not taking any of them seriously.' I scan Max's face for signs of disgust or anger but can find none. In fact, he continues to look at me with a clear empathy and understanding.

'Hey, you know me. I've never wanted or needed a partner to complete me. But I loved the buzz of meeting new people. I got onto a dating site, the one you used when we first met.'

He nods.

'I found it exciting. I enjoyed the freedom of having no commitments...'

'And then you met Will's father?'

I nod, but my thought stream's interrupted. I was going to explain about Vince.

Max continues as I'm stopped in my tracks. 'And although this frog didn't turn into a prince, it did end with the birth of your son, Will? I wanted to ask you about his dad. I guess he's the only frog I have wondered about, but I'd thought if you'd wanted to tell me more you'd do so in your own time. And maybe that's now?'

He stares at me intently.

How did we get here? I was going to explain about Spontaneous Encounters and Vince. I feel thrown off course and my thoughts take an about-turn to focus on Will's dad. I swallow hard.

'Well, there's not much to tell there. Will's dad, I met him at Penelope's wedding. It was a one-night stand. Literally. So, when I found out I was pregnant I knew it'd be my only chance of becoming a mum. So I took it.'

'Did you tell the father?'

'Yep. Turns out he had his own family. And neither he nor I wanted him to play daddy.'

'And how does Will feel about that?'

'I... What? Well, I haven't exactly told him.'

Max pulls back and stares at me, his eyebrows raised.

'Dev – his dad – made it clear he didn't want Will searching for him. I told Will I'd chosen to get pregnant using clinical means... Hey, Max, don't look at me like that.'

'Is that fair to Will?'

I feel a prickle of anger and my heckles rise. After all, Will's upbringing is nothing to do with Max.

Crossing my arms, I respond, 'Look, I've been mother and father to Will. He's completely fine with my choice to bring him into the world as a single parent.'

'But you lied to him.'

'Woah. And this is your problem because...?'

Max looks away downstream and I'm sure I caught his eye twitch.

What the hell?

I can see he's struggling with heavens knows what, so I

touch his shoulder and soften my tone. 'Look, I didn't tell Will the full truth, as it was kinder to say he came from a sperm donation than to say his biological father wanted no part in his life. He'll have enough problems to face in life without adding more.'

Max doesn't speak for a few minutes, but then turns back to me. 'Sorry.' He pulls me into his arms. 'Sorry, you're quite right. It's none of my business. He's your son.'

'Correct. And apology accepted.'

The clock chimes out from the bell tower of the cathedral.

We listen and then look at each other before both saying, 'The bells... the bells...' And burst out laughing.

'Oh heck, is that really the time? I need to get back. We're dancing soon.'

'Can I watch?'

'Really?'

'I'd love to see your gorgeous body gyrating on stage.'

I smile and kiss him on the lips, and he responds eagerly.

'Yes. I'm sure I can sneak you in. Just walk with me into the theatre foyer with a balletic step and the doorman will think you are one of the dancers.'

'Show me.' Max's eyes twinkle.

We walk back joking and laughing and trying out a variety of dance-walking styles, which wouldn't have been out of place in a *Monty Python* sketch.

By the time we get back to the Opéra House, our conversation about past dates and Will's father are completely forgotten.

Max tells me he's booked into a hotel nearby and invites me to join him there tonight.

'Oh damn. My nightwear's in our awful hotel, miles away.'

'Well, you won't need pyjamas and I always carry a spare toothbrush.'

'I not even asking why you do that but offer accepted.'

At the *Opéra Bastille*, I get Max through security without a hitch and deposit him in the amphitheatre before dashing back to the changing rooms.

I'm a little regretful I haven't told Max about Vince, but I figure I don't need to. After all, Monica is the past. Max is the future.

18

INGRIDA

The competition has started, and we have only one hour until our first dance. We are eating the delicious French snacks Monica has brought as we watch the other dancers on the television screen high on the wall. The teams all look very glamorous in their costumes and with the special lighting, different effects for each number.

Sheila's group, who are now ready for their first dance, they wear tight pink sparkly leotards with bunches of large pink feathers on both their heads and sticking out in a clump on their behinds – I smile when I recall what Ruby say at the airport, that they look like flamingos.

'Wouldn't be out of place in Las Vegas,' Cath mutters to Bonnie.

We all watch the screen and Sheila talks very loudly, giving a commentary on each performance.

'Look at this lot.' Sheila points to the screen where a group of women in wide peasant-style skirts are turning full circles on the stage with little variation in the routine. She snorts with laughing. 'Totally uncoordinated. Like the Sound of Music on speed. How did they get into the bloody semis?'

Although I agree the dance is not very good, I do not nod like the dancers in Sheila's group. They bob their heads up and down every time she speak; it make them look even more like flock of birds.

Fay whispers to me that Sheila has verbal diarrhoea, and this make me giggle so much I have to pretend to blow my nose to cover the sound. Sheila's language is full of swearing. Bonnie calls it effing and blinding and this also creases me up as this is probably not correct expression knowing Bonnie. I am quick to laughing as I am feeling a combination of being nervous and also of being excited.

I look at Monica as she glances up at the screen now and then. She was very quiet when she returned from what she said was a good walk to clear her head. She did not say much at all, although she is now smiling more. Fay say she has a spring in her step.

Maybe Asha make a mistake when she tell us about Ruby and her husband?

I think perhaps it would have been a good idea if I had gone out on a walk too but I do not want to miss Neil's call if he rings me. I am hoping he will ring when we are inside the Opéra House; the theatre has wonderful Wi-Fi so I will not be charged for taking a call here. The cost of using phones outside is very high. After Kazimieras called last night at our hotel without any Wi-Fi, there was a large fee added to my bill. I checked before bed.

I also checked my bank account which is not yet closed and can see I do not have much money left. Perhaps I will stop my nurse salary going into the new joint account? I think I will need it. I can always tell Neil it takes the NHS a long time to do the changes, but I know as I think it, I cannot lie to Neil – not if I do not want him to lie to me.

I finish my baguette and thank Monica again for getting us all lunch. Fay asks her for the receipt, saying she will deduct it from Monica's total and divide it up, adding it onto what everyone else owes.

I must have frowned again as Fay says, 'Ingrida, you must not worry about these costs. Janine will be paying us back. I will ensure this happens.'

I am tempted to tell Fay I hand all my worries to God, but I know she does not go to church anymore, so I keep quiet.

Now we have eaten something, I am eager to get ready for our first dance. But it is a bit squashed, and we are pushed very close together. Sheila's group, they are taking up a lot of the space. Asha says we can change when they leave for the stage.

Monica has her phone in one hand all the time and looks at it almost continuously. She must be waiting for a call, as I am waiting for Neil to call. Her mobile buzzes and she reads a text message before smiling and typing in a reply.

'Happy message?' Asha asks.

'Oh, just planning a surprise get together.'

'Lovely. Er… Monica, do you know when Ruby is coming back?'

Monica shrugs. 'No, and if she doesn't, we can manage without her.'

I am not at all sure we could do this. We have not

practised the dances without Ruby, and it would leave a gap for all the times we move together. "Dancin' Fool" especially would not work correctly. Even Asha say it would throw the dance out and this is exactly what it would do.

Sheila's group finally leaves the dressing room in a flurry of feathers to go to the stage.

'Thank goodness for that,' Bonnie says. 'Those blasted feathers have got everywhere.' She pulls a feather from her hair.

'And finally, we have room to spread out,' Cath sighs.

'Time to get changed,' Asha grabs her costume. 'I just hope Ruby will be back in time.'

All but Monica murmur agreement and we change into our costumes: black jazz trousers and bright red tunic tops. We all have the same colour red, but we wear different styles, made by Monica. Some are one-shouldered, some are halter neck. Mine is what Monica she call 'cold shoulders', with a little slit at the top of each arm. It is not as loose-fitting as it was when it was first made, as I have gained a little weight, but I can see it still looks flattering for my figure.

We also have a small swatch of the same red material to place in our hair. Mine is a wide headband, and it holds my hair back in a pretty way. Monica has a red scrunchie – I think that is what she called it – and a thick strip of red ribbon. She has tied her lovely hair up in a high ponytail and the red material hangs down her back. When she dances her solo, it will fly around with every head roll and catch the eyes of those watching. Monica is such a very attractive lady; like a film star. She is also an excellent dressmaker, and her dancing is close to that of a professional. I think she could have make a career as a dancer if she had wanted.

'Right, we need to set up our outfits for the next dance so we can put them on quickly. There is only a short gap to change before our second number.' Asha announces.

We get our white pin-striped trousers, matched waistcoat and brightly coloured bowler hats from the central rail and drape them over and around the backs of our chairs. We all have a different colour hats – mine is orange – and wrist bands in matching colours for the "Dancin' Fool" jazz number. Monica, she has make cloth flowers in each colour and she carefully uses pin to put them on each waistcoat. They look like professional costumes. I cannot help but smile when I see them all lined up waiting for us to step into them until I realise one outfit is missing. Where is Ruby?

Asha shrugs when I look from the gap to her eyes. Without words, we all lean into the mirrors to line our eyes with black liner pencil and put on bright red lipstick. It is the same red as the tops so we all match. Clarissa always insists on what she calls 'attention to the detail' and I like this detail very much.

I do not usually wear make-up, only moisturiser and a little lip gloss. Fay helps me with putting on the false eyelashes and bronzer. She has even put the bronzer on the small patch of arm showing at my cold shoulders, which make me smile.

'You look very pretty, Fay... Fay?' I say this again, but I do not think she hear me. I am not sure I have seen her so full of excitement and anticipation as she is today. She keeps looking at the television screen and then the programme fixed to the mirror and then her watch, which she has left on the dressing table as we cannot wear watches on stage.

I think she is wanting to look at a particular dance on the screen; I can guess the one. It was the best one we saw this morning. I also want to see the four dancers of *Corps et Ame* in their actual costumes for the Coldplay "Fix You" routine. They look like professional dancers, not amateurs like rest of us.

'There. That is your bronzer done.' Fay smiles, glancing up at the screen again. 'You look like you have been in the sun for a week.'

I turn my head from side to side to see my new face. It is a lot of make-up. I have tanned flawless skin and very big eyes. To me, it looks like a mask, and it make me feel very good as I think no one will see Ingrida Valenko – I mean, Ingrida Goodman – they will see me as one of the group of Clarissa's ladies capturing music in a scintillation of dance.

'Oh look, Sheila's on next.' Bonnie points to the screen and we all watch the women strut to their opening positions.

I do not know how they will check their spacing is correct as they did not have a run-through after they were ejected from the rehearsals. Their dance starts and even though we cannot hear the music, we can see it is not very good. Some of the arm moves look very awkward and angular and I see Sheila make a mistake in the first few bars.

'Did Sheila just bump into that woman on the left? Was that supposed to happen?' Bonnie asks Cath.

'She's made a right mess of that move. Look, it's befuddled the rest of them, they don't know who to follow.'

'What a mess.' Asha has a smile on her face, but I feel sorry for Sheila. I know what it is like to go wrong in front of many people. I am, however, relieved Bold as Brass have left our dressing room. They not only swear all the time, but I saw them pull ugly faces at us when they think we are not looking.

Before they went on stage, Sheila shared a tin of something alcoholic for what she called Dutch courage. Clarissa told us alcohol was prohibited. But perhaps this is Clarissa's rule, not the competition rule. I do not know. I do know a little sip of vodka might calm my nerves, which right now feel very much on edge after seeing Sheila's mistake.

I look at my phone again to see if there is a message from Neil, but he has not sent anything since last night when I told him I had arrived in Paris. I go to put his numbers in the phone to give him a quick call, but I hesitate. Neil told me he would call me and I was *not* to call him. I go to put the phone back in my bag, praying Neil has now told Rita and Terry all about our being married when the device makes a single ring and my heart leaps. But then I see the Latvian words on the screen, and I know immediately it is a message from Kazimieras. I frown and open it.

Ingrida, guess where I am? I am in Manchester. I know you have moved to live with a man called Neil Goodman. I have the address. What are you doing with a widower man and his children? Does he know about me? Does he know you stole from your uncle?

INGRIDA

> *What would he think if he knew you had criminal connections? Would he even want you in the house if he found out? Ingrida, you make sure you meet me next week or I will be paying this Neil Goodman a visit to tell him all about your theft and your uncle. In fact, I may pay him a visit before you return if I do not have your assurance you will meet me.*

My stomach does a knot twist and I quickly send a reply in Latvian.

> *Kazimieras, if you go anywhere near my house I will not help you in any way. Not ever. We will meet on Tuesday as we have arranged. You need to know that I will not give you a single penny if you should dare to even approach Neil Goodman or his children. I also know the police are looking for you. So, watch your step or I will report you. You do not know me and you do not know what I am capable of. Do not test me on this. So, for the last time, keep away from my house. I MEAN IT.*

I throw my phone in my bag and take a large gulp of water. I should not have said *my* house… but it is too late now. I look at myself in the mirror. *Ingrida*, I tell myself, *get a grip* – as Fay would say – and put this out of your mind for the dancing. I also say a prayer in my head, and I know that God, he hears me.

The other ladies give a loud cheer and I glance up and there is Ruby, just arrived and smiling at me.

'Looks like you've made your mind up about something, Ingrida?'

I nod and reach to pat Ruby's hand. 'I am so glad you are here, Ruby.'

'Sorry I'm late, folks, but better late than never,' she calls to the others as she hurriedly gets changed.

'Thank goodness you're back,' Bonnie calls. 'Asha was having kittens.'

I watch her as she grabs her costume from the hanger. I am a little surprised she look so happy after what happened with Monica.

'Ruby, you scared us to death,' Asha calls. 'Now we are all good and can dance our hearts out, ladies.'

Ruby gives Asha a thumbs up in the air and puts on her jazz shoes. She then attends to her make-up, but she does not need much with her ebony skin. She is very striking with her shortly cropped hair and wide eyes. I watch her brush her face, neck and exposed flesh with sparkling powder. It glitters in the light. Ruby's top is cut very low. It shows her big chest, but it is flattering. She looks full of curves and very sensual as she adds glitter to her bosom. Her hair has only one splash of red material on a hair clip. At the time Monica said her hair needed just the merest hint of red. Today Monica pays Ruby no attention and moves away to warm-up by herself in the vestibule.

'Would you like some, Ingrida?' Ruby asks me. She shows me her loaded powder brush and I nod and let her make my exposed skin sparkle, too.

'Where did you go?' I ask.

She leans in to tell me it was big surprise, but her Max

is actually here, in Paris and she has smuggled him into the theatre to watch our performance. I can see her eyes shine when she talks about this man and I feel a little – what is it called? – ah yes, twinge. I feel a little twinge because I am not sure my eyes shine like this when I see Neil. He is a very kind and gentle man, and I am growing to love him, but I would like also my eyes to shine like this when I see him.

'Ingrida.' Ruby leans into me. 'What did Asha say to you about Monica's blow up?'

I do not know how to reply. I cannot tell her full truth of what Asha said, as it does not seem the right thing to do.

'Well?'

'Asha told us you and Monica...' I check to see Monica is far enough away not to overhear. 'Well, you and Monica would not be able to... to make up your differences but she say she hope we could all pull together for the competition.'

'Did she say why we'd fallen out?'

'I am not sure... it was very difficult to hear. Sheila's ladies were making very much noise and also my English is still not complete so I am not sure if I comprehen—'

'It's OK. I don't care if you know, Ingrida.' Ruby speaks in a quiet voice so only I can hear. 'Something happened one night a few years ago. I met a man, just once, but I didn't know it was Monica's husband. I've only just found out and while I'm very sorry, Monica will never see it from my point of view, I just need to move on. Don't worry. I'm good.'

I do not know what to say to this, so I say nothing and nod as if I know what she means. Sometimes I do not understand English people.

19

FAY

When I have finished helping Ingrida with her make-up, I add a few finishing touches to mine. The effect is rather marvellous; I look ten years younger. The red top, red combs in my hair, bronzer and lipstick all contrive to give me a wonderful, healthy glow.

My thoughts drift to Edith and I feel butterflies in my stomach. I cannot believe she is here. And I cannot help feeing this is more than coincidence. I no longer subscribe to any religious beliefs, thanks to Andrew, but maybe this was pre-ordained? I find myself saying a silent prayer that it indeed be so.

It may be a few years since Edith and I were together, but the minute I saw her on the stage, there was no mistaking her. My heart began to race and while I briefly acknowledged it could just be a strange coincidence of watching someone who was her spitting image, I needed no further confirmation when she took her first steps. I know the way Edith dances. Her movements are ingrained in me. She has always danced beautifully and today it was clear she is even better than she used to be. Her performance was completely breathtaking. I was so enraptured I could not concentrate on anything other than her movements and that of her dance partner. At the end, when everyone in the auditorium burst into spontaneous applause, I found I was overcome with awe and pride.

It took a great deal of self-control not to tell Asha the reason for my attention, but I fear Asha takes an unhealthy interest in the affairs of others and does not know when to hold her tongue. I was perfectly outraged when she gleefully told us the reason for Monica and Ruby's fall out. This is an extremely private matter, and in my opinion, it should not be bandied around as if it were a tasty morsel of inconsequential gossip. I am relieved I did not explain to Asha my relationship to Edith. The rest of the dance group would no doubt have heard it by now had I done so.

When Edith and her group had left the stage – they must have allowed them access from the wings due to them being barefoot – I began to wonder how I could approach her and more importantly, if she would be happy to see me.

I have scoured the competition information and the programme, so I have learnt Edith's quartet is called *Corps et Ame*. Ingrida says the name translates to Body and Soul. Had I not witnessed their dance I would have thought this a somewhat overdramatic, bordering-on-pretentious name, but it is entirely suitable as they most definitely put every ounce of themselves into the performance.

In fact, it was a bit of a light bulb moment for me.

Clarissa said I needed to dance from the soul and up until that point, I had not truly realised what she meant. It has made me resolve to give my dancing more than just the correct rhythm and steps. I need to feel the music as Edith does. I am a little nervous to try this out, but I have rehearsed our numbers in my head using more expression, and I think I can elevate my performance. Besides, Edith may be watching me from her dressing room, and I would like her to be as proud of me as I am of her.

I keep glancing up to the screen to see if she is on stage. I could not bear to miss Edith dancing in costume. My programme says they are on after our first dance, but I notice some of the other entries are not appearing in the planned order, so I keep checking the screen just in case Edith's slot has been altered. What a pity we cannot hear the music, as this would alert me if the "Fix You track started to play.

If Edith's ensemble is indeed on after our first number, I have a plan. I will stay in the wings and watch them close up. I know we must get changed quickly for our next dance, but I cannot miss this opportunity. It will only take a few minutes extra to linger on the side of the stage and watch my daughter. The others will barely notice I am a little late back into the dressing room.

I think back to the last time I saw Edith. It was way back before the pandemic. It is not a pleasant memory. She had driven to my flat with some of my personal effects after I refused to go back to the family home, knowing Andrew had since installed his mistress there. OK, not his mistress, as we were no longer married, but I was not going to set foot back inside that house now tainted by her presence. Andrew had already delivered all my clothes and the items I insisted would be mine, like the crockery and cutlery we had accumulated over the years. Why should I go to the extra expense of replacing these items when it was Andrew who wanted to end our marriage?

Edith made a final trip to bring over additional items Andrew thought I should have, including the photograph albums of when they were little girls. I suppose I should have been grateful for that.

I think back to our last conversation, which, like all our exchanges of the previous decade, was awkward and strained.

'Would you like to come in and see the flat, Edith?'

'I don't think so, Fay.'

Edith and Bethan stopped addressing me as Mum quite a few years before. It was all part of their adolescent rejection of me, and I refused to rise to it. I will never give them the satisfaction of knowing how much this hurt.

'You wouldn't even let us into your bedroom at home. You've made it clear you have your separate personal space where Bethan and I are not welcome. So, I will say goodbye here from the outside, where I have always been.'

'Edith, there is no need to be so melodramatic. This situation does not call for hysteria. I was merely asking you if you wanted to see the small flat in which I am now forced to live.'

'Nobody forced you. Dad tried his best. It was you who turned your back on Bethan and I and then on Dad. You brought this on yourself.'

'You always did have an overinflated sense of self-righteousness, Edith.'

'I wonder where I got that from?'

'Here we go again, rudeness and insolence. One day you will become a mother, Edith. And perhaps then you will realise the sacrifices and devotion I put into caring for you. I must say, all I ever wanted was the best for you and your sister.'

'Well, you had a bloody funny way of showing it.' Edith then turned on her heels and it was the last time I saw her. I confess I was on the brink of tears.

Over the past few years, I sent Edith and Bethan cards and money every birthday and Christmas. Annoyingly, I had to send them via Andrew, as I did not know where either girl was living. But I have not received a single message back. Most ungrateful. That was years ago now. I sigh.

In the last few days, I have had a recurring niggle that I may have been a little extreme in my reactions to my teenage girls. Ingrida recently borrowed a book on parenting from my library. When she returned it, I looked through the section of self-help guides to see what else was on offer and I found a book about adolescents. After thumbing through its pages, I decided to bring it with me on this trip. I read it on the train journeys here. It cited several scientific studies and the information contained within has left me feeling somewhat uncomfortable. I thought I knew about the terrible teens everyone talks about, but I had not appreciated teenage children have a different chemical make-up in their brains to adults, to the point where belligerence and awkwardness are often a manifestation of hormone imbalance and over which they had no control. It certainly made for interesting reading, and it has started me questioning if I had been a little too harsh on occasions.

I frequently wonder: if I had known my own mother or been raised in a traditional home rather than the orphanage, would I have been better prepared for the changes in my girls?

I consider the opportunity I now have with Edith here in this very theatre. I had always envisaged being reunited with my daughters once they became parents. Perhaps my new relationship with Edith will start before she is a mother. I vaguely acknowledge she may already have a family, after all, I have had no contact for so long. Although it would be disgraceful if Andrew had not told me if I had become a grandmother.

Perhaps I can make a connection with Edith using our common bond of dance? I give a little shiver of anticipation. She must remember it was I who instilled this love of dancing into her and her sister at an early age. I encouraged them to keep up ballet and just look at Edith now.

I can barely listen to the others gossiping in the changing rooms as all I can think about is Edith and the best way to approach her.

I had asked a few of the competition officials if they could direct me to the dressing room for *Corps et Ame* but they did not understand me. Perhaps it was my attempt at a French accent. I have never been proficient in foreign languages. I admit it would be marvellous to be as fluent as Ingrida. I was most grateful she acted as interpreter at the Charbon Hotel for our group.

I went on a foray down the adjoining corridors to look for Edith's group, but I was unable to locate them in the rooms near ours. There are over thirty dance troupes in the competition, and we are spread out over several floors – the place is quite a labyrinth. However, on reflection, it is perhaps as well I have not stumbled into her yet as I need to prepare myself.

'All right, Fay?' Bonnie asks and I realise I have been looking in her direction but with my eyes unfocussed. 'A penny for them?'

'Sorry?'

'Oh Lor, have I said that wrong? You just looked like you were far away.'

'No, I mean, penny for your thoughts is the correct idiom.'

'Who are you calling an idiot?' Bonnie and Cath laugh out loud.

'No, I said *idiom* not idiot…'

'Only kidding.' Bonnie smiles. 'You look fabulous, Fay. In fact, we all look fabulous. Not long until we're on stage.'

'Less than fifteen minutes,' Asha reminds us. 'Come on, ladies, we need to warm-up.'

Cath starts to sing about the final countdown but is cut short and before we can take over the vestibule, Sheila's group bursts back into the changing room. They are arguing and shouting loudly. We stand back to admit them.

'You silly bitch.' Sheila is admonishing a large-bosomed female who has clearly been crying as her mascara is now panda-like around her eyes.

'Why the fuck did you suddenly stop, Bridget?'

'I went blank. The steps, I just couldn't remember them—'

'Well, that collision could cost us a place in the final—' Sheila stops short when a pink feather flutters into her mouth. She spits it out and only then appears to realise we are all staring at her, so she turns on our group and hisses, 'And you lot can mind your own bloody business.'

We all turn away without saying a word and exit the changing room.

'That's what I call spitting feathers.' Ruby nudges Ingrida as we hurry towards the green room. I find myself tittering with the rest of our ladies.

In the green room, which is just outside the stage entrance, Asha leads us in a stretch out and warm-up.

We limber up and watch the huge wall screen showing the gymnastic-styled group perform. The loud Elton John song, "I'm Still Standing" blasts out even behind the closed stage door.

Not long now. I am full of anticipation. We all exchange excited smiles as we swing our arms and roll our shoulders back.

Monica's phone buzzes and she slides it out of her trouser pocket.

'You cannot take a mobile on stage, Monica,' I cry.

'I forgot it was there.' Monica checks the screen. 'Oh, a message from Clarissa. She says, I do not need to wish you all good luck as luck has nothing to do with the outcome. You are all not only capable but wonderful dancers, and Hazel and I know you will put everything into your performances.'

Monica gives a little cough and looks slightly embarrassed as she reads the final part of the message.

*Ladies, sprout wings on your feet, reach for the sky,
let your souls soar, and do your absolute best.*

Clarissa loves this sort of gushy language, but I can see the others appreciate her sentiments, well perhaps not Ruby, who stifles a giggle. We all nod our agreement with Clarissa's good intentions.

An official opens the door, and the previous entrants pour past us, fresh from their dance, all glowing and slightly breathless.

The official checks her sheet and asks Asha, 'Êtes-vous *le groupe DICK? Excusez-moi – DECK?*'

'That's us.' Asha winks at the rest of the group.

The official indicates for us to go out on stage.

'Monica, what will you do with the phone?' Asha asks. 'There is no time to take it back to the dressing room.' Monica flounders, unsure what to do with the device.

At that moment, the four dancers from *Corps et Ame* enter the room and I freeze to the spot as Edith walks straight past me. She is dressed in a stunning, pale blue chiffon dress cut on the bias with a rustically styled multi-layered hem. The other female dancer is in a matching dress and the men wear three-quarter length cream leggings with an open pale blue shirt. They are all barefoot. Even without lighting, the four dancers look superb.

I realise Edith has not seen me and would probably not recognise me even if she had. Not with me in costume and all made-up. Why should she? She will have no idea I have returned to dancing, let alone entered a Paris competition where she is also competing.

Ingrida grabs Monica's phone and places it on a chair. She points to it and speaks directly to Edith in perfect French.

'*Excusez-moi, pouvez-vous garder ça pendant que nous dansons?*'

'*Mais oui*,' Edith replies in a beautiful French accent.

'*Merci beaucoup*,' Ingrida smiles and we all enter the stage door. I am the last to go through, so when Edith calls, '*Bonne chance*.' I turn and call, 'Thank you.'

I do not have time to see if she recognises me as we all move to our starting positions.

The theatre lights dim, the audience goes quiet. This is it. My daughter will be watching from the green room. Clarissa and Hazel will be watching behind the line of judges. I certainly am going to do my best to put my body and soul into it and give the performance of my life.

20

ASHA

I have been feeling a little nauseous all day and as we step onto the stage, for one horrible moment I think I am going to throw up. I had not expected my nerves to get the better of me. Thankfully, the feeling subsides the moment the lights dim. We all stand facing the audience, heads dipped down, one hand outstretched towards the floor. All I can see are my feet. My heart pounds and I take a deep breath.

The first notes fill the air. One heel beats to the rhythm as our heads slowly lift and the arm simultaneously reaches up to the ceiling, fingers spread wide. We are in perfect unison with Adele's opening words about a fire within... We move across the stage threading in and out of each other. On the word *dark* and in canon, we lift our arms into a wide full circle, jack-knifing towards a raised leg with pointed toes. Our isolation moves are sharp and coordinated with head rolls on the title words. I do not think about the audience or the judges.

ASHA

When we get to Monica's solo, the rest of us spread out in a semicircle behind her. Our moves are slow and exaggerated, hers are fast, a synthesis of jazz and balletic styles. I can see her out of the corner of my eye, and she is incredible. This has to be the best she has ever danced her part.

On the same count, as Adele repeats her reflection about what could have been, we move as one to the edge of the stage, reaching out our hands to the audience, all at different levels. None of us smile. Clarissa has rehearsed us to glare and simmer in this number and I can feel power emanating from our every step. I can see members of the audience sitting forward in their seats as the pace of the dance intensifies.

We come to the line about souls and doors, and Fay and I turn to face each other as the other dancers swirl towards their designated partner. This is where we do our high five – our joke for the move – which is in fact a most effective hand slap that stops before it connects before flying above our heads as we go into jazz reaches. I give Fay a double take, she is usually a little expressionless, but I can feel her eyes burn into mine as she puts her heart into it. I have never seen her dance so well. At one time she could be accused of cutting short some of the movements, but not today. It spurs me on to dance with equal fervour.

When we reach the end of the dance, turning in canon, hands raised in fists and heads lifted to the sky, we hold our positions, and I am breathless.

There is rapturous applause from the auditorium. We stay frozen in tableau and wait for Monica to move first then all drop to a low bow. Even our exit has been rehearsed and we peel off one by one, departing the stage with shoulder rolls and drag walks.

I swear I see Ruby give a low wave to someone out in the audience, but I cannot be sure, and I am so ecstatic we danced so well I miss looking in the direction she waved.

So, this is what is like to feel as if you are walking on air.

We bunch up as soon as we are off stage, and our faces split into wides smiles. We are breathless with exertion and excitement. Even the backstage hands applaud us.

We are ushered through the door into the green room as we bubble and chatter.

'That could not have gone any better, could it?' Bonnie is aglow like the rest of us.

'What a feeling – better than being blootered.' Cath squeezes Bonnie's arm.

Bonnie looks puzzled.

'Tipsy to you.'

'Ha ha. It is like being on a high, isn't it? Ingrida, you didn't make a single mistake.'

'*Ja*, I know. I am so happy. It went by too quickly. I want to do it again.' Ingrida laughs.

The quartet of dancers are also applauding us in the green room and one of the two elegant French ladies hands Monica back her phone.

'*Bravo, bien dansé*,' she says to each of us as she strains her neck to survey our group.

I swear she is looking for someone.

'*Merci*,' Ingrida responds for us all. 'This kind lady say well done.'

The kind lady then switches to perfect English with a slight Manchester twang. 'You're from the North West in England? Can I ask exactly where?'

Ingrida and I do a double take.

'Cheadle, near Manchester,' I answer.

She nods her head enthusiastically.

'Do you know it?'

'Yes. I was born near there.'

'Really?'

But the woman is no longer looking at Ingrida or I, she is scanning the faces of the rest of Clarissa's ladies, nervously rubbing her hands together.

Before we can say anything, the official calls the quartet to go through to the stage and Ingrida calls to them, '*Bonne chance à vous aussi.*'

We head back to the dressing room, and it suddenly strikes me – they were the dancers Fay had sat forward to watch. What was the name she muttered? I cannot think of it. Ah well, it will come to me but for now I am buzzing.

'That was the best we have ever done it.'

Monica's phone sounds and she reads Clarissa's message as we navigate the busy corridors.

'Clarissa said we were magnificent.' Monica's eyes sparkle as she reads the text aloud.

> *I could not be prouder of you ladies. You shone like the brightest stars in the firmament. But now you must descend like comets and return to Earth. You will need to keep your heads for "Dancin' Fool". Remember, it is a change in tempo and approach.*

Bright smiles – goofy moves – you can go over the top with facial expressions in this one. Send it up. Think Charlie Chaplin in silent movies. Ladies, give it your all.

We all race to the dressing room but stop short at the entrance. Our euphoria evaporates. All our carefully placed costumes are now strewn all over the floor, our hats, our white pin-striped waistcoats, and matching trousers. Sheila's group is nowhere to be seen.

'Oh, my goodness.' I stare at the mess.

'What bitches. Look what they've done to our outfits.' Ruby marches into the room.

'My bowler is dented,' Bonnie cries as she bends to retrieve her damaged purple hat from under a dressing table and attempts to push the hat back into shape.

'I can't believe what those vile wee hallions have done.' Cath starts to pick up all the waistcoats now spread round the room.

'I'd like to give them a slice of my mind,' Bonnie declares.

'A slice? Is mean slice of cake?' Ingrida asks as she picks another hat off the floor.

Ruby bangs the costume rail with her fist. 'Piece, slice, I want to shove an entire cake into their faces. Wait until I get my hands on that bloody woman and her cronies…'

Monica interjects. 'We cannot afford to be distracted by this. We are on stage again after the next two numbers. Quick, everyone, find your costumes and change.'

'We have no idea whose trousers are whose…' I start

before Monica pulls a pair off the floor and checks the back seam.

'Thankfully, I labelled each pair on the inside hem. Ingrida, these are yours. And the waistcoats are easy. They have the matching flower to our hats.'

'Brilliant.' I sigh with relief and help Ingrida to sort the rest of the trousers as Bonnie and Cath pair up the waistcoats, wristbands, and bowlers.

Time is marching, so we hurriedly strip off our red tunics and leggings, discarding them where we stand, and start to pull on the new outfits. Some of the flowers have been damaged, so Monica, still in her underwear, deftly pulls out her pocket sewing kit from her bag and retrieves a tiny pair of scissors. She trims the satin petals to neaten them up.

When Monica has finished, Ruby, who is the first to be dressed, calls, 'Here, I'll take those, Monica.'

I see this as Ruby's attempt to make reparations – offering to put the scissors away – but Monica simply hands them over without looking at Ruby and turns to pull on her own costume. Any anger Monica might be showing towards Ruby is surpassed by our combined fury at the actions of Sheila's group.

'How dare they? Can we report them to the organisers?' Bonnie asks.

'They're not worth the energy it would take,' Cath tuts in the mirror as she quickly brushes her hair. 'So spiteful. And just because their dance went so badly wrong, as if that was our fault. To be sure, I should have guessed when we were out of the room, they'd be acting the maggot.'

Ingrida and I exchange a baffled look.

'Maggot?' We all start to chuckle.

'Maggot is too good a word for them,' I say, zipping myself into my trousers. I am glad Cath has lightened the moment.

'What is this word maggot?' Ingrida looks up from lacing her jazz shoes.

'A disgusting little grub that feeds on rot,' Ruby calls as she crosses to the rail where the Bold as Brass costumes hang ready for their second and final number.

'Accurate description I think.' Cath laughs. 'They are rotten to the core.'

'And Sheila has rotten teeth,' I add. 'What? What are you laughing at, Ruby? Well, it is true. Her mouth is full of amalgam fillings. Every time she laughs you can see them glinting.'

'Asha, you're a hoot.' Cath sniggers. 'Well, I think we should call those Bold as Brass women Sheila's Maggots from now on.'

'Ha ha. I like it.' Bonnie applies more bronzer to her face and neck. 'Well, we'll show them. Their grubby little tactics won't stop us dancing our best.'

'Well said.' Monica removes her red ribbon and undoes her ponytail to brush it straight and flat.

My fingers fly over my waistcoat buttons, but I cannot pull the top one close enough to fit in the buttonhole. 'Are you sure this is mine?' I call to the others. 'I am struggling to do it up.'

'Yes, look – yellow flower like your hat, Asha.'

Monica is right. This has to be mine, but it is much

tighter around the bust than it used to be. I have not put on weight, have I? I flatten my chest to squeeze the top buttons in place and sigh with relief when they fasten. Perhaps it is my new sports bra purchased especially for the competition? I should have worn it in. I feel a small niggle at the back of my mind, but my attention is taken up as I catch Ruby in my peripheral vision.

The scissors are in her hand as she determinedly starts to quietly snip at the costumes on the rail in front of her. I open my mouth in shock, planning to say something to stop her, but my words dry up. Sheila's group has tried to scupper our chances after all. I am not close enough to see exactly what Ruby is doing with those scissors, so I deliberately look away. No one else appears to have noticed her and it is better I do not witness whatever it is she is doing, so I am not complicit in her actions.

Truthfully, inside I find I am cheering Ruby on. Sheila's group deserves to be punished for what they have done.

Ingrida, also now changed, is removing her red head band when she points to the screen. 'Oh *ne*. We have missed the Body and Soul group. Look. They have just finish. They are smiling and bowing. I think they are getting very much clapping. I did so want to watch them.'

'Whose costume is this?' Bonnie holds up the green bowler hat and pin-striped suit.

'Fay. That is Fay's costume. Where on earth is she?' I cry.

Cath dashes to the door to look down the corridor. We all stop in our tracks and look anxiously at each other. We need Fay.

'Panic over. She's coming,' Cath shouts.

Fay races in, her face glowing and eyes moist.

There is no time to ask where she has been as we help her strip off her red costume and get into her pinstripes.

'What on earth has happened here?' Fay surveys the mess of our previous costumes haphazardly strewn about the room.

'Sheila's group. They trashed our outfits,' I tell her.

'What?'

'Come on, we can tidy up after. We are on after the next dance.' Monica points to the screen where the next troupe is assembled and ready to start.

I quickly pull a brush through my hair and tie it into a low ponytail, which will not interfere with my hat. We all put on new lipstick and head back to the stage carrying our brightly coloured bowlers.

'We need to show those bloody women they haven't phased us or put us off,' Ruby calls as we run. 'Are we going to give "Dancin' Fool" our all?'

In unison, we respond, 'Yes we are.'

We make it to the green room just as the official is calling for us.

My heart is racing, and I feel a little sick again as we rush to our places on stage and each of the ladies places her hat down on the floor before assuming a jazz pose and freezing above each hat.

I lean slightly back, one knee inverted. My arms are raised, elbows bent at shoulder height, the fingers of each hand are splayed with my palms down high above the yellow bowler. We joked in rehearsal it was as if I was poised to levitate the hat upwards to meet my hands.

ASHA

I know all the other ladies are all in different stances, a leg or arm outstretched or bent at a jaunty angle. We are briefly backlit, giving us a silhouette shaping as we look intensely at our own hats, a wide smile fixed on each face.

Awaiting the first note, I am aware of the audience watching with bated breath. You could hear a pin drop were it not for my heart thumping in my ears.

The first beat starts. The lights blaze. Monica and one of the other ladies reach for their hats first with a variety of sharp kicks and flicks and freeze with one hand on their hat rim. Then the next two launch into their steps to each hat and finally my group executes our precise moves to place a hand on our hats before we all pick them up in unison.

I quell the nausea and tell myself to focus and stay sharp.

At this very moment, nothing else matters.

21

MONICA

The "Dancin' Fool" routine is fantastically high energy. We are all dripping when we come off stage. It was going perfectly, but then Ingrida made one major mistake, which could have thrown us all. However, she dealt with it brilliantly. It happened near the end of the dance. At the point where we all travel stage left, one behind the other in those crazy back-bent-forward-at-right-angles-walks, swinging our arms with our heads turned to the audience, Ingrida went stage right. At first, I hadn't noticed. I was at the front of the line. But as I led the walks round full circle, I could see she was the wrong side of the stage. Ingrida acted spontaneously and, as if it was part of the dance, she gave an exaggerated move, raising her hand to her open mouth and did an about turn. Speeding up the walk to double time, she raced to the end of the line and tagged on just in time for the fast Charleston sections. It was inspired. In fact, as we returned to the dressing room, we all joked it should be included as part of the routine next time.

'I was so shocked I had danced to wrong side, I had to think – how you say – on my feet what to do to make it look as if it had been put in the actual dance. I still cannot believe I managed to hide mistake. I hope Clarissa will not be cross.'

'Cross? She'll be delighted. It was brilliant, Ingrida. Completely in time with the music. What a pro.'

Although it's just what I would have said, I'm tiring of Ruby taking every opportunity to reaffirm her new best buddy. However, nothing can take away the sense of euphoria which started when we threw our hats into the air on the last note of the music. There was incredible applause, and I had turned to smile at all the dancers before indicating when to take our choreographed exit. Ruby had winked at me. She had tears in her eyes and for a split second I forgot why I was so angry with her. I had to fix the wide smile to my face for the audience before I gave her the nod, the cue for a few bars of music to replay and for her to clown-act gathering up the hats. We each placed our hats individually into Ruby's hands, one on top of the other before dancing to the exit and Ruby pretended to almost over balance with the topsy-turvy stack held at arm's length. We watched her from the wings as she milked this for everything she could, and the audience laughed and clapped in time to the music when she pantomimed catching up the precariously teetering pile as if it was out of control.

Watching her, my jaw momentarily tensed but I have vowed to put thoughts of her betrayal out of my head. I'm here to dance and immerse myself in the positivity it creates. My life is going to take a different direction and I'm going to dance to a tune of my own making from now on.

The others chatter happily down the corridors to the dressing room but quieten when we approach the door. From the shouts and shrieks that greet us, it is clear Sheila's group is back.

We arrive in the vestibule to see them changing into skimpy black and red costumes. The split black skirts are teamed with tight crimson tops, half-torn-half-ripped in what I think is a punky goth style. They also wear red lacy wrist gloves with no fingers and black fishnet stockings held by bright red suspender belts.

Heavens. There's a lot of flesh on display.

Asha turns her head and nods to us all, and we stop talking as we enter the room in silence. We move to our line of mirrors, sit on our chairs, and turn our backs on Bold as Brass.

In the green room, we had all agreed we would completely ignore the women.

'We will not dignify their actions with a response,' Asha had urged us. 'They should not have the satisfaction of knowing they upset us.'

'Besides, there're other ways of getting even,' Ruby had added cryptically, but I am getting into the habit of switching off the moment she speaks.

The voices of Sheila's women slowly peter out when they are met with a barrage of silence. They soundlessly touch up their make-up and place squares of red-edged black netting in their hair, fixed with combs. These form short veils over one side of each face, and I have to grudgingly admit they are subtle but effective and give the minimal costumes a much-needed sophisticated, almost French, touch.

Sheila eventually breaks the quiet and looks at me through the mirrors.

'Left the dressing room in quite a mess, didn't we, ladies? Stuff everywhere.' She puts her hands on her hips and exchanges grins with her group.

When we say nothing, she adds, 'Oh dear, have all the dickie-chickies lost their voices?'

Ruby bangs her fist on the table – causing Asha and Ingrida to recoil – and swivels round in her chair to face Sheila. 'Christ, how old are you, Sheila? Twelve?'

A couple of the Bold as Brass women snigger.

'What did you bloody say?' Sheila steps forward with a backward glare at the offenders in her group. One of her dancers holds up her phone to film what they no doubt hope will be a blazing row.

Ruby stands up and steps forward. She is a good six inches taller than Sheila and when she is up close, she looks down on her. Ruby speaks slowly and clearly, 'FOR – FUCK'S – SAKE – GROW – UP.'

Sheila's face goes crimson. Her lips appear to try to form words, but nothing comes out of her mouth.

The stand-off lasts half a minute before the large-busted member of Bold as Brass lightly taps Sheila's shoulder and says softly, 'Sheila, we need to go. We're on after this dance.' She points to the screen.

Sheila breaks eye contact with Ruby, mutters a barely

audible, 'Fucking DECKs,' and the group mobilises, picking up bright red concertina fans and leaving for the stage without another word.

'Good for you, Ruby,' Cath and Bonnie slap Ruby on the back.

Ruby smiles, grabs her bag, and also heads for the door. 'Gotta go.'

'You're not supposed to go out in costume,' Asha calls but Ruby has left, and we all start to change into our rehearsal wear.

'Where's Fay?' Bonnie asks.

'She did not wait for Ruby's exit off stage.' Asha starts to undo her waistcoat. 'She dashed ahead of us. Look, her coat has gone so I guess she has put it over her costume and gone out for a bit.' Asha shrugs as she pulls on her black DECK top.

'Well, we have a good hour or more until our next dance. There's a break after Sheila's group has performed,' Cath adds.

'Let's go for a coffee at the theatre café. I could do with a change of scene.' Bonnie takes off her jazz shoes and stops as Asha slumps down into one of the chairs next to her. 'You all right, Asha? You've gone very pale...'

Asha gives a small nod and puts her hand up to her head. 'I... I came over a bit dizzy.'

Ingrida crosses to her and squats to look at her. 'You probably need something to eat and drink after the energy we expend in "Dancin' Fool". Come on, we will get some cake, *ja?*' Ingrida passes Asha a bottle of water and we all quickly change.

MONICA

I check my phone and smile to see Bruce has sent a text.

Butch, baby, I'm bringing Curtis and Divinity, from the Friends of Dorothy show. Are we are going to have some fun! See you later, you hunky cowboy, you.

I send a thumbs up emoji and quickly delete the message even though there is no chance of Vince seeing it.

'Oh look,' Bonnie cries, finger pointed at the screen. 'Sheila's group is about to start.'

The television shows the dozen women get into their places. Under the lights, the tops look shockingly see-through, leaving nothing to the imagination. I cannot quite make up my mind if they are in the worst possible taste or an inspired and quirky design. They certainly hold the eye.

Bold as Brass form a tableau in the centre of the stage with open fans, each dancer holding theirs at arm's length at different angles.

I stare at the positioning of the fans; this looks more than familiar. Then an image flashes across my mind and I realise why. We had similar costumes in a show we did several years ago – tight black skirts over red and gold leotards – except our tops were not so sensual and definitely did not show our underwear. Tame in comparison to Sheila's garb.

The dance starts and I instantly recognise the moves.

'What the…?'

'What is it, Monica?'

'This number. It's one of Clarissa's former winning routines.'

'No!'

'Where's the programme?'

Bonnie leans forward and runs her finger down the listing on the mirror.

'Oh, my goodness. You're right. It's "Roxanne". We did this, let me see… in 2019 I think.'

'The sly, wee hallions. This is Clarissa's dance.' Cath slams her hand down on the dressing table.

'Monica, is this right? Are you say to us Sheila has steal this dance from Clarissa? All of the choreography steps?' Ingrida stares at the screen.

'Stolen it move for move. Look.' I stand and place myself under the screen where I dance the moves on the spot in exact time with the women out on stage.

'I don't believe it! They have not even attempted to disguise Clarissa's steps.' Asha has perked up and is on her feet, looking from the screen to me. 'It is phrase for phrase. That woman is outrageous. I hope Clarissa is watching this. She should put in a complaint. We will rally round her.'

The routine picks up in tempo and I pull back to watch it critically. I have to admit they are dancing it well and even without being able to hear the soundtrack, the number has impact.

This'll get a high score.

'Watch. At the end, they'll all swirl into a group around a central figure. Then they'll each stretch out a leg to run a hand down to the toe. And right on the last phrase of "Roxanne", they'll all make a sudden move to open their fans and raise them high to the ceiling. If you remember, Bonnie, we had to have those stretch leotards under our skirts as the tops we were going to use kept snapping or riding up.'

'Oh yes, I do remember. Those leotards were sparkly red and gold. I think I still have mine somewhere.'

The women do exactly as I predicted, but as they make the final dramatic reach with the fans held high to the ceiling, the bra tops of two of the dancers dramatically tear at the shoulders and drop down.

'Oh my God.'

'No.'

We all put our hands to our mouths as we watch the women struggle to cover their bare breasts. The large-bosomed woman is floundering as she tries to drag the top from under her sizeable wobbling chest. It's the same dancer Sheila had berated for making a mistake in their first number – I think her name's Bridget.

Sheila makes a dash to assist Bridget with her costume malfunction. She stands in front of the woman and leans over to help hitch up the broken top, but as she does so, her skintight skirt rips from the top of the rear split to her waistband exposing a sparkling thong framing her large white buttocks for all the audience to see.

I give an involuntary gasp. What a nightmare.

We are too shocked to say anything at first. Although I'm sure Asha muttered some remark about Ruby as she shakes her head in disbelief.

'Well, she's certainly giving a holy show of herself. Gives a whole new meaning to something going arseways.' Cath begins to snigger.

'I don't think that was quite the end they had planned.' Bonnie chuckles.

Ingrida is also starting to laugh. 'It was a very big end. *Ja?*'

I have to smile. 'They certainly fleshed it out.'

'Oh, my goodness. Look here. The programme describes the routine as a cheeky tango number.' Asha points at the description with glee.

'Not just cheeky but delivered with bare-faced cheek.' Cath is now laughing heartily.

'All that bare flesh.' Asha starts to titter. 'And that horrible rhinestone thong. So crude.'

'Krude?' Ingrida gives a belly laugh that is infectious. 'Ha ha. This word, *krutis*. In Latvian it mean breast or tits.'

I find myself laughing too and we all rock about guffawing as more witticisms are added.

'You can definitely say it went tits up.' Bonnie is dabbing her eyes.

'They were busting out all over.' Asha laughs.

'I've heard of the bottom dropping out of your world, but that takes the biscuit,' Bonnie adds.

Ingrida is now holding her cheeks as she laughs.

'What? Ingrida, what is so funny?' I ask, chuckling with her.

'This… This words Bonnie say. Biscuit and bottom… it is very funny.' Ingrida is shaking as she chortles aloud.

'Oh Ingrida, you crease me up.' Bonnie starts, but

Ingrida goes into hysterics, which sets everyone else falling about with laughter.

'That finale was a bit of a bummer.' Cath is holding her sides.

Bonnie raises her water bottle and on cue we all shout, 'Bottoms up.'

Our laughter starts to die down and we see on the screen that Sheila's group is leaving the stage.

'Quick. We have to go out.' Asha announces.

'What? We're dancing in another hour or so,' I say.

'We do not want to be here when the Maggots get back. I, for one, will not be able to keep a straight face. Come on, we can go to the café. Give it twenty minutes – we will still have plenty of time to get ready – and hopefully Sheila's lot will have left by then. They have done their last dance.'

We grab our bags and pull on our jackets.

'We must find Clarissa and see what she wants to do about the theft of her number.' Asha leads the way as we hurriedly leave before Sheila's group returns.

'You have really happy glow, Monica,' Ingrida tells me as we head for the café.

'I guess the dance, the laughter has been cathartic...'

Ingrida looks puzzled.

'It means cleansing, liberating...'

Ingrida nods understanding and I repeat the words in my head. Cleansing... liberating... An image of Jean-Claude flicks across my mind and my buoyancy is instantly accompanied by a pleasant flush of desire.

22

RUBY

I sneak into the amphitheatre to find Max. He's in the back row, right where I left him. Creeping down, I slide into the seat next to him. He turns, and I'm rewarded with a beaming smile as he opens his arms to hug me.

'My God, Ruby, you were incredible,' he whispers into my ear.

'Honestly?'

'Honestly. I'm not sure what I was expecting, but your dancing was far better than anything I could've imagined. The "Dancin' Fool" routine was inspired. I couldn't take my eyes off you. You have real stage presence.'

I bask in his praise and cuddle in close.

'This is nice,' I murmur.

'When are you on again?'

'In just over an hour. We're doing a Bollywood number. Different again.'

'Now that I must see. Want to slip down to the theatre café for a drink?'

'Yes, let's. But I must keep an eye on the clock and make sure I get back to the dressing room in time to change into my sari. It's dead complicated to put on.'

'I need to see if I'm right as to which lady is which. I barely remember Saint Monica from our brief meeting on the train. And I can't wait to meet Batty Bonnie, Celtic Cath, Gnasher-Asha, Frosty Fay, and Happy-To-Be-Here-Ingrida.'

'I bet you'll have them all correct.'

We start to make a move when I see Sheila's group strutting onto the stage in their skimpy outfits.

'Wait. Let's just watch this. These are our big rivals from the North West.'

'Wow. Those costumes don't leave much to the imagination.'

I smack his arm lightly. 'No lusting after other dancers, you. Besides, this group's vile. We have to share a dressing room with them and to say relations are strained is a gross understatement.'

The lights dim and Bold as Brass start their "Roxanne" number.

What the... I move from Max and sit up, back erect, staring at the stage.

'What's the matter?'

'Frigging hell. It's Clarissa's dance.' I scan the tiers for Clarissa and Hazel but can't see them anywhere.

Max sits forward too and gives me a quizzical look.

I whisper sideways to him as I stare at the stage. 'They didn't generate the choreography to this – it's Clarissa's number. We won the Expression Cheshire competition with the exact routine a few years ago. It's... well, it's cheating.'

I watch with a growing rage as the group repeats the steps still held in my muscle memory. How dare they?

'Am I allowed to say they're good?'

'No. Even if it's true. Although, to be fair, they're dancing really well,' I mutter grudgingly. In fact, they're outstanding. Perfectly in time, full of sass, and looking way sexier than we had in our cover-all leotards. Damn them.

The sharp tango moves hold our eyes to the end when the spectacular costume disaster unfolds. The entire audience gasp and I can't tear my eyes away from the calamity on stage.

'Grief. That's a surprise ending.' Max pretends to hide his eyes behind his hands.

When Sheila's skirt splits open, revealing her shiny white ass, I find myself stifling a laugh and rushing Max from our bench to the exit.

'Are we running away?'

'Yes.'

'Should I ask why?'

'No.'

We laugh all the way to the main foyer area.

I don't feel an ounce of guilt. I only cut a few stitches on a couple of the tops. I didn't touch Sheila's skirt.

I spot Clarissa and Hazel in the café. Hazel's in her wheelchair and they are at a quiet table each sipping a glass of red wine. I cross to introduce Max and tell them about Sheila, but I then realise Clarissa is crying, dabbing her wet eyes with a handkerchief.

I quickly cut short what I was going to say and instead pass the table with a quick, 'Hi, Hazel and Clarissa. Just having a break.'

Hazel gives a small wave and smiles – I see in her eyes she is grateful I have not intruded on their conversation – and we hurriedly find chairs on the other side of the café.

'Is that the great Lady C herself?'

'Yes, but she's having a tough time of it. Her friend Hazel is terminally ill. This is probably their last trip away.'

Max nods sadly and gives a barely audible sigh. Again, I wonder if this has touched a nerve like the business with Will's dad. It makes me realise we need to speak more about the past. Our conversations focus on music, festivals, travel and politics – where we're in surprising agreement with each other. And much of the time, conversation isn't needed. I smile to myself.

He goes to the bar and buys me a coffee and himself a beer and when he returns, we move our chairs to be right next to each other.

'So, are you enjoying watching the dancing?'

'Surprisingly, yes. There were a fair few mediocre numbers, but I have to confess, one of the dances moved me to tears.'

'Besides Sheila's arse you mean?!'

'Yes, besides Sheila's voluptuous ass.'

'You're not allowed to say voluptuous.'

'Curvaceous?'

'Definitely not.'

'Ample?'

'No.'

'Meaty?'

'I'll allow meaty, but tell me which dance moved you to tears?'

'It was a French quartet. Ballet, I think. They did it to a Coldplay track.'

'"Fix You"? Yes, we saw it in rehearsal. It was fantastic. Very moving.'

'I was quite taken aback at the effect it had on me. I hadn't realised dance could do that.'

I smile at Max and take his hand and kiss it, leaving a large imprint of my red lipstick on his knuckles. 'Oops. Sorry.'

'I shall not wash it for a week.' His eyes twinkle. 'Hey, isn't that one of the dancers from the "Fix You" number over there?'

I turn to see where he is looking. A few tables away, a young woman sits opposite Fay. They are deep in conversation. Seeing them close up, I realise they look very alike. The conversation appears strained, and when Fay glances up and sees me smiling at her, she quickly looks away.

Max grabs my hand. 'So, you're coming to my hotel tonight, Ms Anderson?'

'You betcha. But my poor, aching dancing bones may need a complete massage.'

'It would be my pleasure.' Max rubs his hand up my leg under the table and I squirm with delight.

'I think the pleasure could be all mine...' I start to say when I spy Asha, Monica, and the others bound into the foyer.

They home straight in on Clarissa and Hazel, who hurriedly sit back in their seats and listen to Asha. The others join in, and I can see from their animated discussion they are telling Clarissa all about Sheila stealing her moves to "Roxanne" and the unfortunate wardrobe malfunctions.

Ingrida spots me sitting with Max and smiles. I wave her over.

'Max, this is Ingrida. Ingrida, Max.'

Max stands and shakes her hand. 'Pleasure to meet you. Your dancing was fantastic. I loved the section in "Dancin' Fool" where you had to dash back to the group. It put a real smile on my face.'

'It was terrible mistake.' Ingrida laughs. 'But it work out OK. Very nice to meet you, Max.'

'Ingrida, did you see what happened to Sheila's Maggots?'

'*Ja*. We see from the dressing room. It was very bad, but I could not stop laughing.'

'Us too.'

'I laugh so much I cry off one of my false eyelashes.' She holds up the eyelash between her finger and thumb. 'I will have to ask Fay to stick it back on.'

'She's just there, but I think she's a bit preoccupied.'

Ingrida glances at Fay and nods back at me. Max indicates for her to take one of the spare chairs at our table.

The rest of the group heads towards us, apart from Monica who is crouched next to Clarissa and has a comforting arm around her.

'Poor Clarissa. She is just having a moment,' Asha tells me. 'She did not see Sheila's dance. Did you?'

I nod but before I can say more Bonnie and Cath gush, 'Who have we got here Ruby?' and 'Are you going to introduce us to your friend?'

'Bonnie, put your tongue back in your mouth.' I wink at them. 'This is Max.'

'Max, this is Asha, Bonnie, and Cath. Monica is over there.'

I hold my breath as Max smiles at each one, giving a brief lingering look at Monica in the distance. He gives nothing away but smiles at me as he raises an eyebrow to indicate he'd guessed each dancer correctly.

'Delighted to meet you all, ladies. Your dancing was excellent. Can I get you all a drink? You certainly deserve one.'

'Five gin and tonics.' Cath smiles before adding, 'To be sure I'm only kidding. We can't go on the gargle until we've finished dancing for the day. Mine's a Diet Coke.'

The others politely add their orders for soft drinks or water and lots of cake and Max goes to the bar.

We chat and giggle about the Bold as Brass debacle. And then I see Monica walk to the bar where she ends up right next to Max. I find myself tensing. I see Max introducing himself and he goes to shake her hand. She declines and the conversation around me dulls to background noise as I freeze, watching their interaction but unable to hear their exchange. My stomach is churning.

Monica is listening to Max. She's not smiling. Her arms are crossed and at one point she briefly looks back to where I'm sitting before unfolding her arms and addressing Max again. One hand is now on her waist and the other is raised palm up, moving sharply up and down as she speaks. The hairs on the back of my neck prickle. I then realise Ingrida has been speaking to me as she leans her head in front of my face, blocking my line of vision to Max and Monica.

I focus on Ingrida. 'Sorry, what?'

'Are you OK, Ruby? You do not look well.'

'What? No... I'm fine...' I move my head until I can see Max again. Monica's returning to Clarissa's table and Max has his back is to me as he pays for the drinks.

Oh God, I should have told him about Vince. It'll be much worse to have come from Monica. He won't understand. Hell, she doesn't understand.

I bite the inside of my lip and feel the metallic taste of blood as I pierce the soft flesh under the pressure. Damn.

By the time I've rummaged for a tissue in my bag to dab at the wound, Max has returned to the table with a tray of drinks and cakes. His expression is unreadable, but he doesn't make eye contact with me.

'How long are you in Paris?' Asha asks Max.

'I'm not sure. I may be travelling back tonight.' Max doesn't even look in my direction.

I bend to put the tissue back in my bag, so the table hides my face.

'Well, Ruby has certainly kept you a secret, Max.' Bonnie jokingly nudges him.

Bonnie, shut up. I want to kick her.

'Oh, Ruby likes her secrets.'

I lift my head and Max is staring straight at me. The others giggle and I slowly shake my head at him. Max, don't do this...

'Did you watch both dances?' Cath asks, but I cannot focus on his reply or the ensuing conversation about the competition, the *Opéra Bastille*, Paris, and hotels. All I can hear is the blood pounding around my head.

I need to speak to Max – alone.

'What's our hotel called again?' I vaguely hear Bonnie ask.

'Charbon. It's pretty dreadful.'

'I'm not surprised,' I hear Max reply. 'In French, *charbon de blé* means coal product or smut.'

'*Ja*, that is what I say…'

'Oh, my goodness.' Asha springs up from her chair, pointing to the café clock. 'Look at the time. We need to go get changed for our last dance.'

Everyone hurriedly downs the last of their drinks. They thank Max again and leave the table. I linger. He stands to leave, and I grab his arm.

'Max?'

'What?'

'What Monica told you…'

'Yes?'

'She… well she…'

'Is it true?'

'No, I mean yes, but you have to know…'

'Know what? If I think about it, I don't think I know that much about you at all, Ruby.'

'You're fucking kidding me…'

'Look, I need to clear my head.' He turns away and then back again as he adds, 'Thing is, I've had it with relationships based on lies and deceit. I thought you were different.'

'Max, what the fuck—'

'Ruby, hurry up, you can talk to lover boy later,' Bonnie calls loudly across the café.

'Max. Talk to me. For crying out loud...' I fold my arms and challenge him with my eyes.

'I'm not sure. I'm not sure about anything right now.'

Max walks away and exits through the main Opéra House doors.

I slump down into the chair and press my fist into my forehead.

Fuck... fuck... fuck.

'Ruby?'

I look up to see Clarissa staring anxiously at me.

'Oh dear, I do not know what has happened, but you do know you will be on soon?' She taps her watch. 'I hope you can compose yourself and that you will you be able to dance?'

I nod.

'Are you sure? We must put our dance performance above and beyond any personal concerns.'

'Yes, sure... No problem.' I give Clarissa a weak smile and mechanically head for the dressing rooms.

Well, Monica. Thanks a bunch. You've had your revenge good and proper.

23

INGRIDA

It is good to see Sheila and her group are not in the dressing room. We take it in turns to use the ladies' toilets, as it will not be easy once we are dressed in our saris. I take my phone and look at it as I wait for a free cubicle.

There is still no message from Neil, and I cannot wait any longer, so I call him. There is no answer and just when I think it will put me on the answer service to record a message, another voice comes onto the phone. I know this voice. It is Rita, Maya's mother.

'Hello, Neil Goodman's phone, can I help you?'

'Hello, Rita. Is Neil there?'

'Who is this?'

'It is me. Ingrida. Can I speak to Neil?'

'Hang on I need to put this on speaker phone. Sorry, who is this?'

'Ingrida.'

'Ingrid? Oh, yes, the nanny. Can it wait? Neil is just out with my husband, Terry. And I am rather busy with the children.'

I can hear Lizzy crying in the background, and my stomach has a knot. When Rita says, "Oh, yes, the nanny", I know this mean Neil has not told them we are married. I do not know why he has not when he promised he would.

Lizzy cries even louder and shouts, 'I want Guy-da.'

I feel my heart spasm. 'Rita, please can I talk to Lizzy?'

'Good grief, no – you are on holiday, are you not? Why on earth would you want to speak to the children? Now I am sorry, but I must get back to my granddaughter. She probably needs a rest...'

'No, Lizzy does not have a daytime rest.' I am unable to make myself heard as Lizzy is now wailing right next to phone. I want to pick her up and tell her everything is OK, but I cannot even speak with her.

'Stop that crying this minute, Elizabeth.'

I hear Rita's shout and clap of the hands. Or is it a smack? Please do not be a smack.

I grip the phone tightly. 'Lizzy...'

'What? Sorry, I cannot hear a word with this din. I have to go. I will tell Neil you called, Ingrid. Enjoy your holiday. Goodbye.'

I cannot believe it. I steady myself against the sink and take a deep breath. The children are OK. Rita is their grandmother. She would not hurt them.

I turn on the tap and flick a little water on my face and frown at myself in the mirror. Why has Neil not told them? I need to warn him about my uncle. Oh, why has Neil not called me? The Latvian word *glevulis*, it goes round and round in my head. Neil, he is *glevulis*... What is the English word? Then I remember, it is coward.

'*Bez mugurkaula glevulis*,' I say aloud.

'Wow, you sound angry, Ingrida.' Bonnie appears from one of the cubicles.

I had forgotten she was in here.

'What does that mean, then?'

'It means coward, with no bones in the back.'

'Well, I hope you are not referring to your lovely new husband.'

A cubicle door opens, and I quickly go in and shut the door. Inside my head I say, *Ja, Bonnie, I was speaking of my new husband*. He is perhaps not so lovely. He is weak man. I see it now. He is too weak to tell Maya's parents we are now married. He is like frightened little boy. I am full of disappointment with Neil. Why did he ask me to marry him if he will not say this to others? I do not understand. And I do not like being here when the children need me. All I want to do is go home. I try to say prayer, but the words they do not come so I flush the toilet and go to wash up my hands.

'Ingrida, are you OK?' Asha joins me at the washing area.

I nod to Asha and blink back a tear.

'Trouble at home?' She looks at the phone I have put down next to the sink.

I merely nod, then I realise her breath smells a little of vomit. 'Asha, are you sick?'

'I think all the nervous tension of the competition has got to me. That cake has come straight back. Although I feel better now.' She lightly splashes water on her face and dabs it dry with a paper towel.

'I am sorry to hear this. You are not pregnant, are you?'

Asha's face looks at me in a very startled way. She looks quickly to her stomach area and then she holds onto the sink as if it will stop her from slipping down to the floor.

'Oh, my goodness.' Asha's voice goes very quiet, and her breaths come very quickly. I lean into her so I can hear her.

'Ingrida, no… I cannot be pregnant. I mean, I do not want children. I mean, not yet…' She puts a hand to her stomach.

'Do not worry, being sick is not always sign of pregnant. The main one is missing your… *menstrualais*… what is English word?'

'The same.' Asha starts to pace the floor. 'I am not sure if I have missed. I am not very regular. It has been a month, maybe more…' She suddenly puts her hands to her breasts. 'They are swollen…' And stares at me wildly.

'This is also sign. But only true way to know is to have an actual pregnant test, *ja*? We can buy one at a *kimikis* – a chemist.'

'Yes, you are right. After the dance… Ingrida?'

'*Ja?*'

'Will you come with me? I have no idea how to ask for this in French.'

'Of course.'

'Thanks. Oh, and Ingrida, please do not say anything to the others.'

'Of course,' I nod. I do not know why Asha would think I would tell others, but I am not paying so much attention to her as I am thinking too much of Neil. I also remember Kazimieras, he is in Manchester.

I rub my head and find the words to say to God, *please rub my worries away.*

I cannot help but think if Asha is going to have a baby, this should not be a big worry for her in whole scheme of things. She is about to be married to her true love, Jay. The wedding is soon, so she will be a married lady when her baby is born. She is a very fortunate person… And – God, he remind me – I am also fortunate to have three beautiful stepchildren.

Back in the dressing room, we change into our saris. They are different pale shades of blue and green. Mine is light azure. It remind me of the colour of the sea. We also put on our ballet shoes. Fay told us she could not go barefoot – she did not say for what reason – but we all agreed we would wear ballet shoes instead. They remind me of when I was a little girl in my ballet class. I think Grace and Lizzy will like ballet… when they are older. As soon as I think of Neil's children my face creases up, but this is not with laughing, it is with worry. I miss them and I know they miss me.

Asha quietly adjusts the beautiful sari material for each of us until it is looking correct.

Cath and Bonnie ask her if she is OK – I see them looking at each other with a question in their eyes. Asha says she is anxious for the dance to go well as she knows this will be performed at her wedding and today is the dress rehearsal for the big day. But I think this is not her main worry.

I try to remember the opening steps for our Bollywood routine, but my mind is blank.

Everyone is quiet in the dressing room.

I do not feel like making conversation. I try to concentrate, but I cannot make the first part of the dance come into my head; I cannot even think how the music goes.

I look around to ask Monica to remind me how the dance begins, but she is brushing her hair and does not make eye contact with me or anyone.

Fay also looks very preoccupied and when I ask her to help me stick the false eyelash back on, she does it without saying a word to me. I think this has something to do with the young lady she met in the café. I think this must be one of Fay's estranged daughters Neil told me about, but the young lady had her arms crossed and she did not look at Fay's eyes.

Ruby arrives a few minutes later. Her shoulders are slumped, and she quickly put on her costume with her back to us. She is very quiet and there is barely any noise in the room.

'What's up with everyone?' Bonnie asks. 'It's so quiet in here. You could hear a pin prick.'

Fay shakes her head but does not say anything.

There is no more joking or laughter.

'I don't know about anyone else,' – Cath turns to examine her mint-shade sari in the mirrors – 'but I'm shattered. What we all need is a good rest and a stiff drink.' She starts to sing in a quiet voice a song about wanting to be shown the way home and going to bed.

I do not know this song, but I am also tired, but I would not like to go to bed. I would like to go home.

'Ladies.'

We all turn, and Clarissa is in the doorway, smiling at us.

'How are we all feeling? Sheila's group has descended on the café. They are making a terrible show of themselves. Such vulgarity. Many of the customers walked out. Apparently, someone has posted an online clip of her skirt ripping and it is being watched across the internet. You would have thought they would be ashamed of the incident, but on the contrary, they appear to be as proud as punch. That woman's coarseness never ceases to amaze me.'

We all nod in agreement, but no one speaks. Even Fay, who I think would normally say something to Clarissa, just shakes her head.

Clarissa looks surprised no one say anything. She waits a moment, then clasps her hands together. 'Anyway, I have come to wish you the best. You all look wonderful, and you danced splendidly in the first two numbers. I think at least one of them stands a good chance of getting into the finals and perhaps the best is yet to come?'

Clarissa's eager face looks about the room and appears to fall as she see our not so happy expressions.

'Oh, and I must tell you, Hazel and I have a treat in store for you later.'

Monica smiles. 'How lovely. What treat is that, Clarissa?'

'Hazel is treating us all to a dinner cruise on the River Seine. We can sit and take in the sights of Paris from the comfort of the boat and eat wonderful French cuisine.'

'Well, that is marvellous,' Bonnie jumps up and takes Clarissa's hand and gives it a squeeze. 'I just hope it won't be snails, or frogs' legs, on the menu. Ha ha.'

We all thank Clarissa, but I can see there is not the excitement nor grateful thanks she is expecting.

Monica is smiling, but she does not smile with her eyes.

Ruby is chewing her lip.

Fay is gently rubbing her toes in her ballet shoes, and I think to myself, maybe her feet, they are sore.

Asha has a hand over her mouth, and I wonder if she might be sick again. She looked a little green when Bonnie mentioned the snails and legs of the frogs.

'Ladies, you all look a little tired.' Clarissa pats Monica's arm. 'And it is no wonder. You had a full day of travel yesterday on top of the trauma of Janine's thievery. However, I do urge you to dig deep and to give the Bollywood dance your all. Would it help to walk it through? We have a few minutes before you need to go to the green room.'

I jump up. '*Ja*. Thank you, Clarissa.' If she can demonstrate to me the first steps, I think I will be able to remember the rest.

After the walk-through, Clarissa takes a photograph of us all in costume in a dance pose. We smile for the camera, but I do not think many of us are smiling inside.

'Now, ladies, I must head back to the auditorium to watch you all. I will not say good luck but as they say in theatre circles, *break a leg*.'

In the green room, we watch the screen for the

previous dance to finish. It is some kind of street dance. Three young men are wearing baggy clothes and baseball caps. They spin on their backs, punch the air, do high kicks and point at the audience many times. There is loud rap music that blares out from behind the stage entrance.

'Well, our dance will be quite a contrast to this.' Bonnie laughs.

'As long as they think it is from the ridiculous to the sublime and not the other way around, I'll be happy.' Cath tucks in a piece of material that is hanging down at the back of Bonnie's costume.

Within minutes, the street dancers bounce out of the stage door, and we all line up in our correct order.

When the music starts, we will run on from the wings holding our matched coloured scarves high in the air, so they float behind us. We must keep the scarves high as we cross through each other. Clarissa, she tell us it is lethal to slip on the material, so we must be careful to stop it dropping to the floor.

Once we are in our actual positions, we must each tie our scarves around our waist as our hips move with the beat of the music. We will then begin the fast mixture of Indian steps. It is a complicated dance with many arm movements.

I am in Janine's place right at the front of the line.

I say a quick prayer, please God, let me dance this well as I am not as confidence in the footsteps, and I do not want to make mistake.

My heart is beating very loud in my head. We rush onto the stage. I am holding my scarf high and when I reach the other side of the stage, I turn and run to cross between Ruby and Monica and then Fay and Bonnie. I feel as light as air in my ballet shoes. The steps are still in my feet even if they are not in my head. I feel wonderful.

We surge – Clarissa loves this word, surge – to the front of stage in two groups, then I hear a loud scream, follow by Bonnie's voice.

'Oh dear.'

I turn and Fay is down on the floor. One foot is bent back beneath her. It is wrapped up in a pale blue length of material. Her eyes, they blink and I think she has hit her head on the floor. I can see she is badly hurt, so I drop my scarf and rush to her side.

The music stops and the main lights go on.

I am no longer a dancer but a professional nurse. My training takes over and I call for help.

24

FAY

My leg is broken. I felt it crack. The X-ray shows a hairline fracture of the fibula just above the ankle. I am to wear something called an airboot and use crutches until I can weight-bear again. I have no idea what this will cost, and I am concerned what excess my insurance will expect me to pay.

Still, I must consider myself fortunate not to have a bad head wound, just bruising. At least I will be allowed to travel home provided that it is by train. Perhaps Janine did me a favour after all when she did not use our money for flights? Going home by aeroplane would have been out of the question.

'*Attendez ici s'il vous plaît?*' a nurse asks me.

I look blank, so she asks, '*Êtes vous indienne?*' pointing to my outfit; I am still dressed in the sari costume.

I shake my head and reply, '*Ju-swees-englaze.*'

She smiles and says, 'Wait here, please.'

I sigh. As if I can do anything else.

It will no doubt be a long wait to have this boot fitted and I will probably miss the dinner cruise on the Seine, now my only opportunity to see a little of Paris. And when on earth will I be able to get changed?

Pull yourself together, Fay. It could have been a lot worse.

I am glad I am by myself. I sent Ingrida and Asha back to the theatre – thankfully just a short distance away – as soon as they confirmed I could be a while. Ingrida kindly said she would come back for me. I was most appreciative she was able to translate the doctor's diagnosis.

Goodness, it has been a day full of incidents, and I decide to relive it as I sit in the treatment area of the Saint Antoine Hospital.

The accident was not my fault. But it is true to say my mind was not on the Bollywood dance, that is for sure. The conversation I had had with Edith in the café was going round and round endlessly in my head.

It had been such a relief she had indeed recognised me just before we went on stage to perform the Adele number. She had not known I had hidden in the wings to watch her dance at close quarters. "Fix You" was magnificent and the applause in the amphitheatre had been thunderous.

'Bravo.' I had clapped when they came off stage. 'Edith, you were superb.'

She had half-smiled, unsure how to respond. However, I was unable to engage in a lengthy conversation as I had to rush back to the dressing room to change for "Dancin' Fool".

'Will you meet me in the foyer café after our next dance? We are on again soon.'

She had nodded, but her face betrayed a degree of uncertainty. Indeed, she appeared to have clamped her mouth shut. Perhaps she feared saying the wrong thing. I realise this is exactly how I felt. I did not want to say anything that would cut off communication before it had begun.

I decided there was insufficient time to change after "Dancin' Fool", so I threw on my coat over my costume and rushed to the café, forcing down a rush of unchecked emotions. This was not the time to be losing my head.

My voice felt a little constricted when I sat down opposite her. She was sipping from a bottle of water, and I resisted the temptation to advise her to drink it from a glass. Unsure of how to start, I was quite sure alluding to the lazy habits of people drinking directly from tins and bottles was not what she would want to hear.

'Edith, I...'

'You danced really well, Fay.'

'Ah, you watched "Dancin' Fool".' I am pleased with her compliment but my heart sinks when she addresses me with my forename.

'Yes. The choreography was excellent. How long have you been dancing?'

'Almost four years now. And you, Edith, are you living in Paris?'

'No. We are living in Nice. Just staying in Paris for the competition.'

'We?'

'Yes, we.'

When Edith did not elaborate, I glanced around the

café and noticed Clarissa and Hazel sitting together. I was glad they had not seen me. I wanted my conversation with Edith to be private.

'You danced beautifully, Edith.'

'Thank you.'

'Are you working in Nice?'

'Yes.'

'Have you been living there long?'

'Just over a year.'

'I would like to see Nice. Did you know it has the longest seafront on the French Riviera?'

'Yes, I live there remember?'

'Quite.'

We both stared at the table for what seemed like a good few minutes. I saw Ruby enter the café with a male companion. They sat a few tables away, but she was too far to overhear, and I resolved to deliver my rehearsed oration before I changed my mind.

'Edith?'

She looked at me and nodded.

'I am not one to make speeches, but I would like to say a few things and I would appreciate it if you would hear me out.'

She folded her arms.

'I did not have a mother when I grew up. Please do not sigh. I know this information is not new to you. The reason I mention this is I did not have the benefit of a kindly mother to show me how to be a parent to pubescent girls. My upbringing was rather austere – oh, I am not looking for sympathy, I did perfectly well at St Eulalia's – and well… what I am trying to say is I may not have handled your adolescent years as well as I could have.'

'Understatement of the century.'

'If you would hear me out, Edith?'

She shrugged, but I feared I had lost her attention.

'I did my best, or what I thought was my best, but perhaps I should have…'

'Should have what?'

'Should have sought some assistance. I mean, you and Bethan were quite a force…'

'Oh, here we go.'

'What I am trying to say is I am sorry—'

'And?'

'I am sorry we have drifted apart.'

'Oh, you're not sorry for turning your back on us when we most needed you.'

I sat back, startled. This was not going at all how I had planned.

I saw some of the other ladies joining Ruby at her table. I did not want them coming over to me, so put my head down and studiously ignored them.

We sat in silence for a good long time. I sipped at my coffee and Edith finished her bottle of water.

Eventually, Edith looked at her watch and began to tap the table with her fingernails.

I knew I only had this one chance, and it was fast fading, so I turned to her and tried again.

'Edith, I know we cannot turn the clock back. We cannot alter the past. But I do not want to be a stranger to you or Bethan. I was hoping we could…'

'Play mother and daughters? Glance over those years where you ignored us and pick up as if they hadn't happened?'

I knew then she was not in a receptive mood, and this had been an error of judgement on my behalf. I slowly moved my chair back and stood up. 'I am sorry. This was a mistake. I had only wanted to say I was sorry. I also wanted to have… well to have some contact… but I can see I have misjudged the situation. Edith, I am happy I have seen you. I am delighted you are dancing. I hope you… well, I hope everything will go well for you in life. Please send my… my regards to Bethan.'

Edith had stared at the table, and I had walked away.

I forced myself to go to the dressing room. If it were not for the final dance, I would have left the theatre that instant and wandered around Paris to gain some equilibrium, but I was duty-bound to perform with the others. I could not let Clarissa down.

And now this. A broken leg. I can hardly take it in. They wanted me to inject myself daily with an expensive drug for the next week. Apart from what will no doubt be a ridiculous cost, I have a deep-seated fear of injections dating back to my school days when I was held down for a tetanus jab. This is more than being a little squeamish. I was diagnosed with trypanophobia, an extreme fear of medical needles after that. I had to see a specialist doctor to have gas and air in order to have my Coronavirus vaccines. I would be unable to explain this to the young French doctor who asks if I know how to inject myself. I merely nod. I am given seven days' supply. The hypodermics are thankfully hidden in a box. I am deeply relieved I do not have to look at them. I have absolutely no intention of using them and will leave them on my chair. I heard them say the word *préventif*, so I know the medication is only precautionary. I just want to get out of this hospital.

I press my fingers into my forehead as I contemplate what lies ahead. There will be so much to sort out. Insurance, transport, weeks of rehabilitation and no more walks or dance for months. How will I manage stairs? Getting in and out of a bath? Going to work… I quickly stop myself before sinking into a quagmire of self-indulgent pity. This is not the way I was brought up. Perseverance, steadfastness, and practicality; I can visualise Sister Josephine telling me so.

I stare at my swollen foot. I am unsure exactly what happened; it is all a bit of a blur. One minute we were crossing through each other, our scarves held high; the next minute, I was on the ground. I banged my head on the floor and my ankle was in agony. I tried to stand up – I certainly did not want to make a spectacle of myself – but my leg would not hold my weight. It was dreadful to be out there, everyone looking at me. I had to be supported to get off the stage. Monica was on one side and Ingrida on the other. I could not have been more embarrassed.

They deposited me on a chair in the green room and Ingrida placed my foot up on a low table. She carefully removed my ballet shoe and examined my ankle while they fetched the theatre first aider.

'It may be broken, or it could be sprain.' Ingrida had turned to one of the backstage staff to ask, '*Avez-vous un bloc de glace?*'

'What is that you are asking for?'

'Ice. I am afraid this will *uxbriest*... what is English word?' Ingrida puffed out her cheeks.

'Swell up?'

'*Ja*. Swell up. You need rest leg.'

I stared down at my foot and realised my foreshortened toe was on display for all to see. Ingrida must have seen the look of alarm on my face as she gently placed my scarf over the foot to hide it and smiled at me. I have not been wrong in judging her to be a kind soul.

Monica shook her head and sat down next to me. 'You'll not be able to dance for a while, Fay. Even if it's only a sprain, sometimes that can be worse than a broken bone. James was weeks recovering from a sprained ankle playing rugby last term.'

'I think you are right,' I responded. 'I may have some difficulty getting back to the Charbon Hotel. Oh dear, I do not know how this happened. Perhaps it was my scarf? Did I drop it?'

'You tripped on part of Bonnie's sari – it'd come loose at the back.' Ruby crouched down next to me. 'Poor you.'

I must say, they were all being very kind.

'Oh dear, was it my fault? I'm so sorry, Fay.' Bonnie went to pat her open hand on my raised foot, but thankfully Ingrida caught it mid-air and stopped her.

'*Ne*.'

'Oh, my word. I'm so sorry. What was I thinking? If I had hit your foot, it would certainly have been adding upset to injury...'

'*Insult*.' I grunted out the word at exactly the same time

as Monica, Asha, Ruby, Cath and even Ingrida.

Despite the circumstances, we found ourselves smiling at each other when we saw Bonnie's consternation at the combined correction.

'Well, that's me told.' Bonnie grinned good-naturedly. 'Adding *insult* to injury? Who'd have thought that was the right saying?'

A competition official motioned for Monica to go and speak to him. Within a few minutes, she was back.

'What shall we do? The organisers want to know if we want to start again?'

'Can we do it without Fay?' Asha had a deep frown in her forehead.

I was grateful they at least contemplated not dancing without me even if they then decided to go ahead.

'We can try. We could just leave a gap where Fay normally dances,' Ruby suggested.

'We have to go now if we are going to dance.' Monica indicated the official tapping his watch.

'You must dance. Go. I will be fine,' I urged. I knew Clarissa would want them to continue, and this is, after all, Asha's special wedding dance.

So, with a wave, the ladies disappeared through the stage door.

I heard the music start and watched them on the screen. I found myself welling up and had to exert supreme control not to give in to tears. It was more than being excluded from the performance of a dance I loved; our time together had bonded us in a way I had not expected. I had felt an integral part of the ensemble, but not any longer. This injury has put paid to that. Of course, I wanted them to dance well, but I felt so utterly useless and suddenly quite alone.

Then a voice pulled my attention back to the green room.

'Mum. Are you OK?'

I found myself unable to speak when I looked up at Edith. She had not addressed me thus in years and I confess, I could not find any words and my lower lip began to tremble.

'Oh, Mum.' Edith crouched down and put her arms around me.

I blinked back a tear and placed my arms around her, too.

We did not talk much. The first aider arrived and said I should see a doctor. Edith called the hospital and arranged for me to get an X-ray. I loved listening to her speaking in fluent French on her phone. Living in France has certainly developed her language skills. Edith then conversed with the theatre manager and found they had a wheelchair they would allow me to borrow. She explained the hospital was only a twenty-minute walk away and offered to push me, but it was clear she was due somewhere else when one of the male dancers of *Corps et Ame* arrived in the green room to indicate they needed to hurry away. As it happened, as soon as Ingrida came off stage, she and Asha insisted they would take me.

I did not introduce Edith to the others as my daughter, the situation seeming delicate and precariously balanced, but I was aware Asha was looking Edith up and down and about to question her. Before she could say anything, I talked deliberately loudly about requiring my insurance details and made a big show of finding the information I had saved on the notes app of my mobile. As I checked them, Edith leant in and asked for my device. When she handed it back, she whispered in my ear that she had put her telephone number in my contacts list.

'Let me know how you get on.'

'Thank you. I will and Edith?'

'Yes?'

'Bless you.'

There, I said it directly to her. After years of going to bed and saying, 'Bless you,' to both girls in the photograph in my flat, I have finally said it to Edith in person. Maybe one day I will say it to Bethan too.

25

ASHA

'We're in the finals.' Bonnie punches the air.

'Wonderful.' Cath claps Bonnie's back. 'I'm just annoyed Sheila's Maggots have made it too. Purely down to stealing Clarissa's dance routine to "Roxanne". The dirty wee hallions.'

I should be delighted we are through and furious about Sheila's group, but all I can feel is a mental numbness.

The announcement was made just after Ingrida and I returned from the hospital where we had left Fay to wait for her airboot to be fitted. All the groups were called into the amphitheatre for the rollcall.

Now back in the dressing room, Clarissa distributes the judges' written notes, her face beaming.

'Will you look at this?' Cath waves the sheet of paper. 'Apparently, "Dancin' Fool" has won the judges' second highest commendation, and this is what they want us to perform in the finals tomorrow. Asha, did you hear?' Cath taps my shoulder.

'Sorry?'

'We got a commendation. For "Dancin' Fool".'

I manage a thumbs up with a smile and a nod. I should be over the moon; it was all I wanted. But now there is only one thing on my mind.

I glance at the notes and feel only a mild sense of disappointment to see there were no remarks – positive or negative – about my Bollywood number. Though in truth, we did not dance our best. Not with one person down and so many of us distracted, me included.

'Ladies, we need to get going if we are to make our river cruise,' Clarissa calls.

Ingrida and I hastily change out of our saris.

The sun is low in the sky as we wait for our bus at *Place de la Bastille*. I hold my bag tightly. The test is inside. Ingrida and I went to the chemist on our way back from the hospital.

Pregnant? I cannot get the thought out of my head. I am still hoping I am not. What will I say to Jay? I resolve not to call him until I know. It seems a leap too far to contemplate becoming a mother. Maybe these waves of nausea are purely psychosomatic; the autosuggestion of expecting a baby inducing the symptoms. I mean, I am getting married, travelling the world. A child is not part of the equation.

Our bus arrives and we show our passes. Ruby has taken over as our guide in Fay's absence, but I can see she is flicking between the map screen and her messages in a distracted way. No doubt waiting for a call from Max. The tension sparking between them in the theatre café was downright obvious.

All the buses are equipped with a disabled ramp, so Ruby offers to push Hazel on and off in her wheelchair.

Within a few minutes, we are getting off again.

'Where now, Ruby?' Cath asks.

'Hang on... Right, this is the *Place de la Concorde*. Hey, wow. It's massive isn't it. Oh look, the *Champs-Élysées* starts just there.' She points.

'I read Marie Antoinette was executed here,' Cath comments.

'Was she really? This place is so full of history.' Bonnie links arms with Cath.

'And here is the Luxor Obelisk.' Hazel stares up at the gold-tipped Egyptian relic at the centre of the square. 'That's said to be over three thousand years old.'

Bonnie whistles and we all take in our surroundings.

I take a deep breath of fresh air and turn full circle. 'Hey, those buildings by the trees look a bit like Buckingham Palace.'

'Marvellous. I had almost forgotten we were in Paris after being inside the theatre all day,' Clarissa points to the other end of the square to a large, light stone structure topped with a glass-domed roof. 'If I remember rightly, I think that is a palace just over there.'

'The map says it's the *Grand Palais*.' Ruby glances up. 'It's a pity Ingrida is not with us. She could've told us more.'

I had offered to go back to the hospital with Ingrida to collect Fay – she called to say she had been seen quicker than expected – but Ingrida told me to go ahead. She knew I wanted to do the test as soon as possible.

Stop thinking about the test.

Instead, I reflect on Fay's injury. She has been told she can collect crutches tomorrow, but they said she must not weight-bear and risk displacing her fracture in the first few days, so using a wheelchair will be a necessity. I do not know how we will get her back to the UK. I can see it will be fraught with difficulties.

I wonder about the dancer from the French quartet who had rushed to Fay's side. Ruby wondered if she could be Fay's daughter, but I had always thought Fay was a spinster. I mean, I cannot imagine her being married.

Ruby studies her phone for a few minutes before saying, 'We're only a thirty-minute walk from the Eiffel Tower... Now which way?'

'I hope Ingrida can manage Fay in the wheelchair.' Monica speaks to Clarissa.

'She assured me she would be fine.' Clarissa responds. 'It has turned out to be a huge asset to have a trained nurse as part of our number.'

I do not say anything. I think the other dancers have forgotten that as a trained dentist I have far more medical training than Ingrida. However, I did not want to be lumbered with Fay and besides, if Ingrida needs everyone to know she is a nurse and her sense of self depends on it, then who am I to comment?

Ruby calls to us. 'We could cross the river here, or walk along the banks until we're nearer the Eiffel Tower?'

'Let's see which is wheelchair friendly,' Hazel suggests.

Ruby sets off and waves us over to indicate a gentle ramp down to the walkway on our side of the river.

We follow and walk along the waterfront for about

twenty minutes before the river turns and the Eiffel Tower comes into view.

'OK, the *Bateaux Parisiens* is where our boat's moored, over there. We need to cross at the next bridge.' Ruby helps Clarissa push Hazel up the slope to the bridge and a few minutes later we are beside a line of cruisers below the Eiffel Tower.

There are artists dotted around the pavement, painting the iconic structure in the early evening light with the sun low and the clouds in the sky beginning to shimmer shades of pink. We stop to admire their efforts as Clarissa and Hazel go to a small ticket booth to confirm our arrival.

'I wish we had had time to get out of our black dance tops.' Monica talks to Cath and Bonnie.

'We wouldn't have made it to our hotel and back in time.' Cath shakes her head. 'It's right on the outskirts of Paris.'

'I didn't bring a change of clothes, anyway.' Bonnie laughs. 'I should have guessed you had, Monica. You're always impeccably dressed.'

'I thought about wearing my sari – Fay is still in hers – but we need the costumes in good condition for my wedding…' I peter out. I do not want to think about the wedding.

'I'm just glad it's a warm evening and we don't need extra layers.' Cath stares up at the Eiffel Tower and sighs. 'But it's cracking to be here in the centre of Paris.'

Clarissa pushes Hazel towards us and – to my relief, as I am starting to feel sick again – we sit down on a couple of benches.

'All sorted,' Hazel announces. 'We just need to wait a short while before we can board.'

'I have to say, I am delighted we have reached the finals, ladies.' Clarissa glows. 'And with the "Dancin' Fools" routine. I am so proud of your performance.'

'What are you going to do about Sheila?' Bonnie asks.

'We should tell the judges.' Cath nods her head vigorously. 'They need to know she stole your choreography.'

'They should be kicked out of the competition,' I add.

'I must say I agree, Asha. But Hazel has a different take on this.'

Hazel sits forward in her wheelchair. 'I think that providing Sheila accepts the routine is Clarissa's choreography, they should be allowed to dance. After all, it's another of Clarissa's numbers in the final. And she should get the rightful credit she deserves.'

I am not sure I agree. Personally, I think Bold as Brass should be stopped. Their theft of Clarissa's dance steps is every bit as bad as Janine's theft of our Paris money.

'We do, however, have to prove it *is* your routine first,' Hazel adds.

Monica holds up her phone. 'I can get Joanne to forward me the video of the original dance to show the judges. I have it saved on my home computer, and she can send it to my phone. Once they see it is identical, there will be no question it is your dance, Clarissa.'

'Thank you, Monica. At present I would be happier to see Bold as Brass thrown out of the competition. They are a discredit to the dancing profession.'

'True, but who knows what revenge they'll take if we get them booted?' Ruby interjects.

Ruby has a point. But I realise I am losing interest in the discussion. My mind keeps reverting to my impending test. I resist the temptation to go the nearby public toilet. We must surely be getting on the boat soon.

'Hello, we are here, *ja*.' Ingrida, slightly breathless, arrives with Fay in the wheelchair, which she pushes next to Hazel's.

'Well, look at us. We are a pair.' Hazel squeezes Fay's hand.

Fay smiles, despite looking incredibly pale. 'I have to say this fall has taken it right out of me. I would not have been up to finding my way here, but Ingrida has been marvellous navigating the Paris transport.' Fay turns to Ingrida and smiles at her.

'You are welcome. It is good to see some of Paris, *ja?* Look at the Eiffel Tower. We are so close.'

Ingrida sits down next to me on the bench and looks at me expectantly. I give a small shake of my head and lightly pat my bag so she knows I have not yet done the test.

Fay lifts her sari to show everyone the large airboot with Velcro fastenings.

'That's one big boot, Fay,' Ruby comments.

'At least my outfit hides it from view,' Fay responds with a smile.

'How are we going to manage "Dancin' Fool" without Fay? We need someone to take her place.' Cath and Bonnie go and stand in front of Clarissa and exchange looks before they continue.

'And on that point, we've had an idea.' Cath encourages Bonnie to continue.

'So, Clarissa, well… we thought perhaps you would dance with us. You know the routine; you taught us, after all. I expect you will fit into Fay's costume, too.' Bonnie cocks her head to one side, awaiting Clarissa's response.

I must admit this sounds like a good solution to me, but I know Clarissa has not danced with the group publicly in aeons and may not be comfortable on stage. Plus, "Dancin' Fool" is a very energetic dance and Clarissa is getting on in years.

'Goodness, no.' Clarissa looks horrified. 'My days of performing in public are over.'

'Nonsense.' Bonnie pats Clarissa's arm but I can see from the way Clarissa returns her entreaty with a hard stare that she is unlikely to budge on this.

'As it happens, there may be a solution,' Hazel remarks. I am sure she glances at Fay when she says this. 'But I cannot say more. Not until tomorrow. For tonight, let's all relax and enjoy the food and the Paris sights. You have all done brilliantly today.'

I cannot think what Hazel means. Unless Fay's leg miraculously heals overnight, we are a person down, which will present problems whichever way you look at it. I expect Hazel plans to persuade Clarissa during the course of the evening.

I stand up and pace the pavement. Come on. Let us get on.

Finally, we are allowed to board the boat and I rush to the ladies to use the test. I am grateful Ingrida read the instructions for me outside the chemist.

This is it. Please, please, do not let me be pregnant.

Sample taken; the three minutes seem to go on forever... And ever.

Eventually, a word comes up on the small display, '*Enceinte*'. What? Oh, for goodness' sake; it would be in French. But then I see below in the same window it says '*3-4 sem*'. No. I google the translation of 'Enceinte' but I hardly need the confirmation when the answer appears on my screen. I am pregnant.

My first reaction is to call Jay, but I stop myself. I need time to think.

'Asha, are you OK?' Ingrida's voice comes from outside my cubicle. I did not hear her come in. It must be the noise of the boat engines covering the sound of doors opening and closing.

'Not really.' I open the door and when Ingrida sees my face, she pats my arm and I hand her the test while I wash my hands.

'*Enceinte*. Pregnant. It say 3-4 weeks...'

As the words leave her lips, Bonnie and Cath enter the ladies and stop short as they catch the word, pregnant. Cath spies the test in Ingrida's hand.

'Is that what I think it is?' Cath claps her hands together with delight. 'Oh, Ingrida, how wonderful. Congratulations. Already 3-4 weeks? How exciting.'

'What?' Bonnie looks blank. 'What is it?'

'Oh, Bonnie, can you not see? Ingrida is expecting.'

Ingrida looks anxiously at me, and I give a slight shake of the head. Please let them think it is her for now – they all know she is happily married. I told her at the chemist that no one could know I was pregnant if the test was positive, not when they are dancing at my wedding. If I have a termination, I do not want anyone but Jay to know. My parents must not catch wind of it. I look at Ingrida and plead with my eyes. She promised.

'You dark horse, Ingrida,' Bonnie begins. 'Fancy you expecting. Ha. No wonder you got married so hurriedly. What wonderful news.'

'Is not reason I get married.' Ingrida steps back from Bonnie, glares at me and slaps the test down on the side of the sink. She marches out and Bonnie looks aghast.

'Oh dear, is it something I said?'

With Ingrida gone, I am definitely not owning up to it being my test; not in front of these two gossiping women. 'I think it is a private matter, Bonnie. Not to be discussed.'

'Oh dear, of course. I didn't mean to put my foot in it.'

Cath adds, 'Asha please assure Ingrida we won't say a word, will we, Bonnie?'

'No, of course not.' Bonnie looks earnestly. 'Mum's the word… oh dear, mum's the word. Ha ha.'

Bonnie and Cath giggle and I quell a rising nausea. I hurriedly dispose of the test and wash my hands.

Before I can leave, Cath grabs my arm. 'Asha, we came to find you to say you missed all the drama. Outside. After you boarded the ship, Monica was only mugged – right here. Some eejit tried to steal her phone.'

'What?'

'We saw the whole thing. He got away but not before Ruby rugby tackled him to the ground.'

I do not know what to say but I would rather speak to Monica and Ruby than listen to the story second-hand, and I need to speak to Ingrida urgently, so I mutter something incomprehensible and hurriedly leave.

26

MONICA

It all happened so quickly I can barely recall the detail. I'd been on my phone… No wait… I was about to answer my phone. Yes, I was hoping to have a response from Jean-Claude…

I scratch my head to summon up the chain of events as I recover in a comfortable chair in the boat lounge. A waiter brings me a glass of water. Clarissa is next to me, gently patting my arm. Ruby is sitting at some distance with an ice pack on her raised leg. I nurse my sprained hand and rewind the events in my head.

Let me think, I had called Joanne to check all was OK and to tell her we made the finals. I also asked her to send the clip of our "Roxanne" performance.

'Has your father called?'

'No. Isn't he at that conference thingy? James tried ringing him earlier, but it went to voicemail.'

I had checked my watch. I knew exactly where Vince was, or where he was heading. Not long before his first *spontaneous encounter* of the evening.

Joanne wished me good luck in the finals and – phone-in-hand – I'd stared up at the Eiffel Tower and contemplated my twenty-year marriage.

Vince had been a monumental mistake, but at least I'm in no doubt about my next moves. I'm ready to take back control of my life and Vince is out of it.

I'd then texted Jean-Claude about the finals, a fleeting fantasy of attending fashion shows with this attractive Frenchman skittering through my mind. Imagine being with someone who shares your interests... My imagination took another flight of fancy as I daydreamed managing my own business, meeting lots of exciting fashion gurus, taking my time choosing someone I really wanted to share my life with. Heck, I could even use dating sites like the ones Ruby used...

I'd then snapped back to the moment and looked across to Ruby. She was by herself, leaning against the railings at the edge of the river and staring despondently at her phone. I've never seen her so miserable.

I felt a stab of guilt. Did I have to tell Max? Yes, how else was I to have responded when he'd asked me why I wouldn't forgive Ruby a silly mistake. Those bloody words again. Infuriated with this minimisation of her actions, I had lashed out. Max – who I have to say seems a nice enough person – was incredibly shocked when I told him, 'She's sleeping with my husband. Hardly a silly mistake.' OK, I know this implied it was recent and ongoing... Not kind, Monica. I know, I know.

But at that moment I wanted Ruby to experience

the hurt I felt. Seeing her so dejected, I began to regret my words. Two wrongs don't make a right. Besides, my future's waiting for me to grab it and run – new job, new relationships, new Monica – but there's no denying Ruby was hoping for a future with Max.

As if she could hear my thoughts, Ruby had suddenly looked up and our eyes met. I expected her expression to change to one of accusation, but instead she dipped her head and turned away.

My stomach had churned. Oh, Ruby. Then my phone vibrated in my hand. Thinking it could be Jean-Claude, I lifted it to look at the screen when it was suddenly snatched from my fingers, and I found myself pushed to the floor. It's a miracle I was able to reach out with one hand to break my fall. A small, hooded person dressed in dark clothes was racing away from me, my phone in his or her hand.

'Stop!' I screamed, but all the dance ladies apart from Ruby were on the boat. A few passers-by rushed to my aid as I cried, 'My phone.'

They tried to help me up, and I lost sight of the thief. But then I heard a shout and cry from others in the area and a screech above it all.

'Take that, you little prick.' Ruby's voice was unmistakeable.

I wobbled to my feet and strained to see Ruby on the ground, grappling with my assailant, who could have only been a young teenager. They both had my phone and were tussling to get sole possession of it.

The thief twisted and kicked out at Ruby. The phone

flew up in the air and the youth sprang up and ran off into the distance, quickly disappearing into the crowds.

Ruby shouted a good number of obscenities before slowly getting to her feet. She picked up the phone and started to hobble across to me when a deckhand from the cruise ship ran down the gangplank, jumped on her and pulled her arm behind her back.

'*Voleur.*'

'What the fuck?' Ruby tried to pull away from the man.

'Let her go,' I screamed.

'*Voleur*. Thief,' the man shouted.

'You bastard.' Ruby turned her head to scream in his face, 'Let me go.'

'Let her go this minute. She is not the thief you bloody bigot.' I rushed to Ruby to pull her away from him.

The deckhand glared at Ruby, spat on the floor, and returned to the boat.

'What an arse.' Ruby rubbed her arm and glared in his direction.

'Are you OK?'

She nodded. 'You?'

'Just hurt my hand when that kid pushed me to the ground.'

'Little bastard kicked me in the shin.' She bent to rub her leg. 'Ouch. I'm afraid your mobile's smashed.' Ruby handed me the phone. The screen was completely shattered and blank.

'Thank you. But honestly, Ruby, you put yourself in such danger. You could have been badly injured. I mean, he could've had a knife.'

'Yeah, I know,' Ruby mumbled. 'Guess I was lucky. Although it would've been no more than I deserve... after I've stabbed someone in the back, even if I didn't know it at the time.'

I watched her limp away as Bonnie and Cath rushed across from the boat, gushing out their concerns and wrapping me in their arms.

'Oh, Monica.'

'Are you OK, lass?'

'We saw the whole thing from the boat.'

'It was spectacular how Ruby managed to jump that gobshite... Oh no. Will you look at your mobile? That's well and truly smashed.'

'Shall we call the police?'

'No, I'm OK. I just need to sit down.'

They helped me onto the cruiser where Clarissa dismissed them and took over my care.

Now Ruby's words are going round and round in my head. *Even if I didn't know it at the time...* I rack my brains to recall any occasion where Ruby had been in the same place as Vince and it dawns on me I can't remember a single one. Of all the school plays, fundraisers, parents' evenings, sports days and socials, Vince hadn't attended one. He saw that as my role, plus he was away most of the week. We had never had Ruby round to our house when Vince was at home. He always maintained he hated socialising, as he had to do so much for work. Ha. The lying bastard. The more I think about it, I realise none of my friends have met Vince. Hell, it wasn't just Ruby who assumed I was a single parent. I give an involuntary shudder as any remnants of outrage start to ebb away.

'Are you all right, Monica?' Clarissa's voice interrupts my thoughts. 'You are shivering. I hope you are not going into shock. You need to be in good shape for the finals tomorrow.'

'Sorry, I was far away. I'm fine, thank you, Clarissa. Just a bit bruised. Annoyed my phone is broken but it could have been much worse. I'm extremely glad the thief didn't get away with my bag. My passport and cards are all in that. Far less easy to replace than a handset.'

'Well, the captain has reported the matter to the *Gendarmes*, but he says they will do nothing other than give you a log number so you can claim insurance. He says there is a lot of theft near the key tourist spots. I am glad we will be on this cruise for the evening where no one can target us. The key thing is that you and Ruby are able to dance tomorrow. We are already one dancer down.'

I see Ruby stand and tentatively test her leg. She smiles at Clarissa when she manages a few steps and puts her thumbs up. 'All good here. Loads better. Now I need a good stiff drink after all that drama.' She moves towards the door leading to the dining area.

'Ruby, wait a minute.' I touch the chair next to me. 'Clarissa, can you give us a moment?'

Clarissa nods and discreetly leaves saying no more.

Ruby looks reluctant, but I pat the chair. She shrugs, joins me and sits down.

'Thank you. For out there.'

'No problem. It was a bit mad really. I wasn't thinking.

I mean that little shit could've had a knife. It was a stupid risk to take.'

'You always take stupid risks. It's who you are.'

'I guess.'

'And as for that horrible deckhand…'

'Bastard. Did you see he had a tattooed swastika on his neck?'

'Vile. What a lowlife.'

Ruby looks down at her feet and there is a long awkward silence.

I attempt to rehearse what I am going to say in my head and wait for Ruby to look up at me.

As she does, we say in unison, 'We need to talk.'

Ruby smiles nervously. 'What can I say? I've committed the ultimate crime. I can't change that no matter how much I wish I could. I slept with your husband. Not that I knew that at the time, but I guess ignorance is no defence. I can't begin to say how sorry I am…'

'I know. I mean, I've finally realised you didn't know it was Vince. I've thought about it and ridiculous as it is, I can't remember you ever having met him.'

'I haven't, not once. I mean how nuts is that? But Monica, if I'd known it was him, I would never have met up with him and I would've told you he was using the site and cheating on you. You surely knew I would never deliberately hurt you like that?'

I nod and we go quiet for a few minutes before I explain, 'What can I say? I flipped… I guess it's testament to how little Vince is involved in my life when you think that in all these years you've not as much as encountered him. Same goes for my other friends. When he was at home, he just wanted it to be the twins and us; no visitors, no one else. Plus, we had completely separate social lives.'

'It's crazy I never met him... although as it turns out I have, but only the one night.' Ruby grimaces. 'Oh God, Monica, I'd no idea. I assume you saw my photo when you trawled through his SE profiles.'

'The one and only Sassy Scarlet.'

'Please. Don't remind me.'

'Can you imagine if you had met Vince since and then realised who he...'

'I'm so glad I didn't. I would probably have had a heart attack.'

'It might have given him one too. In fact, there's an idea.'

'No way. I never want to meet him again. Not as Clint or Vince. Besides dying of embarrassment, I'd want to punch him after what he's done to you. Have you decided what you're going to do?'

'I'm going to kick him out. I deserve better.'

'Bloody right you do. Good for you, Monica.'

'I've been doing a lot of thinking over the last few weeks and I'm going to make a lot of changes. I want to start my own wedding dress business, for starters.'

'Go girl. You're amazing at design. I hope you tell Arsy-Annabelle where to go. She's been stealing your work for years. Hey, will you need a seller? IT guru? Someone to make the tea?'

'Why? You are not quitting your job, are you?'

'I may have no choice. Besides, if I'm truthful my heart isn't in it anymore.'

'You could do loads of other jobs. You are amazing at IT.'

'I guess. You know, I've been wondering if I could start my own business too.'

'Really? Doing what?'

'I hardly dare tell you, but I've wondered if I could set up a new dating agency. Before you look at me like that, it'd be a vast improvement on Spontaneous Encounters. It'd be open and transparent. We would check ID and have a policy of complete honesty. I've been planning the whole thing in my head – on and off – for a year or two. Speed dating online, quiz evenings teaming up singles into couples, virtual holidays together without the pressure to meet up or have sex, that sort of thing. And definitely no creeps...'

'Like Vince. Good. I may even join myself once I'm free and single again.'

'Now there's a change in tune. Is it possible the previously saintly Monica is developing a wicked side?'

'Who knows? This could be the start of my sexual awakening.'

'Now I *am* all ears. What's changed?'

'I couldn't possibly say.' I smile to myself. I am not quite ready to share with her that I found her gift at the bottom of my wardrobe. My fury with Vince's adultery and added resentment about our unsatisfactory sex life led me to uncover Ruby's present...

'What's that smile about?'

'Let us just say I've begun to realise what I've been missing.'

'Monica Thornton, has this anything to do with that dishy bloke you were talking to on the Eurostar? No? Well, something has changed, and it's not just discovering Vince is a cheating bastard. A sexual awakening sounds a step in the right direction to me.'

'I may not go quite as over the top as you...'

'Charming. Scarlet had a good time in her day.' Ruby shakes her head and pauses. 'Seriously though, can you ever forgive me?'

'Ruby, I was completely enraged thinking you had not only slept with Vince, but had also been laughing about it behind my back. You may well look offended, but I can only say I went a bit mental; thought I couldn't trust anyone. Guess it was paranoia; thought everyone was against me, including you. But I can see now that I got that wrong. Vince can take a hike, but I couldn't lose you, I know that now. So, of course I forgive you. Can you forgive me?'

'Whatever for?'

'Telling Max.'

'Oh, that.' Ruby's face falls.

'I feel terrible...'

'Well, it was a shitty thing to do but I guess I should've told him myself. I nearly did. Anyhow, turns out he was badly hurt in the past and although I don't know the details, he hasn't given me a chance to explain and has backed off. I've never seen that side of him before...'

'I was so angry with you, Ruby. But it was wrong of me to make out you were having a full-blown affair with

Vince and… well, inferring it was ongoing… What can I say? I'm so, so sorry.'

'Jeez. No wonder Max was so pissed…' Ruby bites her lip and stares at the floor.

We are silent for a good few minutes, then Ruby looks up and sighs.

'Hey, my happiness has never depended on a bloke and anyway, if he's half the man I thought he was, he'll call back. I've sent a recorded message explaining the Vince thing and telling him he should've talked to me instead of going off on his high horse…'

'I hope you sent it to the right number this time.' I hold up my broken phone and grin.

'Oh hell. That awful, recorded message. I'm dead sorry about that too.'

'What? Sorry for calling me Practically-Perfect-In-Every-Way-But-Never-Had-An-Orgasm-Monica?'

'Don't.' Ruby mimes putting her fingers in her ears as she drops her head, shaking it from side to side.

'Anyway, it's technically inaccurate now.'

Ruby looks up, her eyes questioning.

'And before you ask, I'm still practically perfect.'

'Oh, Monica.' Ruby's mouth splits into a wide smile and she pounces on me to pull me into a huge bear hug.

I find myself filling up and hugging her tightly in return.

'What're we like?' She smiles and I grab a tissue to blow my nose loudly.

'You definitely need to develop a quieter blow. That's atrocious.' Ruby and I both snigger.

Batty Bonnie pokes her head around the door. 'What's going on here, then? Oh good, you two have buried the widget.'

'The widget? Grief, Bonnie, where the hell do you get your sayings from?' Ruby starts to giggle, and it's infectious.

'Did I get that wrong? Oh dear. I'm making a complete spectre of myself today. What? Well, I'm glad you find that funny. But really, I keep making a mess of everything. First, Asha seems to be cross with me, and I have no idea why and second, I've gone and upset Ingrida by mentioning her condition at the table.'

'Her condition?'

'Oh Lor, I'm not supposed to have told you. Cath is right. I really do need to learn how to put a sock in it, although why that is a saying I do not know. I mean who uses socks to shut anyone up… What? Look at you two laughing at me. Ha ha. Oh, I don't know. Come on you pair, Hazel has ordered champagne and this wonderful menu. They want to serve the starters. Oh, and you'll be glad to know there's not a single snail in sight.'

We get up and Ruby and I follow Batty Bonnie into the dining area, arm in arm, injuries forgotten.

27

RUBY

The champagne – ordered in copious amounts by Hazel – is going straight to my head, and I feel wonderful. Monica and I sit together at a circular table accommodating all our group in a large glass-covered dining deck. We are slightly apart from the other tables in a near-private area.

'Hazel must've paid a pretty penny to get this spot,' Bonnie says to Cath.

'And would you just look at Paris lit up now the sun has set? It's a sparkling backdrop for our river cruise. Cheers,' Cath responds, chinking her flute with Bonnie.

'Ingrida, could you possibly translate some of the menu?' Fay holds up the typed sheet as the first course arrives. 'Ingrida? Hello...'

Ingrida, who has been staring out at the night sky through the amazing glass floor-to-ceiling windows, looks startled and asks Fay to repeat her request.

'Oh, *ja*. It say *dégustation*, it mean taste, so a tasting menu. We are to have six courses. *Confit de canard*, that is duck. Salade niçoise is same in English. *Boeuf bourguignon* and *cassoulet*, they are like stew, and also the *coq au vin*, which is chicken.'

'And we all know what chocolate soufflé is. How wonderful.' Fay licks her lips.

Ingrida goes back to looking out of the window and our first course arrives; a small but beautifully presented plate worthy of MasterChef.

As we tuck into the delicious fare, Monica and I catch-up on all the chatter we've missed in the last few weeks. I forget there's anyone else at the table and I almost forget we're on a ship, only glancing out to the sites when others call out or point to a famous attraction.

I congratulate Monica for tackling Arsy-Annabelle. She roars with laughter when I tell her about my work appraisal. We talk about our kids and how they were desperate for us to repair our relationship.

Monica asks me how she should go about telling the twins she and their father are splitting up. 'Do I tell them he's been unfaithful? I mean, they'll still need to have some kind of relationship with him and despite what he's done, I don't want them thrown off course.'

'Difficult one. It's like my dilemma, not wanting to hurt Will with regard to his biological father.'

'What if Vince doesn't agree to an amicable separation?'

'I guess you could threaten to tell Joanne and James about his adultery if he doesn't go quietly? When are you going to have it out with him?'

'Good question. Soon, but the thing is, I don't want

to speak to him at the house. The twins can't be anywhere within earshot…'

'Perhaps you should catch him out?' I suggest. 'Maybe set up a spontaneous encounter under a false name and turn up to confront him?'

Monica's face splits into a wide smile as she playfully punches my arm. 'I am ahead of you there. Although I didn't consider turning up myself…'

'Explain?'

Monica glances at her watch. 'Vince is currently sat in a Birmingham pub about to meet his latest SE date, Venus.'

My eyes widen as Monica explains how she hacked into his account, set up a new profile and hid it from Vince.

'I sent all the messages to my phone and several somewhat questionable dates will be arriving at the Cock and Bull simultaneously in just half an hour. If my phone was not bust I'd show you the profiles for Greta Grinder, Cindy-Just-Cindy – oh and her dog – Titania and finally Bruce with several of his drag artist friends.'

'Frigging brilliant. Where have you been hiding this new Monica? Respect girl.'

We both laugh aloud as Monica describes each of the dates and their messages.

'God, Monica, I take it all back. Don't go on social media, you'd wipe the floor with everyone else. Oh, to be a fly on the wall at the Cock and Bull…'

'Yours is a good idea though, Ruby. For me to turn up and have it out with him. Wish I'd thought of it.'

'You can still do it. Arrange to meet him before he gets home – send him a date request on Spontaneous

Encounters as yourself. It'll then be obvious you've sussed him so he can't squirm out of it. I can look after the twins for you...'

'He's due back the same day as me. I could do with getting home first then intercepting him. I need to work out something,' Monica sighs.

Hazel interrupts our conversation by tapping her spoon to her glass.

'I hope you will indulge me ladies, but I would like to say a few words.'

We all sit back in our chairs and listen.

'I'm so glad we all made it to Paris despite the difficulties that have arisen. It was my dearest wish to see Clarissa's wonderful dance numbers performed in this competition. And now you are through to the finals. Well done all of you. I know Clarissa could not be prouder of you.'

We all smile at one another, although I notice Gnasher-Asha looks rather glum and Ingrida, who sits between Celtic Cath and Frosty Fay, seems to be forcing her smile. Her demeanour is a far cry from her nickname, Happy-To-Be-Here-Ingrida. I guess she's not happy to find she's pregnant. Who'd plan to have a baby on top of three young stepchildren?

Lady C's eyes shine as she looks at Hazel, but there's a slight wobble to her lower lip. No wonder. Monica seems to think Hazel's unlikely to see the year out.

'Today has been quite the day of drama and unfortunate incidents. What with Fay's accident and the attack on Monica, never mind Sheila Bold's exposé on stage.' Hazel raises her eyebrows.

'It reminds me life can be full of drama and unfortunate incidents. But I think we should be careful not to let these moments take on a significance they do not warrant. The peaks and troughs, while providing endless hours of entertainment or trauma, are not the essence of life. Life's treasures are in the more commonplace normality of everyday living. Friendships that endure…'

I glance briefly at Monica, and we smile at each other.

'…A walk in the park. Watching a sunset. Sitting quietly without having to talk. Dancing. A hug. And more dancing.'

There are a few shouts of 'Yes' and 'Dancing forever' before Hazel continues.

'I don't normally take kindly to those who give of their opinions freely and copiously, but if you will allow a woman in the twilight of her life to give a little counsel, I'd be most grateful.'

We all seem to hold our collective breath as Hazel continues and Clarissa's eyes pool.

'A wise person once said to me, don't be afraid to take risks. Life passes far too quickly to play it safe. They added, don't take yourself too seriously. We all need to act the fool on occasion to keep our sanity. I pass on this advice knowing it has stood me in good stead. So, give me a racy rhythm – I am a dancing fool.'

'Right on,' I shout as others clap.

'I will not say much more but now I have reached this… this crossroad – no, I refuse to be sad – I must tell you I've discovered life's greatest treasure is to be at peace with oneself. At peace with who you are and with those you care for. I can honestly say...' Hazel takes a deep breath and Clarissa places her hand on Hazel's arm, which she covers with her own palm.

'I can honestly say I am completely at peace with myself and with my life.' She gives Clarissa a significant look as she smiles and blinks back a tear.

Without looking around the table, I know Hazel's words are touching everyone.

'I've had a truly wonderful life, surrounded by talented and wonderful people. If I did it all over again, I wouldn't change a single thing.'

Tears cascade down Clarissa's face, but she makes no attempt to wipe them away as she tightly holds Hazel's hand.

'So, I would like you to raise your glasses to toast my lifelong companion, my confidante and my closest friend.'

Hazel struggles to stand but with Clarissa's help gets to her feet as do we all, apart from Fay who is wheelchair bound.

'To the wonderfully talented Clarissa Kirkland.'

'To Clarissa,' we raise our glasses and look at each other. There is not a dry eye among us and a great deal of sniffling and reaching for serviettes and tissues.

'And to Hazel,' Bonnie adds.

'Hear, hear,' Clarissa helps Hazel back into her chair.

'Clarissa and Hazel,' we all shout, sip our champagne then dab at our eyes as we smile self-consciously at each other.

Hazel gives a little cough to get our attention again.

'Finally, I would like to say life really is too short to hold onto resentments and anger. I say we let Bold as

Brass perform in the finals on the proviso it's made clear it's Clarissa's choreography.'

Gnasher-Asha mutters and Frosty Fay frowns. It's clear they have mixed feelings about this proposition.

'As long as they don't put in the same stark ending as today,' I laugh.

'Or should that be starkers?' Bonnie quips.

We all smile, and I'm relieved the sombre mood starts to lighten.

'Well I for one am sorry I missed the Bold as Brass performance,' Hazel grins. 'Ladies, for your final dance tomorrow, I won't say break a leg. That didn't turn out too well the last time it was uttered…'

We giggle and look to Fay who is smiling good-naturedly back at Hazel.

'But I will wish you well as they do here in France, *bonne chance. Bonne chance* to you all.'

We toast another glass and collapse back into our chairs.

'Wow. What a tearjerker.'

'I'm emotionally drained,' Monica admits. 'I also need to order a coffee. After all that champagne, I think I can see double of the Paris skyline.'

'That's just the reflection in the ship windows. But I know what you mean. I'll go and order us some.'

'Thanks, Ruby.'

I walk to the bar suddenly realising I haven't checked my phone all evening. I retrieve it from my bag. Two missed calls. Max? I hurriedly go to the missed call log. They're not from Max but Will. I frown.

I dial Will's number but can't get a signal to call back. I hope he's all right. I realise, a little guiltily, I haven't checked in with him since this morning when I sent a message from the hotel.

'Excuse me, does the boat have Wi-Fi?'

The barman, who has had his back to me wiping down the bar surface, turns around and I realise he's Swastika-man. He glares at me, grunts and walks purposefully away from the bar muttering some obscenities in French. He's not going to serve me. Bastard.

A waiter rushes past placing empty glasses and a half bottle of red wine on the bar surface next to me. When he's gone, I gently and deliberately tip the bottle onto its side, so red wine leaks all over the bar and drips onto the floor before I brush my hands and walk away.

Up yours.

I return to the table to find coffee pots are being delivered by a waitress.

Monica pours us both a large, steaming cupful and Fay taps her cup with a teaspoon.

'Not another speech,' I mutter to Monica. 'I'm not sure I can cope with any more.'

Fay, her voice taut – and for some reason sounding alarmingly like that of the late queen – begins, 'On behalf of us all I would like to express our enormous gratitude to Clarissa and Hazel for this wonderful meal.'

We start to clap. I whisper in Monica's ear, 'Her Royal Highness, Queen Frosty,' but Fay hushes our applause with her hand and continues in earnest.

'The river cruise, and wonderful food and drink is well

above and beyond anything we had been expecting...'

Hazel is looking embarrassed and wags a finger to indicate Fay should stop.

'...and I hardly need remind you Hazel's extraordinary munificence in paying for us all to drink genuine French champagne...'

'Fay, thank you, but please, no more. You're all most welcome.'

Fay, with just a hint of an indignant frown, peters out. Her displeasure is short-lived as we all clap heartily and Bonnie shouts, 'Well said, Fay.'

'Absolutely. Thank you, Hazel.'

'Yes, thank you.'

'It was very nice meal.'

'Hear, hear.'

Our boat will be mooring again soon, and Monica and I take our coffees out onto the deck to look at the Eiffel Tower – all lit up – looming large.

'It's magical, is it not?'

I lift my phone above my head and point it in all directions. 'No flaming reception.'

'Checking if Max has called?'

'Yes. And no, he hasn't. Damn. I've missed two calls from Will too.'

'I would lend you my phone, but it is as dead as a dodo. Besides...'

'...there's no flaming reception,' we say together.

'Grrr. This is infuriating. I mean we're in the middle of Paris for God's sake.'

'*Mesdames et messieurs, nous sommes arrivés.*' The

announcement prompts us to return to the dining room for our jackets so when the ship moors, we are ready to disembark.

'Hazel has got the captain to order two large taxis to take us back to our hotels. They're to be minivans that will fit in wheelchairs,' Cath tells us.

This is a big relief; no one fancies navigating the Paris transport system at this time of night. We thank Hazel and I push her out to wait on the deck.

Every few seconds, I check my screen to see if I have any 'Gs'. I look at the pedestrians strolling along the riverside. If only I could conjure up Max standing there waiting for me, contrite and eager to talk. Dream on, Ruby.

The boat docks and I ready myself to push Hazel along the gangplank. I balance the phone with one hand on the edge of the chair, glancing at the screen to see if any bars appear.

Monica goes in front to steady our descent and as I start to manoeuvre the chair over the small lip, someone barges into me from behind and my phone slips from between my hand and the chair and drops down into the river.

'No!' I screech as the handset hits the murky water, frothing and churning with the motion from the boat's engine. It instantly disappears below the surface.

I turn to see who crashed into me just in time to see the smirking face of Swastika-man before he retreats into the boat.

'Oh, Ruby. Your phone.' Monica, one hand on Hazel's wheelchair arm, leans over the gangplank and shakes her head. 'It's gone. What happened?'

'That shit of a deckhand deliberately barged into me.' I turn to go and give him a piece of my mind, but there are fifty or more passengers pressing into us to move forward and get off the boat. How the hell am I going to contact Will or Max now?

'You bastard!' I shout.

'Ruby, have a little decorum please.' Clarissa is right behind me. 'You are representing Dance Excellence with Clarissa Kirkland.' She points to the insignia on my top. 'It is most unfortunate about your mobile phone, but I am sure that man only bumped into you due to the motion of the boat.'

'Oh, for crying out loud, Clarissa, he did it deliberately the little...' My expletive is drowned by the ship's horn.

Passengers start to complain and shout '*Dépêchez-vous*' and '*Allez*'.

I have no choice but to clamp my mouth shut and push Hazel forward.

'Oh, Ruby.' Monica puts her arm around me as I look despondently into the now still river water. 'That's both of us without phones now.'

*

Even by taxi it takes almost an hour to get back to our hotel. We see distant fireworks going off in the Paris night sky.

'Must be some kind of celebration. It is too early for Bastille Day. That is not until July,' Fay remarks.

We watch the display from the taxi windows and lapse into a sleepy silence until Cath, in her beautiful lilting Irish voice begins to sing about Roman candles burning in the night. Those of us who know the Ash song, 'Shining Light', join in quietly one by one and as we finish the song the emotion is palpable. I don't know who everyone else is thinking about, but when I think about the light in my life, I can't get Max's face out of my head.

We're all knackered when we finally get back to our room having found the Smut Hotel lift was still broken but eventually locating a service elevator for Fay in her wheelchair. Fay is almost faint with relief to get to a bathroom where Ingrida offers to help her.

I feel like someone has cut off my arm without my phone. I keep going to check it forgetting it's gone. Asha lets me borrow hers and I try to call Will, but it goes to answer phone. In the end, I have to leave a message.

Will, I'm sorry I missed your calls. I hope you're OK. We were on a boat without Wi-Fi or a decent reception. Anyhow, now my phone's at the bottom of the River Seine – long story – and Monica's phone is smashed, so can you send me a message on this number? This is Asha's phone and if you need to speak to me, ring here. But even if you don't need to speak to me, send a message anyway. I just need to know you're OK. Love you.

I hand Asha her phone back. She gives me a smile having heard the voicemail.

'I can leave my phone on overnight in case your son calls.'

'Thanks, Asha.' She doesn't look well, and I wonder if the food has disagreed with her. I also vaguely wonder what's up between Asha and Ingrida as there's definitely a bit of an edge between them. I guess tempers fray when you're with others twenty-four-seven.

I think about Max. It would be tempting to call him from Asha's phone, but I can't for the life of me remember his number. Anyway, I expect he is on a flight home. I wonder if he got my voicemail? I guess if he can't be bothered to let me explain, he isn't worth bothering with. Probably just as well he hasn't become a permanent fixture. I just need to get over this stupid prevailing sense of loss…

We're all settled in our beds quickly, and I toss and turn to the sounds of Bonnie's snoring before falling into a fitful sleep.

Stark images bombard me; I'm drowning in churning water. The face of the vile deckhand is gloating above the water line as I sink. A phone is ringing. It's just out of reach and I can't get to it. I end up awake and unable to sleep for hours. As a distraction to the awful nightmare, I force my thoughts into planning my new dating business in fine detail, determined to write it all down in the morning.

28

INGRIDA

Dear God, I am... what is English word for *niknās*? Ah yes, furious. I am furious with Asha who let Bonnie and Cath think it is me with the positive pregnant test. I am also furious with Neil. He has not called. Not once. And I need to warn him about Kazimieras. *Please God, get Neil to call me and please give me strength and take away my worry, anger and pain.* I pause and try to remember how it is Reverend Prudence ends her prayers. Ah yes, *please guide my ways. Paldies Dievam.*

I say this prayer when I am in the toilets on the boat. I hear someone enter the ladies and Asha calls, 'Ingrida, are you there? I need to speak to you.'

I do not reply.

'Ingrida?'

I stay silent and after a few minutes the outer door closes. I will speak with Asha soon but not now. God, he tell me, 'Speak to Asha tomorrow.'

My phone buzzes and I see Neil has sent me a message – *Paldies Dievam* – and I hurry to open it.

Ingrida, sorry I didn't get a chance to call today. I will try to call tomorrow, but it's full on with the children. You know how it is. Hope you're enjoying your dancing. Grace, Theo and Lizzy send their love XXXX

I want to send message back saying, why have you not told Maya's parents we are married? And why do *you* not send me your love? But I can see Neil has put four kisses, not three. I am in confusion and cannot find words to reply so I put my phone away.

I try my best to enjoy the boat meal, especially as it did not cost any money because Hazel kindly pay. Although I am sitting with all the dance ladies, I do not feel part of the conversation. So, I sip the champagne, which is very good, eat the excellent food and look at the lights of Paris as others chat.

Ruby and Monica, they are leaning into each other and laugh loudly on and off. I do not understand how they are friends again if Ruby has been sleeping with Monica's husband, unless Asha has told us wrong. Ruby, she has not speak to me since our dance performance.

I sit next to Fay but she spend the evening talking with Hazel and they speak in quiet voices and do not include me. Once I hear Fay say something about hatching some wonderful plan, but I have no idea what this mean.

I think I drink a little too much champagne and when Hazel makes her speech, I find myself close to crying.

Fay, she turn to me after the speeches and she say to me, 'Well, Hazel has certainly given us food for thought.'

I smile at her, repeating her words in my head. 'I like this idea, Fay. Food to fatten up thoughts…'

'Interestingly enough, the idiom originates from the French revolution when people started to reject traditional beliefs with a fresh diet of ideas. It began the era of reason.'

'A French phrase for meal in Paris with French food.'

'Precisely. And both a delicious meal and a delicious phrase.' Fay hiccups.

'How is your leg?'

'I think I have possibly anaesthetised the pain. Hic.' Fay raises her flute before draining the last drop of her champagne. 'But thank you for asking, Ingrida. You are a kind soul.'

At the hotel, I help Fay to change in the bathroom and she sits on the toilet seat to brush her teeth. Her leg is swollen so I slightly loosen the Velcro of her airboot.

'You need to rest your leg on a few pillows tonight, to raise it high. Fay, did the hospital give you injections for the thinning of the blood?'

'What? Oh… I can get those when we get home.'

'They did not give you Heparin or similar medicine?'

'Ingrida, it will be fine. They are only a precautionary measure.'

'Is very important you have this medicine. It is anticoagulant.'

'Quite… is it not splendid we are in the finals? I shall miss dancing with you all…'

I know Fay, she deliberately change the subject and I suddenly feel very tired. I rub my eyes and a sigh, it escape my mouth.

Fay looks at me with questions in her eyes. 'Ingrida, I could see you were not your usual self tonight. And I could not help overhearing Bonnie refer to your condition. Do you mind me asking, are you expecting?'

'*Ne*. I am not. I am not pregnant.'

'Oh dear, another of Bonnie's gaffes. What then? I am a very good listener.'

I sit on the side of the bath and my worries bubble to the surface.

'I will never be pregnant. I have cancer when I was younger.'

'How terrible. But you now have three lovely stepchildren?'

'*Ja*, but Neil, he does not tell Rita and Terry we are married.'

'Maya's parents?'

'*Ja*. And now my uncle, Kazimieras, he is not a nice man, he is in the United Kingdom, and he say I must give him money but I do not have any and...' I start to speak quickly as my troubles, they pour out and only when I finish do I realise I have been saying the words in half-English and half-Latvian.

Fay nods her head and I think she is comprehension what I say.

'So, you are going to meet this Kazimieras next week?'

'*Ja*.'

'I can come with you if you like? If you need some moral support.'

I look at the big hospital boot on Fay's leg and I think of her in a wheelchair next to me when I meet Kazimieras.

Then I think of his huge muscles and how he make many threats. It is a very big contrast and the thought of it brings a smile to my face.

'You are very kind, Fay. But I will not need help. My uncle, I will not let him frighten me.'

'Well, please just let me know. I need to repay you for your first-rate assistance since my fall.'

'It help just to speak my worries out loud and for you to listen, so thank you.'

'Well, they say a trouble shared is a trouble halved.'

I am not sure this is a good saying as my troubles are still big, but I give Fay a quick hug before helping her into bed.

I do not think I will sleep, even after a prayer, but it is big surprise to find I do not wake until morning and most of the other ladies are already up and quietly getting dressed. I take my phone from under my pillow. There are no further messages. I think it will be best to have long talk with Neil when I get home.

'*Labrit,* Ingrida,' Bonnie and Cath say to me. 'Fay said this is Latvian for good morning.'

'*Ja. Labrit.*'

I help Fay with getting washed up and dressed. When she is ready, she ask me to wheel her into the corridor outside our room so she can make a private call. She seem to be very excited. This surprises me as she is not able to dance with us and has to face a long journey back to the United Kingdom with a broken leg. But I do not ask her why she is so happy.

Cath, she produce a little kettle from her case and is

making for us cups of tea as she sings a song I do not know about liking a nice cup of tea in the morning.

We dress and brush our hair as we drink the not so nice tea from the plastic cups Bonnie find in her case.

'I can't believe you brought long-life milk and sugar too, Bonnie and Cath. It's like having our own Mary Poppins on board with all the stuff in your cases.' Ruby laughs as she puts on her underwear.

'Nurse Ingrida,' Ruby shouts to me. 'Any advice on my leg? Just look at this.'

I look to Ruby's leg. There is large bruise starting to grow on her shin.

'Is it hurt?'

'Yes, it's dead sore, but I'm hoping I will be OK to dance.'

'It maybe hurt more to dance but dance will not make bruise any worse. How is your hand, Monica?'

Monica shows me her hand. 'It is still a bit swollen, but it feels better than yesterday.' She flexes and extends her fingers.

'As long as you can still do jazz reaches, Monica,' Ruby imitates Clarissa's voice. 'After all, the dance must be your top priority.'

We all smile and I listen to all the ladies chatter as I finish dressing.

'It's driving me mad having no phone,' Ruby moans. 'I've tried calling Will on Asha's mobile but not had a single message back. I've left him three voicemails now but at least I know he is OK. I rang my dad to check on him and to tell him I don't have a phone. He said Will was right as rain as far as he knew. He had no idea why Will had called me. I guess it could just be pocket dials – typical teenager – so there's no point worrying.'

'Where are we going to have breakfast?' Bonnie asks in a loud voice. 'Hopefully not that dreadful café we went to yesterday. My croissant was flaccid.'

'Bonnie, whatever can you mean?' Cath laughs out loud.

I smile. As a nurse, I know this word.

'Well, it was.'

'What? Limp and lifeless?' Ruby asks with a wink.

'Wait a minute, do I mean flaccid? No, what's the word I'm looking for?'

'To be sure I think you mean rancid,' Cath pushes Bonnie with her hand and Bonnie gives a big roar of laughing.

Fay knocks on the bedroom door and I wheel her back in.

Cath then asks Fay how much we owe Monica, and I listen with much care.

Fay gets out her notebook and lists many things – return train fares from Manchester to London, London to Paris, travel cards, snacks… It is a very long list. She finally gets to the end and says, 'So, with everything all told we will each owe Monica four hundred and ninety pounds and eighty-seven pence. Of course, we will need to add on anything else we put on her card between now and getting home.'

I am shocked. This is much more money than I realise. Where will I find this? I am not holding onto much hope

Janine will give us our money back. In fact, I think she will not have this anymore. Perhaps Monica will let me pay her back a little every week?

'There's no rush.' Monica smiles and Ruby nudges her in the ribs.

'I will give you a cheque, if that is OK, Monica?' Fay says.

'As long as you don't want cash.' Bonnie grins.

'Bonnie's husband doesn't let her deal with cash. Not after what happened,' Cath adds.

'Oh, don't remind me.' Bonnie throw her hands into air and they start to giggle.

'Come on, spill the beans.' Ruby's eyes twinkle.

'I still don't feel it was my fault.'

Cath laughs loudly, and it is what Fay would call an infectious laugh as it makes us laugh too.

'Well, how was I supposed to know Clyde had sold his car and put the money in a plain brown envelope? He didn't tell me.'

I see Ruby turn to Monica, her eyebrows high. She say, *Clyde?* in silent way and she and Monica snort with laughing. I am not sure what is funny.

'I put my letters on top of the plain brown envelope and naturally I posted them all at the earliest opportunity – not realising this envelope contained cash. Oh dear, Clyde didn't think it was funny. He had to wait four hours by the postbox until it was emptied and even then, he had to go to the post office with the postie to sign declarations and whatnots before they allowed him to have the money back. I mean, I can laugh now, but at the time it wasn't at all funny.'

Fay asks how much money was in envelope.

'Oh, I think it was about eight thousand pounds.'

'Oh my God, Bonnie.' Ruby makes big hands in air. 'You posted eight thousand pounds of Clyde's cash in an unmarked envelope in a letter box? What're you like?'

'Well, at least he got it back. I never got my engagement ring back.'

'You posted that too?' Monica shakes her head as she giggles.

'Oh, not deliberately. It was a few years before, when we were on holiday. The ring was a bit loose, and it must have happened when I pushed a postcard into the gap of this yellow postbox. I didn't realise until later in the day. The ring must have come off in there. It cost a fortune to replace.'

I touch my ring. It is very tight. I will have to get it cut off when I go to work.

Asha also puts her hand to her big engagement ring. She looks very tired. Perhaps she did not sleep well? She goes towards the bathroom.

'I can't believe you and your hubby are called Bonnie and Clyde.' Ruby makes a big laugh and I think I will ask Fay to explain later.

Cath sings a song about Bonnie and Clyde I have not heard before.

'Oh, now that is deliberate,' Bonnie say. 'I hated my name. I mean, who wants to be called Betty for goodness' sake? So, a friend suggested I became Bonnie when Clyde and I got together. We've made lots of friends on our holidays over the years as soon as we introduce ourselves. Turns out to be a marvellous way to break the ice...'

From the corner of my eye, I see Asha at the bathroom door. She waves for me to come over. I take a deep breath. Now is right time.

When I am inside, she closes the door.

'Ingrida, I am sorry about yesterday.'

I do not say anything and shrug.

'I was a bit in shock. I had not expected to be... well, expecting.'

When I say nothing, she continues.

'And I have not told Jay and I am not sure what we will do and I just cannot have these women knowing about this.' She point to her stomach. 'Especially as they will be at my wedding. I know I can trust you, Ingrida. And I am sorry Cath and Bonnie got the wrong end of the stick yesterday. But I did not actually tell them you were pregnant, they just assumed that... Look, all I am saying is please do not say anything to them.'

'Asha, I will not tell them about you. But I will not lie and say I am expectant with baby.' I look Asha in her eyes. 'It is not possible for me to lie about this. Hazel and Clarissa, they already know I cannot have children. I have cancer many years ago and I no longer have womb. This is not secret. It is fact.'

'Oh, Ingrida, I... I did not know. I am so sorry.' Asha drains of colour and before I can say it is OK and she was not to know this, she rushes to the toilet and wretches. She waves a hand behind her back for me to go and I turn and leave the bathroom.

I think to myself, I will not lie to Rita and Terry either. If Neil does not tell them we are married, then I will.

'Ladies,' Fay calls for our attention. 'Wonderful news; Hazel is sending the same taxi for us this morning. We are to have breakfast with her and Clarissa at their lovely hotel. What a treat. And I have to tell you we have come up with an excellent solution to my incapacitation for our dance entry.'

We all look at each other with surprise.

'Does it depend on a miraculous healing of your leg?' Cath starts to sing, 'I believe in miracles…'

'Most amusing, Cath. No, it does not, but I can say no more until we are at the hotel.'

Bonnie gets a message on her phone and suddenly flaps her hand in the air. She shouts, 'Oh my goodness. Ladies, listen to this. I've just had a text from Maureen, Janine's old neighbour. She was watching the *North West Tonight* programme last night and suddenly saw her old house. You're not going to believe this, but the report said police had to break into Janine's property to remove the dead body of a fifty-seven-year-old woman…'

'What?'

'Said it had been there for a week or more. Apparently, the police had called on what was said to be an unrelated matter and discovered the body.'

'Oh my God.'

'Frigging hell.'

'Maureen said a young woman was being held for questioning, but they were not looking for anyone else connected with the investigation.'

'So, the dead person must be Janine's mother?'

'That's terrible.'

'*Ja*, poor Janine. I know what it is like to lose a mother.'

'What a state she must have been in if her mother had died, and she couldn't tell anyone.' Monica shakes her head.

'How terrible to be in a house with a dead body all that time,' Asha says, stepping out of the bathroom. She puts a hand up to her mouth and swallows hard.

'Really, ladies,' Fay says with a cross voice. 'We cannot know exactly what has happened. I mean, for all we know, the poor woman could have been murdered by Janine. Well, do not look at me like that. It *is* a possibility. All that is clear is Janine is not the person we thought she was. She has embezzled our funds and now it is clear that something most untoward has occurred in her house. I am sure we will find out more on our return, but I do not think it is helpful to speculate. I also do not think it is a good idea to relay this information to Clarissa or Hazel yet. They do not need additional worries when they are trying to enjoy what could be a final weekend away together. I am sure we will learn the truth of the matter soon enough. I suspect it will mean trouble for our claims against Janine, but at the end of the day, all that matters for now is our dancing.'

Everyone start to talk quietly about Janine. Cath, she sing in a soft voice from a song from *Les Misérables* about how at the end of the day there'd be nothing but trouble. But she does not smile.

Fay drums her fingers on the arms of her wheelchair and calls out, 'Come along. Less of the tittle-tattle. The taxi will be outside. Now, can someone help me get to the service lift? I fear the regular one is still out of order.'

I hear Ruby whisper, 'Yes Miss,' and she winks at me.

I think Fay should not try to sound like a teacher. It rubs people the wrong way up, but I help her and take her down in the lift.

'Are you feeling any better Ingrida?' she ask me.

'A little. I want to go home to speak to Neil and stop my uncle causing trouble. Also, I am missing the children.'

'Of course, you are. Now take stock, my dear. Rise above your concerns. These finals are of the utmost importance to Clarissa and Hazel. You must put aside your worries and dance the best you can. You were wonderful in the "Dancin' Fool" number yesterday. You can do it again. It would be marvellous to get a trophy and beat Sheila's dreadful group.'

I nod. I know Fay is right. I make a promise in my head, I will make Clarissa and Hazel proud.

29

FAY

My leg aches, my back aches and my head is very sore where I hit it on the stage floor yesterday. However, I am determined not to complain. The last thing these ladies need is a Moaning Minnie in their group. I take a few more paracetamol, sipping the water from a small bottle in my bag, as we are driven through Paris in our taxi.

Sleeping with this ridiculously large airboot on my leg proved almost impossible. I was unable to turn over or stretch out. However, I must have drifted off for a short duration as I awoke in the early hours needing the bathroom. It was then I almost made the most dreadful mistake of putting my weight on my bad leg before I remembered my injury. Ingrida had kindly left my wheelchair next to the bed, brake on, so I was able to slide myself into the chair and quietly push myself backwards across the room using my good leg. Every move is more complicated than I had appreciated and needs thinking through thoroughly. I managed to hop from the chair to the toilet, but as I looked up the chair slowly slid away from me on the uneven floor. I had forgotten to put the brake back on. Once I had flushed, I was reluctant to hop to the chair, now on the other side of the room, in case I overbalanced. I began to wonder what on earth I should do. It was an enormous relief to hear Cath's whispered voice at the door.

'Fay, are you OK?'

I called her in and she kindly helped me back into my chair, assisting me to the bidet – I could not reach the high sink – to wash my hands. She then helped me back to bed, and I was most grateful.

Ingrida was in the bed next to me in a fitful sleep. Now and then she would mutter and give a little moan. Poor Ingrida. Apart from the issues with her husband, this Kazimieras – her uncle – sounds an absolute thug. I looked up the translation for the Latvian '*Iebiedēt*' and '*Mafijas*', the words I remembered her saying before I went to bed. They mean intimidate and Mafia. After all Ingrida has done for me, I find myself feeling most protective towards her.

We all press our faces up against the taxi windows as we arrive at *Le Pavillon de La Reine*, Clarissa and Hazel's four-star hotel. Set back from *Place des Vosges* – which my guidebook describes as the most beautiful square in the world – the seventeenth-century building is magnificent, bedecked in flowers and foliage.

'Oh, my goodness. Would you just look at this place.' Bonnie gives a whistle.

'Stunning.' Asha steps outside and breathes deeply. She

looks a little off colour. Perhaps she had motion sickness in the taxi?

'I walked here yesterday. It's beautiful.' Monica admires the distinctive frontage.

'What a contrast to our smutty dive of a hotel.' Ruby shakes her head.

I grit my teeth and decide not to take umbrage. Ruby cannot know how difficult it was for me to find a hotel in Paris capable of accommodating all of us and within our price bracket. I would like to have seen her sort out a better hotel in the time.

Our group walks into the courtyard, Ingrida pushing me in my wheelchair.

We all stop to take in the fabulous building, which is awash with greenery.

'I bet it costs a pretty penny to stay here,' Cath remarks.

'It is very beautiful.' Ingrida sighs. 'And very romantic. I would like come to hotel like this for honeymoon.'

'Did you not have a honeymoon?' Monica asks.

'No but Neil, he say maybe we will go one day…'

Ingrida pushes me away from Monica toward the hotel entrance a little quicker than I would have perhaps liked. I hold tightly onto the arms of the chair.

I hurriedly remind the ladies not to say a word about Janine and the latest turn in events.

The hotel lobby is quite a contrast to the wonderful classical exterior. It is furnished with plush, contemporary furniture on a deep-pile purple carpet that sweeps up the vertical front of the reception desk. A little modern for my taste.

Ruby and Monica walk arm in arm and sink into two of the chairs. They are back to being as thick as thieves. I fleetingly wonder what hotchpotch Bonnie would make of this saying. Oh dear, the woman is a walking disaster. I cannot for the life of me imagine being so careless with a large sum of money. And why on earth would any couple want to be named after violent bank robbers? Even so, Bonnie is pleasant enough. Indeed, my accident seems to have brought out the best in everyone in our group. I find myself warming to them all – well perhaps not Asha, who has turned rather sullen and quiet – and I rather wish we were not returning home tomorrow, especially now I have made contact with Edith.

We wait at the hotel reception while Asha enquires about our arranged breakfast.

Ruby and Monica exchange words and burst out laughing. I am beginning to get sorely tired of Ruby's loud cackle. They really should keep it down now we are in this superior hotel. We are representing Clarissa now.

'*Par ici s'il vous plaît.*' The concierge leads us down a corridor.

Ingrida pushes my chair forward and I give a little shiver of excitement. I cannot wait to tell the ladies of the solution Hazel and I dreamt up yesterday. We have been exchanging secret texts all morning after devising our plan over dinner on the cruise ship. When I sent my proposition by text message, I had held my breath, but to my delight I had an immediate and positive response. A follow-up call put the arrangements in place, and I cannot wait to inform the ladies.

We are taken to a private hotel dining room where

Hazel is already seated. The smell of freshly baked bread and percolated coffee fills the air. We all take a seat around the single large table. Well, all apart from Asha who dashes from the room. *Rather rude*, I think to myself. She did not even say hello to Hazel first, but I expect she needed the ladies urgently. She does at least thank Hazel when she eventually returns to the dining room.

'Please help yourselves to breakfast, ladies.' Hazel throws an arm out to indicate the large array of food on offer on the buffet table. 'Clarissa will be with us shortly.'

'This looks amazing.' Bonnie takes a plate to help herself.

'And not a flaccid croissant in sight.' Cath winks.

I do wish they would keep their voices down. If Hazel has heard them, she does not react, and she indicates for Ingrida to manoeuvre my wheelchair next to her seat.

'What can I get you, Fay?' Ingrida asks.

'Oh, perhaps a continental selection? Croissants, cold meats, cheeses… Oh and if they have olives… and those French pastries look very tasty…'

There is a wonderfully congenial atmosphere in the room as the ladies help themselves to the generous buffet.

'Yum, look at these.' Cath and Bonnie point to some Cruller donuts. 'And what are those? Radishes with butter and salt. Is that a thing?'

'I'm trying everything. We need to build-up our strength for our dance.' Cath loads her plate.

'Ingrida, I'm glad to see you have two plates. You need to eat plenty.' Bonnie curves her hand over her stomach as she smiles.

Ingrida replies sharply, 'This is for Fay.'

'Is that all you're having, Asha? A single croissant...' Before Bonnie can say more, Cath pulls her away and steers her to the table.

Waiters pour us coffee and fresh orange juice and if it were not for the ache in my leg, I would be feeling on top form, especially with the news I have in store for our group.

When we have all finished eating, Hazel prompts me to make the announcement.

'Ahem. You will all know I am unable to dance today, which poses a problem for the "Dancin' Fool" routine.'

'Hey. We could incorporate the wheelchair into the dance. It would add to the comedy of the performance.' Ruby nudges Monica.

'That would take entirely new choreography, Ruby.' Clarissa's voice comes from the open door. 'But dancing with wheelchairs is not unheard of. You will remember *Strictly* had a wheelchair dancer in one of their shows. However, that is not what we will be doing.'

Ruby winks at Monica as Clarissa continues. I do not think Clarissa realises almost every utterance from Ruby's mouth is a joke or chide. I must say I preferred it when Monica and Ruby were not speaking. Ruby's constant patter – now she is back to her usual self – is grating on me.

'No, Hazel and Fay have come up with a much better solution. Ladies, please meet Edith, Fay's daughter.'

Clarissa stands aside and ushers Edith into the room. The majority of the ladies look from Edith to me with surprised expressions.

'Hi again.' Edith, who is dressed in dance leggings, a black T-shirt and jazz shoes, looks a little self-conscious as everyone waves a hand to her.

'Edith has kindly agreed to perform in Fay's place,' Clarissa continues. 'We have just run through the routine several times in the hotel gym, and I have to say Edith has picked up the dance with incredible speed.'

Edith dips her eyes and fidgets with her hands.

Clarissa continues, 'We will need to rehearse together so Edith can dance in situ with the group. To this end, I am pleased to say we have been given additional rehearsal time on the main stage in recompense for Fay's unfortunate accident yesterday. I hardly need tell you, Edith is a magnificent dancer – a tour de force – and we are incredibly lucky to have her.'

Edith lingers by the door a little awkwardly and I am relieved when Cath stands and crosses to shake Edith's hand.

'Welcome. How did you pick up the dance in just a few run-throughs? It took us months to learn it.'

'Edith is a natural dancer with a memory for pattern. She assimilated the steps with ease. She could be a professional dancer,' Clarissa responds.

Edith blushes and Cath takes her arm to lead her to the table.

I beam, unable to hide my delight.

'I hope you don't mind me joining you,' Edith sounds a little shy as she addresses everyone. 'I just love the routine. It is such a contrast to the numbers my group normally dances. I'm honoured to be allowed to dance with you.'

'The honour is all ours,' Asha signs 'thank you' with her fingers to her chin. 'Your "Fix You" performance was outstanding.'

'That's kind of you to say. Thankfully, we are doing that later in the finals show. I had to check the programme before agreeing to come and try out "Dancin' Fool". You know, give me time to change costume and get into a different frame of mind.'

I hang onto Edith's every word, delighted with the reception she has been afforded by the others.

Clarissa goes to the breakfast table to help herself to some food and Ruby and Monica stand to greet Edith across our table.

'Edith, I'm Ruby. Welcome to the DICKs,' Ruby laughs as she points to the insignia on her top.

Edith peers at the badge and then giggles.

'It is supposed to read D-E-C-K. Dance Excellence – Clarissa Kirkland,' I quickly interject. Trust Ruby to lower the tone.

'Yes, welcome. I'm Monica.' Monica and the others introduce themselves to her.

'Please don't be upset if I don't remember all your names, but I'm delighted to meet you. I can't wait to dance with you. I loved your costumes too.'

'Oh dear.' I look at Edith's trim figure. 'I fear my outfit may be rather large on you, Edith. I am a couple of sizes bigger than you, I am sure.'

'I can sort that.' Monica smiles. 'I knew there had to be a reason for bringing my sewing kit and at least you are both a similar height.'

Edith is invited to get some breakfast, and I sit back and listen as she tells them about herself. She answers much more readily than if I had asked and I am able to glean a little more about her life.

I learn she and one of the male dancers in her group, Peter, are a couple and *Corps et Ame* performs in bars on the French Riviera for tourists.

'How exciting. I would love to visit the South of France. And Monaco particularly,' Asha says.

'We performed in Monaco once. In fact, we learnt afterwards that the Prince of Monaco was in attendance, although I am glad we didn't know it at the time. I might have been overcome with nerves.'

I find I am holding my breath in anticipation of Edith's responses and I force myself to relax and savour her answers.

'I bet it gets a bit tiring to perform in public on a daily basis,' Ruby comments. 'I mean, I love dancing, but every single night? Just one day of this competition has knackered me.'

Edith smiles, despite Ruby's crude remark.

'It can get tiring dancing night-in-night-out, and there's no guarantee we will have bookings every week so it can be a bit hand to mouth. But I'm hoping there may be an opportunity here in Paris.'

I sit up straighter to hear more.

'Ooh. That sounds exciting,' Bonnie nods enthusiastically. 'Go on.'

'Well, since dancing in the heats we've been approached by a professional dance company in Paris with a view to joining them.'

'Wowzers.' Bonnie claps her hands. 'How marvellous.'

'This is very good news. You must be very happy,' Ingrida adds.

'The director's coming to watch us today in the finals. To be honest with you, that did influence my decision about doing the "Dancin' Fool" routine with you. The contrast will hopefully show my versatility. And of course, I just love Clarissa's choreography.'

Clarissa beams at Edith and I cannot help saying, 'Dancing with a professional Paris dance company. It is like a dream come true.'

Edith gives me a strange look but smiles all the same.

When the breakfast plates have been cleared, we take coffee in the hotel lounge and I manage to speak to Edith by myself.

'It really is very good of you to help us out, Edith.'

'My pleasure. I am sorry about your leg. How is it?'

'Sore, but they warned me there would be a lot of bruising on the site of the injury. I am supposed to get my crutches later today, but I am not keen on using them. I do not want to fall over and do myself a worse injury. Plus, they are charging a small fortune – I would have to buy them outright – and the insurance may not cover this cost. So, I plan to only use a wheelchair until I can weight-bear. I have to return this one to the theatre but Hazel has arranged to purchase for me a folding chair – here in Paris – that I can use on the journey home. It is being delivered to the *Opéra Bastille* this morning.'

'Very generous of Hazel.'

'Indeed. She wants to donate it to St Ann's Hospice when I no longer require it.'

Edith studies me for a few minutes. 'It's had an amazing effect on you.'

'What, the broken leg?'

'No, being with these lovely women in Clarissa's group.'

'Yes, I wish I had found it sooner.'

'Me too.'

There is a short and awkward silence between us.

'How is Bethan?'

'She's good. She's living in Melbourne with her partner.'

'The one she was travelling with? I have forgotten his name.'

'No, a different one. And he is a she.'

'A she? Oh.' I do not know what to say.

'She's called Emma.'

'Right.'

Edith scans my face, and I am quite sure my reaction will dictate her opinion of me, so I fight to find the right words.

'Is she happy?'

'Very. She's selling real estate over there. Bethan and Emma have just purchased a fantastic place outside Melbourne close to the sea. I hope to go and visit next year.'

'I am told Australia is wonderful. Erm… Edith, I would love to contact Bethan. Perhaps you would ask her if I could have her phone number or email address?'

'Yes, I will.'

'Thank you. And Edith, thank you so much for dancing in my place. It means a great deal to me.'

'No problem.'

Hazel retires to her hotel room to save her energy for the finals show and Ingrida pushes me the short distance back to the theatre. Returning to the *Opéra Bastille*, I watch Edith chat with Ruby and Monica, realising it is a long time since I heard her laugh so heartily.

My new folding wheelchair has been delivered to the theatre and I sit in it to one side of the stalls in the main auditorium when rehearsals are underway.

The space is immense. I realise I would have been quite daunted to dance in front of such a large audience. Tickets to the final have been sold to theatre and dance schools across Paris. We are told the theatre will be almost half full. Just over a thousand people. Extraordinary.

Our ladies run through the "Dancin' Fool" routine several times. They repeat sections when required and also incorporate Ingrida's impromptu change from yesterday as part of the sequence. They are not in costume, but they use the bright bowler hats as props.

Edith is magnificent. She is a natural dancer, and I can see she is having a positive effect on the others, who all up their performance in an attempt to match hers.

Clarissa is on stage with them, giving instructions and sharpening up the moves. From here I can see precisely what she wants as she issues her instructions.

'Bonnie, arms higher and fingers wide...'

'Ingrida, exaggerate those shoulder rolls more. This is large theatre, and we must magnify each movement.'

'Ruby, keep low on those three-step-turns... down into the ground, jazz-style.'

'Monica, can you demonstrate the lyrical sequence to the others? Please pay attention to Monica's arms and how she finishes every move which melts into the next…'

'Splendid Edith, you have a wonderful stage presence…'

They are part-way through a full run-through when the music is suddenly cut and a male voice over the speaker says, *'Pardon. Excusez l'interruption.* Clarissa Kirkland, is it possible for you to come to the stalls for to be in a meeting, *tout de suite? Merci.'*

Clarissa leaves the stage – where the ladies continue – and ends up standing next to me.

She leans in to tell me, 'This will be about Bold as Brass. I am glad you are here, Fay… Ah, Frédéric.' Clarissa steps forward to greet the French organiser who, a giant of a man, emerges from the closest theatre entrance.

He folds her tiny hand inside his huge ones as he beams at her. *'Bonjour,* Clarissa. *Merveilleux de vous voir, ma belle dame.'*

He kisses the back of her hand but Clarissa's wide smile freezes on her face as Sheila then emerges from behind Frédéric. She stands next to him and folds her arms tightly across her chest.

'Clarissa.'

'Sheila.'

'Mesdames, we must talk about the forthcoming show together.' Frédéric ushers Clarissa and Sheila into the seats in front of me. They leave an empty seat between them and Frédéric moves to the row forward of theirs and kneels on the chair to face them. His large frame only just squeezes into the chair, but he covers his grimace with a smile.

'Clarissa, *félicitations. Votre chorégraphie est fantastique...* Sorry, I am saying...'

'Yes, I understand, Frédéric. Thank you. But we are here to discuss the Bold as Brass rendition of "Roxanne" and I can assure you it is entirely my choreography that they have used.'

'Not all of it,' Sheila objects.

'Every last step and I can prove it.' Clarissa holds up her phone.

'Indeed,' I echo from behind the group, keeping perfectly still as I know full well we do not have the clip Monica had promised now her phone is smashed.

Frédéric indicates for Clarissa to continue but thankfully Sheila, shuffling awkwardly in her chair flicks her hand in the air and says, 'Fine. It is Clarissa's dance, but I have enhanced it with our costumes and dramatic interpretation...'

Clarissa starts to object, but Frédéric turns to her and opens his hands. 'The dance, it is yours, Clarissa. It will be announced it is yours. You will get the fullest accolade for this wonderful number.'

Clarissa pauses, as though deep in thought before adding, 'I would not normally agree to such a proposition. It is, after all, dance plagiarism.'

Sheila tuts loudly, but Frédéric throws her a warning look before continuing.

'I must inform you, Clarissa, we have many, many more people coming to watch the show tonight. Indeed, we are *épuisés*... that is, sold out. Yes, *c'est vrai*. Every seat has been sold overnight. Any idea why? Clarissa, they want to see your "Roxanne" dance.'

'I do not understand.' Clarissa glances back at me and I shrug.

'The final section of the dance, it was on the French television last night. The clip has gone viral on the internet…'

'Bold as Brass are properly famous…' Sheila starts.

'Infamous,' I mutter under my breath.

Frédéric flaps his hands to shush Sheila and appeals directly to Clarissa.

'Now the theatre, it is full to capacity and they all want to see your incredible routine…'

'I do not for a minute think it was my choreography that caused this public interest.' Clarissa glares at Sheila, but before Sheila can retort, Frédéric quiets her with a finger to his lips before turning to Clarissa.

'It will be the largest audience ever in the history of the Expression competition. And Clarissa, you know what they say, there is no such thing as bad publicity. Indeed, this could be the making of the Expression show. Think of the press interest, the exposure…'

I bite my tongue.

'…our dance competition could finally hit the big time: *un succès retentissant!*'

'Yes, well, I can see that.'

Frédéric holds his breath as Clarissa rubs her forehead.

'Very well. Providing I am acknowledged as the choreographer for "Roxanne", Sheila's group may perform it later today.'

Frédéric reaches forward and clasps Clarissa's hands. 'Excellent. Thank you, Clarissa.' He turns to Sheila and nods at her expectantly.

Sheila picks at her nails, shrugs and mumbles, 'Right. Ta. I must get going.' She gives Frédéric what I can only describe as an unashamedly insincere smile and leaves the auditorium.

'Well, she could have apologised at the very least,' I say.

'Sheila does not know the meaning of the word apology.' Clarissa shakes her head.

Frédéric stands, rubbing his squeezed thighs. 'Regrettably, it is too late to change the programme, but we will ensure it is announced that "Roxanne" is your dance.'

'Thank you, Frédéric.'

Frédéric then approaches me and – much to my surprise – drops down into a crouch position to address me. 'Fay, how is your leg?'

'Thank you for asking. As good as can be expected.'

'The press, they would like to interview you, Fay.'

'Why on earth would they want to do that?'

'You know, about your unfortunate accident...'

'I hardly think that is headline news.'

'And the wonderful coincidence of discovering your daughter, Judith...'

'Edith.'

'Edith. That she is in the same competition...'

'I beg your pardon?'

'It makes a wonderful story, how you say *une histoire réconfortante*? A comfort to the heart? You know, your long-lost daughter reunited with her mother and how she... a *sauvé la journée* by dancing for her *maman* in the final of the competition...'

'No. Absolutely not. I will not have my private life

bandied about by the gutter press. And gutter press they must be if their interest has only been prompted by pornographic images of Sheila and her dancers.' I turn to Clarissa to appeal to her, but her eyes are focussed on the stage and the rehearsal.

'But Fay,' Frédéric opens his huge hands to plead with me. 'It will be additional publicity. And I understand a well-known director is coming to the finals to watch Judith…'

'Edith.'

'*Oui*… Edith, your daughter, with a view to recruiting her to a Paris theatre. It would reflect well on her; do you not think? Her magnanimous act to save Clarissa's dance, yes? Perhaps you could be interviewed together?'

I find myself speechless and Frédéric rises, pats my shoulders and leaves, presumably under the impression I will comply, which I most certainly will not. I rub my forehead. I have a bad feeling in my bones – from my head to my broken ankle – about all this press interest.

30

ASHA

I am finally alone. I stand and stare at myself in the mirror of the dressing room and run a hand over my flat stomach. How long before it will start to show? I know most pregnant women caress their bumps affectionately, but I cannot imagine doing this. It feels like there is an alien inside me. How dare it implant itself in there, making me sick and threatening to take over my whole life. I then think what a terrible person I must be to react in this way – Rashmi was over the moon when she first got pregnant. I slump into a chair.

At least I am alone. Sheila Bold's group has – thankfully – moved to a different dressing room. With several groups knocked out of the competition, a few rooms became empty, and the organisers felt it best to move Bold as Brass, giving our group some much-needed peace, let alone space.

Clarissa told us to take a well-earned break before the finals show this evening and all the other women have left the theatre. We have the whole afternoon to ourselves, and I would have loved to go sightseeing, but I feel so sick. Here I am in one of the most famous capital cities and I end up being stuck in this theatre dressing room.

Fay has gone back with Clarissa to her hotel to have a lie down. She had dark circles under her eyes; I think her injury is taking its toll on her.

Cath and Bonnie have gone sightseeing, using their travel passes. It would not surprise me if they got lost, but they always seem to land on their feet whatever happens to them. Cath would call it the luck of the Irish and heaven knows what Bonnie would call it.

Ruby and Monica have gone out and said they would look for a cheap phone. I think they could see I was beginning to get a bit annoyed with them using my phone every five minutes. I am sorry theirs are broken or lost, but it is a bit of a cheek to use mine all the time. They could have used anyone's phone in the group, but somehow mine was the only one they requested… Oh dear, Jay would tell me I am being bad-tempered. I have to speak to him. I look at his messages on my mobile. He is wondering why I have not got back to him.

I go to select his number but quickly stop as Ingrida enters the dressing room.

'Ingrida, I thought you had gone out with the others?'

'*Ne*. How are you feeling?'

'Pretty sick. It is not so bad when I am sitting down.'

'I think it is good idea to eat little and often. I nurse pregnant ladies in hospital and they say this advice to me. I buy you these.'

Ingrida hands me a bag of plain crisps and a bottle of sparkling water.

'Thank you.' I realise I am a little faint after only a small breakfast and the exertion of our rehearsal. I sip the water and nibble on the crisps. The effect is immediate as my feelings of nausea are quelled.

'Have you told Jay?'

I shake my head. I do not think Ingrida would understand my negative feelings, knowing how much she loves her stepchildren and being unable to have her own baby.

'I am going to phone him now.'

Ingrida pats my arm and suggests we go for a walk into Paris when I am ready.

'I think fresh air will do you good, *ja?* I will wait in theatre café.'

I smile at her gratefully and when she has left the dressing room, I take a deep breath and video-call Jay.

'Ash. I was beginning to get worried about you. How's Paris and how are you, my darling?'

'Jay, I need to talk to you...'

'What's wrong? You look worried.'

'I have been unwell. Feeling sick and under the weather.'

'Have you seen a doctor?'

'No, I know what the matter is...'

'Well, tell me.'

'Jay, I am...'

'You're not going to say pregnant?' He laughs and I stay silent.

'Ash?'

'Yes. I am pregnant.'

It is his turn to go quiet, and he stares back at me.

'I know. I cannot take it in either...'

'Are you sure?'

'Yes. Quite sure. I took a test. It said I am already three to four weeks.'

'Three to four weeks. Oh, my word.'

I can see him doing a calculation in his head.

'It will be full term at the end of the year. Jay, what are we going to do?'

'What are we going to do? I guess we're going to become parents.'

'Jay, be serious. I thought you did not want children, well not yet.'

'I am being serious. I mean, I never said I didn't want any, and I always thought we would end up with children one day... Ash this is big... I mean huge. Just think, our child is growing inside of you.'

'You mean, you do not mind?'

'Well, we could have got the timing a bit better, but – oh wow – I am going to be a father.'

'But our wedding? Our travel plans? I mean I probably will not be showing for the ceremony, but our big trip away, travelling the world?'

Jay chews his lip and then looks at me, his eyes shining. 'Wait, we don't need to change anything.'

'What?'

'We can travel for three, maybe four months, come home to have the baby and then take the child with us to complete our trip.'

'That sounds crazy.'

'No, it'll be the perfect time. It'll be easier while the baby is tiny and not mobile. No extra airfares and you'll be paid maternity leave for the trip rather than taking an unpaid sabbatical. More money for us to spend on nice baby-friendly hotels.'

'I suppose that could work… but Jay, slow down. I am not sure I am ready to be a mother. I feel like my body has been invaded, and the sickness is terrible.'

'You *have* been invaded. By a tiny creation made from our love. I hope it's a girl. She will be as beautiful as you and dance just like you.'

'And what if I want a little boy who will look just like you – but with my teeth, obviously…'

'Obviously.'

'…and be as positive as you no matter what bad news comes their way, well what then?'

'Boy or girl, I don't mind. And anyway, it could be twins. One of each.' Jay laughs and I wag my finger at him.

'Do not even dare suggest that. Getting used to having one baby will be enough for now.'

I feel nauseous again, so sip more water and nibble another crisp.

'What are you eating?'

'Crisps, for the sickness… Jay, you realise I am going to get big and fat.'

'No, you won't. You'll be swollen with our baby, not fat. And you'll be as beautiful then as you are now.'

'But look at Rashmi.'

'Your sister never took care of herself. She's not like you. You'll be a very yummy mummy!'

I think of Monica. She is stunningly beautiful and trim despite having twins. Jay is right. Just because I am pregnant, I do not need to let myself go. I am not Rashmi.

'You'll be a wonderful mother, Ash. And I reckon I'll be a terrific father. I can't wait to see you. I love you.'

'I love you, too. Now do not go saying anything to Ma and Baba or anyone else for that matter. I need time… and we should not tell anyone before the wedding anyway…'

'My lips are sealed. Good luck in the finals too, or should I say break a…'

'No! Do not say that.'

I tell him all about Fay's accident and Sheila Bold and the competition. And I also tell him about Janine.

'That was her house? I saw it on the news – there was a dead body in there. Awful. Has anyone contacted her to see what's happened?'

'No, I don't think anyone has messaged her since she left our chat group the day we travelled. Perhaps I should send her a text? I am the closest in age to her in the group and I would love to know what is going on.'

'Yes, perhaps you should. Although she may not reply, given she stole your Paris money.'

'And possibly all our lottery money, too. But we cannot know that for sure.'

By the time Jay and I say our goodbyes, I feel infused with his positivity.

I look down at my stomach. Will I make a good mother? It seems a ridiculous thought. Me, a mother. But I realise I am slowly warming to the idea.

ASHA

I write a short text to Janine, choosing my words carefully.

Janine, are you OK? We have heard your house was on the news. Has your mother passed away? If so, we all send our condolences.

I start to type.

We do not know what happened with the Paris money, perhaps you can explain?

But on reflection, it does not seem right to include this when her mother has most probably died, so I delete this line and instead write,

We want to know if you are OK. If you want to talk, you can call me anytime. Asha.

I grab my things and find Ingrida in the café.

'You look much better, Asha.'

'I feel much better. I have sent Janine a text asking about her mother.'

'*Ja*, I send one to her yesterday. I hope she is OK. Ready for Paris? The theatre receptionist, she give me good tips for us to see many top sites in one afternoon.'

'Lead the way, Ingrida.'

'First, we catch a bus to the *Place de la Concorde*. It is only a short distance. Then we can walk through the *Jardin des Tuileries*. It is public gardens and there is no entrance fee.'

'That sounds lovely. And plenty of fresh air.'

'From there it is a thirty to forty-minute walk up the *Champs-Élysées* to the *Arc de Triomphe*.'

'*Très bien*, Paris here we come, and I shall buy you a French pastry for being my personal tour guide, and... well and for all that upset I caused.' I scan Ingrida's face for annoyance but find none there.

She slips her arm inside mine and within half an hour we are ambling through the many walkways of the Tuileries gardens in the spring sunshine. Cherry trees, full of blossom, sway in a gentle breeze and we admire the bright spring tulips that fill the formal flower beds and frame the stone frontage of the *Tuileries Palace*.

By nibbling tiny amounts of crisp and sipping small mouthfuls of sparkling water every time nausea threatens, I manage the whole afternoon without vomiting once. Ingrida dubs it her salt and sparkle therapy.

'You should tell everyone about it.' I pat her hand. 'It is like a miracle cure.'

Everywhere we go my eyes are drawn to parents pushing babies in prams, tiny children held in slings and pregnant women. While Ingrida gives me a potted history of Paris.

'The *Tuileries Palace*, it was built by Catherine de' Medici...'

I find myself scanning the expectant mothers, thinking, *will I be that big?* Or *there is a nice maternity outfit*, or *what a cute baby*. I am sure Ingrida notices my focus, but she does not mention my condition. I find myself completely relaxing in her company.

Ingrida tells me about her life in Latvia before she moved to the UK. She tells me about her cancer and hysterectomy at such a young age. And about her nursing job and her horrid Uncle Kazimieras. I tell her about my family and my annoying sister, Rashmi. And I talk about my dentistry training and how I moved in with Jay and our future travel plans.

We take the Metro from *Charles de Gaulle* station to *Sacré Cœur* and climb the steps to the massive white cathedral before sitting at the top to take in the views over Paris.

'Look at that. You can see how all the Paris streets are laid out, and over there, the Eiffel Tower. You get a real sense of the scale of it from here.'

'I love to look at the rooftops. When I live here, this place it was my favourite place to come and sit and think.'

'Why did you leave Paris?'

'My uncle, he follow me here. So, I disappear. He did not know I went to United Kingdom, not until recently. He is a bad person… but I know God, he will protect me and my family.'

'You must have a strong faith, Ingrida?'

'*Ja*. And you?'

'I guess it is always there in the background, but I do not really think about it much.'

We are quiet as we take in the expanse of Paris in front of us and I decide to risk asking about Neil.

'How is it being married?'

'*Ja*, it is good. And Neil, he is a good man… why you laugh?'

'His surname – Goodman.'

Ingrida's face splits into a smile. '*Ja*, it is good name for him. Is very funny. But I am worried he does not want other people to know we are married. This weekend he was to say to Rita and Terry, Maya's parents but he has not. I call on my phone and Rita think I am still just nanny.'

'What did Neil say?'

'He not speak with me yet.'

'Well, call him.'

'He say he will call me.'

'Blow that. If Jay or I want to speak to each other, we call there and then. It does not matter what we are doing, we always prioritise calls to one another. You should get in the habit of doing the same with Neil.'

'This is good idea. It would be good habit to make, to talk whenever he or I feel this need. I like this.'

'So, call him…'

'I will. As soon as we are back in the theatre when we have Wi-Fi. I…' Ingrida pulls at her tight wedding ring and does not make eye contact. 'Asha, can I ask you something?'

'Sure.'

'You and Jay, do you tell each other everything? I mean, do you have secrets? I mean, from each other?'

'Absolutely not. It nearly killed me to hold back telling him I am pregnant for just one day. We tell each other everything. How about you and Neil?'

Ingrida shrugs and before I can reach over to touch her arm, she gets to her feet and heads towards the cathedral entrance. I want to ask her more, but the moment is gone.

'Come and see inside the basilica.'

We enter the church, and all eyes are immediately drawn to the ceiling above the altar. The first sight of the incredible mosaic of the risen Christ takes my breath away.

'It is beautiful, *ja*?' Ingrida whispers. 'One of the largest ceiling mosaics in the world.'

We walk about the vast interior, our eyes fixed on the mosaic and the central dome as we take in the Roman-Byzantine architecture in complete silence.

The church has a calming effect on us both and before we leave, Ingrida turns to me to say, 'I will be only minute.' She kneels before the bronze altar and closes her eyes, and her lips move in silent prayer.

When she rises, I ask, 'Praying for something?'

'*Ne*. Just praising God.'

We leave the church and I give a little smile when I find my hand has subconsciously moved protectively to my stomach as we descend the many steps of *Montmartre*. We take the Metro back to *Notre Dame* and slowly walk back to the theatre where we head for the café.

'Did you see there was a film crew setting up outside? Wonder what that is about. Come on, Ingrida, I will buy you something to eat. I can't believe we have seen so much of Paris and spent practically nothing.'

'*Ja*, the receptionist, she tell me all the free places and it seem good idea to use our Metro passes as we already have them.'

I buy us each a light snack to set us up for dancing and remind her to call Neil. 'You can call from here and I can go back to the dressing room.'

'*Ne*, if you do not mind, I would like you to listen to call and listen to what Neil say. I can put it on speaker. I do not want to make any mistake with the English.'

'Well, only if you are sure?'

Ingrida nods and dials Neil's number.

'Hiya.' The voice is that of a small child.

'Grace, is that you?'

'Guy-da.'

'Hello, my lovely girl. How are you?'

'Guy-da, when are you coming home?'

'Tomorrow, sweetie. Where is your daddy?'

'He's downstairs. Nanna was cross with me and sent me to my room. I was very sad, so Theo came up with daddy's phone. Daddy told him to tell me I could play some games.'

'Grace, why your nanna cross with you?'

'I told the big secret to Nanna and Gramps.'

'What big secret?'

'That Daddy put Great-Granny's gold ring on your finger.'

'Oh, that big secret.' Ingrida looks at me wide-eyed.

'What did Nanna say when you tell her this?'

'She said a very rude word, so I told her it was a very naughty word and she sent me to my... my...' Grace bursts into tears.

'Grace, it is OK. Do not cry. I am here. Shh.'

My hormones must be playing havoc as I find myself filling up, listening to Ingrida try to comfort the little girl.

'I don't like Nanna. She is mean,' Grace stutters out with sobs. 'She said I was lying... that I was a naughty girl.'

Ingrida grips the phone so the whites of her knuckles show, but her tone is calm and soothing.

'Grace. Listen to Guy-da. Nanna, she not mean to say those things. She was upset. She miss your mummy very much. You are a very good girl and you have not done wrong thing. Tomorrow, I will give you big hug when I am home.'

'Guy-da?'

'Yes?'

'I love you.'

'I love you too, Grace,' Ingrida puts a finger to her lip and then to the phone even though the child cannot see her. They say goodbye and Ingrida looks directly at me.

'Well?'

'Well, they must know now.'

She slowly nods her head.

'I mean, that is good is it not?' I ask her. 'Neil will be forced to tell them you are now married, right?'

'Yes, he will have to tell full truth. It is better it is out in the open but I do not think they will be very happy.'

'Is it really his grandmother's ring?'

'*Ja.*' Ingrida touches the ring fixed tightly on her finger.

'It is too tight Ingrida, and anyway you should have your own ring. When you get back, you must tell Neil to get a new ring for you. This is a symbol of your marriage, not his grandmother's.'

'You are right.' Ingrida snaps her phone away decisively.

I look past Ingrida to see a large number of people entering the theatre.

'People are starting to arrive,' I say. 'There are lots of

them. We had better go and get changed… Wait. That man, is it not Ruby's boyfriend, Max?'

Ingrida looks to where I am pointing and nods.

Max is pulling a small suitcase along as he scans the faces of those in the café. When he spots us, he waves and comes across.

'Hi, have you seen Ruby?'

'She and Monica, they go out for afternoon,' Ingrida replies.

'She's out with Monica?'

'*Ja*. They are best friends.'

Max scratches his head. 'I've been trying to call her mobile, but it says it's unobtainable.' Max's eyebrows are furrowed, and he looks incredibly tense.

'She drop phone into River Seine.'

'She did what?'

'Not deliberately,' I interject. 'Ruby wanted to call you from my phone, but she could not remember your number.'

Max's features soften.

'You come to watch final show?' Ingrida smiles. 'We are doing "Dancin' Fool".'

'No, I mean I'd love to watch, but I have a late flight home tonight and I need to set off for the airport in a while.'

'Well, the show starts in just over an hour and we are first on the programme,' I explain.

'Right. So, Ruby should be back soon?'

'She may already be in the dressing room. We have not gone down there yet.'

'If she is, can you tell her I'm here.'

'Sure. Nice to meet you again, Max. Come on Ingrida, we need to get ready to be Dancing Fools.'

31

MONICA

Ruby and I have a wonderful afternoon in Paris. The sun is shining and after a stroll around some of the key exhibits in the Louvre, we head for the river, and I use Vince's credit card to pay for us to go to the top of the Eiffel Tower to take in the views.

'Is it just me, or is this tower wobbling?' Ruby grips the handrail tightly.

'I guess it moves in the breeze. Wait, are you scared of heights?'

'No. Well maybe a little.'

'And you let me bring you up here? Mad woman. Besides, I didn't think Ruby Anderson was scared of anything.'

'Hey, the only thing that really scares me is the thought of Will staying a teenager forever.' She laughs but then folds her arms and adds, 'Or never forgiving me when he finds out about his biological father.'

'You're going to tell him, right?'

'Yes, but no matter how many times I rehearse it, it all comes out wrong.' Ruby puts on a sugary voice. 'Darling, you were a moment of passion, a freak sperm and an impossible egg... Nah. Or, Will, the truth is, your birth father and I had a quick fling, but he wanted nothing to do with you, and besides it turned out he was a dirty rotten cheat, anyway.'

'Ouch.'

'Or, I had a load to drink on my thirtieth birthday and ended up pregnant. Best birthday present ever...'

'That's better.'

'But when he asks if Dev knows about him...'

'You have to say yes. But he has to know Dev chose not to be involved.'

'How hurt will that make him feel?'

'You're just going to have to steel yourself for it, but Ruby you've been a great mum and Will knows that, deep down. I expect Joanne will be histrionic and James will go ballistic when they find out I'm divorcing their father, but I'm banking on them eventually realising it's for the best.'

'Will you tell them he's a cheat?'

'I've thought about that. If I'm honest, the adultery was just the final straw. We were never happily married; forced into it by my mother. We almost split up, but then I found I was pregnant with the twins. It worked out when they were little, but since they started school, he and I have been living separate lives. Anyone who saw us together – yes, barely anyone – must wonder how we lasted this long. I need to speak to him away from the twins and maybe he'll agree to an amicable separation on the proviso we don't tell them about the *coup de grâce*.'

'Ooh. Get you with your French. Swotting up in case you see the lovely Jean-Claude again?'

'Nothing could be further from my mind...'

'Monica Thornton, you damn well know he'll be coming to watch you later. OK, go quiet on me. Hey, talking of dates I wonder how Vince got on last night. You do realise he'll know you set him up when he finds your mobile number on the dummy profile?'

'I guess. It wouldn't take the brain of Britain to discover who hacked his account. He may well have tried to call me, but I've resolved to only to speak to him face-to-face. Turns out it was meant to be – my phone getting smashed.'

'I'd love to know if Max has tried to get me.' Ruby's eyes glaze over before she snaps out of it and smiles. 'Damn it. Why did he have to be so cute. Come on, let's get back to *terra firma*. My stomach's flipping every time I look down.'

The smell of freshly made crêpes greets us at the base of the Eiffel Tower and we buy a portion each from the kiosk. The River Seine sparkles in the April light as we walk along the banks, biting into the hot pancakes and licking our fingers as chocolate drips over our hands.

'You won't continue to work with Arsy-Annabelle, will you?'

'I've been thinking about that. Jean-Claude started his business from scratch, so there's no reason I can't do the same. Besides I can launch it with my festival wedding dress – after all it was my creation – and Annabelle can't claim any different.'

'Go, Monica. We have to think up a name for your bridal wear. How about Drop-Dead Dresses? Monica's Marriage Moulds?'

'Mould? Not a good word in the same sentence as marriage.' I laugh. 'Well unless you're referring to my marriage. Groan.'

'Hey, Fabulous Frocks to Get Hitched In, or Get Saddled in Style…'

'Saddled?'

'Now you're being picky.'

We cross the river and traverse the large square of *Place de Concorde* to slowly walk through the *Jardin des Tuileries*, admiring the foliage and breathing in the warm Paris air. A wedding party is having photographs in front of the box hedges beside the palace, and we stop to admire the outfits.

'Got it. How about Wed-in-Style by Monica? You could weave the W of Wed into the M of Monica as your logo?'

'Now you're talking. I can visualise that. Wed-in-Style by Monica. Maybe I should employ you as my media consultant?'

'Hey, I'm going to be too busy setting up my new online dating agency.'

'You're going to do it, then?'

'I'm not going to be outdone by my best mate.'

'And what will you call this new agency?'

'Let me think, Core Connections? Date or Dump…'

'No.'

'How about Pick-and-kiss? Or Insta-men?'

'Terrible. Maybe something with the word match?'

'Match... MatchFix. I like that.'

I can't bring myself to say it sounds like a site for those wanting to fiddle the football results and let Ruby bubble on about how her site will be uniquely different to anything currently out there.

'It'll be a real opportunity to get to know someone before meeting up in person. I may even discourage photos until the third or fourth communication. You know how some people only go by looks... Hey, lookey over here...'

The scent of exotic perfume along with a swanky shop front forces us to divert to a fashionable perfumery outside the gardens where we try out some of the latest brands.

'This smells divine.' Ruby liberally sprays some *Yves Saint Laurent* on her wrists and breathes it in. 'Blow the expense, I'm going to get a teeny bottle.'

'Good idea. I need a new scent, something that fits my new business persona.'

Ruby looks at the brand name of the bottle I've picked and whistles. 'Jeepers! That costs a fortune.'

I wave the credit card and wink. Ruby gives my arm a light punch.

Strolling back towards the theatre, our conversation drifts back to Vince when Ruby spots an internet café.

'Monica, let's grab a cuppa and you can use the computer to go on the Spontaneous Encounters site and set up a meeting with him. There's a calendar section of the app where you can put in details, and it'll come up on his mobile.'

'I thought about that but unfortunately I won't be able

to intercept him before he gets home tomorrow. Our train out of Paris is not until lunchtime. He'll be home long before me. If only I could get back tonight, I could have it out with him while the twins are in school during the day. I can't bear the thought of stewing over it for another week or more...'

'We could see if there're any flights home after the show.'

'Good idea.'

Ruby searches the internet as we sip our coffees. 'No. Nothing. There's a late flight to Manchester but it's fully booked.'

'Oh well, it was worth a try. My turn.' We swap seats and load the SE site.

'That's a surprise. I can still access it.'

'Maybe he hasn't figured out you set up the dummy profile?'

I scroll through his account. 'He has shut the Butch profile down. Perhaps he thinks he was hacked and doesn't realise I did it?'

'What an idiot not to change his access password.'

'Ruby, look. He has cleared all the dating history on his other profiles. Not a single date record...'

'Trying to cover his tracks, the shit. I bet he panicked after yesterday. And I guess he still may not have twigged it was you.'

'And look, he's emptied his message box... Wait. There's an unopened message in the inbox from Venus. It's only just come in.' I click on the envelope icon.

Ruby peers eagerly over my shoulder and reads aloud.

'Well Clint, or should I call you Butch? I was going to report you for multi-dating without permission – a category one offence – but as it happens, I ended up having a blast with the guys from the Friends of Dorothy Show and I'm glad I left you to it with those three women and that horrid little dog. I hope your bite heals but it is no more than you deserve, you greedy cowboy. Next time you want a one-to-one I may consider it – you're kinda cute – but if you're looking for the same kind of showdown, don't howdy me. Laters.'

Ruby laughs. 'That pooch had the right idea. What, Monica – why the frown?'

'I was sure he'd find out. I mean, I was banking on it. I want him to know it was me. I want it crystal clear that I know everything, and this is the end of our marriage.'

'You need to send him a message. I can't think how you can do this from his profile… Hey, what if I log on as Scarlet and you send your message from there?'

'Do it.'

Within a few minutes, I have devised my message.

Vince. This is not Scarlet. This is me, Monica, and I know everything. I will make myself very clear. It is over. You will pack up and leave. We will talk arrangements away from the children as soon as possible.

I press send.

'There, done. Are you all right Ruby.' I watch her jump to her feet.

'Frigging hell, look at the time? We're dancing soon.'

'Damn. Come on, we can warm-up by sprinting to the *Opéra Bastille*.'

We race along the dual carriageway leading to the theatre. As we approach the circular steps, we see large crowds gathering outside and spilling down the road.

'Are all these people coming to watch the show?' I shout to Ruby as we slow from our run.

The place is heaving with large groups making their way up to the entrance where a long queue has formed.

'What're they doing here?' Ruby starts to push her way through as she points to a number of camera crews outside the foyer.

'*Excusez-moi*. Pardon…'

A technician diverts us to sidestep a reporter who is giving a live bulletin about the Expression show. Ruby and I raise our eyebrows at each other.

'What the hell's going on?' Ruby mutters as we finally push past the film crews to get inside the theatre.

I glance at the clock, 'Ruby, we're so late. When are we dancing?'

'No idea. Quick, grab one of those programmes and let's leg it to the dressing room.'

I squeeze through a few groups queuing for tickets, the foyer abuzz with chatter and laughter, and manage to grab a programme from a small stand. When I flick it open, my stomach drops.

'Oh no. Ruby, "Dancin' Fool" is the first number. We're opening the show.'

'Shit. We only have twenty minutes.'

We exchange a panicked look and sprint to the backstage door, weaving our way through the throng.

'They're here.' Cath screams as we fly into the dressing room. 'Now that's what I call cutting it fine. We'd given you up for lost.'

'Thank goodness you are back. I was about to text Clarissa to tell her we would not be able to go on.' Asha gives a loud sigh before sipping from a bottle of water and nibbling on a crisp.

She shouldn't eat so close to dancing, but I'm too busy rushing to get out of my clothes to say anything.

All the other women are changed and ready in their white pin-striped trousers and waistcoats, including Edith who is wearing Fay's outfit – thank heavens I altered it before we left the theatre earlier. They're all stage-ready with full make-up.

My heart thumps as Ruby and I race to get ready. 'Sorry, sorry...'

I see Ingrida wave a finger to get Asha's attention before pointing to Ruby. Asha puts a finger to her lips and mouths, 'Not now.'

No idea what that's about but I kick my shoes off as Ruby yanks at her top, saying, 'We lost track of time.'

'It is OK. You are here now, *ja*? Breathe slow and stay calm.'

'Have you seen all the press interest in the show?' Ruby asks breathlessly as she rips off her clothing.

'*Ja*.'

'The place is swarming with reporters. What's going on?

'They are trying to catch a glimpse of Sheila Bold's women,' Asha shakes her head.

'What?'

'Yes, Bold as Brass have shot to fame,' Bonnie says as she puts on another layer of lipstick. 'Or rather, their rear ends have. Earlier they did a photo shoot outside the theatre entrance. Cath and I watched them. Very cheeky it was too. Apparently, their costume malfunction featured on the main French news last night – their exposed flesh pixelated – and its gone vinyl.'

'Viral, Bonnie, you daft eejit.'

'That's what I said.'

'You're kidding me?' Ruby shakes her head. 'Must've been a slow news day to show Sheila's arse on French TV.'

Edith giggles.

'Frédéric, the Expression manager, he is over moon – Clarissa tell us.' Ingrida adds. 'Many people buy tickets for show and it is sold out.'

'Grief. That explains the crowds.'

Cath continues, 'Yes, apparently this one incident has achieved more publicity than the combined promotions from all the previous years in the history of Expression.'

'All down to the Bold as Brass mishap? That's so nuts,' I say.

'I know, and now they are saying the British press is also over it like a rash,' Asha adds. 'They got wind of Fay's accident and tried to interview Fay and Edith, and then it would seem they heard about the rivalry between our two dance groups and the alleged plagiarism of Clarissa's

"Roxanne" number. They are going to have a field day with that, I imagine.'

'I don't think my mother is too happy about it.' Edith chews her lip. 'They caught us outside as we arrived. I think Frédéric told them about her fall. Anyway, they started off asking her about her broken leg and how I'm taking her place in the dance, but they then moved onto questions about why we'd been… well, estranged. I said nothing, apart from it being none of their business. I mean, I don't even know how they knew about that. Anyway, Mum… Fay got all tongue-tied and said it was disgraceful – the press trying to poke their noses into a family rift. But the reporter wouldn't let it go and the next minute the interviewer asked about the bad blood between the UK dance groups. I tried to indicate for her to stop, but she was so indignant and in full flow. She ended up saying some very inflammatory statements about the Bold as Brass group. I couldn't stop her…'

'Jeez. Frosty Fay needs to learn when to stick a sock in it.'

I quickly nudge Ruby with my elbow.

'Sorry, Edith… Er, I didn't mean…'

'It's OK. Frosty's a pretty good name for my mother. Although I think you ladies have managed to thaw her out a bit between you.'

'Ladies, look at time. We need to warm-up, *ja*? We are on stage very soon.' Ingrida encourages Asha to lead a hasty warm-up as Ruby and I quickly plaster on our stage make-up.

It is a real honour to be opening the show, but I wish

we had a little longer. I force myself to breathe slowly as I pull back my hair into a low ponytail and put on the bright lipstick.

Ruby and I barely have time to do a few warm-up moves when an organiser arrives at the door and hurries us towards the stage.

'*Dépêchez-vous. Vous êtes les premiéres. Vite.*'

We fast walk behind her down the corridors, bowler hats in our hands.

We stop in the green room and watch the TV screen to listen to Frédéric introducing the finals show in French.

Ingrida translates for us as we take the opportunity to do a few plié squats.

'Frédéric say, he applaud all dancers, teachers and organisers. He say a lot of hard work has gone into show. He also mention the press interest.' Ingrida pauses to listen to more. She starts to giggle, as do the audience. 'He make joke about derrière – it mean behind – he make audience laugh.'

Frédéric's next joke is drowned out by laughter. Ingrida did not catch it but we all smile anyway. He then starts to announce Dancing Excellence Clarissa Kirkland and we catch the words, DECK, DICK and then *zizi*. The audience roar with laughter and clap.

We look to Ingrida for an explanation.

She shrugs. 'He say something I do not comprehension. I do not know this word, *le zizi*, but it make everyone laugh very much.'

Frédéric then says Edith's name and the name of her group, *Corps et Ame*. We all guess *remplacer* means Fay's replacement.

'He say *jambe cassée*. Is broken leg.'

'We get the gist, Ingrida.' Ruby smiles.

In Clarissa's absence I feel duty-bound to fire everyone up and encourage them to do their best. I wave everyone across to me and we form a tight huddle.

'OK, ladies. This is it. The audience should be well in the mood for "Dancin' Fool" after Frédéric's jokes. Let's give this our all. Comedy, smiles, exaggerated moves, and fun. We need to make the biggest fools of ourselves yet, Clarissa-style.'

We have a group hug, and the organiser calls us to go through.

'*Mesdames et Messieurs, Barry Manilow qui chante, "Dancin' Fool" exécutée par DICK… pardon… par DECK.*'

We march onto the stage to loud applause and spread out. I am at the front, centre stage. We place our bowler hats on the floor and all assume our jazz poses.

The house lights dim to blackness. The back-light shines behind us as we are silhouetted. The audience cheers and claps. We hold our positions until they finally settle down.

The track starts. A deep male voice introduces the song with 'Ladies and Gentlemen' and how it's showtime at the Copacabana. Then the spotlights come on and the music starts with loud, fast drumbeats.

The first clash of the cymbals is my cue. I'm in the zone; my focus is on nothing else.

Clash – I move, as does Edith, in a prepared kick and flick so we end in a new jazz position, our hands poised over our hats.

Clash – Ruby and Ingrida click their fingers as they drop their arms, raise one knee and change position directly behind their hats.

Clash – Cath, Bonnie and Asha all do sharp head isolations before pointing to their hats.

Then the trumpets briefly flare.

One Blast. In unison, we all drop. We hold our hats between our fingers and thumbs.

Two Blasts. We take sharp steps lifting the hats in front, elbows wide.

Three Blasts. We lift and lower the hats in staccato moves onto our heads. Our hands are paused on the hat rim, three fingers lifted high. The music then surges as we lean at a jaunty angle, take a hand up and out to the side in a huge sweeping movement and walk around in a full circle.

Barry's words kick in about the band blasting out… and we launch into the fast-all-action routine.

We hit every beat with our bent train-wheel arms. Our hands and fingers form trumpets and trombones. We raise and lower our hats. There is a sharp isolation for every word of the song.

When the rhythm switches to a brief lyrical section, our moves are soft and flowing before the pace charges up again to high-speed jazz.

I'm aware only of us on the stage. We're one cohesive unit, completely in step. Our wide smiles are genuine. This is the best feeling ever.

The instrumental interlude sees us forming a tight group at the front of the stage. We all sharply raise our hands high – fingers wide – and back. Then again, splayed out so we are framed in a circle of open hands. We twist to the side and slide-step on the spot as we look to the wings, then as one we turn our heads to the front.

We turn, sidestep, then lurch away from each other and back and start the crazy walks. Our backs are bent forward, our hands swing high and low, our faces turn to face the audience.

Ingrida, on cue, goes the wrong way and play-acts wide mouth horror before catching us up in double time.

The air between us is charged. By the time we get to the final line about being a dancing fool, we're all crossing through each other, mock speed-running, raising our hats and finally stepping into the frantic Charleston section, hands thrown wide, eyes bright and faces animated with fun. On the final note when Barry shouts 'Yeah.' We all throw our hats high into the air and freeze with our arms raised.

The applause is thunderous. Tears prick the back of my eyes as I take it all in.

We take a short bow, then the instrumental music replays as we pile the hats – one on top of each other – into Ruby's hands and dance off the stage.

Wolf whistles can be heard along with further clapping as we leave the auditorium and green room behind.

Back in the dressing room, we all talk at once.

'It was over too quickly,' I say, panting like the others after the sheer exertion of the dance.

'It went by in a flash.'

'Edith, you were amazing.'

'I loved it. What brilliant fun that was. I need to come down off the ceiling before we do the "Fix You" number.'

'I'm dripping, but so happy.' Ruby high-fives Cath, Bonnie and Ingrida. 'Did you hear that applause?'

'Beat that, Sheila Bold.' Bonnie punches the air with her fist.

'It was very good, *ja?* I think it was best we ever do dance.'

'It was. And now I think we deserve to get ossified.'

'Is that an Irish term?'

'Sloshed to you, Bonnie.'

'Ha ha. You were marvellous, Ingrida, fancy dancing with such high energy in your condition... oops.'

'I do not have condition, Bonnie. You make mistake.'

'Oh, I am so sorry, Ingrida, I must have got the wrong end of the stick... Asha, are you OK? You look a bit pale. Do you need to sit down?'

Asha shakes her head and rushes out in the direction of the toilets.

Bonnie looks at Cath with her eyebrows raised.

Edith strips off her costume and puts on her blue dress ready for her next dance before we all thank her again and she waves goodbye from the door.

'Good luck and stay in touch,' I call to her.

'Will do.'

When our chatter calms, a buzzing noise can be heard. I see it is Asha's phone on the dressing table so, in her absence, I lift it and press the flashing green answer button.

'Hi, Asha's phone – Monica here... Hi Hazel,

everything OK? Yes, thank you. Yes, it was the best we have ever danced it. So glad Clarissa agrees.' I call out to the others, 'Hazel said we moved Clarissa to tears. Who? Oh, Ruby? Yes… really? Yes… OK, I will send her up.'

'Ruby, Hazel said there's someone to see you. He'll meet you in the café if you can go up there now.'

Ruby questions me with her eyes and I give an almost imperceptible nod, smiling when I see the flash of comprehension hit home. She turns and rushes from the dressing room.

32

RUBY

Slow down, Ruby. He may not be here to talk. Quite the opposite. This could be a final goodbye. And if it is, it's his loss.

There is no sign of anyone in the café, so I lean against the bar, my back to the seating area, determined I won't be discovered scanning for his entrance. The staff are busy preparing interval drinks, but one smiles and crosses to serve me. I order a cold drink, staring out of the window at the darkening Paris sky as I wait. There's a band of tension flickering across my forehead.

A familiar voice calls from behind.

'Ruby?'

I swing round. 'Max, you came back.'

'I wanted to speak to you before I left. I'm catching a flight soon. My taxi's on the way.'

I glance down at his suitcase, and my stomach sinks as I force a smile.

'I tried to get you on your phone...'

'Yes, it's…'

'At the bottom of the River Seine, I know.'

'How?'

'Gnasher-Asha. She told me before the start of the show.'

'Asha didn't tell me she'd seen you. Mind, we were dead late getting back and only just got on the stage in time.'

'"Dancin' Fool" was brilliant, by the way. Clarissa snuck me in to watch it. The new dancer was amazing.'

The waitress delivers my drink and I take a sip as we stand, saying nothing.

'Ruby, I… think we should make a date to talk, when you get back.' Max's phone buzzes and he looks at the screen before adding, 'Ah. The taxi's outside.'

'Fine by me. But Max, I can tell you now, I am not apologising for anything that happened before we met. Believe it or not, I don't do lies and deceit either.'

'Right. Sorry, I must have sounded like a right judgemental prick.'

'Just a bit.'

Max grabs the handle of his suitcase and I put my hand on top of his.

'Wait. Are you on the late flight to Manchester?'

'Yes.'

'Max, two things. One, we can talk this over tonight if you're willing? Because, as-it-happens-two… Monica needs to get back to the UK tonight if possible. Could you change your ticket to her name? I mean, that is…'

'You want me to surrender my flight ticket to Monica? Saint Monica who has ignored you for the last two weeks and let me believe you were cheating on me while having an affair with her husband?'

I put my hands on my hips and start to say, 'It's OK, don't bother...' when I see his eyes are twinkling.

I shake my head and gently poke my finger into his chest in mock annoyance. 'Yes. The same Monica who knows it all happened way before you came on the scene and who knows it was a right frigging mistake... the same Monica who, when she spoke to you, wanted to lash out at me... so making her not-quite-so-bloody-saintly...'

'Right. That Monica. Well, good. And yes.'

'You'll give up your ticket?'

'First, I need to check if I can transfer it. If so, I'll have to go to the airport with her, it's so close to the flight. Plus, we'd need to leave now. Ten minutes tops.'

'Really? You'd do that for me... I mean Monica?'

'Well, I'd then need to get home another way.'

'You could use Monica's Eurostar ticket. I'm sure we can pay an admin fee to sign it over to you. I mean, that's if you were OK with spending the night here and travelling back with us tomorrow?'

'Depends... I need to check my diary to see what's on in the morning.'

Max rubs his forehead and scans his phone. He looks up with a shake of his head, then his face splits into a beaming smile as he says, 'OK. Yes, I can return tomorrow, but I have one condition.'

'Name it.'

'We dine out by ourselves to talk and...'

'And?'

'And decide where we're going to spend the night.'

I leap at him and press my lips against his. He kisses me back but has to pull away when his phone rings.

Max speaks to the taxi driver, '*Pouvez-vous attendre quelques minutes, s'il vous plaît? Merci.*' He then points me in the direction of the backstage area. 'Taxi's waiting. Go and get Saint Monica while I check it can be done. Go.'

'Thank you,' I shout as I dash back to the dressing room, unable to wipe the grin off my face.

Monica takes little persuading and we rush round, helping her change, passing her wipes to quickly remove her make-up and hastily packing her suitcase.

'Why are you rushing back again?' Bonnie asks.

'Childcare arrangements,' I say quickly before Monica can speak.

'Yes. I need to get back. Oh no, I've left a good few things at the Charbon.'

'Me too. Ingrida, can you and the others grab our stuff and bring it with you to the train station tomorrow?'

'Where are you off to?' Bonnie asks.

'Ah, that would be telling.' I wink.

'*Ja*. We can bring your things.' Ingrida smiles.

After Max leaves for the airport with Monica, I sit with the other ladies watching the competition finalists on the dressing room screen. We had hoped to sit at the back of the auditorium but the show is now packed to the hilt after all the publicity.

In between the dances, we chat and laugh.

'Are you OK now, Asha.' Bonnie subconsciously pats

her own stomach as Cath nudges her in the ribs.

'Look, you may as well all know.' Asha throws out her hands. 'I am pregnant, but I must swear you all to secrecy. You have to promise you will not breathe a word to anyone. Not until I have told Ma and Baba. It is a good job I am wearing a sari for the wedding as I can wrap it looser so no one can tell. I have a few very traditional relatives who would be most shocked to know I even live with Jay let alone that I am expecting.' Asha is surrounded by empty crisp packets and discarded bottles of sparkling water.

'How exciting and let's hope you've stopped being sick for your wedding.' Bonnie remarks as her phone buzzes. 'Oh look, it's Maureen again. She wants to know what's going on in Paris. Apparently, the competition has made the local news. Yes, really. The report featured Sheila's costume malfunction, Fay's broken leg, and what they called fierce rivalry between Bold as Brass and the DECKs. DECKs? What can they mean? Oh dear, is that what our new name spells? Goodness, it's as well that second letter is an 'e' and not an 'i' or that would spell something much w...'

'Bonnie, what planet are you on?' I shake my head as Bonnie turns back to the text message.

'Anyway, Maureen says she may need my autograph when we get back. Ha ha. How funny. We could be famous.'

'Is there any more news about Janine?' I ask.

Bonnie sends a text to Maureen and reports her immediate reply. 'Nothing on the TV news but Maureen saw an online bulletin that said it was, in fact, Sharon Young, Janine's mother, who had died. Janine has been charged with not reporting a death – is that really a criminal offence? – but she has been allowed home. Poor girl. What can have happened?'

'Well, clearly her mother died.' Cath rolls her eyes to heaven.

'Oh, you know what I mean.'

'I think it is very sad her mother pass away and no one else know,' Ingrida adds.

It is one of the few times Ingrida says anything. She took a call on her phone earlier, taking it into the ladies, and has retreated into herself since.

'Oh look, Bold as Brass are next.' Cath points to the screen.

We all stop to watch as Sheila's women execute the "Roxanne" dance perfectly.

'Damn. They were good,' I comment. 'I always loved that routine. Wonder what the judges thought?'

'I expect the audience will be disappointed there were no costume disasters this time,' Cath adds. 'They must be getting a lot of applause, they're still bowing and waving. Sheila will be lapping this up.'

Asha's phone rings and she answers before handing it over to me. 'Ruby, your son.'

I thank her and take the phone into the corridor as everyone has stopped talking to watch Edith's group perform the "Fix You" routine.

'Hi, Will. How are you? I missed your calls. Everything OK?'

'Yep. Wanted to see if you'd left me money but Grandpa gave me some.'

'And there's me worried you'd had an accident. Did you get my messages?'

'Yep.'

'Has everything been OK with Grandpa staying?'

'Yep.'

'We danced well in the finals. Opened the show.'

'Sweet.'

'You're doing it again.'

'What?'

'Talking in monosyllables.'

'What do you want me to say? The house burnt down? Aliens landed? My biological father turned up to claim his long-lost son...'

My mouth dries up and I start to say, 'Very funny...' but it's a fraction of a second too late and he instantly picks up on the delay.

'Wait. Hello? I was going to say only kidding, but now I'm guessing that's, like, a real possibility? I mean, you said...'

'Will, we can't talk now. When I get back.'

'What... Are you for real, Mum? I mean, are you having some kind of mid-life crisis?'

'What?'

'Well, first you start seeing Max seriously when you've never been serious about any bloke in your life. And then you and Monica fall out, and you rant on about hating your job. Then you chuck your mobile in a river. And now you're going to have a heart-to-heart with me about this anonymous sperm you used...'

I have to smile. I thought my lad lacked intuition but that's clearly not the case.

'You know, Will, maybe I *am* having a mid-life crisis, but underpinning it is wanting the best for you...'

'Not now, Mum, I'm off out with James. Catch ya.'

He hangs up and I smile to myself. He's a good kid, on the whole.

*

At the end of the show, all the dance groups, in full costume, gather on the stage to hear the results. We stand in a large semicircle as we wait. There's a drum roll as Frédéric steps forward and announces each set of winners.

'*Mesdames et messieurs. Les résultats de L'Expression Paris. En troisième place, c'est le groupe,*' – Frédéric leaves a long dramatic pause – 'Bold as Brass *qui a exécuté la danse "Roxanne".*'

There is a loud blast of music – the first bars from the "Roxanne" track – over the speaker. The audience cheer as Sheila leads her group to the front of the stage. They all turn their backs on the audience and give a saucy wiggle of their rear ends – annoyingly to the flashing of cameras and rapturous applause – before accepting a small shield.

We all clap half-heartedly.

Frédéric then puts his hand up in the air and adds, '*Mesdames et messieurs, la chorégraphe de cette danse était Clarissa Kirkland.*' He starts clapping and points to where Clarissa is sitting in the audience next to Hazel and Fay. She gets to her feet and bows graciously.

We all cheer loudly. Sheila grimaces and gives a slow

handclap, clearly disappointed she's no longer the centre of attention.

'*À en deuxième place…*'

We all hold hands, willing our group to be ahead of Sheila's.

'*…c'est le groupe,* Dance Excellence *avec* Clarissa Kirkland by ze very same Clarissa Kirkland.'

We whoop and grin at each other as the audience applaud and whistle.

'Wowzers, second place.' Bonnie gives Ingrida a high five.

'Result. We beat Sheila's Maggots.' Cath punched the air.

We head for the front of the stage and pass Edith, standing with her quartet. I reach for her hand and pull her along with us to the front of the stage, shoving Fay's green bowler hat into her hands.

A few bars of "Dancin' Fool" play out loudly and we all step to the front of the stage and in unison raise our hats then bow. Asha accepts the shield on behalf of the group, and we all turn to acknowledge Clarissa with our outstretched hands. She again stands and even from this distance we can see she is wearing a grin like a Cheshire cat.

'*Et maintenant, Mesdames et Messieurs, les gagnants d'Expression Paris sont… Corps et Ame.*'

Edith and the other three dancers in her ensemble leap up and down, and we all cheer loudly as they claim their trophy.

'What a result.'

'First and second place for Fay's daughter. She will be very happy, *ja?*'

Clarissa meets us in the dressing room, her eyes sparkling, as she thanks us for all our hard work.

'What a shame Monica missed the awards,' Bonnie says.

'I understand some important family business came up.' Clarissa barely looks at me, but in the briefest of eye contacts I know Monica's told her about Vince and that we won't be sharing this information with the others.

*

Once changed and packed, we all have a celebratory drink in the café, and I wave the other women off in their taxis as Hazel and Clarissa leave for their posh hotel and the others return to Smut Central with Fay.

The night's getting cold and, waiting on the steps of the theatre, I pull my jacket tighter around me. Come on Max. Where are you? If only I had my frigging phone.

His taxi finally appears, and he gets out, tells it to wait and walks to meet me.

I hug him close. 'All go OK?'

'Bit of a rigmarole, but Monica's on the flight. I'd forgotten how far out the *Charles de Gaulle* airport is. Come on, *Mademoiselle*, the taxi's taking us to our dinner date. How did you get on in the competition?'

'You are talking to a runner-up. Second place and Sheila got third.'

'Congratulations.' Max pecks me on the cheek and we

start to walk towards the taxi when I see a man with a vaguely familiar face emerging from the theatre.

'Max, hang on a minute.' I cross to speak to the smartly dressed gent. 'Excuse me?'

'*Oui?*'

'Are you Jean-Claude?'

'*Mais oui.*'

'I'm Ruby, a friend of Monica's.'

'You were one of ze Dancing Fools?'

'Yes, I'm a dancing fool.' I smile. 'I'm afraid Monica had to rush home to the UK. A family matter.'

'*Mon dieu!* I 'ope everything is all right with her family.' He looks genuinely concerned.

'She'll be sorry she missed you.'

'I was hoping she would call me.' Jean-Claude holds up his phone and shrugs.

'Her phone got smashed.'

'Pardon?'

'Er...' I then remembered Frédéric's word for Fay's broken leg. '*Cassée?*' I mime dropping a phone and stamping on it. I then open my arms wide to show there was nothing she could do.

'*Je vois!* I see.'

'I'll ask Monica to call you when she's sorted a new phone.'

'Ah *oui*, thank you.' He pulls out a business card and puts it into my hand. 'In case she has lost ze last one. Please tell Monica I am sorry to miss her. By the way, your dance was magnifique!'

'Thank you.'

'*Au revoir.*'

I watch Jean-Claude hail down a taxi and disappear into the Parisian night. Now that's one lovely-looking man.

'What are you thinking?'

'Nothing. Just that Monica could do a lot worse.'

Max taps my nose, wraps his arm around my shoulder and once in the taxi we hold hands until we get to a small bistro in the Marais district.

We take our seats in the characterful small restaurant with raw-stone walls and exposed wooden beams.

'This is romantic.' I raise my glass of red wine to chink his.

'I booked us into a boutique hotel nearby. We can walk there from here, but for now I need food.'

'Me too. I'm ravenous after all that dancing. You'd struggle to get food this late in Cheadle.'

'Ah, but this is Paris.'

Over a selection of tasty French dishes, Max tells me all about his conversation with Monica on the way to the airport.

'She admitted she'd been disingenuous and apologised.'

'Good.'

'Although I still don't understand how you ended up with Vince?'

'Complete fluke. I take it Monica told you I'd never met her absent husband, crazy as that sounds.'

Max nods.

'So, I'd no idea. I mean I barely remember it; it was eons ago. He was a spontaneous encounter. Didn't use his real name.'

'Like you, Scarlet?'

'Point taken. But I had no idea he was a) married and b) married to Monica. Believe me, I feel completely weird about it.'

'Can you imagine if you'd met up with him after, at Monica's place?'

'That's just what Monica said. Thank God I didn't. She's going back to confront him. End it.'

'She told me. She also told me what a great friend you are.'

'As if you needed confirmation. So, what about you, Max? Why the big I've-had-it-with-relationships-based-on-lies-and-deceit speech?'

Max opens up about a previous partner where he was subjected to all kinds of falsehoods and inventions. It also turns out he never knew his dad; his mum being a single parent who refused to disclose even a name.

By the time we've finished our meal, I've gained a fair understanding of why he's remained single and why he reacted the way he had when he discovered I hadn't been honest with Will about his biological father.

I finish my wine and stare at the table.

'Penny for them, Ruby Anderson?'

'Sorry?'

'Penny for your thoughts.'

'Shouldn't that be a euro?' I smile. 'Max, I'm going to tell Will about his father.'

'Good.'

'I was planning to, anyway. I just don't want the guy in our lives, but I guess that will be Will's choice.'

'I don't want him back in your life, that's for sure.' Max's brow furrows.

He purses his lips and I see a flash of something. What is that? Jealousy?

'Max, you do know I'm not and never have been the slightest bit interested in this bloke, right? I haven't clapped eyes on him in fourteen years.' I lift his hand and kiss the backs of his fingers.

Max visibly relaxes. He hugs me close to him and strokes my cheek and neck. It triggers an instant response, and I can sense the feeling is mutual.

We pay the bill and hurry back to our hotel, making all sorts of outrageously sexy suggestions on the way.

33

INGRIDA

It is very hard to concentrate on Fay's words as I help her to get ready for bed. My conversation with Neil, it goes around inside my head, and I cannot make sense of it. He finally called when we were in the dressing room watching the finals show and I took my phone to the ladies to speak with him in private.

'Sorry I didn't call earlier. I've only just got the kids to bed. Lizzy's been playing up rotten without you here. I had to put her down in our bed in the end. How's the dancing?'

I could not bring myself to answer.

'Ingrida? You OK?'

'I speak with Grace yesterday.'

'Really?'

'She tell me Rita and Terry now know big secret.'

'Ah.'

'You did not tell them we are married. They find out from children.'

'Ingrida, it's been hard…'

'Hard for you? To say we are now husband and wife?'

'No. Hard for them. They left. Walked out as soon as they found out. Look, they'll come round. They don't understand… they don't know you…'

'*Ne*, they do not know me. I am not in house to speak with them so they will not know me…'

'Ingrida, in the whole scheme of things, this is of little importance.'

'Little importance. I do not know what you mean.'

'It's just… well, there's a lot of other stuff going on. Look, I will tell you when you get back. Things are… complicated and well, today someone arrived at the house and… well, basically made a lot of threats.'

My heart, it knot and I think of Kazimieras and I was unable to find the words to tell Neil.

'Ingrida, I can't talk about this on the phone.'

'Who… who make these threats?'

'Look, I didn't want to worry you but I need to come clean… There are… well, some things I haven't told you… I haven't been completely honest…'

He go very quiet and I wait until he speak again.

'When you get back… I'll tell you everything. Oh no. Lizzy's crying again. I need to go. See you tomorrow.'

'Neil?'

But he hang up without even saying I love you and I am left in confusion with his words.

The rest of the evening, it went by in a blur. At the theatre I was with the other dancers on stage, but inside my head I was thinking of Neil's words and no matter how much I say to God to take this worry away, my mind would not settle.

Now we are in the hotel room and the others eat a pizza they have delivered to the room.

'Ingrida, you sure you don't want any?' Bonnie ask me. 'It's actually quite good and you can heat it up in the microwave.'

'*Ne*, thank you. I am not hungry. I think I will go to bed and read.'

'Good idea, Ingrida.' Fay puts the crust of her pizza in an empty box and wheels herself to her bed where I help her to get in.

'I haven't even got the energy to brush my teeth.' Fay gives a big sigh when I lift her bad leg onto the bed. 'Oh, what a relief to finally put my foot up.'

'It is still very swollen, *ja*? You can get this checked at the hospital when we get back home. I think this would be good idea.'

Asha appears from the bathroom in her pyjamas. 'It's so quiet in here without Ruby and Monica.'

'What are you reading, Ingrida?' Bonnie asks. 'That's a tiny and well-worn book.'

'My Latvian New Testament,' I tell her. 'I read it every day.' But I do not tell her I cannot see the words clearly and I end up closing the book and my eyes. When Neil's words repeat in my head, *I haven't been completely honest*, I find the only way I can get to sleep is to put myself back on stage and do all the dance steps over and over.

*

Today, it takes much time to pack up and leave the hotel with Fay in her wheelchair, her case on her lap. Asha pulls my case with hers and we cross Paris with our Metro passes. I am relived we do not have expensive taxi but without Monica, no one offers to pay, and we agree we have time to get to the *Gare du Nord* Station using the Underground.

Ruby and Max, they meet us at the station and Ruby, she look very happy. She wink at me and I smile back at her.

Edith is also at the station to say goodbye to Fay. We leave them to have private word before clearing customs and getting on board. Fay's eyes shine and when I ask if everything is all right, she does not say anything, but nods her head and pats my hand.

The Eurostar journey seem to go by quickly and I listen to the others chatter as the train carries us to London.

'That's the third time your phone has rung Fay,' Cath points to Fay's bag.

'I am not answering it. It is that dratted reporter again. Wants some sort of scoop. Well, he is not getting another word from me.'

Ruby laughs, 'Fay, I think you gave him plenty of words to be going on with. I've just been reading the news report online.' She reads aloud from Max's mobile screen. '"A bunch of squawking, self-absorbent harlots, is how Fay Langridge of the Dance Excellence – Clarissa Kirkland ensemble described the Bold as Brass dancers" – Fay that's priceless.'

Fay shakes her head and bites her lip.

'What else does it say?' Asha and Bonnie ask.

Ruby reads the full article.

'"Fierce rivalry between two UK amateur dance groups came to a head in France this weekend in the competition, Expression Paris. Dance Excellence with Clarissa Kirkland led by Clarissa Kirkland, known as the DECK group, went up against fellow North West residents, Sheila Bold's Bold as Brass ensemble. In a weekend full of drama, the DECKs arrived at Manchester Airport only to discover they had no flight bookings. Forced to travel to Paris by train, a source close to the group told the *Manchester Evening News* that a former dancer had embezzled both the flight and hotel funds."...'

'Who the hell told them that?' Ruby looks at Fay.

She shakes her head and mumbles an unconvincing reply about being assured her comments were 'off the record'.

'Go on, Ruby,' Cath points to the phone.

'"The DECKs arrived in Paris only to discover there had been a further theft. Their rivals, Bold as Brass had stolen one of their dance numbers. When Sheila Bold's ladies performed this sexy fan dance to "Roxanne" by The Police, a full-blown costume boob unfolded – literally – on stage. Several of the lacy tops tore and breasts were exposed. The unexpected titillation was eclipsed when Sheila Bold herself mooned at the audience. Ms Bold's skirt ripped to reveal her bottom complete with cheeky thong, pictured here."...'

Ruby turns the screen to show us the image.

'Is Sheila's big ending, *ja?*'

'Yeuw. Gruesome,' Cath giggles.

Ruby turns the phone back and continues reading.

'"Film of the costume malfunction, taken by a Bold as Brass friend in the audience, went viral and made headline news in both France and the UK. There followed un-substantiated claims that the costumes had been sabotaged."'

Asha takes a sharp intake of breath and Ruby mutters a swear word under her breath before continuing.

'"I suspect one of the Clarissa Kirkland's women interfered with Sheila's back seam, Bridget Davies from Bold as Brass speculated, adding there had been an incident with costumes being damaged earlier in the day."...'

Ruby shakes her head. 'The little bitch. Frigging sour grapes if you ask me.'

'Keep reading,' Bonnie urges.

'"Further drama dogged the competition when one DECK dancer had her phone stolen by thieves near the Eiffel Tower. Another was reported to have been subject to a racist attack."... Who the hell told them that?'

Fay stares studiously out of the window as Ruby continues reading.

'"In a day of disasters, DECK dancer and local librarian, Fay Langridge, then broke her leg on stage at the start of their Bollywood entry. The drama kept giving when Ms Langridge, who was estranged from her two daughters for many years, was to discover her eldest daughter, Edith was also a competitor."...'

Ruby looks up at Fay who rubs her forehead and

continues to stare at the distant French countryside flashing past. Ruby coughs and carries on.

"'Edith Langridge was dancing in a balletic French quartet, Body and Soul – the group which went on to win the show with their rendition of "Fix You" by Coldplay. The tense reunion between Fay and Edith resulted in the daughter taking the mother's place in the aptly named finals dance, "Dancin' Fool", which took second place, narrowly beating Bold as Brass."...'

'Narrowly my arse...' Cath starts before Bonnie slaps the table and roars with laughter.

'Very funny, Cath.'

"'Sheila Bold eventually acknowledged her group's entry was in fact choreographed by Clarissa Kirkland, the head of the DECKs, and with this admission, they were allowed to proceed to the final where they achieved third place. Our reporter watched the finals show in the packed main theatre of the *Opéra Bastille*. 'A showcase of exciting, fast-paced dance enthralled the Paris audience. Expression, the formerly little-known competition, is now set to gain an unprecedented following.' The show's director, Frédéric Montrer, was delighted the initially unwelcome incidents gave way to some extremely welcome publicity. '*Vive la compétition!*' were his final words.'"

'You bet Frédéric was pleased. And I bet it was him who gave them lots of juicy titbits.' Ruby hands the phone back to Max.

Asha then speaks up. 'Hey, I hope they do not connect the former dancer they mentioned at the beginning with Janine and find out about Janine's mum.'

'You're right, Asha,' Cath agrees. 'They'll have a right field day with that.'

Ruby turns to Max to explain what we have heard about Janine's mother.

I think about Janine, and I realise my problems, they are not so big. Whatever Neil has to tell me, even if Kazimieras make big threats, we can sort it out. I just want to be home to see him and the children.

*

After many hours, we finally make the train from London to Manchester, and I help Fay into one of the few seats not pre-booked where Cath and Bonnie agree to sit in the aisle to look after her. Max folds her wheelchair and places it in the nearby luggage area. There are no other seats, so we squeeze our way through to the buffet car where I stand with Asha, Ruby, and Max.

Ruby and Max talk quietly to each other all the way and Asha and I have a conversation about what it is like being a mama.

Asha's phone rings and as she sees who is calling, she points at the screen frantically, answering in a loud voice, '*Janine*. How are you?'

She waves for me to come closer and puts the phone between us so I can hear Janine's voice.

'Asha, I...' Janine's voice stops.

'It is OK, Janine. It is good to hear from you. We missed you in Paris. We are sorry to hear about your mother.'

When Janine says nothing, Asha tries again.

'We came second. In the competition. We beat Sheila's group. They came third. Janine, are you OK?'

'Yes. I am now. It's been a bad few weeks.'

Again, Janine goes very quiet.

'Janine, here's Ingrida.'

Asha pushes the phone to me and makes a big face for me to say something. She leans right into me to listen.

'Hello, Janine. I am also very sorry to hear about your mama. It is very sad news. I remember when my mama passed away only a few years back.'

'Really?'

'*Ja*. It was very sad.'

'Oh, you know how I feel then… I mean, I know my mum was not well, but it all happened so quickly…' She goes quiet again.

'Do you have anyone stay at home with you?' I ask.

'Yes, my sister came home. Eventually. She is helping me sort out the house. It got into a bit of a state…'

'That is good news that your sister is helping you,' Asha says into the phone.

'Yes. Angela's been very supportive. Helped me clear up and put things in order. It's why I am phoning.'

Asha looks at me and raises her eyebrows.

'Go on,' she says.

I think to myself perhaps Janine will say she is very sorry about our Paris money, but I do not think she will say she has our money to give back to us. I listen with much care when she speaks.

'We… well, we cleared the house and then I found it. I found the slip. It was with all the others. I had not checked any of them. Just bought them and stored them. I forgot about them. But Angela checked and, well… there it was.'

I do not understand, but Asha pulls the phone close to her head and says, 'Which slip?'

I do not hear Janine and can only see Asha as she puts a hand to her mouth and her eyes go very wide.

'Janine, are you sure? I mean, are you absolutely sure?'

I wait and watch Asha's face as she listens.

'Oh, my word, I do not know what to say.'

Asha's eyes they shine, and she flaps her hand and mouth to me the words, 'Tell you in a minute'.

Ruby taps me on the shoulder.

'What's going on? Is that Janine Asha's talking to?'

I nod and put my finger to my lips.

Asha says, 'Yes,' and 'No,' and nods many times as she stares out of the window. Finally, she finishes her call. She puts her phone in her bag and squeezes her eyes shut very tight. Then she opens them wide and jumps up and down. She pulls Ruby and me across to hold hands.

'What? What the hell is it, Asha?' Ruby, she smiles as we watch Asha leap up and down as she takes our hands with hers.

'You are not going to believe this.'

'Try us.'

'Janine has found the winning lottery ticket. The one that is about to expire. It is ours. We have won.'

'What?'

'We have won.' Asha shouts at the top of her voice and the other passengers look round to see who makes this noise.

Ruby puts her hands on Asha's shoulders. 'Shh. Now, slowly, calmly, quietly… tell us what you mean. Start at the beginning.'

'OK, OK. I am just so excited.' Asha takes a deep breath and pulls us both close to her.

'Janine said she had got into debt. Something about a betting app. She borrowed the Paris money, thinking she would be able to win it all back in time to book our flights and hotel, but everything got out of hand. She basically lost the plot. Could not bring herself to tell us and at the same time she was being hounded by debt collectors. Anyway, her mother died, and I think she shut herself away until the police turned up and managed to contact her sister. Her sister has been helping her sort out her affairs and they came across all the lottery tickets stuffed into a jar and left unchecked. It was Janine's sister who discovered one of them was the winning ticket from almost six months ago and she is helping Janine claim the money for our syndicate.'

'This is like fairy tale,' I say.

'Bloody hell. How much have we won?'

Ruby has a very loud voice and other passengers again look at us.

Max he is also listening, and he say, 'Ladies, let's keep this to ourselves, shall we?'

Asha nods and whispers, 'Two million pounds.'

'What? Fuc— I mean, frigging hell!'

'That's the total, but obviously it needs to be shared out between all Clarissa's dance ladies. Everyone was in the syndicate, not just the Expression dancers. I was trying to work it out. I think Janine said there were eighteen of us…'

'Eighteen – two million. So how much? My brain's just frozen.'

Max uses his phone to do the calculation. 'That would amount to one hundred and eleven thousand pounds each, more or less.'

Ruby whistles loudly.

'Amazing.' Max smiles. 'Congratulations.'

'I cannot take this in. Is it true we have won this much money? It does not seem possible.' I look from Ruby's face to Asha to Max.

'What else did Janine say?' Ruby asks.

'We have to go and meet the lottery rep with our syndicate agreement and then they will pay out. Janine's sister has set up the meeting for tomorrow.'

'We need to tell the others. Although, hold that thought.' Ruby frowns. 'Let's check this is for real first. Janine hasn't been the world's most reliable person to date. Oh my God. One hundred and eleven thousand pounds. It's incredible.'

'Definitely worth a celebration. What're we all drinking?' Max asks. 'Bearing in mind this is a train buffet.'

'Gin and tonic tinnie for me.' Ruby laughs.

'Sparkling water,' Asha and I say at the same time.

'And crisps,' Asha adds.

We all laugh and smile. It is a good feeling.

We agree we will not say a word to the other ladies about the money until we are sure it is true but I am hoping it will be true so I can pay some to Kazimieras so he will stop harassing us and go home and I can also buy the children good presents and maybe even a new ring for myself.

INGRIDA

*

Neil is waiting for me when my taxi finally arrives home after I have delivered Fay to her flat. Fay kindly paid the full fare. This was big relief, as I did not have enough money. I wanted to say to Fay, soon we will all have a lot of money for taxis and nice things, but I do not say anything as I promised Ruby and Asha we would wait.

Neil, Grace, Theo, and Lizzy all rush to the door to greet me. My heart is very full as the children put their arms around me and cry, 'Guy-da, you're home. We missed you.'

I have only little presents for the children. I kept the snacks Fay got for me at Euston Station. They do not seem to care I do not have expensive gifts and they are very happy to each have their own small packet of biscuits. They eat as I make a cup of tea and Neil, he hug me from behind.

'How was Paris?'

'Many things happen. It was full of incident I think is right saying.'

'I guessed as much. Saw some of the commotion on the news.'

'*Ja*, we are famous. But I think the other dance group, they have more fame with big exposure.'

Neil laughs and squeezes me around my waist, but I take his arm away and turn to look at him.

'We need to talk, *ja?*'

'We do. When the children are in bed.'

When I have kissed them all goodnight, I find Neil

pacing the floor in our lounge and I sit down on the sofa and wait for him to talk.

'Ingrida, I don't know where to start. I haven't been exactly honest with you...'

I do not know why but I find I am close to tears, and he comes to sit down next to me and takes my hand in his. He look so sad and shake his head many times before taking deep breath.

I cannot stop myself as the words burst from my mouth, 'Neil, you are going to tell me you do not love me?'

'What? No. I mean, yes, of course I love you.' He leans in to kiss me gently on the lips before saying, 'But I should have told you, I have money problems... a lot of them. Look, there's no easy way to say it, but my business has gone bankrupt.'

'*Bankrotējis? Ne.* But you will be able to find new job?'

'Maybe, I mean I owe a lot of money... the house, I didn't keep up the insurance payments and when Maya died, well the mortgage wasn't paid off. It started back in the pandemic when I got all those extra medical supplies to sell but I hadn't realised much of it wasn't up to scratch. Then I borrowed more against the house thinking I could sell the items on eventually... Anyhow, the bottom line is I have a room full of stuff upstairs that I cannot sell and we're going to have to move out of this house in order to pay all the business debts. I can't tell you how sorry I am... Ingrida, you're smiling?'

'*Ja.* I was worried it was serious problem not just money.'

'Well, money problems are serious. Especially if we have to sell the house. There's not enough equity to buy somewhere else and I don't imagine finding a rental will be easy for a known bankrupt.'

'Was it Kazimieras who came to the house to make threats?'

'Who?'

'My uncle, Kazimieras Valenko. *Ne?*'

'Your uncle? What? No. Who's he when he's at home?'

'He is not nice man. He say I take his money when my mama died, but it is not true and now he has track me down and he want me to give him money...'

'He'll have to get in line.'

'So, if it was not Kazimieras, who did come here with threats?'

'Bailiffs. They took the car and served an ultimatum for the balance of payment. I'm so sorry to have put you in this position, Ingrida. You wanted a home, security, and a reliable husband. I've completely failed you.'

'So, these are the things you hide from me? You have no money, your business it go *kapút*, you have secret room full of things you cannot sell... and you did not tell me any of this because...? Why, Neil? Why did you not tell me?'

'I didn't want to frighten you away. I thought if you knew all this, you wouldn't marry me. After everything you've been through, you need stability. I'm sorry. I've let you down.'

I sit back and look at Neil who has put his head in his hands.

'How much money you owe?'

'I hardly dare say it but it's just over one hundred thousand pounds.'

I shake my head.

'I know. It's terrible. What? Why are you smiling? Ingrida, we cannot pay it…'

'I think we can sort something out.' I kiss him on the lips. 'First, no more secrets, *ja*? I do not like secrets between us.'

'No. No more secrets. Oh Ingrida, I don't deserve someone as loving and gracious as you.'

I stroke the worried lines on his forehead. 'I too have a secret but only one and it is a good secret, but we must wait until tomorrow. For now, I want you to know I did not marry you for your money or your house or security. Nothing is secure in this life. I marry you because I grow in love with you and I love your children.'

Neil, his eyes shine like Ruby's eyes shine when she speak of Max and my heart, it feel very full. We embrace and go up to bed without clearing up the kitchen or setting up for breakfast.

34

FAY

I have never felt so useless. My folding wheelchair is too tight a fit into the narrow entrance of my flat and Ingrida has to support me as I hop into the lounge. At least I can use the wheelchair in here and can get to the bathroom as everything is on one level but answering the door will not be easy.

'Fay, do you have spare key so I can call tomorrow?'

'Yes. Thank you, Ingrida. There is one hanging up on the key rack by the door.'

'I have unpacked your case for you, *ja*? And put it under the bed.'

'Ingrida, I cannot thank you enough.'

'I will make for you a cup of tea before I go. The taxi said it would wait.'

I take out my purse and hand Ingrida a few notes. 'For the taxi fare. Please, you must take it. What would I have done without you?'

'Thank you, Fay. You are very kind. I think tomorrow,

you must make appointment with fracture clinic so they can check your leg. I may be able to take you.'

'Most kind. And I hope you do not mind me saying so, but Ingrida, you seem very much happier today.'

'*Ja*. I have very good news and I hope I can share this with you tomorrow, but I must wait for now.'

'Well, that sounds intriguing.'

'How is leg feel?'

'Throbbing and hot but I suspect once I have rested it overnight, it will be vastly improved. You get on now. And again, many thanks.'

Ingrida waves as she takes the key and heads off.

I feel utterly spent, but no wonder after the long journey home from France. It was exhausting.

As I sip my tea, I smile thinking of our weekend in Paris and I glance at the photograph of Edith and Bethan with a renewed hope in my heart.

I take more painkillers and close my eyes, not caring if I sleep all night in my chair.

35

ASHA

It is finally the first day of my wedding celebration. The sun is due to shine all weekend and I am eternally grateful I have stopped being sick. I have no idea how Ma guessed I was pregnant. I am sure Rashmi said something even though I had told her to keep it secret. Typical. Anyway, Ma is delighted. We will not tell Baba until after Jay and I are back from our mini moon. Not because he will be shocked. No, because Ma said he would be so happy he would be sure to blurt it out to everyone at the wedding. I certainly do not want my old-fashioned relatives talking about my condition at the ceremony.

Jay has been wonderful. He has done all the cooking while I lie on the sofa after work. He also frequently goes out to the late shop to get me ice cream or chocolate or sparkling water and crisps. He is going to be a very attentive father, I am sure.

I cannot decide if I want to know the sex of the baby. Jay says he does not care but I think I am favouring a little girl. She can dance with me when she is older, like Monica's daughter, Joanne, who is going to join Clarissa's class.

At least the first scan showed I was not having twins! I do not know how Monica managed having two babies at the same time. I said as much last night when we had the final rehearsal of my Bollywood number.

I think everyone at dance is looking forward to the celebration of my wedding, especially after the recent funeral. It was a very miserable affair. Barely twenty-minutes at the sparse chapel of the local crematorium. There were no prayers, no singing, and it was all painfully flat. I only counted a dozen people and most of those were the dance ladies, as we had all agreed to give a show of support.

This is the first English funeral I had been to, and it is nothing like an Indian funeral. There was not even a small gathering afterwards. Twenty minutes for a life. It seems woefully pitiful for any human being. And so little said about the deceased. At the end of the service, I was certainly none the wiser as to who Sharon Young had been.

'It was the least we could do,' Bonnie had said as we walked to the car park afterwards. 'After all, Janine could so easily have claimed the winning lottery ticket was her own and run off with all our money.'

'She would never have done that,' Cath exclaimed.

'Well, there have been enough television dramas on the subject.'

'To be sure, but Janine has been through a rough time. I am glad we've supported the wee girl. It's a terrible thing to lose your mother at such a young age.'

ASHA

'*Ja*, I agree.' Ingrida had given Janine a large bunch of flowers outside the chapel.

'Do you have big Indian funerals as well as big weddings, Asha?' Bonnie asks.

'We most certainly do. Any major events, births, marriages, deaths, are celebrated by the full family. We are very closely bonded together.' I did not add that I could not imagine a tiny funeral like this for any of my extended family.

Now my wedding is here. I am not even going to think about the second funeral next week.

I told Jay it was not funny, when he joked it could be a film, *Two Funerals and a Wedding*.

No, I am putting all my energies into making this a memorable weekend. I can hardly believe the date has arrived and tonight we do my dance.

The Bollywood spectacular will kick off the dancing mid evening. I am wearing the first of my wedding outfits, a Lehenga of tangerine and gold. I will stand out against the other dancers as they will be in the blue and green shaded saris we wore for the competition. Tomorrow I will wear the traditional red Lehenga, and I even have a sparkling white off-the-shoulder dress for the final day as a shout-out to my English upbringing.

Monica has designed the beautifully cut lace dress that hides my slight bump. I am the first customer of Wed-in-Style by Monica. No one else will have worn this design before me. My hair will be adorned with bright red roses to complete the look. Monica even said she wants to use one of my official photographs for her new promotional site. Imagine. I could be the face of her new company.

I study the henna patterns on my hands painted there earlier by my aunts. The henna stain is very dark. This is perfect, as they say, the darker the colour, the stronger the bond will be between Jay and me. All my friends giggled and laughed when I had Jay's name and mine hennaed onto the top of my thigh. It is a good custom for the groom to have to find the names and I assured them this will not happen until we are completely by ourselves after the ceremony.

I have seen Jay's Sherwani, and he looks magnificent in it. Everyone says what a handsome couple we will make.

I practise the dance steps inside my head and think through the rehearsal. It all went well. With no Fay, it will be Janine who will be dancing with us.

Janine seems like a new person since her mother's death and her sister coming back to live with her. I am glad I opened the line of communication between the dance ladies and Janine. It was a good move on my part, and I can now pride myself that this no doubt made all the difference as to how events unfolded.

Janine now talks to me a lot, and I even persuaded her to come in and have her teeth whitened for free.

During her treatment, I was able to glean more information about what happened. I booked her in for double the normal time so I could pause the procedure for her to speak to me.

'Thank you for doing this for me, Asha.'

'It is no problem, Janine. You have nice teeth and I promise this will enhance your smile. I tell all my patients how it does wonders for the confidence. Now, before we do the lower jaw, you need a break. Tell me how it is going with your sister living back with you.'

'It's going well. Angela and I are both glad to have each other.'

I smiled and waited for her to say more.

'I started back at my job last week too, at the theatre. Only part-time, but it's good to get back to some normality.'

'That is good news. And the police, are they going to pursue the charge of not reporting your mother's death?'

'No. They gave me a fine and a caution. I was so relieved. They know I wasn't in a good place, mentally. My community nurse said I was in a state of denial when Mum passed away.'

I patted her arm and said nothing.

'I mean, I know it sounds ridiculous now, but I convinced myself she was asleep. I couldn't face dealing with it and then I had come to rely on her weekly payments to pay Ryan...'

'Ryan?'

'He's a debt collector, although my nurse called him a loan shark. The payments went up every week and before I knew it, I was handing over both Mum's disability benefit and my carer's allowance. We had nothing, and he was threatening getting us kicked out of the house next.'

'How terrible.'

'That is why... why I took the Paris payments. I thought I could win it all back...'

I patted her arm again, and she went quiet for a long time. Eventually, she spoke again.

'I was in a cycle of gambling, borrowing more, losing more, borrowing more… It was never-ending. When the police finally came, it was a relief. And they put me in touch with Step-Change, a debt charity. They're helping me sort out all the issues.'

'You will be able to pay off this Ryan person now we have the lottery win?'

'They've drawn up an agreement for me to pay him at a set rate over the next two years and he has to stay away from my house. They also said it wouldn't be a good idea if Ryan got wind of the winnings; it would make me a target. So, I'm keeping that quiet. It's such a relief Clarissa's group agreed not to have publicity.'

'I think we have had enough press interest over the dance competition to last us a lifetime,' I laughed.

'I'm sorry I missed Paris. In particular the dancing. It was one of the few things that kept me going over the last few years. I'm so excited to be dancing at your wedding.'

'Could you imagine yourself married one day?' I asked her.

'Not thought about it. I haven't really been out much in the last few years. But Ruby says I must try her new dating site when it's up and running. Although, I'm not so sure about that.'

'It may be worth a try. Now lie back and open your mouth again.'

I did not say it would not suit me, finding a match online. But I guess not everyone is as lucky as I have been in meeting my true love without any forced blind dates.

Ingrida and I have been out a couple of times since

Paris. I went to the park with her and Lizzy the other day to feed the ducks. Watching her with the little stepdaughter, I can see Ingrida is a natural mother. I hope I will be the same.

'How are things with Neil?' I asked her.

'Good. He is searching for new job. Also, we are planning church blessing for our marriage and Rita and Terry, they have said they will come.'

'Really? That is great.'

'It is answer to prayer.'

'How about that uncle of yours? Did you meet up with him?'

'*Ja*. I gave him some money…'

'No. Ingrida, surely he will just keep coming back for more?'

'That is what Neil say. But maybe giving Kazimieras this money will help him to start something worthwhile? Maybe it will give him chance to make a better life and maybe it will be his only chance. Some people have very hard time in life and just need a helping hand.'

'I suppose. You will not have much of your winnings left after paying off Neil's debts and giving your uncle money.'

'It is only money. What are you spending your winnings on?'

'Most of it is going into our travel funds. We are having a mini moon to a fantastic game reserve in South Africa for a week; no expense spared, not for our last holiday before the baby. Then we are going to have the best and longest honeymoon ever after our child arrives. We are booking the most luxurious hotels and resorts around the world, and Ma and Baba will join us in India for a month, so they will not miss too much of watching our little one grow. They can also look after the infant in Delhi while we see the Taj Mahal and Jaipur. I have always wanted to visit the Golden Triangle.'

'That sound like a brilliant plan.'

'Do you know how the others are spending their winnings? I mean, I know Ruby and Monica have started up their own businesses.'

'I think Bonnie and Cath, they are going to Las Vegas including sightseeing in the Grand Canyon. Cath also say she wants to tour Ireland and see all the places she miss as a child.'

An ice-cream van next to us in the park then turned on a loud track of music. "Yellow Submarine" by The Beatles blares out and Lizzy pulls Ingrida's arm to whisper in her ear.

'Does she want an ice cream?'

'*Ne*. She wants to dance.' Ingrida laughed, and we each took one of Lizzy's hands and danced round in a circle next to the pond.

*

Bang on time, the dance ladies arrive, and we gather in a room to the side of the large community hall for a final practice of my dance.

'Ingrida. Who has been treating herself to new jewellery then?' I grab her hand and examine her new rings. The engagement ring has a single diamond set on white gold, matching the plain wedding band.

'*Ja*. I am so happy. They had to cut the old ring off my finger at the hospital.'

'Ouch.' Ruby and the others crowd around to look at the rings, too.

'*Ja*, my hand it had turn blue. It was a bit of emergency procedure, but I choose this last week and it fit me perfectly.'

Both rings are a little plain for my taste, but Ingrida seems to love them.

'You look amazing, Asha.' Monica comes close to look at the detail on my dress. 'What a fabulous outfit.'

'Shall we do the dance barefoot?' Cath points to my feet, decorated with henna in my light sandals. 'It would be such a shame to cover those ornate patterns.'

'It would look more authentic,' I reply.

'Well, without Fay there's no reason to wear ballet slippers…' Bonnie bites her lip.

'Yes, let's go barefoot. Thank goodness I put nail varnish on my toes.' Ruby pulls off her ballet shoes and all the other dancers follow suit.

We all get into position, holding our scarves high – I have an embroidered tangerine one for the occasion – and we run through the dance. The beat of the drums reverberates through the room and our bodies. In costume, the entire dance is lifted, and the rehearsal is excellent.

'Now remember, it is to look a bit like a flash dance. I will give you the nod and you will grab your scarves, and all come from different directions to join me on stage. I cannot wait to see Jay's face.'

'You did not tell him?' Ingrida looks surprised.

'It is the only secret I have kept from him,' I whisper in her ear.

Ma appears at the door and says it is time to go and greet our first guests, who are all gathered in the enormous community centre we have decorated for the wedding venue.

I look at myself in the mirror and check my teeth, which sparkle beautifully in contrast to my dark red lipstick. I have butterflies in my stomach. By the end of the weekend, Jay and I will be married. Finally. And I will have performed my dance on stage to hundreds of our adoring relatives.

36

THE SECOND FUNERAL

It is a wet gloomy day. A small crowd of around fifty people shelter under their umbrellas outside the place of worship as the hearse arrives. The vicar of the pretty village church hosting the funeral gently ushers the guests into the sanctuary. Their brightly coloured dripping umbrellas gradually fill three buckets at the porch door. The congregants emerging from under the umbrellas wear equally bright clothing of every hue. It had been agreed: no black. Although a few had clearly not got the memo and self-consciously smooth down their black suits or skirts, muttering apologetically to anyone who will listen that they had not known.

The coffin is bedecked in bright yellow sunflowers. It is lifted and carried into the church.

'I am the resurrection and the life...' Reverend Prudence intones as she leads the way.

Several mourners follow behind the coffin. All but one, who is wearing a stunning dress suit of yellow and black echoing the flowers on the coffin, are attired in white pin-striped trousers and matching waistcoats. Each holds a brightly coloured bowler hat to their chests, which matches a satin flower sewn onto each garment. One of their number is in a wheelchair – she holds a green bowler hat. She is pushed by a slightly chunky lady carrying an orange hat. They sit in the front pews reserved for their number.

Following the opening prayers, a large drop-down screen displays images of the deceased. She is shown in an array of dance costumes in various tableaux with others from her former dance group. The mourners smile and point to the photographs, chattering quietly under the upbeat jazz music that fills the church.

'Oh, will you look at that one now.' Only the front two rows could discern the soft Irish accent. 'That was Expression Margate, wasn't it? We all look so young.'

'Well, you do. It's a terrible photograph of me. Look at my hair. I look like I've been dragged through a hedge backwards.'

'You daft eejit, that's not your hair. It was the scarf headdress we wore for the peasant skirt number. Aw. Look at this one.'

'Is that Hazel and Clarissa as teenagers?' The black lady with closely cropped hair waves her red bowler hat towards the screen.

'We were only fifteen years old there, Ruby,' the sunflower-suited woman turns to smile, a tear slipping down her cheek. 'We had only met a few months earlier.'

A beautiful auburn-haired lady holding a pink hat leans forward to pat the yellow-suited lady on her arm. 'You both look wonderful,' she says before blowing her nose a little too loudly.

'Oh look. There we are in Paris,' an Indian lady points. Her other hand, hidden beneath her yellow bowler, gently strokes the barely discernible bulge of her stomach.

'I like this photograph very much. We are on dinner cruise boat. I think it is after Hazel say her speech. It was very good speech. I remember it as if she say it yesterday.'

'We were all in tears then too, ladies. Hazel's "Dancin' Fool" speech. She meant every word. I think she knew then she did not have long… long to…'

A few more pin-striped-clad women reach out to touch the chief mourner.

'I wish I had been there.' The smallest and youngest of the costumed ladies nods her head sorrowfully.

The photographs give way to short video clips of the deceased and her laugh rings around the church. The ladies stop talking and quietly watch the clips as they sniffle and dab their eyes with tissues. The presentation closes on a still of her smiling face.

Reverend Prudence takes the lectern.

'We are gathered here today to remember our dearly departed friend, Hazel Bull. I had the pleasure of speaking with Hazel at length during her recent and sadly final hospital stay at St Ann's where I am chaplain. I know she wanted this to be a happy occasion. A celebration of her life. A life full of colour, dance and love…'

The vicar gives a brief history of the key dates in Hazel's

life before inviting the chief mourner to say a few words. 'Please, Hazel's closest friend, Clarissa Kirkland.'

Clarissa takes the lectern and puts a rigid smile on her face before taking a deep breath. She reads from a typed sheet as she embarks on a faltering and flowery accolade to Hazel, which, in her efforts to contain her emotions, is rendered rather dispassionate and flat.

'...her support for me in all manner of things but especially choreography will be sadly missed. Having danced her last dance, she now takes her place where she moves with the angels and saints on the heavenly stage in the sky. Farewell my dear, dear confidante and most treasured friend.' Clarissa finishes and there is a short burst of polite applause.

The ladies in costume look mainly at invisible specs of dust on their clothing or at the floor during the speech but clap politely as Clarissa retakes her seat.

Reverend Prudence then indicates for another of the key mourners to come forward to the microphone.

'The ladies of Dance Excellence – Clarissa Kirkland have been asked to nominate one of their number to give a final tribute to Hazel and they have chosen Ingrida Goodman to summarise their feelings for this much-loved lady.'

The ladies all nod and smile encouragingly to the chosen speaker who bites her lip and fidgets nervously with her orange bowler hat before handing it to the lady in the wheelchair. She walks to the front. She has no typed notes.

'It is very great honour to speak about Hazel. She

is very special and lovely lady. She find she have cancer many years ago. I am professional cancer nurse, but I also know what it is like to have this terrible disease and I am sorry she is not recover from it like me. Hazel say to me if everyone have diagnosis of cancer maybe they live life in better way. She say it change her outlook and I think she have point. She say to me one day this cancer will be eradicate. I hope she is right. Cancer is truly terrible. Hazel, she say to me we are here for only short time and we must do best to make the world better place. I know Hazel make the world better place. St Ann's Hospice, they ask me to say big thank you to Hazel. She leave her lottery prize, some to the hospice and rest to research to find cancer cure.' Ingrida's lower lip wobbles as she says her final words. 'Before she pass away, Hazel say to me, Ingrida live and dance like there is no tomorrow. I think this is very good advice. Thank you, Hazel, for being lovely lady. We all love you and will miss you very much.'

The congregation applaud loudly and all the pin-striped women stand to hug or pat Ingrida when she returns to her seat.

The service concludes with another of the dance ladies singing 'Amazing Grace,' her lilting Irish accent prompting further tears.

*

The wake is held in the circular function room above the Lowry theatre in Manchester. Balloons adorn every table and photographs of Hazel and Clarissa are prominently displayed at the entrance. The almost three-hundred-and-sixty-degree views through the windows look out to Media City, the Manchester Ship Canal and Salford Quays. They let light flood in from the clearing sky. Despite the occasion, the mood is upbeat, and the dance friends take their buffet lunch to a central circular table where they chat freely.

'This place is incredible. I wish I had known you could hire it before I had my wedding in the community hall.'

'Asha, you would never have fitted all your wedding guests in here. I mean, I've never seen so many people at one wedding,' Ruby laughs.

'That is true, and Jay and I could always hire this place for our first anniversary.'

'You may have your hands full by then.' Cath smiles as she indicates Asha's stomach.

'Cath, you sang beautifully. And, Ingrida, you did a fantastic speech. Well done.'

'Thank you, Monica. I was little nervous in my words, but I think of Hazel inside my head, and I stay strong for her.'

'You made a brilliant job of it...' The wheelchaired lady stops to catch her breath. 'I wish I could have said something... but I find it hard to... to complete a sentence with this terrible... terrible pulmonary hypertension.' She coughs into a handkerchief and Ingrida gently pats her arm.

'You need slow down, Fay. This recover, it will take much time. It is very lucky you are still here with us.'

'Yes, you had a narrow squeeze from what I heard...' Bonnie starts.

'Escape… Narrow escape.' Fay splutters.

'Exactly, but escape you did. Just think if Ingrida had not called on you or if she had not had your flat key? No one would have known you were on the point of collapse.'

Fay nods her head and wordlessly reaches for Ingrida's hand to clasp it before choking out, 'I fear it will take months and months to get right again.'

'Don't get despondent, after all it's still early days for you, Fay.' Monica pats her shoulder. 'You only moved from the hospital to the rehabilitation home last week. It's lovely you were able to join us today, but you need to give yourself time. Plus, your leg will need lots of physio.'

'At least Edith is coming over from France to visit me soon…' Fay catches her breath. 'And did I tell you I had an email from Bethan? She, she sounds very happy living in Australia.'

'That's great news, Fay. Tell Edith to send us a text. We can have a "Dancin' Fool" reunion.' Monica and Ruby nod enthusiastically.

When Fay has been collected by her adapted taxi, the ladies applaud Ingrida for her swift action.

'You really did save her life, Ingrida.' Ruby hugs her lightly.

'Remind me, what was it she had?' Bonnie asks.

'A threatened PE. Pulmonary embolism to you,' Cath shakes her head.

'And what's that again?'

'A blood clot. If it detach, it can travel to the lungs,' Ingrida explains. 'Is very dangerous and common with people who break leg. Fay did not take anticoagulant medicine.'

'What a stroke of luck you went to call on her then, Ingrida,' Bonnie slaps Ingrida on her back.

'Not luck. I knew I had to go there.'

'Really? How?'

'*Dievs pavêlêja.*'

'Oh, what does that mean?'

'It translate, God command.'

'Really? God told you to go to Fay's?'

'*Ja.*'

Bonnie looks somewhat perplexed before saying, 'Well thank goodness for that.'

Late that evening, Ruby and Monica deliver Clarissa to her door before the taxi takes them home.

'What a day.'

'I think Hazel would have been pleased. Clarissa held up well.'

'What time are you dropping Will off tomorrow, Ruby?'

'Not too early. Eleven-ish OK? Thanks so much for having him while we're away. We're going to take our time driving all the way down the Welsh coast. The hotel's perched on a clifftop overlooking Saundersfoot. It looks amazing. A great way to celebrate walking away from First Bite and setting up MatchFix. Three cheers for the lottery win.'

'Has Max said anything about moving in?'

'I think he might this weekend. He keeps talking about the next step in our relationship, so maybe this is it. Can you sound out Will? Make sure he's OK about it?'

'Will thinks Max is great. I'm sure he'll be happy about it. But of course, I'll check.'

'You know he wants to meet Dev? I haven't bitten the bullet and called the bloke yet. It's going to be tricky. And although Will is dead cool about it on the outside, he must be in bits on the inside.'

'Ruby, he's a really level-headed kid; he's like you. I can see if James will talk to him. Although James is still furious with me that his father has moved out.'

'I guess they were close.'

'Closer than I'd realised. Deep down, James must know our marriage had been on the rocks for ages, but he refuses to discuss the whys and wherefores. And anyway, Vince agreed to go quietly if we told the twins it's an amicable separation – no mentioning his adultery. Not that Joanne believes a word of it. She's guessed her father has done something unforgivable. The next problem will be my lottery winnings. Vince is determined he has an equal right to half of them.'

'You're kidding me? What a bastard.'

'You know what? I don't care. He can have half. I just want him out of my life.'

'Hey, I wouldn't give him as much as the time of day! But respect, Monica, you've really taken control of your life. And what's this I hear about a fashion fair in Paris next month? Hosted by the delicious Jean-Claude.'

'Put your tongue away, Ruby Anderson. Purely business and all you need to know is it'll be your weekend to babysit.'

'No problem. But be sure to find your inner Scarlet.'

'Ruby!'

PostScript

ONE YEAR LATER

Expression London
Press Announcement

North West troupe, Dance Excellence with Clarissa Kirkland, and the French ensemble, *Corps et Ame*, will be headlining Expression London as last year's winners. It promises to be a spectacular fusion of dance and ballet, having attracted more entrants than in any previous year. The competition will take place in the Royal Albert Hall.

Sheila Bold, who shot to fame after her group's costume disaster on stage last year, has strenuously denied allegations that Bold as Brass have copied one of the professional numbers from the television show *Strictly Come Dancing* for the competition.

'The routine to "Fever" is choreographed by me and me alone,' she insisted when challenged on a recent talk show.

Ms Bold has made countless appearances on games and chat shows since Expression Paris and now has a following of over two million people on Instagram.

Her Twitter feed was recently suspended following complaints regarding pornographic images. Ms Bold denies posting these, saying her account was hacked. Unconfirmed reports now suggest she has signed up to take part in the celebrity game show, *Love Island*.

Tickets for Expression London will be available from next week.

ACKNOWLEDGEMENTS

Finding the time to start write Dancing Fools was one of the few silver linings to the cloud of the pandemic – thankfully now a distant memory. Back then, with my dance classes cancelled, I frequently danced solo in my lounge to keep the routines fresh in my mind and in my writing. Three years on, after putting the manuscript down for a long break, I have now given Monica, Ruby, Ingrida, Fay and Asha a brushing down and a new lease of life. How they fare and their next adventure has been niggling away at me for some time, so work has begun on the follow-up novel.

My heartfelt thanks go first to my rock and ever supportive hubby, Julian. Massive thanks to my wonderful daughter, Katie Hawley, and fabulous friends, Liz Hughes, Alison Newell, Val Tweed and Louise Gough for beta reading. *Merci beaucoup* to Val Tweed for correcting and polishing my French and my grammar. Respect and appreciation to Shelley Routledge and Emma Mitchell for

ACKNOWLEDGEMENTS

their initial professional edits. And finally, I am indebted to Suzanne Brown, my real-life dance teacher, whose fantastic routines I have shamelessly replicated in the pages of this novel. Suzanne showed me how to point my toes, keep my jazz moves down in the ground and open my fingers wide for jazz hands! She also instilled in me a passion for dance for which I am forever grateful.

More information about my books and me can be found on my website: www.bfleetwood.com

ABOUT THE AUTHOR

B Fleetwood lives in the North West of England with her husband. A mother of four and now a hands-on granny, she writes while managing a lively toddler group and a foodbank. She previously authored a YA science fiction trilogy, The Chroma Series. Dancing Fools and All That Jazz is her first piece of UpLit fiction, inspired by her own amateur dance group.